© Charmian Reading

KHALED HOSSEINI was born in Kabul, Afghanistan, the son of a diplomat whose family received political asylum in the United States in 1980. He lives in northern California, where he is a physician. *The Kite Runner* is his first novel.

continued . . .

"A more personal plot, arising from Amir's close friendship with Hassan, the son of his father's servant, turns out to be the thread that ties the book together. The fragility of this relationship, symbolized by the kites the boys fly together, is tested as they watch their old way of life disappear. Hosseini's depiction of pre-revolutionary Afghanistan is rich in warmth and humor but also tense with the friction between the nation's different ethnic groups. . . . Full of haunting images: a man, desperate to feed his children, trying to sell his artificial leg in the market; an adulterous couple stoned to death in a stadium during the halftime of a football match; a rouged young boy forced into prostitution, dancing the sort of steps once performed by an organ grinder's monkey."
—*The New York Times*

"It is not so much a story of Mideast politics . . . as it is a story of life in a beautiful country torn asunder. Through his characters and the plot, which is captivating and at times quite disturbing, Hosseini offers a lesson on his culture and the history of his beloved homeland."
—*San Antonio Express-News*

"The frame of the story is the rhythm of life. This novel, set in Afghanistan in the 1970s and later in America, is a work of universal interest because of the literary genius of Khaled Hosseini. The culmination of the novel, too brutal and beautiful to reveal, demonstrates the author's capacity to bring life full circle in a great arc of grace and redeeming activity. A profound work of literature with a rare healing power."
—*The Buffalo News*

"Khaled Hosseini brings his native country to life with great sensitivity. [He] richly describes the Afghan customs and traditions that tug on the immigrants as they mourn the loss of their country and struggle to build an American life. In *The Kite Runner* Hosseini has created a wise, thoughtful book in which redemption and happiness are not necessarily the same thing."
—*Houston Chronicle*

"This extraordinary novel locates the personal struggles of everyday people in the terrible sweep of history." —*People*

"Evocative . . . acute and genuine . . . One of the great strengths of *The Kite Runner* is its sympathetic portrayal of Afghans and Afghan culture. Hosseini writes with warmth and enviable familiarity about Afghanistan and its people . . . a descriptive and easily readable account." —*Chicago Tribune*

"A powerful book . . . no frills, no nonsense, just hard spare prose . . . An intimate account of family and friendship, betrayal and salvation that requires no atlas or translation to engage and enlighten us. Parts of *The Kite Runner* are raw and excruciating to read, yet the book in its entirety is lovingly written. Hosseini clearly loves his country as much as he hates what has become of it. . . . A tale told in simple brush strokes, closer to Kawabata's *Thousand Cranes* than Mahfouz's *Trilogy*. Hosseini is at his best describing moments of slow, silent agony." —*The Washington Post Book World*

"Demonstrates a love of storytelling and respect for literary writing in equal measures . . . a big-hearted book with plenty of winning qualities. One of the most appealing aspects of this novel is its deceptively simple prose. Like *Waiting*, Ha Jin's novel of love, politics, and class issues, *The Kite Runner* blesses readers with guileless storytelling." —*The Cleveland Plain Dealer*

"A gripping and moving book that offers a surprising reward: an understanding of, and empathy for, the people of Afghanistan. . . . The book's power resides in Hosseini's ability to bring that culture to life on the page . . . almost impossible to put down." —*Iowa City Press*

"A vivid picture of Afghanistan thirty years ago." —*The Wall Street Journal*

continued . . .

"Hosseini shows how an engaging novel begins—with simple, exquisite writing that compels the reader to turn the page."
—*The Philadelphia Inquirer*

"Provides an extraordinary perspective on the struggles of a country that, until that doleful September day, had been for too long ignored or misunderstood. And despite its grimmer episodes, the novel ends with a note of optimism about Afghanistan's future, an optimism that the whole world would prefer to see unspoiled."
—*BookPage*

"Hosseini does tenderness and terror, California dream and Kabul nightmare with equal aplomb. . . . A ripping yarn and ethical parable."
—*Globe and Mail*

"A wonderfully conjured story that offers a glimpse into Afghanistan most Americans have never seen, and depicts a side of humanity rarely revealed."
—*Contra Costa Times*

"Here's a real find: a striking debut from an Afghan now living in the U.S. His passionate story of betrayal and redemption is framed by Afghanistan's tragic recent past. . . . Rather than settle for a coming-of-age or travails-of-immigrant story, Hosseini has folded them both into this searing spectacle of hard-won personal salvation. All this, and a rich slice of Afghan culture too: irresistible."
—*Kirkus Reviews* (starred review)

"Provides a vivid glimpse of life in Afghanistan over the past quarter century. The characters of Amir and his father, their relationships, and the relationship of Hassan and Amir are all carefully and convincingly described and developed. Hosseini, now a doctor in California, is possibly the only Afghan author writing in English, and his first novel is recommended."
—*Library Journal*

KHALED HOSSEINI

THE KITE RUNNER

RIVERHEAD BOOKS

NEW YORK

Riverhead Books
Published by The Berkley Publishing Group
A division of Penguin Group (USA) Inc.
375 Hudson Street
New York, New York 10014

First Riverhead hardcover edition: June 2003
First Riverhead trade paperback edition: May 2004
Riverhead trade paperback ISBN: 1-59448-000-1

The Library of Congress has catalogued the Riverhead hardcover edition as follows:

Hosseini, Khaled.
The kite runner / Khaled Hosseini.
p.   cm.
ISBN 1-57322-245-3 (acid-free paper)
1. Kåbol (Afghanistan)—Fiction.   2. Male friendship—Fiction.
3. Social classes—Fiction.   4. Afghanistan—Fiction.   5. Betrayal—Fiction.
6. Boys—Fiction.   I. Title.

PS3608.O525K58   2003   2003043106
813'.6—dc21

Printed in the United States of America

25   24   23   22   21   20

This book is dedicated to
Haris and Farah, both
the *noor* of my eyes,
and to the children
of Afghanistan.

ACKNOWLEDGMENTS

I am indebted to the following colleagues for their advice, assistance, or support: Dr. Alfred Lerner, Dori Vakis, Robin Heck, Dr. Todd Dray, Dr. Robert Tull, and Dr. Sandy Chun. Thanks also to Lynette Parker of East San Jose Community Law Center for her advice about adoption procedures, and to Mr. Daoud Wahab for sharing his experiences in Afghanistan with me. I am grateful to my dear friend Tamim Ansary for his guidance and support and to the gang at the San Francisco Writers Workshop for their feedback and encouragement. I want to thank my father, my oldest friend and the inspiration for all that is noble in *Baba;* my mother who prayed for me and did *nazr* at every stage of this book's writing; my aunt for buying me books when I was young. Thanks go out to Ali, Sandy, Daoud, Walid, Raya, Shalla, Zahra, Rob, and Kader for reading my stories. I want to thank Dr. and Mrs. Kayoumy—my other parents—for their warmth and unwavering support.

I must thank my agent and friend, Elaine Koster, for her wisdom, patience, and gracious ways, as well as Cindy Spiegel, my keen-eyed and judicious editor who helped me unlock so many doors in this tale. And I would like to thank Susan Petersen Kennedy for taking a chance on this book and the hardworking staff at Riverhead for laboring over it.

Last, I don't know how to thank my lovely wife, Roya—to whose opinion I am addicted—for her kindness and grace, and for reading, re-reading, and helping me edit every single draft of this novel. For your patience and understanding, I will always love you, Roya jan.

THE KITE RUNNER

ONE

December 2001

I became what I am today at the age of twelve, on a frigid overcast day in the winter of 1975. I remember the precise moment, crouching behind a crumbling mud wall, peeking into the alley near the frozen creek. That was a long time ago, but it's wrong what they say about the past, I've learned, about how you can bury it. Because the past claws its way out. Looking back now, I realize I have been peeking into that deserted alley for the last twenty-six years.

One day last summer, my friend Rahim Khan called from Pakistan. He asked me to come see him. Standing in the kitchen with the receiver to my ear, I knew it wasn't just Rahim Khan on the line. It was my past of unatoned sins. After I hung up, I went for a walk along Spreckels Lake on the northern edge of Golden Gate Park. The early-afternoon sun sparkled on the water where dozens of miniature boats sailed, propelled by a crisp breeze. Then I glanced up and saw a pair of kites, red with long blue tails, soaring in the sky. They danced high above the trees on the west end of the park, over the windmills, floating side by side like a pair of eyes looking down on San Francisco, the city I now call home. And suddenly Hassan's voice whispered in my head: *For you, a thousand times over.* Hassan the harelipped kite runner.

I sat on a park bench near a willow tree. I thought about something Rahim Khan said just before he hung up, almost as an afterthought. *There is a way to be good again.* I looked up at those twin kites. I thought about Hassan. Thought about Baba. Ali. Kabul. I thought of the life I had lived until the winter of 1975 came along and changed everything. And made me what I am today.

T W O

When we were children, Hassan and I used to climb the poplar trees in the driveway of my father's house and annoy our neighbors by reflecting sunlight into their homes with a shard of mirror. We would sit across from each other on a pair of high branches, our naked feet dangling, our trouser pockets filled with dried mulberries and walnuts. We took turns with the mirror as we ate mulberries, pelted each other with them, giggling, laughing. I can still see Hassan up on that tree, sunlight flickering through the leaves on his almost perfectly round face, a face like a Chinese doll chiseled from hardwood: his flat, broad nose and slanting, narrow eyes like bamboo leaves, eyes that looked, depending on the light, gold, green, even sapphire. I can still see his tiny low-set ears and that pointed stub of a chin, a meaty appendage that looked like it was added as a mere afterthought. And the cleft lip, just left of midline, where the Chinese doll maker's instrument may have slipped, or perhaps he had simply grown tired and careless.

Sometimes, up in those trees, I talked Hassan into firing walnuts with his slingshot at the neighbor's one-eyed German shepherd. Hassan never wanted to, but if I asked, *really* asked, he wouldn't deny me. Hassan never denied me anything. And he was deadly with his slingshot. Hassan's father, Ali, used to catch us and get mad, or as mad as someone as gentle as Ali could ever get. He would wag his finger and wave us down from the tree. He would take the mirror and tell us what his mother had told him, that the devil shone mirrors too, shone them to distract Muslims during prayer. "And he laughs while he does it," he always added, scowling at his son.

"Yes, Father," Hassan would mumble, looking down at his feet. But he never told on me. Never told that the mirror, like shooting walnuts at the neighbor's dog, was always my idea.

The poplar trees lined the redbrick driveway, which led to a pair of wrought-iron gates. They in turn opened into an extension of the driveway into my father's estate. The house sat on the left side of the brick path, the backyard at the end of it.

Everyone agreed that my father, my Baba, had built the most beautiful house in the Wazir Akbar Khan district, a new and affluent neighborhood in the northern part of Kabul. Some thought it was the prettiest house in all of Kabul. A broad entryway flanked by rosebushes led to the sprawling house of marble floors and wide windows. Intricate mosaic tiles, handpicked by Baba in Isfahan, covered the floors of the four bathrooms. Gold-stitched tapestries, which Baba had bought in Calcutta, lined the walls; a crystal chandelier hung from the vaulted ceiling.

Upstairs was my bedroom, Baba's room, and his study, also known as "the smoking room," which perpetually smelled of tobacco and cinnamon. Baba and his friends reclined on black leather chairs there after Ali had served dinner. They stuffed their pipes—except Baba always called it "fattening the pipe"—and dis-

cussed their favorite three topics: politics, business, soccer. Sometimes I asked Baba if I could sit with them, but Baba would stand
in the doorway. "Go on, now," he'd say. "This is grown-ups' time.
Why don't you go read one of those books of yours?" He'd close
the door, leave me to wonder why it was *always* grown-ups' time
with him. I'd sit by the door, knees drawn to my chest. Sometimes
I sat there for an hour, sometimes two, listening to their laughter,
their chatter.

The living room downstairs had a curved wall with custom-
built cabinets. Inside sat framed family pictures: an old, grainy
photo of my grandfather and King Nadir Shah taken in 1931, two
years before the king's assassination; they are standing over a dead
deer, dressed in knee-high boots, rifles slung over their shoulders.
There was a picture of my parents' wedding night, Baba dashing
in his black suit and my mother a smiling young princess in white.
Here was Baba and his best friend and business partner, Rahim
Khan, standing outside our house, neither one smiling—I am a
baby in that photograph and Baba is holding me, looking tired and
grim. I'm in his arms, but it's Rahim Khan's pinky my fingers are
curled around.

The curved wall led into the dining room, at the center of
which was a mahogany table that could easily sit thirty guests—
and, given my father's taste for extravagant parties, it did just that
almost every week. On the other end of the dining room was a
tall marble fireplace, always lit by the orange glow of a fire in the
wintertime.

A large sliding glass door opened into a semicircular terrace
that overlooked two acres of backyard and rows of cherry trees.
Baba and Ali had planted a small vegetable garden along the eastern wall: tomatoes, mint, peppers, and a row of corn that never
really took. Hassan and I used to call it "the Wall of Ailing Corn."

On the south end of the garden, in the shadows of a loquat tree, was the servants' home, a modest little mud hut where Hassan lived with his father.

It was there, in that little shack, that Hassan was born in the winter of 1964, just one year after my mother died giving birth to me.

In the eighteen years that I lived in that house, I stepped into Hassan and Ali's quarters only a handful of times. When the sun dropped low behind the hills and we were done playing for the day, Hassan and I parted ways. I went past the rosebushes to Baba's mansion, Hassan to the mud shack where he had been born, where he'd lived his entire life. I remember it was spare, clean, dimly lit by a pair of kerosene lamps. There were two mattresses on opposite sides of the room, a worn Herati rug with frayed edges in between, a three-legged stool, and a wooden table in the corner where Hassan did his drawings. The walls stood bare, save for a single tapestry with sewn-in beads forming the words *Allah-u-akbar*. Baba had bought it for Ali on one of his trips to Mashad.

It was in that small shack that Hassan's mother, Sanaubar, gave birth to him one cold winter day in 1964. While my mother hemorrhaged to death during childbirth, Hassan lost his less than a week after he was born. Lost her to a fate most Afghans considered far worse than death: She ran off with a clan of traveling singers and dancers.

Hassan never talked about his mother, as if she'd never existed. I always wondered if he dreamed about her, about what she looked like, where she was. I wondered if he longed to meet her. Did he ache for her, the way I ached for the mother I had never met? One day, we were walking from my father's house to Cinema Zainab for a new Iranian movie, taking the shortcut through the military barracks near Istiqlal Middle School—Baba had forbidden us to take that shortcut, but he was in Pakistan with Rahim Khan at the time. We hopped the fence that surrounded the barracks, skipped over a little creek, and broke into the open dirt field where old, abandoned tanks collected dust. A group of soldiers huddled in the shade of one of those tanks, smoking cigarettes and playing cards. One of them saw us, elbowed the guy next to him, and called Hassan.

"Hey, you!" he said. "I know you."

We had never seen him before. He was a squatty man with a shaved head and black stubble on his face. The way he grinned at us, leered, scared me. "Just keep walking," I muttered to Hassan.

"You! The Hazara! Look at me when I'm talking to you!" the soldier barked. He handed his cigarette to the guy next to him, made a circle with the thumb and index finger of one hand. Poked the middle finger of his other hand through the circle. Poked it in and out. In and out. "I knew your mother, did you know that? I knew her real good. I took her from behind by that creek over there."

The soldiers laughed. One of them made a squealing sound. I told Hassan to keep walking, keep walking.

"What a tight little sugary cunt she had!" the soldier was saying, shaking hands with the others, grinning. Later, in the dark, after the movie had started, I heard Hassan next to me, croaking. Tears were sliding down his cheeks. I reached across my seat, slung my arm around him, pulled him close. He rested his head on my shoulder. "He took you for someone else," I whispered. "He took you for someone else."

I'm told no one was really surprised when Sanaubar eloped. People *had* raised their eyebrows when Ali, a man who had memorized the Koran, married Sanaubar, a woman nineteen years younger, a beautiful but notoriously unscrupulous woman who lived up to her dishonorable reputation. Like Ali, she was a Shi'a Muslim and an ethnic Hazara. She was also his first cousin and therefore a natural choice for a spouse. But beyond those similarities, Ali and Sanaubar had little in common, least of all their respective appearances. While Sanaubar's brilliant green eyes and impish face had, rumor has it, tempted countless men into sin, Ali had a congenital paralysis of his lower facial muscles, a condition that rendered him unable to smile and left him perpetually grimfaced. It was an odd thing to see the stone-faced Ali happy, or sad, because only his slanted brown eyes glinted with a smile or welled with sorrow. People say that eyes are windows to the soul. Never was that more true than with Ali, who could only reveal himself through his eyes.

I have heard that Sanaubar's suggestive stride and oscillating hips sent men to reveries of infidelity. But polio had left Ali with a twisted, atrophied right leg that was sallow skin over bone with little in between except a paper-thin layer of muscle. I remember one day, when I was eight, Ali was taking me to the bazaar to buy some *naan*. I was walking behind him, humming, trying to imitate his walk. I watched him swing his scraggy leg in a sweeping arc, watched his whole body tilt impossibly to the right every time he planted that foot. It seemed a minor miracle he didn't tip over with each step. When I tried it, I almost fell into the gutter. That got me giggling. Ali turned around, caught me aping him. He didn't say anything. Not then, not ever. He just kept walking.

Ali's face and his walk frightened some of the younger children in the neighborhood. But the real trouble was with the older kids. They chased him on the street, and mocked him when he hobbled by. Some had taken to calling him *Babalu*, or Boogeyman.

"Hey, Babalu, who did you eat today?" they barked to a chorus of laughter. "Who did you eat, you flat-nosed Babalu?"

They called him "flat-nosed" because of Ali and Hassan's characteristic Hazara Mongoloid features. For years, that was all I knew about the Hazaras, that they were Mogul descendants, and that they looked a little like Chinese people. School textbooks barely mentioned them and referred to their ancestry only in passing. Then one day, I was in Baba's study, looking through his stuff, when I found one of my mother's old history books. It was written by an Iranian named Khorami. I blew the dust off it, sneaked it into bed with me that night, and was stunned to find an entire chapter on Hazara history. An entire chapter dedicated to Hassan's people! In it, I read that my people, the Pashtuns, had persecuted and oppressed the Hazaras. It said the Hazaras had tried to rise against the Pashtuns in the nineteenth century, but the Pashtuns had "quelled them with unspeakable violence." The book said that my people had killed the Hazaras, driven them from their lands, burned their homes, and sold their women. The book said part of the reason Pashtuns had oppressed the Hazaras was that Pashtuns were Sunni Muslims, while Hazaras were Shi'a. The book said a lot of things I didn't know, things my teachers hadn't mentioned. Things Baba hadn't mentioned either. It also said some things I *did* know, like that people called Hazaras *mice-eating, flat-nosed, load-carrying donkeys*. I had heard some of the kids in the neighborhood yell those names to Hassan.

The following week, after class, I showed the book to my teacher and pointed to the chapter on the Hazaras. He skimmed through a couple of pages, snickered, handed the book back. "That's the one thing Shi'a people do well," he said, picking up his papers, "passing themselves as martyrs." He wrinkled his nose when he said the word Shi'a, like it was some kind of disease.

But despite sharing ethnic heritage and family blood, Sanaubar joined the neighborhood kids in taunting Ali. I have heard that she made no secret of her disdain for his appearance.

"This is a husband?" she would sneer. "I have seen old donkeys better suited to be a husband."

In the end, most people suspected the marriage had been an arrangement of sorts between Ali and his uncle, Sanaubar's father. They said Ali had married his cousin to help restore some honor to his uncle's blemished name, even though Ali, who had been orphaned at the age of five, had no worldly possessions or inheritance to speak of.

Ali never retaliated against any of his tormentors, I suppose partly because he could never catch them with that twisted leg dragging behind him. But mostly because Ali was immune to the insults of his assailants; he had found his joy, his antidote, the moment Sanaubar had given birth to Hassan. It had been a simple enough affair. No obstetricians, no anesthesiologists, no fancy monitoring devices. Just Sanaubar lying on a stained, naked mattress with Ali and a midwife helping her. She hadn't needed much help at all, because, even in birth, Hassan was true to his nature: He was incapable of hurting anyone. A few grunts, a couple of pushes, and out came Hassan. Out he came smiling.

As confided to a neighbor's servant by the garrulous midwife, who had then in turn told anyone who would listen, Sanaubar had taken one glance at the baby in Ali's arms, seen the cleft lip, and barked a bitter laughter.

"There," she had said. "Now you have your own idiot child to do all your smiling for you!" She had refused to even hold Hassan, and just five days later, she was gone.

Baba hired the same nursing woman who had fed me to nurse Hassan. Ali told us she was a blue-eyed Hazara woman from Bamiyan, the city of the giant Buddha statues. "What a sweet singing voice she had," he used to say to us.

What did she sing, Hassan and I always asked, though we already knew—Ali had told us countless times. We just wanted to hear Ali sing.

He'd clear his throat and begin:

> *On a high mountain I stood,*
> *And cried the name of Ali, Lion of God.*
> *O Ali, Lion of God, King of Men,*
> *Bring joy to our sorrowful hearts.*

Then he would remind us that there was a brotherhood between people who had fed from the same breast, a kinship that not even time could break.

Hassan and I fed from the same breasts. We took our first steps on the same lawn in the same yard. And, under the same roof, we spoke our first words.

Mine was *Baba*.

His was *Amir*. My name.

Looking back on it now, I think the foundation for what happened in the winter of 1975—and all that followed—was already laid in those first words.

THREE

Lore has it my father once wrestled a black bear in Baluchistan with his bare hands. If the story had been about anyone else, it would have been dismissed as *laaf*, that Afghan tendency to exaggerate—sadly, almost a national affliction; if someone bragged that his son was a doctor, chances were the kid had once passed a biology test in high school. But no one ever doubted the veracity of any story about Baba. And if they did, well, Baba did have those three parallel scars coursing a jagged path down his back. I have imagined Baba's wrestling match countless times, even dreamed about it. And in those dreams, I can never tell Baba from the bear.

It was Rahim Khan who first referred to him as what eventually became Baba's famous nickname, *Toophan agha*, or "Mr. Hurricane." It was an apt enough nickname. My father was a force of nature, a towering Pashtun specimen with a thick beard, a wayward crop of curly brown hair as unruly as the man himself, hands that looked capable of uprooting a willow tree, and a black glare that would "drop the devil to his knees begging for mercy," as Rahim Khan used to say. At parties, when all six-foot-five of him thundered into the room, attention shifted to him like sunflowers turning to the sun.

Baba was impossible to ignore, even in his sleep. I used to bury cotton wisps in my ears, pull the blanket over my head, and still the sounds of Baba's snoring—so much like a growling truck engine—penetrated the walls. And my room was across the hall from Baba's bedroom. How my mother ever managed to sleep in the same room as him is a mystery to me. It's on the long list of things I would have asked my mother if I had ever met her.

In the late 1960s, when I was five or six, Baba decided to build an orphanage. I heard the story through Rahim Khan. He told me Baba had drawn the blueprints himself despite the fact that he'd had no architectural experience at all. Skeptics had urged him to stop his foolishness and hire an architect. Of course, Baba refused, and everyone shook their heads in dismay at his obstinate ways. Then Baba succeeded and everyone shook their heads in awe at his triumphant ways. Baba paid for the construction of the two-story orphanage, just off the main strip of Jadeh Maywand south of the Kabul River, with his own money. Rahim Khan told me Baba had personally funded the entire project, paying for the engineers, electricians, plumbers, and laborers, not to mention the city officials whose "mustaches needed oiling."

It took three years to build the orphanage. I was eight by then. I remember the day before the orphanage opened, Baba took me to Ghargha Lake, a few miles north of Kabul. He asked me to fetch Hassan too, but I lied and told him Hassan had the runs. I wanted Baba all to myself. And besides, one time at Ghargha Lake, Hassan and I were skimming stones and Hassan made his stone skip eight times. The most I managed was five. Baba was there, watching, and he patted Hassan on the back. Even put his arm around his shoulder.

We sat at a picnic table on the banks of the lake, just Baba and me, eating boiled eggs with *kofta* sandwiches—meatballs and pickles wrapped in *naan*. The water was a deep blue and sunlight glittered on its looking glass–clear surface. On Fridays, the lake was bustling with families out for a day in the sun. But it was midweek and there was only Baba and me, us and a couple of long-haired, bearded tourists—"hippies," I'd heard them called. They were sitting on the dock, feet dangling in the water, fishing poles in hand. I asked Baba why they grew their hair long, but Baba grunted, didn't answer. He was preparing his speech for the next day, flipping through a havoc of handwritten pages, making notes here and there with a pencil. I bit into my egg and asked Baba if it was true what a boy in school had told me, that if you ate a piece of eggshell, you'd have to pee it out. Baba grunted again.

I took a bite of my sandwich. One of the yellow-haired tourists laughed and slapped the other one on the back. In the distance, across the lake, a truck lumbered around a corner on the hill. Sunlight twinkled in its side-view mirror.

"I think I have *saratan,*" I said. Cancer. Baba lifted his head from the pages flapping in the breeze. Told me I could get the soda myself, all I had to do was look in the trunk of the car.

Outside the orphanage, the next day, they ran out of chairs. A lot of people had to stand to watch the opening ceremony. It was a windy day, and I sat behind Baba on the little podium just outside the main entrance of the new building. Baba was wearing a green suit and a caracul hat. Midway through the speech, the wind knocked his hat off and everyone laughed. He motioned to me to hold his hat for him and I was glad to, because then everyone would see that he was *my* father, *my* Baba. He turned back to the microphone and said he hoped the building was sturdier than his hat, and everyone laughed again. When Baba ended his speech, people stood up and cheered. They clapped for a long time. Afterward, people shook his hand. Some of them tousled my hair and shook my hand too. I was so proud of Baba, of us.

But despite Baba's successes, people were always doubting him. They told Baba that running a business wasn't in his blood and he should study law like his father. So Baba proved them all wrong by not only running his own business but becoming one of the richest merchants in Kabul. Baba and Rahim Khan built a wildly successful carpet-exporting business, two pharmacies, and a restaurant.

When people scoffed that Baba would never marry well—after all, he was not of royal blood—he wedded my mother, Sofia Akrami, a highly educated woman universally regarded as one of Kabul's most respected, beautiful, and virtuous ladies. And not only did she teach classic Farsi literature at the university, she was a descendant of the royal family, a fact that my father playfully rubbed in the skeptics' faces by referring to her as "my princess."

With me as the glaring exception, my father molded the world around him to his liking. The problem, of course, was that Baba saw the world in black and white. And he got to decide what was black and what was white. You can't love a person who lives that way without fearing him too. Maybe even hating him a little.

When I was in fifth grade, we had a mullah who taught us about Islam. His name was Mullah Fatiullah Khan, a short, stubby man with a face full of acne scars and a gruff voice. He lectured us about the virtues of *zakat* and the duty of *hadj*; he taught us the intricacies of performing the five daily *namaz* prayers, and made us memorize verses from the Koran—and though he never translated the words for us, he did stress, sometimes with the help of a stripped willow branch, that we had to pronounce the Arabic words correctly so God would hear us better. He told us one day that Islam considered drinking a terrible sin; those who drank would answer for their sin on the day of *Qiyamat*, Judgment Day. In those days, drinking was fairly common in Kabul. No one gave you a public lashing for it, but those Afghans who did drink did so in private, out of respect. People bought their scotch as "medicine" in brown paper bags from selected "pharmacies." They would leave with the bag tucked out of sight, sometimes drawing furtive, disapproving glances from those who knew about the store's reputation for such transactions.

We were upstairs in Baba's study, the smoking room, when I told him what Mullah Fatiullah Khan had taught us in class. Baba was pouring himself a whiskey from the bar he had built in the corner of the room. He listened, nodded, took a sip from his drink. Then he lowered himself into the leather sofa, put down his drink, and propped me up on his lap. I felt as if I were sitting on a pair of tree trunks. He took a deep breath and exhaled through his nose, the air hissing through his mustache for what seemed an eternity. I couldn't decide whether I wanted to hug him or leap from his lap in mortal fear.

"I see you've confused what you're learning in school with actual education," he said in his thick voice.

"But if what he said is true then does it make you a sinner, Baba?"

"Hmm." Baba crushed an ice cube between his teeth. "Do you want to know what your father thinks about sin?"

"Yes."

"Then I'll tell you," Baba said, "but first understand this and understand it now, Amir: You'll never learn anything of value from those bearded idiots."

"You mean Mullah Fatiullah Khan?"

Baba gestured with his glass. The ice clinked. "I mean all of them. Piss on the beards of all those self-righteous monkeys."

I began to giggle. The image of Baba pissing on the beard of any monkey, self-righteous or otherwise, was too much.

"They do nothing but thumb their prayer beads and recite a book written in a tongue they don't even understand." He took a sip. "God help us all if Afghanistan ever falls into their hands."

"But Mullah Fatiullah Khan seems nice," I managed between bursts of tittering.

"So did Genghis Khan," Baba said. "But enough about that. You asked about sin and I want to tell you. Are you listening?"

"Yes," I said, pressing my lips together. But a chortle escaped through my nose and made a snorting sound. That got me giggling again.

Baba's stony eyes bore into mine and, just like that, I wasn't laughing anymore. "I mean to speak to you man to man. Do you think you can handle that for once?"

"Yes, Baba jan," I muttered, marveling, not for the first time, at how badly Baba could sting me with so few words. We'd had a fleeting good moment—it wasn't often Baba talked to me, let alone on his lap—and I'd been a fool to waste it.

"Good," Baba said, but his eyes wondered. "Now, no matter what the mullah teaches, there is only one sin, only one. And that is theft. Every other sin is a variation of theft. Do you understand that?"

"No, Baba jan," I said, desperately wishing I did. I didn't want to disappoint him again.

Baba heaved a sigh of impatience. That stung too, because he was not an impatient man. I remembered all the times he didn't come home until after dark, all the times I ate dinner alone. I'd ask Ali where Baba was, when he was coming home, though I knew full well he was at the construction site, overlooking this, supervising that. Didn't that take patience? I already hated all the kids he was building the orphanage for; sometimes I wished they'd all died along with their parents.

"When you kill a man, you steal a life," Baba said. "You steal his wife's right to a husband, rob his children of a father. When you tell a lie, you steal someone's right to the truth. When you cheat, you steal the right to fairness. Do you see?"

I did. When Baba was six, a thief walked into my grandfather's house in the middle of the night. My grandfather, a respected judge, confronted him, but the thief stabbed him in the throat, killing him instantly—and robbing Baba of a father. The townspeople caught the killer just before noon the next day; he turned out to be a wanderer from the Kunduz region. They hanged him from the branch of an oak tree with still two hours to go before afternoon prayer. It was Rahim Khan, not Baba, who had told me that story. I was always learning things about Baba from other people.

"There is no act more wretched than stealing, Amir," Baba said. "A man who takes what's not his to take, be it a life or a loaf of *naan* ... I spit on such a man. And if I ever cross paths with him, God help him. Do you understand?"

I found the idea of Baba clobbering a thief both exhilarating and terribly frightening. "Yes, Baba."

"If there's a God out there, then I would hope he has more important things to attend to than my drinking scotch or eating pork. Now, hop down. All this talk about sin has made me thirsty again."

I watched him fill his glass at the bar and wondered how much time would pass before we talked again the way we just had. Because the truth of it was, I always felt like Baba hated me a little. And why not? After all, I *had* killed his beloved wife, his beautiful princess, hadn't I? The least I could have done was to have had the decency to have turned out a little more like him. But I hadn't turned out like him. Not at all.

IN SCHOOL, we used to play a game called *Sherjangi,* or "Battle of the Poems." The Farsi teacher moderated it and it went something like this: You recited a verse from a poem and your opponent had sixty seconds to reply with a verse that began with the same letter that ended yours. Everyone in my class wanted me on their team, because by the time I was eleven, I could recite dozens of verses from Khayyám, Hãfez, or Rumi's famous *Masnawi.* One time, I took on the whole class and won. I told Baba about it later that night, but he just nodded, muttered, "Good."

That was how I escaped my father's aloofness, in my dead mother's books. That and Hassan, of course. I read everything, Rumi, Hãfez, Saadi, Victor Hugo, Jules Verne, Mark Twain, Ian Fleming. When I had finished my mother's books—not the boring history ones, I was never much into those, but the novels, the epics—I started spending my allowance on books. I bought one a week from the bookstore near Cinema Park, and stored them in cardboard boxes when I ran out of shelf room.

Of course, marrying a poet was one thing, but fathering a son who preferred burying his face in poetry books to hunting...well, that wasn't how Baba had envisioned it, I suppose. Real men didn't read poetry—and God forbid they should ever write it! Real men—real boys—played soccer just as Baba had when he had been young. Now *that* was something to be passionate about. In 1970, Baba took a break from the construction of the orphanage and flew to Tehran for a month to watch the World Cup games on television, since at the time Afghanistan didn't have TVs yet. He signed me up for soccer teams to stir the same passion in me. But I was pathetic, a blundering liability to my own team, always in the way of an opportune pass or unwittingly blocking an open lane. I shambled about the field on scraggy legs, squalled for passes that never came my way. And the harder I tried, waving my arms over my head frantically and screeching, "I'm open! I'm open!" the more I went ignored. But Baba wouldn't give up. When it became abundantly clear that I hadn't inherited a shred of his athletic talents, he settled for trying to turn me into a passionate spectator. Certainly I could manage that, couldn't I? I faked interest for as long as possible. I cheered with him when Kabul's team scored against Kandahar and yelped insults at the referee when he called a penalty against our team. But Baba sensed my lack of genuine interest and resigned himself to the bleak fact that his son was never going to either play or watch soccer.

I remember one time Baba took me to the yearly *Buzkashi* tournament that took place on the first day of spring, New Year's Day. Buzkashi was, and still is, Afghanistan's national passion. A *chapandaz*, a highly skilled horseman usually patronized by rich aficionados, has to snatch a goat or cattle carcass from the midst of a melee, carry that carcass with him around the stadium at full gallop, and drop it in a scoring circle while a team of other *chapandaz* chases him and does everything in its power—kick, claw, whip, punch—to snatch the carcass from him. That day, the

crowd roared with excitement as the horsemen on the field bellowed their battle cries and jostled for the carcass in a cloud of
dust. The earth trembled with the clatter of hooves. We watched
from the upper bleachers as riders pounded past us at full gallop,
yipping and yelling, foam flying from their horses' mouths.

At one point Baba pointed to someone. "Amir, do you see that
man sitting up there with those other men around him?"

I did.

"That's Henry Kissinger."

"Oh," I said. I didn't know who Henry Kissinger was, and I
might have asked. But at the moment, I watched with horror as
one of the *chapandaz* fell off his saddle and was trampled under a
score of hooves. His body was tossed and hurled in the stampede
like a rag doll, finally rolling to a stop when the melee moved on.
He twitched once and lay motionless, his legs bent at unnatural
angles, a pool of his blood soaking through the sand.

I began to cry.

I cried all the way back home. I remember how Baba's hands
clenched around the steering wheel. Clenched and unclenched.
Mostly, I will never forget Baba's valiant efforts to conceal the dis-
gusted look on his face as he drove in silence.

Later that night, I was passing by my father's study when I
overheard him speaking to Rahim Khan. I pressed my ear to the
closed door.

"—grateful that he's healthy," Rahim Khan was saying.

"I know, I know. But he's always buried in those books or shuffling around the house like he's lost in some dream."

"And?"

"I wasn't like that." Baba sounded frustrated, almost angry.

Rahim Khan laughed. "Children aren't coloring books. You
don't get to fill them with your favorite colors."

"I'm telling you," Baba said, "I wasn't like that at all, and neither were any of the kids I grew up with."

"You know, sometimes you are the most self-centered man I know," Rahim Khan said. He was the only person I knew who could get away with saying something like that to Baba.

"It has nothing to do with that."

"Nay?"

"Nay."

"Then what?"

I heard the leather of Baba's seat creaking as he shifted on it. I closed my eyes, pressed my ear even harder against the door, wanting to hear, not wanting to hear. "Sometimes I look out this window and I see him playing on the street with the neighborhood boys. I see how they push him around, take his toys from him, give him a shove here, a whack there. And, you know, he never fights back. Never. He just...drops his head and..."

"So he's not violent," Rahim Khan said.

"That's not what I mean, Rahim, and you know it," Baba shot back. "There is something missing in that boy."

"Yes, a mean streak."

"Self-defense has nothing to do with meanness. You know what always happens when the neighborhood boys tease him? Hassan steps in and fends them off. I've seen it with my own eyes. And when they come home, I say to him, 'How did Hassan get that scrape on his face?' And he says, 'He fell down.' I'm telling you, Rahim, there is something missing in that boy."

"You just need to let him find his way," Rahim Khan said.

"And where is he headed?" Baba said. "A boy who won't stand up for himself becomes a man who can't stand up to anything."

"As usual you're oversimplifying."

"I don't think so."

"You're angry because you're afraid he'll never take over the business for you."

"Now who's oversimplifying?" Baba said. "Look, I know there's a fondness between you and him and I'm happy about that. Envious, but happy. I mean that. He needs someone who...understands him, because God knows I don't. But something about Amir troubles me in a way that I can't express. It's like..." I could see him searching, reaching for the right words. He lowered his voice, but I heard him anyway. "If I hadn't seen the doctor pull him out of my wife with my own eyes, I'd never believe he's my son."

THE NEXT MORNING, as he was preparing my breakfast, Hassan asked if something was bothering me. I snapped at him, told him to mind his own business.

Rahim Khan had been wrong about the mean streak thing.

FOUR

In 1933, the year Baba was born and the year Zahir Shah began his forty-year reign of Afghanistan, two brothers, young men from a wealthy and reputable family in Kabul, got behind the wheel of their father's Ford roadster. High on hashish and *mast* on French wine, they struck and killed a Hazara husband and wife on the road to Paghman. The police brought the somewhat contrite young men and the dead couple's five-year-old orphan boy before my grandfather, who was a highly regarded judge and a man of impeccable reputation. After hearing the brothers' account and their father's plea for mercy, my grandfather ordered the two young men to go to Kandahar at once and enlist in the army for one year—this despite the fact that their family had somehow managed to obtain them exemptions from the draft. Their father argued, but not too vehemently, and in the end, everyone agreed that the punishment had been perhaps harsh but fair. As for the orphan, my grandfather adopted him into his own household, and told the other servants to tutor him, but to be kind to him. That boy was Ali.

Ali and Baba grew up together as childhood playmates—at least until polio crippled Ali's leg—just like Hassan and I grew up a generation later. Baba was always telling us about the mischief he and Ali used to cause, and Ali would shake his head and say, "But, Agha sahib, tell them who was the architect of the mischief and who the poor laborer?" Baba would laugh and throw his arm around Ali.

But in none of his stories did Baba ever refer to Ali as his friend.

The curious thing was, I never thought of Hassan and me as friends either. Not in the usual sense, anyhow. Never mind that we taught each other to ride a bicycle with no hands, or to build a fully functional homemade camera out of a cardboard box. Never mind that we spent entire winters flying kites, running kites. Never mind that to me, the face of Afghanistan is that of a boy with a thin-boned frame, a shaved head, and low-set ears, a boy with a Chinese doll face perpetually lit by a harelipped smile.

Never mind any of those things. Because history isn't easy to overcome. Neither is religion. In the end, I was a Pashtun and he was a Hazara, I was Sunni and he was Shi'a, and nothing was ever going to change that. Nothing.

But we were kids who had learned to crawl together, and no history, ethnicity, society, or religion was going to change that either. I spent most of the first twelve years of my life playing with Hassan. Sometimes, my entire childhood seems like one long lazy summer day with Hassan, chasing each other between tangles of trees in my father's yard, playing hide-and-seek, cops and robbers, cowboys and Indians, insect torture—with our crowning achievement undeniably the time we plucked the stinger off a bee and tied a string around the poor thing to yank it back every time it took flight.

We chased the *Kochi,* the nomads who passed through Kabul on their way to the mountains of the north. We would hear their caravans approaching our neighborhood, the mewling of their sheep, the *baa*ing of their goats, the jingle of bells around their camels' necks. We'd run outside to watch the caravan plod through our street, men with dusty, weather-beaten faces and women dressed in long, colorful shawls, beads, and silver bracelets around their wrists and ankles. We hurled pebbles at their goats. We squirted water on their mules. I'd make Hassan sit on the Wall of Ailing Corn and fire pebbles with his slingshot at the camels' rears.

We saw our first Western together, *Rio Bravo* with John Wayne, at the Cinema Park, across the street from my favorite bookstore. I remember begging Baba to take us to Iran so we could meet John Wayne. Baba burst out in gales of his deep-throated laughter—a sound not unlike a truck engine revving up—and, when he could talk again, explained to us the concept of voice dubbing. Hassan and I were stunned. Dazed. John Wayne didn't really speak Farsi and he wasn't Iranian! He was American, just like the friendly, longhaired men and women we always saw hanging around in Kabul, dressed in their tattered, brightly colored shirts. We saw *Rio Bravo* three times, but we saw our favorite Western, *The Magnificent Seven,* thirteen times. With each viewing, we cried at the end when the Mexican kids buried Charles Bronson—who, as it turned out, wasn't Iranian either.

We took strolls in the musty-smelling bazaars of the Shar-e-Nau section of Kabul, or the new city, west of the Wazir Akbar Khan district. We talked about whatever film we had just seen and walked amid the bustling crowds of *bazarris.* We snaked our way among the merchants and the beggars, wandered through narrow alleys cramped with rows of tiny, tightly packed stalls. Baba gave us each a weekly allowance of ten Afghanis and we spent it on warm Coca-Cola and rosewater ice cream topped with crushed pistachios.

During the school year, we had a daily routine. By the time I dragged myself out of bed and lumbered to the bathroom, Hassan had already washed up, prayed the morning *namaz* with Ali, and prepared my breakfast: hot black tea with three sugar cubes and a slice of toasted *naan* topped with my favorite sour cherry marmalade, all neatly placed on the dining table. While I ate and complained about homework, Hassan made my bed, polished my shoes, ironed my outfit for the day, packed my books and pencils. I'd hear him singing to himself in the foyer as he ironed, singing old Hazara songs in his nasal voice. Then, Baba and I drove off in his black Ford Mustang—a car that drew envious looks everywhere because it was the same car Steve McQueen had driven in *Bullitt*, a film that played in one theater for six months. Hassan stayed home and helped Ali with the day's chores: hand-washing dirty clothes and hanging them to dry in the yard, sweeping the floors, buying fresh *naan* from the bazaar, marinating meat for dinner, watering the lawn.

After school, Hassan and I met up, grabbed a book, and trotted up a bowl-shaped hill just north of my father's property in Wazir Akbar Khan. There was an old abandoned cemetery atop the hill with rows of unmarked headstones and tangles of brushwood clogging the aisles. Seasons of rain and snow had turned the iron gate rusty and left the cemetery's low white stone walls in decay. There was a pomegranate tree near the entrance to the cemetery. One summer day, I used one of Ali's kitchen knives to carve our names on it: "Amir and Hassan, the sultans of Kabul." Those words made it formal: the tree was ours. After school, Has-

san and I climbed its branches and snatched its bloodred pomegranates. After we'd eaten the fruit and wiped our hands on the
grass, I would read to Hassan.

Sitting cross-legged, sunlight and shadows of pomegranate
leaves dancing on his face, Hassan absently plucked blades of
grass from the ground as I read him stories he couldn't read for
himself. That Hassan would grow up illiterate like Ali and most
Hazaras had been decided the minute he had been born, perhaps
even the moment he had been conceived in Sanaubar's unwel-
coming womb—after all, what use did a servant have for the written word? But despite his illiteracy, or maybe because of it,
Hassan was drawn to the mystery of words, seduced by a secret
world forbidden to him. I read him poems and stories, sometimes
riddles—though I stopped reading those when I saw he was far
better at solving them than I was. So I read him unchallenging
things, like the misadventures of the bumbling Mullah Nasruddin
and his donkey. We sat for hours under that tree, sat there until
the sun faded in the west, and still Hassan insisted we had
enough daylight for one more story, one more chapter.

My favorite part of reading to Hassan was when we came
across a big word that he didn't know. I'd tease him, expose his
ignorance. One time, I was reading him a Mullah Nasruddin story
and he stopped me. "What does that word mean?"

"Which one?"

"'Imbecile.'"

"You don't know what it means?" I said, grinning.

"Nay, Amir agha."

"But it's such a common word!"

"Still, I don't know it." If he felt the sting of my tease, his smiling face didn't show it.

"Well, everyone in my school knows what it means," I said. "Let's see. 'Imbecile.' It means smart, intelligent. I'll use it in a sentence for you. 'When it comes to words, Hassan is an imbecile.'"

"Aaah," he said, nodding.

I would always feel guilty about it later. So I'd try to make up for it by giving him one of my old shirts or a broken toy. I would tell myself that was amends enough for a harmless prank.

Hassan's favorite book by far was the *Shahnamah*, the tenth-century epic of ancient Persian heroes. He liked all of the chapters, the shahs of old, Feridoun, Zal, and Rudabeh. But his favorite story, and mine, was "Rostam and Sohrab," the tale of the great warrior Rostam and his fleet-footed horse, Rakhsh. Rostam mortally wounds his valiant nemesis, Sohrab, in battle, only to discover that Sohrab is his long-lost son. Stricken with grief, Rostam hears his son's dying words:

If thou art indeed my father, then hast thou stained thy sword in the life-blood of thy son. And thou didst it of thine obstinacy. For I sought to turn thee unto love, and I implored of thee thy name, for I thought to behold in thee the tokens recounted of my mother. But I appealed unto thy heart in vain, and now is the time gone for meeting...

"Read it again please, Amir agha," Hassan would say. Sometimes tears pooled in Hassan's eyes as I read him this passage, and I always wondered whom he wept for, the grief-stricken Rostam who tears his clothes and covers his head with ashes, or the dying Sohrab who only longed for his father's love? Personally, I couldn't see the tragedy in Rostam's fate. After all, didn't all fathers in their secret hearts harbor a desire to kill their sons?

One day, in July 1973, I played another little trick on Hassan. I was reading to him, and suddenly I strayed from the written story. I pretended I was reading from the book, flipping pages regularly, but I had abandoned the text altogether, taken over the story, and made up my own. Hassan, of course, was oblivious to this. To him, the words on the page were a scramble of codes, indecipherable, mysterious. Words were secret doorways and I held all the keys. After, I started to ask him if he'd liked the story, a giggle rising in my throat, when Hassan began to clap.

"What are you doing?" I said.

"That was the best story you've read me in a long time," he said, still clapping.

I laughed. "Really?"

"Really."

"That's fascinating," I muttered. I meant it too. This was . . . wholly unexpected. "Are you sure, Hassan?"

He was still clapping. "It was great, Amir agha. Will you read me more of it tomorrow?"

"Fascinating," I repeated, a little breathless, feeling like a man who discovers a buried treasure in his own backyard. Walking down the hill, thoughts were exploding in my head like the fireworks at *Chaman*. *Best story you've read me in a long time,* he'd said. I had read him a *lot* of stories. Hassan was asking me something.

"What?" I said.

"What does that mean, 'fascinating'?"

I laughed. Clutched him in a hug and planted a kiss on his cheek.

"What was that for?" he said, startled, blushing.

I gave him a friendly shove. Smiled. "You're a prince, Hassan. You're a prince and I love you."

That same night, I wrote my first short story. It took me thirty minutes. It was a dark little tale about a man who found a magic cup and learned that if he wept into the cup, his tears turned into pearls. But even though he had always been poor, he was a happy man and rarely shed a tear. So he found ways to make himself sad so that his tears could make him rich. As the pearls piled up, so did his greed grow. The story ended with the man sitting on a mountain of pearls, knife in hand, weeping helplessly into the cup with his beloved wife's slain body in his arms.

That evening, I climbed the stairs and walked into Baba's smoking room, in my hands the two sheets of paper on which I had scribbled the story. Baba and Rahim Khan were smoking pipes and sipping brandy when I came in.

"What is it, Amir?" Baba said, reclining on the sofa and lacing his hands behind his head. Blue smoke swirled around his face. His glare made my throat feel dry. I cleared it and told him I'd written a story.

Baba nodded and gave a thin smile that conveyed little more than feigned interest. "Well, that's very good, isn't it?" he said. Then nothing more. He just looked at me through the cloud of smoke.

I probably stood there for under a minute, but, to this day, it was one of the longest minutes of my life. Seconds plodded by, each separated from the next by an eternity. Air grew heavy, damp, almost solid. I was breathing bricks. Baba went on staring me down, and didn't offer to read.

As always, it was Rahim Khan who rescued me. He held out his hand and favored me with a smile that had nothing feigned about it. "May I have it, Amir jan? I would very much like to read it." Baba hardly ever used the term of endearment *jan* when he addressed me.

Baba shrugged and stood up. He looked relieved, as if he too had been rescued by Rahim Khan. "Yes, give it to *Kaka* Rahim. I'm going upstairs to get ready." And with that, he left the room. Most days I worshiped Baba with an intensity approaching the religious. But right then, I wished I could open my veins and drain his cursed blood from my body.

An hour later, as the evening sky dimmed, the two of them drove off in my father's car to attend a party. On his way out, Rahim Khan hunkered before me and handed me my story and another folded piece of paper. He flashed a smile and winked. "For you. Read it later." Then he paused and added a single word that did more to encourage me to pursue writing than any compliment any editor has ever paid me. That word was *Bravo*.

When they left, I sat on my bed and wished Rahim Khan had been my father. Then I thought of Baba and his great big chest and how good it felt when he held me against it, how he smelled of Brut in the morning, and how his beard tickled my face. I was overcome with such sudden guilt that I bolted to the bathroom and vomited in the sink.

Later that night, curled up in bed, I read Rahim Khan's note over and over. It read like this:

Amir jan,

I enjoyed your story very much. *Mashallah,* God has granted you a special talent. It is now your duty to hone that talent, because a person who wastes his God-given talents is a donkey. You have written your story with sound grammar and interesting style. But the most impressive thing about your story is that it has irony. You may not even know what that word means. But you will someday. It is something that some writers reach for their entire careers and never attain. You have achieved it with your first story.

My door is and always will be open to you, Amir jan. I shall hear any story you have to tell. Bravo.

Your friend,
Rahim

Buoyed by Rahim Khan's note, I grabbed the story and hurried downstairs to the foyer where Ali and Hassan were sleeping on a mattress. That was the only time they slept in the house, when Baba was away and Ali had to watch over me. I shook Hassan awake and asked him if he wanted to hear a story.

He rubbed his sleep-clogged eyes and stretched. "Now? What time is it?"

"Never mind the time. This story's special. I wrote it myself," I whispered, hoping not to wake Ali. Hassan's face brightened.

"Then I *have* to hear it," he said, already pulling the blanket off him.

I read it to him in the living room by the marble fireplace. No playful straying from the words this time; this was about me! Hassan was the perfect audience in many ways, totally immersed in the tale, his face shifting with the changing tones in the story. When I read the last sentence, he made a muted clapping sound with his hands.

"*Mashallah*, Amir agha. Bravo!" He was beaming.

"You liked it?" I said, getting my second taste—and how sweet it was—of a positive review.

"Some day, *Inshallah*, you will be a great writer," Hassan said. "And people all over the world will read your stories."

"You exaggerate, Hassan," I said, loving him for it.

"No. You will be great and famous," he insisted. Then he paused, as if on the verge of adding something. He weighed his words and cleared his throat. "But will you permit me to ask a question about the story?" he said shyly.

"Of course."

"Well..." he started, broke off.

"Tell me, Hassan," I said. I smiled, though suddenly the insecure writer in me wasn't so sure he wanted to hear it.

"Well," he said, "if I may ask, why did the man kill his wife? In fact, why did he ever have to feel sad to shed tears? Couldn't he have just smelled an onion?"

I was stunned. That particular point, so obvious it was utterly stupid, hadn't even occurred to me. I moved my lips soundlessly. It appeared that on the same night I had learned about one of writing's objectives, irony, I would also be introduced to one of its pitfalls: the Plot Hole. Taught by Hassan, of all people. Hassan who couldn't read and had never written a single word in his entire life. A voice, cold and dark, suddenly whispered in my ear, *What does he know, that illiterate Hazara? He'll never be anything but a cook. How dare he criticize you?*

"Well," I began. But I never got to finish that sentence.

Because suddenly Afghanistan changed forever.

FIVE

Something roared like thunder. The earth shook a little and we heard the *rat-a-tat-tat* of gunfire. "Father!" Hassan cried. We sprung to our feet and raced out of the living room. We found Ali hobbling frantically across the foyer.

"Father! What's that sound?" Hassan yelped, his hands outstretched toward Ali. Ali wrapped his arms around us. A white light flashed, lit the sky in silver. It flashed again and was followed by a rapid staccato of gunfire.

"They're hunting ducks," Ali said in a hoarse voice. "They hunt ducks at night, you know. Don't be afraid."

A siren went off in the distance. Somewhere glass shattered and someone shouted. I heard people on the street, jolted from sleep and probably still in their pajamas, with ruffled hair and puffy eyes. Hassan was crying. Ali pulled him close, clutched him with tenderness. Later, I would tell myself I hadn't felt envious of Hassan. Not at all.

We stayed huddled that way until the early hours of the morning. The shootings and explosions had lasted less than an hour, but they had frightened us badly, because none of us had ever heard gunshots in the streets. They were foreign sounds to us then. The generation of Afghan children whose ears would know nothing but the sounds of bombs and gunfire was not yet born. Huddled together in the dining room and waiting for the sun to rise, none of us had any notion that a way of life had ended. *Our* way of life. If not quite yet, then at least it was the beginning of the end. The end, the *official* end, would come first in April 1978 with the communist coup d'état, and then in December 1979, when Russian tanks would roll into the very same streets where Hassan and I played, bringing the death of the Afghanistan I knew and marking the start of a still ongoing era of bloodletting.

Just before sunrise, Baba's car peeled into the driveway. His door slammed shut and his running footsteps pounded the stairs. Then he appeared in the doorway and I saw something on his face. Something I didn't recognize right away because I'd never seen it before: fear. "Amir! Hassan!" he exclaimed as he ran to us, opening his arms wide. "They blocked all the roads and the telephone didn't work. I was so worried!"

We let him wrap us in his arms and, for a brief insane moment, I was glad about whatever had happened that night.

THEY WEREN'T SHOOTING ducks after all. As it turned out, they hadn't shot much of anything that night of July 17, 1973. Kabul awoke the next morning to find that the monarchy was a thing of the past. The king, Zahir Shah, was away in Italy. In his absence, his cousin Daoud Khan had ended the king's forty-year reign with a bloodless coup.

I remember Hassan and I crouching that next morning outside my father's study, as Baba and Rahim Khan sipped black tea and listened to breaking news of the coup on Radio Kabul.

"Amir agha?" Hassan whispered.

"What?"

"What's a 'republic'?"

I shrugged. "I don't know." On Baba's radio, they were saying that word, "republic," over and over again.

"Amir agha?"

"What?"

"Does 'republic' mean Father and I will have to move away?"

"I don't think so," I whispered back.

Hassan considered this. "Amir agha?"

"What?"

"I don't want them to send me and Father away."

I smiled. "*Bas,* you donkey. No one's sending you away."

"Amir agha?"

"What?"

"Do you want to go climb our tree?"

My smile broadened. That was another thing about Hassan. He always knew when to say the right thing—the news on the radio was getting pretty boring. Hassan went to his shack to get ready and I ran upstairs to grab a book. Then I went to the kitchen, stuffed my pockets with handfuls of pine nuts, and ran outside to find Hassan waiting for me. We burst through the front gates and headed for the hill.

We crossed the residential street and were trekking through a barren patch of rough land that led to the hill when, suddenly, a rock struck Hassan in the back. We whirled around and my heart dropped. Assef and two of his friends, Wali and Kamal, were approaching us.

Assef was the son of one of my father's friends, Mahmood, an airline pilot. His family lived a few streets south of our home, in a posh, high-walled compound with palm trees. If you were a kid living in the Wazir Akbar Khan section of Kabul, you knew about Assef and his famous stainless-steel brass knuckles, hopefully not through personal experience. Born to a German mother and Afghan father, the blond, blue-eyed Assef towered over the other kids. His well-earned reputation for savagery preceded him on the streets. Flanked by his obeying friends, he walked the neighborhood like a Khan strolling through his land with his eager-to-please entourage. His word was law, and if you needed a little legal education, then those brass knuckles were just the right teaching tool. I saw him use those knuckles once on a kid from the Karteh-Char district. I will never forget how Assef's blue eyes glinted with a light not entirely sane and how he grinned, how he *grinned,* as he pummeled that poor kid unconscious. Some of the boys in Wazir Akbar Khan had nicknamed him Assef *Goshkhor,* or Assef "the Ear Eater." Of course, none of them dared utter it to his face unless they wished to suffer the same fate as the poor kid who had unwittingly inspired that nickname when he had fought Assef over a kite and ended up fishing his right ear from a muddy gutter. Years later, I learned an English word for the creature that Assef was, a word for which a good Farsi equivalent does not exist: "sociopath."

Of all the neighborhood boys who tortured Ali, Assef was by far the most relentless. He was, in fact, the originator of the Babalu jeer, *Hey, Babalu, who did you eat today? Huh? Come on, Babalu, give us a smile!* And on days when he felt particularly inspired, he spiced up his badgering a little, *Hey, you flat-nosed Babalu, who did you eat today? Tell us, you slant-eyed donkey!*

Now he was walking toward us, hands on his hips, his sneakers kicking up little puffs of dust.

"Good morning, *kunis*!" Assef exclaimed, waving. "Fag," that was another of his favorite insults. Hassan retreated behind me as the three older boys closed in. They stood before us, three tall boys dressed in jeans and T-shirts. Towering over us all, Assef crossed his thick arms on his chest, a savage sort of grin on his lips. Not for the first time, it occurred to me that Assef might not be entirely sane. It also occurred to me how lucky I was to have Baba as my father, the sole reason, I believe, Assef had mostly refrained from harassing me too much.

He tipped his chin to Hassan. "Hey, Flat-Nose," he said. "How is Babalu?"

Hassan said nothing and crept another step behind me.

"Have you heard the news, boys?" Assef said, his grin never faltering. "The king is gone. Good riddance. Long live the president! My father knows Daoud Khan, did you know that, Amir?"

"So does my father," I said. In reality, I had no idea if that was true or not.

"'So does my father,'" Assef mimicked me in a whining voice. Kamal and Wali cackled in unison. I wished Baba were there.

"Well, Daoud Khan dined at our house last year," Assef went on. "How do you like that, Amir?"

I wondered if anyone would hear us scream in this remote patch of land. Baba's house was a good kilometer away. I wished we'd stayed at the house.

"Do you know what I will tell Daoud Khan the next time he comes to our house for dinner?" Assef said. "I'm going to have a little chat with him, man to man, *mard* to *mard*. Tell him what I told my mother. About Hitler. Now, there was a leader. A great leader.

A man with vision. I'll tell Daoud Khan to remember that if they had let Hitler finish what he had started, the world be a better place now."

"Baba says Hitler was crazy, that he ordered a lot of innocent people killed," I heard myself say before I could clamp a hand on my mouth.

Assef snickered. "He sounds like my mother, and she's German; she should know better. But then they want you to believe that, don't they? They don't want you to know the truth."

I didn't know who "they" were, or what truth they were hiding, and I didn't want to find out. I wished I hadn't said anything. I wished again I'd look up and see Baba coming up the hill.

"But you have to read books they don't give out in school," Assef said. "I have. And my eyes have been opened. Now I have a vision, and I'm going to share it with our new president. Do you know what it is?"

I shook my head. He'd tell me anyway; Assef always answered his own questions.

His blue eyes flicked to Hassan. "Afghanistan is the land of Pashtuns. It always has been, always will be. We are the true Afghans, the pure Afghans, not this Flat-Nose here. His people pollute our homeland, our *watan*. They dirty our blood." He made a sweeping, grandiose gesture with his hands. "Afghanistan for Pashtuns, I say. That's my vision."

Assef shifted his gaze to me again. He looked like someone coming out of a good dream. "Too late for Hitler," he said. "But not for us."

He reached for something from the back pocket of his jeans. "I'll ask the president to do what the king didn't have the *quwat* to do. To rid Afghanistan of all the dirty, *kasseef* Hazaras."

"Just let us go, Assef," I said, hating the way my voice trembled. "We're not bothering you."

"Oh, you're bothering me," Assef said. And I saw with a sinking heart what he had fished out of his pocket. Of course. His stainless-steel brass knuckles sparkled in the sun. "You're bothering me very much. In fact, you bother me more than this Hazara here. How can you talk to him, play with him, let him touch you?" he said, his voice dripping with disgust. Wali and Kamal nodded and grunted in agreement. Assef narrowed his eyes. Shook his head. When he spoke again, he sounded as baffled as he looked. "How can you call him your 'friend'?"

But he's not my friend! I almost blurted. *He's my servant!* Had I really thought that? Of course I hadn't. I hadn't. I treated Hassan well, just like a friend, better even, more like a brother. But if so, then why, when Baba's friends came to visit with their kids, didn't I ever include Hassan in our games? Why did I play with Hassan only when no one else was around?

Assef slipped on the brass knuckles. Gave me an icy look. "You're part of the problem, Amir. If idiots like you and your father didn't take these people in, we'd be rid of them by now. They'd all just go rot in Hazarajat where they belong. You're a disgrace to Afghanistan."

I looked in his crazy eyes and saw that he meant it. He *really* meant to hurt me. Assef raised his fist and came for me.

There was a flurry of rapid movement behind me. Out of the corner of my eye, I saw Hassan bend down and stand up quickly. Assef's eyes flicked to something behind me and widened with surprise. I saw that same look of astonishment on Kamal and Wali's faces as they too saw what had happened behind me.

I turned and came face to face with Hassan's slingshot. Has-

san had pulled the wide elastic band all the way back. In the cup
was a rock the size of a walnut. Hassan held the slingshot pointed
directly at Assef's face. His hand trembled with the strain of the
pulled elastic band and beads of sweat had erupted on his brow.

"Please leave us alone, Agha," Hassan said in a flat tone. He'd
referred to Assef as "Agha," and I wondered briefly what it must
be like to live with such an ingrained sense of one's place in a
hierarchy.

Assef gritted his teeth. "Put it down, you motherless Hazara."

"Please leave us be, Agha," Hassan said.

Assef smiled. "Maybe you didn't notice, but there are three of
us and two of you."

Hassan shrugged. To an outsider, he didn't look scared. But
Hassan's face was my earliest memory and I knew all of its subtle
nuances, knew each and every twitch and flicker that ever rippled
across it. And I saw that he was scared. He was scared plenty.

"You are right, Agha. But perhaps you didn't notice that I'm
the one holding the slingshot. If you make a move, they'll have to
change your nickname from Assef 'the Ear Eater' to 'One-Eyed
Assef,' because I have this rock pointed at your left eye." He said
this so flatly that even I had to strain to hear the fear that I knew
hid under that calm voice.

Assef's mouth twitched. Wali and Kamal watched this
exchange with something akin to fascination. Someone had chal-
lenged their god. Humiliated him. And, worst of all, that someone
was a skinny Hazara. Assef looked from the rock to Hassan. He
searched Hassan's face intently. What he found in it must have
convinced him of the seriousness of Hassan's intentions, because
he lowered his fist.

"You should know something about me, Hazara," Assef said
gravely. "I'm a very patient person. This doesn't end today, believe

me." He turned to me. "This isn't the end for you either, Amir. Someday, I'll make you face me one on one." Assef retreated a step. His disciples followed.

"Your Hazara made a big mistake today, Amir," he said. They then turned around, walked away. I watched them walk down the hill and disappear behind a wall.

Hassan was trying to tuck the slingshot in his waist with a pair of trembling hands. His mouth curled up into something that was supposed to be a reassuring smile. It took him five tries to tie the string of his trousers. Neither one of us said much of anything as we walked home in trepidation, certain that Assef and his friends would ambush us every time we turned a corner. They didn't and that should have comforted us a little. But it didn't. Not at all.

FOR THE NEXT COUPLE of years, the words *economic development* and *reform* danced on a lot of lips in Kabul. The constitutional monarchy had been abolished, replaced by a republic, led by a president of the republic. For a while, a sense of rejuvenation and purpose swept across the land. People spoke of women's rights and modern technology.

And for the most part, even though a new leader lived in *Arg*—the royal palace in Kabul—life went on as before. People went to work Saturday through Thursday and gathered for picnics on Fridays in parks, on the banks of Ghargha Lake, in the gardens of Paghman. Multicolored buses and lorries filled with passengers rolled through the narrow streets of Kabul, led by the constant shouts of the driver assistants who straddled the vehicles' rear bumpers and yelped directions to the driver in their thick Kabuli accent. On *Eid,* the three days of celebration after the holy month of Ramadan, Kabulis dressed in their best and newest clothes and visited their families. People hugged and kissed and greeted each other with *"Eid Mubarak."* Happy Eid. Children opened gifts and played with dyed hard-boiled eggs.

Early that following winter of 1974, Hassan and I were playing in the yard one day, building a snow fort, when Ali called him in. "Hassan, Agha sahib wants to talk to you!" He was standing by the front door, dressed in white, hands tucked under his armpits, breath puffing from his mouth.

Hassan and I exchanged a smile. We'd been waiting for his call all day: It was Hassan's birthday. "What is it, Father, do you know? Will you tell us?" Hassan said. His eyes were gleaming.

Ali shrugged. "Agha sahib hasn't discussed it with me."

"Come on, Ali, tell us," I pressed. "Is it a drawing book? Maybe a new pistol?"

Like Hassan, Ali was incapable of lying. Every year, he pretended not to know what Baba had bought Hassan or me for our birthdays. And every year, his eyes betrayed him and we coaxed the goods out of him. This time, though, it seemed he was telling the truth.

Baba never missed Hassan's birthday. For a while, he used to ask Hassan what he wanted, but he gave up doing that because Hassan was always too modest to actually suggest a present. So every winter Baba picked something out himself. He bought him a Japanese toy truck one year, an electric locomotive and train track set another year. The previous year, Baba had surprised Hassan with a leather cowboy hat just like the one Clint Eastwood wore in *The Good, the Bad, and the Ugly*—which had unseated *The Magnificent Seven* as our favorite Western. That whole winter, Hassan and I took turns wearing the hat, and belted out the film's famous music as we climbed mounds of snow and shot each other dead.

We took off our gloves and removed our snow-laden boots at the front door. When we stepped into the foyer, we found Baba sitting by the wood-burning cast-iron stove with a short, balding Indian man dressed in a brown suit and red tie.

"Hassan," Baba said, smiling coyly, "meet your birthday present."

Hassan and I traded blank looks. There was no gift-wrapped box in sight. No bag. No toy. Just Ali standing behind us, and Baba with this slight Indian fellow who looked a little like a mathematics teacher.

The Indian man in the brown suit smiled and offered Hassan his hand. "I am Dr. Kumar," he said. "It's a pleasure to meet you." He spoke Farsi with a thick, rolling Hindi accent.

"*Salaam alaykum,*" Hassan said uncertainly. He gave a polite tip of the head, but his eyes sought his father behind him. Ali moved closer and set his hand on Hassan's shoulder.

Baba met Hassan's wary—and puzzled—eyes. "I have summoned Dr. Kumar from New Delhi. Dr. Kumar is a plastic surgeon."

"Do you know what that is?" the Indian man—Dr. Kumar—said.

Hassan shook his head. He looked to me for help but I shrugged. All I knew was that you went to a surgeon to fix you when you had appendicitis. I knew this because one of my classmates had died of it the year before and the teacher had told us they had waited too long to take him to a surgeon. We both looked to Ali, but of course with him you could never tell. His face was impassive as ever, though something sober had melted into his eyes.

"Well," Dr. Kumar said, "my job is to fix things on people's bodies. Sometimes their faces."

"Oh," Hassan said. He looked from Dr. Kumar to Baba to Ali. His hand touched his upper lip. "Oh," he said again.

"It's an unusual present, I know," Baba said. "And probably not what you had in mind, but this present will last you forever."

"Oh," Hassan said. He licked his lips. Cleared his throat. "Agha sahib, will it . . . will it—"

"Nothing doing," Dr. Kumar intervened, smiling kindly. "It will not hurt you one bit. In fact, I will give you a medicine and you will not remember a thing."

"Oh," Hassan said. He smiled back with relief. A little relief anyway. "I wasn't scared, Agha sahib, I just . . ." Hassan might have been fooled, but I wasn't. I knew that when doctors said it wouldn't hurt, that's when you knew you were in trouble. With dread, I remembered my circumcision the year prior. The doctor had given me the same line, reassured me it wouldn't hurt one bit. But when the numbing medicine wore off later that night, it felt like someone had pressed a red hot coal to my loins. Why Baba waited until I was ten to have me circumcised was beyond me and one of the things I will never forgive him for.

I wished I too had some kind of scar that would beget Baba's sympathy. It wasn't fair. Hassan hadn't done anything to earn Baba's affections; he'd just been born with that stupid harelip.

The surgery went well. We were all a little shocked when they first removed the bandages, but kept our smiles on just as Dr. Kumar had instructed us. It wasn't easy, because Hassan's upper lip was a grotesque mesh of swollen, raw tissue. I expected Hassan to cry with horror when the nurse handed him the mirror. Ali held his hand as Hassan took a long, thoughtful look into it. He muttered something I didn't understand. I put my ear to his mouth. He whispered it again.

Tashakor. Thank you.

Then his lips twisted, and, that time, I knew just what he was doing. He was smiling. Just as he had, emerging from his mother's womb.

The swelling subsided, and the wound healed with time. Soon, it was just a pink jagged line running up from his lip. By the following winter, it was only a faint scar. Which was ironic. Because that was the winter that Hassan stopped smiling.

SIX

Winter.

Here is what I do on the first day of snowfall every year: I step out of the house early in the morning, still in my pajamas, hugging my arms against the chill. I find the driveway, my father's car, the walls, the trees, the rooftops, and the hills buried under a foot of snow. I smile. The sky is seamless and blue, the snow so white my eyes burn. I shovel a handful of the fresh snow into my mouth, listen to the muffled stillness broken only by the cawing of crows. I walk down the front steps, barefoot, and call for Hassan to come out and see.

Winter was every kid's favorite season in Kabul, at least those whose fathers could afford to buy a good iron stove. The reason was simple: They shut down school for the icy season. Winter to me was the end of long division and naming the capital of Bulgaria, and the start of three months of playing cards by the stove with Hassan, free Russian movies on Tuesday mornings at Cinema Park, sweet turnip *qurma* over rice for lunch after a morning of building snowmen.

And kites, of course. Flying kites. And running them.

For a few unfortunate kids, winter did not spell the end of the school year. There were the so-called voluntary winter courses. No kid I knew ever volunteered to go to these classes; parents, of course, did the volunteering for them. Fortunately for me, Baba was not one of them. I remember one kid, Ahmad, who lived across the street from us. His father was some kind of doctor, I think. Ahmad had epilepsy and always wore a wool vest and thick black-rimmed glasses—he was one of Assef's regular victims. Every morning, I watched from my bedroom window as their Hazara servant shoveled snow from the driveway, cleared the way for the black Opel. I made a point of watching Ahmad and his father get into the car, Ahmad in his wool vest and winter coat, his schoolbag filled with books and pencils. I waited until they pulled away, turned the corner, then I slipped back into bed in my flannel pajamas. I pulled the blanket to my chin and watched the snowcapped hills in the north through the window. Watched them until I drifted back to sleep.

I loved wintertime in Kabul. I loved it for the soft pattering of snow against my window at night, for the way fresh snow crunched under my black rubber boots, for the warmth of the cast-iron stove as the wind screeched through the yards, the streets. But mostly because, as the trees froze and ice sheathed the roads, the chill between Baba and me thawed a little. And the reason for that was the kites. Baba and I lived in the same house, but in different spheres of existence. Kites were the one paper-thin slice of intersection between those spheres.

EVERY WINTER, districts in Kabul held a kite-fighting tourna-ment. And if you were a boy living in Kabul, the day of the tourna-

ment was undeniably the highlight of the cold season. I never slept
the night before the tournament. I'd roll from side to side, make
shadow animals on the wall, even sit on the balcony in the dark, a
blanket wrapped around me. I felt like a soldier trying to sleep in
the trenches the night before a major battle. And that wasn't so far
off. In Kabul, fighting kites *was* a little like going to war.

As with any war, you had to ready yourself for battle. For a
while, Hassan and I used to build our own kites. We saved our
weekly allowances in the fall, dropped the money in a little porcelain horse Baba had brought one time from Herat. When the
winds of winter began to blow and snow fell in chunks, we undid
the snap under the horse's belly. We went to the bazaar and
bought bamboo, glue, string, and paper. We spent hours every day
shaving bamboo for the center and cross spars, cutting the thin
tissue paper which made for easy dipping and recovery. And then,
of course, we had to make our own string, or *tar*. If the kite was
the gun, then *tar*, the glass-coated cutting line, was the bullet in
the chamber. We'd go out in the yard and feed up to five hundred
feet of string through a mixture of ground glass and glue. We'd
then hang the line between the trees, leave it to dry. The next day,
we'd wind the battle-ready line around a wooden spool. By the
time the snow melted and the rains of spring swept in, every boy
in Kabul bore telltale horizontal gashes on his fingers from a
whole winter of fighting kites. I remember how my classmates and
I used to huddle, compare our battle scars on the first day of
school. The cuts stung and didn't heal for a couple of weeks, but I
didn't mind. They were reminders of a beloved season that had
once again passed too quickly. Then the class captain would blow
his whistle and we'd march in a single file to our classrooms, longing for winter already, greeted instead by the specter of yet
another long school year.

But it quickly became apparent that Hassan and I were better kite fighters than kite makers. Some flaw or other in our design always spelled its doom. So Baba started taking us to Saifo's to buy our kites. Saifo was a nearly blind old man who was a *moochi* by profession—a shoe repairman. But he was also the city's most famous kite maker, working out of a tiny hovel on Jadeh Maywand, the crowded street south of the muddy banks of the Kabul River. I remember you had to crouch to enter the prison cell–sized store, and then had to lift a trapdoor to creep down a set of wooden steps to the dank basement where Saifo stored his coveted kites. Baba would buy us each three identical kites and spools of glass string. If I changed my mind and asked for a bigger and fancier kite, Baba would buy it for me—but then he'd buy it for Hassan too. Sometimes I wished he wouldn't do that. Wished he'd let me be the favorite.

The kite-fighting tournament was an old winter tradition in Afghanistan. It started early in the morning on the day of the contest and didn't end until only the winning kite flew in the sky—I remember one year the tournament outlasted daylight. People gathered on sidewalks and roofs to cheer for their kids. The streets filled with kite fighters, jerking and tugging on their lines, squinting up to the sky, trying to gain position to cut the opponent's line. Every kite fighter had an assistant—in my case, Hassan—who held the spool and fed the line.

One time, a bratty Hindi kid whose family had recently moved into the neighborhood told us that in his hometown, kite fighting had strict rules and regulations. "You have to play in a boxed area and you have to stand at a right angle to the wind," he said proudly. "And you can't use aluminum to make your glass string."

Hassan and I looked at each other. Cracked up. The Hindi kid would soon learn what the British learned earlier in the century, and what the Russians would eventually learn by the late 1980s: that Afghans are an independent people. Afghans cherish custom but abhor rules. And so it was with kite fighting. The rules were simple: No rules. Fly your kite. Cut the opponents. Good luck.

Except that wasn't all. The real fun began when a kite was cut. That was where the kite runners came in, those kids who chased the windblown kite drifting through the neighborhoods until it came spiraling down in a field, dropping in someone's yard, on a tree, or a rooftop. The chase got pretty fierce; hordes of kite runners swarmed the streets, shoved past each other like those people from Spain I'd read about once, the ones who ran from the bulls. One year a neighborhood kid climbed a pine tree for a kite. A branch snapped under his weight and he fell thirty feet. Broke his back and never walked again. But he fell with the kite still in his hands. And when a kite runner had his hands on a kite, no one could take it from him. That wasn't a rule. That was custom.

For kite runners, the most coveted prize was the last fallen kite of a winter tournament. It was a trophy of honor, something to be displayed on a mantle for guests to admire. When the sky cleared of kites and only the final two remained, every kite runner readied himself for the chance to land this prize. He positioned himself at a spot that he thought would give him a head start. Tense muscles readied themselves to uncoil. Necks craned. Eyes crinkled. Fights broke out. And when the last kite was cut, all hell broke loose.

Over the years, I had seen a lot of guys run kites. But Hassan was by far the greatest kite runner I'd ever seen. It was downright eerie the way he always got to the spot the kite would land *before* the kite did, as if he had some sort of inner compass.

I remember one overcast winter day, Hassan and I were running a kite. I was chasing him through neighborhoods, hopping gutters, weaving through narrow streets. I was a year older than him, but Hassan ran faster than I did, and I was falling behind.

"Hassan! Wait!" I yelled, my breathing hot and ragged.

He whirled around, motioned with his hand. "This way!" he called before dashing around another corner. I looked up, saw that the direction we were running was opposite to the one the kite was drifting.

"We're losing it! We're going the wrong way!" I cried out.

"Trust me!" I heard him call up ahead. I reached the corner and saw Hassan bolting along, his head down, not even looking at the sky, sweat soaking through the back of his shirt. I tripped over a rock and fell—I wasn't just slower than Hassan but clumsier too; I'd always envied his natural athleticism. When I staggered to my feet, I caught a glimpse of Hassan disappearing around another street corner. I hobbled after him, spikes of pain battering my scraped knees.

I saw we had ended up on a rutted dirt road near Isteqlal Middle School. There was a field on one side where lettuce grew in the summer, and a row of sour cherry trees on the other. I found Hassan sitting cross-legged at the foot of one of the trees, eating from a fistful of dried mulberries.

"What are we doing here?" I panted, my stomach roiling with nausea.

He smiled. "Sit with me, Amir agha."

I dropped next to him, lay on a thin patch of snow, wheezing. "You're wasting our time. It was going the other way, didn't you see?"

Hassan popped a mulberry in his mouth. "It's coming," he said. I could hardly breathe and he didn't even sound tired.

"How do you know?" I said.

"I know."

"How can you *know*?"

He turned to me. A few sweat beads rolled from his bald scalp. "Would I ever lie to you, Amir agha?"

Suddenly I decided to toy with him a little. "I don't know. Would you?"

"I'd sooner eat dirt," he said with a look of indignation.

"Really? You'd do that?"

He threw me a puzzled look. "Do what?"

"Eat dirt if I told you to," I said. I knew I was being cruel, like when I'd taunt him if he didn't know some big word. But there was something fascinating—albeit in a sick way—about teasing Hassan. Kind of like when we used to play insect torture. Except now, he was the ant and I was holding the magnifying glass.

His eyes searched my face for a long time. We sat there, two boys under a sour cherry tree, suddenly looking, *really* looking, at each other. That's when it happened again: Hassan's face changed. Maybe not *changed*, not really, but suddenly I had the feeling I was looking at two faces, the one I knew, the one that was my first memory, and another, a second face, this one lurking just beneath the surface. I'd seen it happen before—it always shook me up a little. It just appeared, this other face, for a fraction of a moment, long enough to leave me with the unsettling feeling that maybe I'd seen it someplace before. Then Hassan blinked and it was just him again. Just Hassan.

"If you asked, I would," he finally said, looking right at me. I dropped my eyes. To this day, I find it hard to gaze directly at people like Hassan, people who mean every word they say.

"But I wonder," he added. "Would you ever ask me to do such a thing, Amir agha?" And, just like that, he had thrown at me his own little test. If I was going to toy with him and challenge his loyalty, then he'd toy with me, test my integrity.

I wished I hadn't started this conversation. I forced a smile. "Don't be stupid, Hassan. You know I wouldn't."

Hassan returned the smile. Except his didn't look forced. "I know," he said. And that's the thing about people who mean everything they say. They think everyone else does too.

"Here it comes," Hassan said, pointing to the sky. He rose to his feet and walked a few paces to his left. I looked up, saw the kite plummeting toward us. I heard footfalls, shouts, an approaching melee of kite runners. But they were wasting their time. Because Hassan stood with his arms wide open, smiling, waiting for the kite. And may God—if He exists, that is—strike me blind if the kite didn't just drop into his outstretched arms.

IN THE WINTER OF 1975, I saw Hassan run a kite for the last time.

Usually, each neighborhood held its own competition. But that year, the tournament was going to be held in my neighborhood, Wazir Akbar Khan, and several other districts—Karteh-Char, Karteh-Parwan, Mekro-Rayan, and Koteh-Sangi—had been invited. You could hardly go anywhere without hearing talk of the upcoming tournament. Word had it this was going to be the biggest tournament in twenty-five years.

One night that winter, with the big contest only four days away, Baba and I sat in his study in overstuffed leather chairs by the glow of the fireplace. We were sipping tea, talking. Ali had served dinner earlier—potatoes and curried cauliflower over rice—and had retired for the night with Hassan. Baba was fattening his pipe and I was asking him to tell the story about the winter a pack of wolves had descended from the mountains in Herat and forced everyone to stay indoors for a week, when he lit a match and said, casually, "I think maybe you'll win the tournament this year. What do you think?"

I didn't know what to think. Or what to say. Was that what it would take? Had he just slipped me a key? I was a good kite fighter. Actually, a very good one. A few times, I'd even come close to winning the winter tournament—once, I'd made it to the final three. But coming close wasn't the same as winning, was it? Baba hadn't *come close*. He had won because winners won and everyone else just went home. Baba was used to winning, winning at everything he set his mind to. Didn't he have a right to expect the same from his son? And just imagine. If I did win...

Baba smoked his pipe and talked. I pretended to listen. But I couldn't listen, not really, because Baba's casual little comment had planted a seed in my head: the resolution that I would win that winter's tournament. I was going to win. There was no other viable option. I was going to win, and I was going to run that last kite. Then I'd bring it home and show it to Baba. Show him once and for all that his son was worthy. Then maybe my life as a ghost in this house would finally be over. I let myself dream: I imagined conversation and laughter over dinner instead of silence broken only by the clinking of silverware and the occasional grunt. I envisioned us taking a Friday drive in Baba's car to Paghman, stopping on the way at Ghargha Lake for some fried trout and potatoes. We'd go to the zoo to see Marjan the lion, and maybe Baba wouldn't yawn and steal looks at his wristwatch all the time. Maybe Baba would even read one of my stories. I'd write him a hundred if I thought he'd read one. Maybe he'd call me *Amir jan* like Rahim Khan did. And maybe, just maybe, I would finally be pardoned for killing my mother.

Baba was telling me about the time he'd cut fourteen kites on the same day. I smiled, nodded, laughed at all the right places, but

I hardly heard a word he said. I had a mission now. And I wasn't going to fail Baba. Not this time.

IT SNOWED HEAVILY the night before the tournament. Hassan and I sat under the *kursi* and played panjpar as wind-rattled tree branches tapped on the window. Earlier that day, I'd asked Ali to set up the *kursi* for us—which was basically an electric heater under a low table covered with a thick, quilted blanket. Around the table, he arranged mattresses and cushions, so as many as twenty people could sit and slip their legs under. Hassan and I used to spend entire snowy days snug under the *kursi,* playing chess, cards—mostly panjpar.

I killed Hassan's ten of diamonds, played him two jacks and a six. Next door, in Baba's study, Baba and Rahim Khan were discussing business with a couple of other men—one of them I recognized as Assef's father. Through the wall, I could hear the scratchy sound of Radio Kabul News.

Hassan killed the six and picked up the jacks. On the radio, Daoud Khan was announcing something about foreign investments.

"He says someday we'll have television in Kabul," I said.

"Who?"

"Daoud Khan, you ass, the president."

Hassan giggled. "I heard they already have it in Iran," he said.

I sighed. "Those Iranians..." For a lot of Hazaras, Iran represented a sanctuary of sorts—I guess because, like Hazaras, most Iranians were Shi'a Muslims. But I remembered something my teacher had said that summer about Iranians, that they were grinning smooth talkers who patted you on the back with one hand and picked your pocket with the other. I told Baba about that and he said my teacher was one of those jealous Afghans, jealous because Iran was a rising power in Asia and most people around the world couldn't even find Afghanistan on a world map. "It hurts to say that," he said, shrugging. "But better to get hurt by the truth than comforted with a lie."

"I'll buy you one someday," I said.

Hassan's face brightened. "A television? In truth?"

"Sure. And not the black-and-white kind either. We'll probably be grown-ups by then, but I'll get us two. One for you and one for me."

"I'll put it on my table, where I keep my drawings," Hassan said.

His saying that made me kind of sad. Sad for who Hassan was, where he lived. For how he'd accepted the fact that he'd grow old in that mud shack in the yard, the way his father had. I drew the last card, played him a pair of queens and a ten.

Hassan picked up the queens. "You know, I think you're going to make Agha sahib very proud tomorrow."

"You think so?"

"*Inshallah,*" he said.

"*Inshallah,*" I echoed, though the "God willing" qualifier didn't sound as sincere coming from my lips. That was the thing with Hassan. He was so goddamn pure, you always felt like a phony around him.

I killed his king and played him my final card, the ace of spades. He had to pick it up. I'd won, but as I shuffled for a new game, I had the distinct suspicion that Hassan had *let* me win.

"Amir agha?"

"What?"

"You know...I *like* where I live." He was always doing that, reading my mind. "It's my home."

"Whatever," I said. "Get ready to lose again."

SEVEN

The next morning, as he brewed black tea for breakfast, Hassan told me he'd had a dream. "We were at Ghargha Lake, you, me, Father, Agha sahib, Rahim Khan, and thousands of other people," he said. "It was warm and sunny, and the lake was clear like a mirror. But no one was swimming because they said a monster had come to the lake. It was swimming at the bottom, waiting."

He poured me a cup and added sugar, blew on it a few times. Put it before me. "So everyone is scared to get in the water, and suddenly you kick off your shoes, Amir agha, and take off your shirt. 'There's no monster,' you say. 'I'll show you all.' And before anyone can stop you, you dive into the water, start swimming away. I follow you in and we're both swimming."

"But you can't swim."

Hassan laughed. "It's a dream, Amir agha, you can do anything. Anyway, everyone is screaming, 'Get out! Get out!' but we just swim in the cold water. We make it way out to the middle of the lake and we stop swimming. We turn toward the shore and wave to the people. They look small like ants, but we can hear them clapping. They see now. There is no monster, just water. They change the name of the lake after that, and call it the 'Lake of Amir and Hassan, Sultans of Kabul,' and we get to charge people money for swimming in it."

"So what does it mean?" I said.

He coated my *naan* with marmalade, placed it on a plate. "I don't know. I was hoping you could tell me."

"Well, it's a dumb dream. Nothing happens in it."

"Father says dreams always mean something."

I sipped some tea. "Why don't you ask him, then? He's so smart," I said, more curtly than I had intended. I hadn't slept all night. My neck and back were like coiled springs, and my eyes stung. Still, I had been mean to Hassan. I almost apologized, then didn't. Hassan understood I was just nervous. Hassan always understood about me.

Upstairs, I could hear the water running in Baba's bathroom.

THE STREETS GLISTENED with fresh snow and the sky was a blameless blue. Snow blanketed every rooftop and weighed on the branches of the stunted mulberry trees that lined our street. Overnight, snow had nudged its way into every crack and gutter. I squinted against the blinding white when Hassan and I stepped through the wrought-iron gates. Ali shut the gates behind us. I heard him mutter a prayer under his breath—he always said a prayer when his son left the house.

I had never seen so many people on our street. Kids were flinging snowballs, squabbling, chasing one another, giggling. Kite fighters were huddling with their spool holders, making last-minute preparations. From adjacent streets, I could hear laughter and chatter. Already, rooftops were jammed with spectators reclining in lawn chairs, hot tea steaming from thermoses, and the music of Ahmad Zahir blaring from cassette players. The immensely popular Ahmad Zahir had revolutionized Afghan music and outraged the purists by adding electric guitars, drums, and horns to the traditional tabla and harmonium; on stage or at parties, he shirked the austere and nearly morose stance of older singers and actually smiled when he sang—sometimes even at women. I turned my gaze to our rooftop, found Baba and Rahim Khan sitting on a bench, both dressed in wool sweaters, sipping tea. Baba waved. I couldn't tell if he was waving at me or Hassan.

"We should get started," Hassan said. He wore black rubber snow boots and a bright green *chapan* over a thick sweater and faded corduroy pants. Sunlight washed over his face, and, in it, I saw how well the pink scar above his lip had healed.

Suddenly I wanted to withdraw. Pack it all in, go back home. What was I thinking? Why was I putting myself through this, when I already knew the outcome? Baba was on the roof, watching me. I felt his glare on me like the heat of a blistering sun. This would be failure on a grand scale, even for me.

"I'm not sure I want to fly a kite today," I said.

"It's a beautiful day," Hassan said.

I shifted on my feet. Tried to peel my gaze away from our rooftop. "I don't know. Maybe we should go home."

Then he stepped toward me and, in a low voice, said something that scared me a little. "Remember, Amir agha. There's no monster, just a beautiful day." How could I be such an open book to him when, half the time, I had no idea what was milling around in his head? I was the one who went to school, the one who could read, write. I was the smart one. Hassan couldn't read a first-grade textbook but he'd read me plenty. That was a little unsettling, but also sort of comfortable to have someone who always knew what you needed.

"No monster," I said, feeling a little better, to my own surprise.

He smiled. "No monster."

"Are you sure?"

He closed his eyes. Nodded.

I looked to the kids scampering down the street, flinging snowballs. "It is a beautiful day, isn't it?"

"Let's fly," he said.

It occurred to me then that maybe Hassan had made up his dream. Was that possible? I decided it wasn't. Hassan wasn't that smart. *I* wasn't that smart. But made up or not, the silly dream had lifted some of my anxiety. Maybe I *should* take off my shirt, take a swim in the lake. Why not?

"Let's do it," I said.

Hassan's face brightened. "Good," he said. He lifted our kite, red with yellow borders, and, just beneath where the central and cross spars met, marked with Saifo's unmistakable signature. He licked his finger and held it up, tested the wind, then ran in its direction—on those rare occasions we flew kites in the summer, he'd kick up dust to see which way the wind blew it. The spool rolled in my hands until Hassan stopped, about fifty feet away. He held the kite high over his head, like an Olympic athlete showing his gold medal. I jerked the string twice, our usual signal, and Hassan tossed the kite.

Caught between Baba and the mullahs at school, I still hadn't made up my mind about God. But when a Koran *ayat* I had learned in my *diniyat* class rose to my lips, I muttered it. I took a deep breath, exhaled, and pulled on the string. Within a minute, my kite was rocketing to the sky. It made a sound like a paper bird flapping its wings. Hassan clapped his hands, whistled, and ran back to me. I handed him the spool, holding on to the string, and he spun it quickly to roll the loose string back on.

At least two dozen kites already hung in the sky, like paper sharks roaming for prey. Within an hour, the number doubled, and red, blue, and yellow kites glided and spun in the sky. A cold breeze wafted through my hair. The wind was perfect for kite flying, blowing just hard enough to give some lift, make the sweeps easier. Next to me, Hassan held the spool, his hands already bloodied by the string.

Soon, the cutting started and the first of the defeated kites whirled out of control. They fell from the sky like shooting stars with brilliant, rippling tails, showering the neighborhoods below with prizes for the kite runners. I could hear the runners now, hollering as they ran the streets. Someone shouted reports of a fight breaking out two streets down.

I kept stealing glances at Baba sitting with Rahim Khan on the roof, wondered what he was thinking. Was he cheering for me? Or did a part of him enjoy watching me fail? That was the thing about kite flying: Your mind drifted with the kite.

They were coming down all over the place now, the kites, and I was still flying. I was still flying. My eyes kept wandering over to Baba, bundled up in his wool sweater. Was he surprised I had lasted as long as I had? *You don't keep your eyes to the sky, you won't last much longer.* I snapped my gaze back to the sky. A red kite was closing in on me—I'd caught it just in time. I tangled a bit with it, ended up besting him when he became impatient and tried to cut me from below.

Up and down the streets, kite runners were returning triumphantly, their captured kites held high. They showed them off to their parents, their friends. But they all knew the best was yet to come. The biggest prize of all was still flying. I sliced a bright yellow kite with a coiled white tail. It cost me another gash on the index finger and blood trickled down into my palm. I had Hassan hold the string and sucked the blood dry, blotted my finger against my jeans.

Within another hour, the number of surviving kites dwindled from maybe fifty to a dozen. I was one of them. I'd made it to the last dozen. I knew this part of the tournament would take a while, because the guys who had lasted this long were good—they wouldn't easily fall into simple traps like the old lift-and-dive, Hassan's favorite trick.

By three o'clock that afternoon, tufts of clouds had drifted in and the sun had slipped behind them. Shadows started to lengthen. The spectators on the roofs bundled up in scarves and thick coats. We were down to a half dozen and I was still flying. My legs ached and my neck was stiff. But with each defeated kite, hope grew in my heart, like snow collecting on a wall, one flake at a time.

My eyes kept returning to a blue kite that had been wreaking havoc for the last hour.

"How many has he cut?" I asked.

"I counted eleven," Hassan said.

"Do you know whose it might be?"

Hassan clucked his tongue and tipped his chin. That was a trademark Hassan gesture, meant he had no idea. The blue kite sliced a big purple one and swept twice in big loops. Ten minutes later, he'd cut another two, sending hordes of kite runners racing after them.

After another thirty minutes, only four kites remained. And I was still flying. It seemed I could hardly make a wrong move, as if every gust of wind blew in my favor. I'd never felt so in command, so lucky. It felt intoxicating. I didn't dare look up to the roof.

Didn't dare take my eyes off the sky. I had to concentrate, play it smart. Another fifteen minutes and what had seemed like a laughable dream that morning had suddenly become reality: It was just me and the other guy. The blue kite.

The tension in the air was as taut as the glass string I was tugging with my bloody hands. People were stomping their feet, clapping, whistling, chanting, *"Boboresh! Boboresh!"* Cut him! Cut him! I wondered if Baba's voice was one of them. Music blasted. The smell of steamed *mantu* and fried *pakora* drifted from rooftops and open doors.

But all I heard—all I willed myself to hear—was the thudding of blood in my head. All I saw was the blue kite. All I smelled was victory. Salvation. Redemption. If Baba was wrong and there *was* a God like they said in school, then He'd let me win. I didn't know what the other guy was playing for, maybe just bragging rights. But this was my one chance to become someone who was looked at, not seen, listened to, not heard. If there was a God, He'd guide the winds, let them blow for me so that, with a tug of my string, I'd cut loose my pain, my longing. I'd endured too much, come too far. And suddenly, just like that, hope became knowledge. I was going to win. It was just a matter of when.

It turned out to be sooner than later. A gust of wind lifted my kite and I took advantage. Fed the string, pulled up. Looped my kite on top of the blue one. I held position. The blue kite knew it was in trouble. It was trying desperately to maneuver out of the jam, but I didn't let go. I held position. The crowd sensed the end was at hand. The chorus of "Cut him! Cut him!" grew louder, like Romans chanting for the gladiators to kill, kill!

"You're almost there, Amir agha! Almost there!" Hassan was panting.

Then the moment came. I closed my eyes and loosened my

grip on the string. It sliced my fingers again as the wind dragged it. And then...I didn't need to hear the crowd's roar to know. I didn't need to see either. Hassan was screaming and his arm was wrapped around my neck.

"Bravo! Bravo, Amir agha!"

I opened my eyes, saw the blue kite spinning wildly like a tire come loose from a speeding car. I blinked, tried to say something. Nothing came out. Suddenly I was hovering, looking down on myself from above. Black leather coat, red scarf, faded jeans. A thin boy, a little sallow, and a tad short for his twelve years. He had narrow shoulders and a hint of dark circles around his pale hazel eyes. The breeze rustled his light brown hair. He looked up to me and we smiled at each other.

Then I was screaming, and everything was color and sound, everything was alive and good. I was throwing my free arm around Hassan and we were hopping up and down, both of us laughing, both of us weeping. "You won, Amir agha! You won!"

"*We* won! *We* won!" was all I could say. This wasn't happening. In a moment, I'd blink and rouse from this beautiful dream, get out of bed, march down to the kitchen to eat breakfast with no one to talk to but Hassan. Get dressed. Wait for Baba. Give up. Back to my old life. Then I saw Baba on our roof. He was standing on the edge, pumping both of his fists. Hollering and clapping. And that right there was the single greatest moment of my twelve years of life, seeing Baba on that roof, proud of me at last.

But he was doing something now, motioning with his hands in an urgent way. Then I understood. "Hassan, we—"

"I know," he said, breaking our embrace. "*Inshallah,* we'll celebrate later. Right now, I'm going to run that blue kite for you," he said. He dropped the spool and took off running, the hem of his green *chapan* dragging in the snow behind him.

"Hassan!" I called. "Come back with it!"

He was already turning the street corner, his rubber boots kicking up snow. He stopped, turned. He cupped his hands around his mouth. "For you a thousand times over!" he said. Then he smiled his Hassan smile and disappeared around the corner. The next time I saw him smile unabashedly like that was twenty-six years later, in a faded Polaroid photograph.

I began to pull my kite back as people rushed to congratulate me. I shook hands with them, said my thanks. The younger kids looked at me with an awestruck twinkle in their eyes; I was a hero. Hands patted my back and tousled my hair. I pulled on the string and returned every smile, but my mind was on the blue kite.

Finally, I had my kite in hand. I wrapped the loose string that had collected at my feet around the spool, shook a few more hands, and trotted home. When I reached the wrought-iron gates, Ali was waiting on the other side. He stuck his hand through the bars. "Congratulations," he said.

I gave him my kite and spool, shook his hand. "*Tashakor*, Ali jan."

"I was praying for you the whole time."

"Then keep praying. We're not done yet."

I hurried back to the street. I didn't ask Ali about Baba. I didn't want to see him yet. In my head, I had it all planned: I'd make a grand entrance, a hero, prized trophy in my bloodied hands. Heads would turn and eyes would lock. Rostam and Sohrab sizing each other up. A dramatic moment of silence. Then the old warrior would walk to the young one, embrace him, acknowledge his worthiness. Vindication. Salvation. Redemption. And then? Well ... happily ever after, of course. What else?

The streets of Wazir Akbar Khan were numbered and set at right angles to each other like a grid. It was a new neighborhood then, still developing, with empty lots of land and half-constructed homes on every street between compounds surrounded by eight-foot walls. I ran up and down every street, looking for Hassan. Everywhere, people were busy folding chairs, packing food and utensils after a long day of partying. Some, still sitting on their rooftops, shouted their congratulations to me.

Four streets south of ours, I saw Omar, the son of an engineer who was a friend of Baba's. He was dribbling a soccer ball with his brother on the front lawn of their house. Omar was a pretty good guy. We'd been classmates in fourth grade, and one time he'd given me a fountain pen, the kind you had to load with a cartridge.

"I heard you won, Amir," he said. "Congratulations."

"Thanks. Have you seen Hassan?"

"Your Hazara?"

I nodded.

Omar headed the ball to his brother. "I hear he's a great kite runner." His brother headed the ball back to him. Omar caught it, tossed it up and down. "Although I've always wondered how he manages. I mean, with those tight little eyes, how does he *see* anything?"

His brother laughed, a short burst, and asked for the ball. Omar ignored him.

"Have you seen him?"

Omar flicked a thumb over his shoulder, pointing southwest. "I saw him running toward the bazaar awhile ago."

"Thanks." I scuttled away.

By the time I reached the marketplace, the sun had almost sunk behind the hills and dusk had painted the sky pink and purple. A few blocks away, from the Haji Yaghoub Mosque, the mullah bellowed *azan*, calling for the faithful to unroll their rugs and bow their heads west in prayer. Hassan never missed any of the five daily prayers. Even when we were out playing, he'd excuse himself, draw water from the well in the yard, wash up, and disappear into the hut. He'd come out a few minutes later, smiling, find me sitting against the wall or perched on a tree. He was going to miss prayer tonight, though, because of me.

The bazaar was emptying quickly, the merchants finishing up their haggling for the day. I trotted in the mud between rows of closely packed cubicles where you could buy a freshly slaughtered pheasant in one stand and a calculator from the adjacent one. I picked my way through the dwindling crowd, the lame beggars dressed in layers of tattered rags, the vendors with rugs on their shoulders, the cloth merchants and butchers closing shop for the day. I found no sign of Hassan.

I stopped by a dried fruit stand, described Hassan to an old merchant loading his mule with crates of pine seeds and raisins. He wore a powder blue turban.

He paused to look at me for a long time before answering. "I might have seen him."

"Which way did he go?"

He eyed me up and down. "What is a boy like you doing here at this time of the day looking for a Hazara?" His glance lingered admiringly on my leather coat and my jeans—*cowboy pants,* we used to call them. In Afghanistan, owning anything American, especially if it wasn't secondhand, was a sign of wealth.

"I need to find him, Agha."

"What is he to you?" he said. I didn't see the point of his question, but I reminded myself that impatience wasn't going to make him tell me any faster.

"He's our servant's son," I said.

The old man raised a pepper gray eyebrow. "He is? Lucky Hazara, having such a concerned master. His father should get on his knees, sweep the dust at your feet with his eyelashes."

"Are you going to tell me or not?"

He rested an arm on the mule's back, pointed south. "I think I saw the boy you described running that way. He had a kite in his hand. A blue one."

"He did?" I said. *For you a thousand times over,* he'd promised. Good old Hassan. Good old reliable Hassan. He'd kept his promise and run the last kite for me.

"Of course, they've probably caught him by now," the old merchant said, grunting and loading another box on the mule's back.

"Who?"

"The other boys," he said. "The ones chasing him. They were dressed like you." He glanced to the sky and sighed. "Now, run along, you're making me late for *namaz.*"

But I was already scrambling down the lane.

For the next few minutes, I scoured the bazaar in vain. Maybe the old merchant's eyes had betrayed him. Except he'd seen the blue kite. The thought of getting my hands on that kite . . . I poked my head behind every lane, every shop. No sign of Hassan.

I had begun to worry that darkness would fall before I found Hassan when I heard voices from up ahead. I'd reached a secluded, muddy road. It ran perpendicular to the end of the main thoroughfare bisecting the bazaar. I turned onto the rutted track and followed the voices. My boot squished in mud with every step and my breath puffed out in white clouds before me. The narrow path ran parallel on one side to a snow-filled ravine through which a stream may have tumbled in the spring. To my other side stood rows of snow-burdened cypress trees peppered among flat-topped clay houses—no more than mud shacks in most cases—separated by narrow alleys.

I heard the voices again, louder this time, coming from one of the alleys. I crept close to the mouth of the alley. Held my breath. Peeked around the corner.

Hassan was standing at the blind end of the alley in a defiant stance: fists curled, legs slightly apart. Behind him, sitting on piles of scrap and rubble, was the blue kite. My key to Baba's heart.

Blocking Hassan's way out of the alley were three boys, the same three from that day on the hill, the day after Daoud Khan's coup, when Hassan had saved us with his slingshot. Wali was standing on one side, Kamal on the other, and in the middle, Assef. I felt my body clench up, and something cold rippled up my spine. Assef seemed relaxed, confident. He was twirling his brass knuckles. The other two guys shifted nervously on their feet, looking from Assef to Hassan, like they'd cornered some kind of wild animal that only Assef could tame.

"Where is your slingshot, Hazara?" Assef said, turning the brass knuckles in his hand. "What was it you said? 'They'll have to call you One-Eyed Assef.' That's right. One-Eyed Assef. That was clever. Really clever. Then again, it's easy to be clever when you're holding a loaded weapon."

I realized I still hadn't breathed out. I exhaled, slowly, quietly. I felt paralyzed. I watched them close in on the boy I'd grown up with, the boy whose harelipped face had been my first memory.

"But today is your lucky day, Hazara," Assef said. He had his back to me, but I would have bet he was grinning. "I'm in a mood to forgive. What do you say to that, boys?"

"That's generous," Kamal blurted, "Especially after the rude manners he showed us last time." He was trying to sound like

Assef, except there was a tremor in his voice. Then I understood: He wasn't afraid of Hassan, not really. He was afraid because he had no idea what Assef had in mind.

Assef waved a dismissive hand. "*Bakhshida.* Forgiven. It's done." His voice dropped a little. "Of course, nothing is free in this world, and my pardon comes with a small price."

"That's fair," Kamal said.

"Nothing is free," Wali added.

"You're a lucky Hazara," Assef said, taking a step toward Hassan. "Because today, it's only going to cost you that blue kite. A fair deal, boys, isn't it?"

"More than fair," Kamal said.

Even from where I was standing, I could see the fear creeping into Hassan's eyes, but he shook his head. "Amir agha won the tournament and I ran this kite for him. I ran it fairly. This is his kite."

"A loyal Hazara. Loyal as a dog," Assef said.

Kamal's laugh was a shrill, nervous sound.

"But before you sacrifice yourself for him, think about this: Would he do the same for you? Have you ever wondered why he never includes you in games when he has guests? Why he only plays with you when no one else is around? I'll tell you why, Hazara. Because to him, you're nothing but an ugly pet. Something he can play with when he's bored, something he can kick when he's angry. Don't ever fool yourself and think you're something more."

"Amir agha and I are friends," Hassan said. He looked flushed.

"Friends?" Assef said, laughing. "You pathetic fool! Someday you'll wake up from your little fantasy and learn just how good of a friend he is. Now, *bas!* Enough of this. Give us that kite."

Hassan stooped and picked up a rock.

Assef flinched. He began to take a step back, stopped. "Last chance, Hazara."

Hassan's answer was to cock the arm that held the rock.

"Whatever you wish." Assef unbuttoned his winter coat, took it off, folded it slowly and deliberately. He placed it against the wall.

I opened my mouth, almost said something. Almost. The rest of my life might have turned out differently if I had. But I didn't. I just watched. Paralyzed.

Assef motioned with his hand, and the other two boys separated, forming a half circle, trapping Hassan in the alley.

"I've changed my mind," Assef said. "I'm letting you keep the kite, Hazara. I'll let you keep it so it will always remind you of what I'm about to do."

Then he charged. Hassan hurled the rock. It struck Assef in the forehead. Assef yelped as he flung himself at Hassan, knocking him to the ground. Wali and Kamal followed.

I bit on my fist. Shut my eyes.

A MEMORY:

Did you know Hassan and you fed from the same breast? Did you know that, Amir agha? Sakina, her name was. She was a fair, blue-eyed Hazara woman from Bamiyan and she sang you old wedding songs. They say there is a brotherhood between people who've fed from the same breast. Did you know that?

A memory:

"A *rupia* each, children. Just one *rupia* each and I will part the curtain of truth." *The old man sits against a mud wall. His sightless eyes are like molten silver embedded in deep, twin craters.*

Hunched over his cane, the fortune-teller runs a gnarled hand across the surface of his deflated cheeks. Cups it before us. "Not much to ask for the truth, is it, a *rupia* each?" *Hassan drops a coin in the leathery palm. I drop mine too.* "In the name of Allah most beneficent, most merciful," *the old fortune-teller whispers. He takes Hassan's hand first, strokes the palm with one hornlike finger-nail, round and round, round and round. The finger then floats to Hassan's face and makes a dry, scratchy sound as it slowly traces the curve of his cheeks, the outline of his ears. The calloused pads of his fingers brush against Hassan's eyes. The hand stops there. Lingers. A shadow passes across the old man's face. Hassan and I exchange a glance. The old man takes Hassan's hand and puts the rupia back in Hassan's palm. He turns to me.* "How about you, young friend?" *he says. On the other side of the wall, a rooster crows. The old man reaches for my hand and I withdraw it.*

A dream:

I am lost in a snowstorm. The wind shrieks, blows stinging sheets of snow into my eyes. I stagger through layers of shifting white. I call for help but the wind drowns my cries. I fall and lie panting on the snow, lost in the white, the wind wailing in my ears. I watch the snow erase my fresh footprints. I'm a ghost now, *I think,* a ghost with no footprints. *I cry out again, hope fading like my footprints. But this time, a muffled reply. I shield my eyes and manage to sit up. Out of the swaying curtains of snow, I catch a glimpse of movement, a flurry of color. A familiar shape materializes. A hand reaches out for me. I see deep, parallel gashes across the palm, blood dripping, staining the snow. I take the hand and suddenly the snow is gone. We're standing in a field of apple green grass with soft wisps of clouds drifting above. I look up and see the clear sky is filled with kites, green, yellow, red, orange. They shimmer in the afternoon light.*

. . .

A HAVOC OF SCRAP AND RUBBLE littered the alley. Worn bicycle tires, bottles with peeled labels, ripped up magazines, yellowed newspapers, all scattered amid a pile of bricks and slabs of cement. A rusted cast-iron stove with a gaping hole on its side tilted against a wall. But there were two things amid the garbage that I couldn't stop looking at: One was the blue kite resting against the wall, close to the cast-iron stove; the other was Hassan's brown corduroy pants thrown on a heap of eroded bricks.

"I don't know," Wali was saying. "My father says it's sinful." He sounded unsure, excited, scared, all at the same time. Hassan lay with his chest pinned to the ground. Kamal and Wali each gripped an arm, twisted and bent at the elbow so that Hassan's hands were pressed to his back. Assef was standing over them, the heel of his snow boots crushing the back of Hassan's neck.

"Your father won't find out," Assef said. "And there's nothing sinful about teaching a lesson to a disrespectful donkey."

"I don't know," Wali muttered.

"Suit yourself," Assef said. He turned to Kamal. "What about you?"

"I ... well ..."

"It's just a Hazara," Assef said. But Kamal kept looking away.

"Fine," Assef snapped. "All I want you weaklings to do is hold him down. Can you manage that?"

Wali and Kamal nodded. They looked relieved.

Assef knelt behind Hassan, put his hands on Hassan's hips and lifted his bare buttocks. He kept one hand on Hassan's back and undid his own belt buckle with his free hand. He unzipped his jeans. Dropped his underwear. He positioned himself behind Hassan. Hassan didn't struggle. Didn't even whimper. He moved his head slightly and I caught a glimpse of his face. Saw the resignation in it. It was a look I had seen before. It was the look of the lamb.

TOMORROW IS THE TENTH DAY of Dhul-Hijjah, the last month of the Muslim calendar, and the first of three days of Eid Al-Adha, or Eid-e-Qorban, as Afghans call it—a day to celebrate how the prophet Ibrahim almost sacrificed his own son for God. Baba has handpicked the sheep again this year, a powder white one with crooked black ears.

We all stand in the backyard, Hassan, Ali, Baba, and I. The mullah recites the prayer, rubs his beard. Baba mutters, Get on with it, under his breath. He sounds annoyed with the endless praying, the ritual of making the meat halal. Baba mocks the story behind this Eid, like he mocks everything religious. But he respects the tradition of Eid-e-Qorban. The custom is to divide the meat in thirds, one for the family, one for friends, and one for the poor. Every year, Baba gives it all to the poor. The rich are fat enough already, he says.

The mullah finishes the prayer. Ameen. He picks up the kitchen knife with the long blade. The custom is to not let the sheep see the knife. Ali feeds the animal a cube of sugar—another custom, to make death sweeter. The sheep kicks, but not much. The mullah grabs it under its jaw and places the blade on its neck. Just a second before he slices the throat in one expert motion, I see the sheep's eyes. It is a look that will haunt my dreams for weeks. I don't know why I watch this yearly ritual in our backyard; my nightmares persist long after the bloodstains on the grass have faded. But I always watch. I watch because of that look of acceptance in the animal's eyes. Absurdly, I imagine the animal understands. I imagine the animal sees that its imminent demise is for a higher purpose. This is the look...

I STOPPED WATCHING, turned away from the alley. Something warm was running down my wrist. I blinked, saw I was still biting down on my fist, hard enough to draw blood from the knuckles. I realized something else. I was weeping. From just around the corner, I could hear Assef's quick, rhythmic grunts.

I had one last chance to make a decision. One final opportunity to decide who I was going to be. I could step into that alley, stand up for Hassan—the way he'd stood up for me all those times in the past—and accept whatever would happen to me. Or I could run.

In the end, I ran.

I ran because I was a coward. I was afraid of Assef and what he would do to me. I was afraid of getting hurt. That's what I told myself as I turned my back to the alley, to Hassan. That's what I made myself believe. I actually *aspired* to cowardice, because the alternative, the real reason I was running, was that Assef was right: Nothing was free in this world. Maybe Hassan was the price I had to pay, the lamb I had to slay, to win Baba. Was it a fair price? The answer floated to my conscious mind before I could thwart it: He was just a Hazara, wasn't he?

I ran back the way I'd come. Ran back to the all but deserted bazaar. I lurched to a cubicle and leaned against the padlocked swinging doors. I stood there panting, sweating, wishing things had turned out some other way.

About fifteen minutes later, I heard voices and running footfalls. I crouched behind the cubicle and watched Assef and the other two sprinting by, laughing as they hurried down the deserted lane. I forced myself to wait ten more minutes. Then I walked back to the rutted track that ran along the snow-filled ravine. I squinted in the dimming light and spotted Hassan walking slowly toward me. I met him by a leafless birch tree on the edge of the ravine.

He had the blue kite in his hands; that was the first thing I saw. And I can't lie now and say my eyes didn't scan it for any rips. His *chapan* had mud smudges down the front and his shirt was ripped just below the collar. He stopped. Swayed on his feet like he was going to collapse. Then he steadied himself. Handed me the kite.

"Where were you? I looked for you," I said. Speaking those words was like chewing on a rock.

Hassan dragged a sleeve across his face, wiped snot and tears. I waited for him to say something, but we just stood there in silence, in the fading light. I was grateful for the early-evening shadows that fell on Hassan's face and concealed mine. I was glad I didn't have to return his gaze. Did he know I knew? And if he knew, then what would I see if I *did* look in his eyes? Blame? Indignation? Or, God forbid, what I feared most: guileless devotion? That, most of all, I couldn't bear to see.

He began to say something and his voice cracked. He closed his mouth, opened it, and closed it again. Took a step back. Wiped his face. And that was as close as Hassan and I ever came to discussing what had happened in the alley. I thought he might burst into tears, but, to my relief, he didn't, and I pretended I hadn't heard the crack in his voice. Just like I pretended I hadn't seen the dark stain in the seat of his pants. Or those tiny drops that fell from between his legs and stained the snow black.

"Agha sahib will worry," was all he said. He turned from me and limped away.

. . .

IT HAPPENED JUST THE WAY I'd imagined. I opened the door to the smoky study and stepped in. Baba and Rahim Khan were drinking tea and listening to the news crackling on the radio. Their heads turned. Then a smile played on my father's lips. He opened his arms. I put the kite down and walked into his thick hairy arms. I buried my face in the warmth of his chest and wept. Baba held me close to him, rocking me back and forth. In his arms, I forgot what I'd done. And that was good.

EIGHT

For a week, I barely saw Hassan. I woke up to find toasted bread, brewed tea, and a boiled egg already on the kitchen table. My clothes for the day were ironed and folded, left on the cane-seat chair in the foyer where Hassan usually did his ironing. He used to wait for me to sit at the breakfast table before he started iron-ing—that way, we could talk. Used to sing too, over the hissing of the iron, sang old Hazara songs about tulip fields. Now only the folded clothes greeted me. That, and a breakfast I hardly finished anymore.

One overcast morning, as I was pushing the boiled egg around on my plate, Ali walked in cradling a pile of chopped wood. I asked him where Hassan was.

"He went back to sleep," Ali said, kneeling before the stove. He pulled the little square door open.

Would Hassan be able to play today?

Ali paused with a log in his hand. A worried look crossed his face. "Lately, it seems all he wants to do is sleep. He does his chores—I see to that—but then he just wants to crawl under his blanket. Can I ask you something?"

"If you have to."

"After that kite tournament, he came home a little bloodied and his shirt was torn. I asked him what had happened and he said it was nothing, that he'd gotten into a little scuffle with some kids over the kite."

I didn't say anything. Just kept pushing the egg around on my plate.

"Did something happen to him, Amir agha? Something he's not telling me?"

I shrugged. "How should I know?"

"You would tell me, nay? *Inshallah,* you would tell me if something had happened?"

"Like I said, how should I know what's wrong with him?" I snapped. "Maybe he's sick. People get sick all the time, Ali. Now, am I going to freeze to death or are you planning on lighting the stove today?"

THAT NIGHT I asked Baba if we could go to Jalalabad on Friday. He was rocking on the leather swivel chair behind his desk, reading a newspaper. He put it down, took off the reading glasses I disliked so much—Baba wasn't old, not at all, and he had lots of years left to live, so why did he have to wear those stupid glasses?

"Why not!" he said. Lately, Baba agreed to everything I asked. Not only that, just two nights before, *he*'d asked *me* if I wanted to see *El Cid* with Charlton Heston at Cinema Aryana. "Do you want to ask Hassan to come along to Jalalabad?"

Why did Baba have to spoil it like that? "He's *mareez*," I said. Not feeling well.

"Really?" Baba stopped rocking in his chair. "What's wrong with him?"

I gave a shrug and sank in the sofa by the fireplace. "He's got a cold or something. Ali says he's sleeping it off."

"I haven't seen much of Hassan the last few days," Baba said. "That's all it is, then, a cold?" I couldn't help hating the way his brow furrowed with worry.

"Just a cold. So are we going Friday, Baba?"

"Yes, yes," Baba said, pushing away from the desk. "Too bad about Hassan. I thought you might have had more fun if he came."

"Well, the two of us can have fun together," I said.

Baba smiled. Winked. "Dress warm," he said.

IT SHOULD HAVE BEEN just the two of us—that was the way I wanted it—but by Wednesday night, Baba had managed to invite another two dozen people. He called his cousin Homayoun—he was actually Baba's second cousin—and mentioned he was going to Jalalabad on Friday, and Homayoun, who had studied engineering in France and had a house in Jalalabad, said he'd love to have everyone over, he'd bring the kids, his two wives, and, while he was at it, cousin Shafiqa and her family were visiting from Herat, maybe she'd like to tag along, and since she was staying with cousin Nader in Kabul, his family would have to be invited as well even though Homayoun and Nader had a bit of a feud going, and if Nader was invited, surely his brother Faruq had to be asked too or his feelings would be hurt and he might not invite them to his daughter's wedding next month and . . .

We filled three vans. I rode with Baba, Rahim Khan, Kaka Homayoun—Baba had taught me at a young age to call any older male *Kaka*, or Uncle, and any older female, *Khala*, or Aunt. Kaka Homayoun's two wives rode with us too—the pinch-faced older one with the warts on her hands and the younger one who always smelled of perfume and danced with her eyes close—as did Kaka Homayoun's twin girls. I sat in the back row, carsick and dizzy, sandwiched between the seven-year-old twins who kept reaching over my lap to slap at each other. The road to Jalalabad is a two-hour trek through mountain roads winding along a steep drop, and my stomach lurched with each hairpin turn. Everyone in the van was talking, talking loudly and at the same time, nearly shrieking, which is how Afghans talk. I asked one of the twins—Fazila or Karima, I could never tell which was which—if she'd trade her window seat with me so I could get fresh air on account of my car sickness. She stuck her tongue out and said no. I told her that was fine, but I couldn't be held accountable for vomiting on her new dress. A minute later, I was leaning out the window. I watched the cratered road rise and fall, whirl its tail around the mountainside, counted the multicolored trucks packed with squatting men lumbering past. I tried closing my eyes, letting the wind slap at my cheeks, opened my mouth to swallow the clean air. I still didn't feel better. A finger poked me in the side. It was Fazila/Karima.

"What?" I said.

"I was just telling everyone about the tournament," Baba said from behind the wheel. Kaka Homayoun and his wives were smiling at me from the middle row of seats.

"There must have been a hundred kites in the sky that day?" Baba said. "Is that about right, Amir?"

"I guess so," I mumbled.

"A hundred kites, Homayoun jan. No *laaf*. And the only one still flying at the end of the day was Amir's. He has the last kite at home, a beautiful blue kite. Hassan and Amir ran it together."

"Congratulations," Kaka Homayoun said. His first wife, the one with the warts, clapped her hands. "Wah wah, Amir jan, we're all so proud of you!" she said. The younger wife joined in. Then they were all clapping, yelping their praises, telling me how proud I'd made them all. Only Rahim Khan, sitting in the passenger seat next to Baba, was silent. He was looking at me in an odd way.

"Please pull over, Baba," I said.

"What?"

"Getting sick," I muttered, leaning across the seat, pressing against Kaka Homayoun's daughters.

Fazila/Karima's face twisted. "Pull over, Kaka! His face is yellow! I don't want him throwing up on my new dress!" she squealed.

Baba began to pull over, but I didn't make it. A few minutes later, I was sitting on a rock on the side of the road as they aired out the van. Baba was smoking with Kaka Homayoun who was telling Fazila/Karima to stop crying; he'd buy her another dress in Jalalabad. I closed my eyes, turned my face to the sun. Little shapes formed behind my eyelids, like hands playing shadows on the wall. They twisted, merged, formed a single image: Hassan's brown corduroy pants discarded on a pile of old bricks in the alley.

KAKA HOMAYOUN'S WHITE, two-story house in Jalalabad had a balcony overlooking a large, walled garden with apple and persimmon trees. There were hedges that, in the summer, the gardener shaped like animals, and a swimming pool with emerald-colored tiles. I sat on the edge of the pool, empty save for a layer of slushy snow at the bottom, feet dangling in. Kaka Homayoun's kids were playing hide-and-seek at the other end of the yard. The women were cooking and I could smell onions frying already, could hear the *phht-phht* of a pressure cooker, music, laughter. Baba, Rahim Khan, Kaka Homayoun, and Kaka Nader were sitting on the balcony, smoking. Kaka Homayoun was telling them he'd brought the projector along to show his slides of France. Ten years since he'd returned from Paris and he was still showing those stupid slides.

It shouldn't have felt this way. Baba and I were finally friends. We'd gone to the zoo a few days before, seen Marjan the lion, and I had hurled a pebble at the bear when no one was watching. We'd gone to Dadkhoda's Kabob House afterward, across from Cinema Park, had lamb kabob with freshly baked *naan* from the *tandoor*. Baba told me stories of his travels to India and Russia, the people he had met, like the armless, legless couple in Bombay who'd been married forty-seven years and raised eleven children. That should have been fun, spending a day like that with Baba, hearing his stories. I finally had what I'd wanted all those years. Except now that I had it, I felt as empty as this unkempt pool I was dangling my legs into.

The wives and daughters served dinner—rice, *kofta,* and chicken *qurma*—at sundown. We dined the traditional way, sitting on cushions around the room, tablecloth spread on the floor, eating with our hands in groups of four or five from common platters. I wasn't hungry but sat down to eat anyway with Baba, Kaka Faruq, and Kaka Homayoun's two boys. Baba, who'd had a few scotches before dinner, was still ranting about the kite tournament, how I'd outlasted them all, how I'd come home with the last kite. His booming voice dominated the room. People raised their heads from their platters, called out their congratulations. Kaka

Faruq patted my back with his clean hand. I felt like sticking a knife in my eye.

Later, well past midnight, after a few hours of poker between Baba and his cousins, the men lay down to sleep on parallel mattresses in the same room where we'd dined. The women went upstairs. An hour later, I still couldn't sleep. I kept tossing and turning as my relatives grunted, sighed, and snored in their sleep. I sat up. A wedge of moonlight streamed in through the window.

"I watched Hassan get raped," I said to no one. Baba stirred in his sleep. Kaka Homayoun grunted. A part of me was hoping someone would wake up and hear, so I wouldn't have to live with this lie anymore. But no one woke up and in the silence that followed, I understood the nature of my new curse: I was going to get away with it.

I thought about Hassan's dream, the one about us swimming in the lake. *There is no monster,* he'd said, *just water.* Except he'd been wrong about that. There was a monster in the lake. It had grabbed Hassan by the ankles, dragged him to the murky bottom. I was that monster.

That was the night I became an insomniac.

I DIDN'T SPEAK TO HASSAN until the middle of the next week. I had just half-eaten my lunch and Hassan was doing the dishes. I was walking upstairs, going to my room, when Hassan asked if I wanted to hike up the hill. I said I was tired. Hassan looked tired too—he'd lost weight and gray circles had formed under his puffed-up eyes. But when he asked again, I reluctantly agreed.

We trekked up the hill, our boots squishing in the muddy snow. Neither one of us said anything. We sat under our pomegranate tree and I knew I'd made a mistake. I shouldn't have come up the hill. The words I'd carved on the tree trunk with Ali's kitchen knife, *Amir and Hassan: The Sultans of Kabul*...I couldn't stand looking at them now.

He asked me to read to him from the *Shahnamah* and I told him I'd changed my mind. Told him I just wanted to go back to my room. He looked away and shrugged. We walked back down the way we'd gone up: in silence. And for the first time in my life, I couldn't wait for spring.

MY MEMORY OF THE REST of that winter of 1975 is pretty hazy. I remember I was fairly happy when Baba was home. We'd eat together, go to see a film, visit Kaka Homayoun or Kaka Faruq. Sometimes Rahim Khan came over and Baba let me sit in his study and sip tea with them. He'd even have me read him some of my stories. It was good and I even believed it would last. And Baba believed it too, I think. We both should have known better. For at least a few months after the kite tournament, Baba and I immersed ourselves in a sweet illusion, saw each other in a way that we never had before. We'd actually deceived ourselves into thinking that a toy made of tissue paper, glue, and bamboo could somehow close the chasm between us.

But when Baba was out—and he was out a lot—I closed myself in my room. I read a book every couple of days, wrote stories, learned to draw horses. I'd hear Hassan shuffling around the kitchen in the morning, hear the clinking of silverware, the whistle of the teapot. I'd wait to hear the door shut and only then I would walk down to eat. On my calendar, I circled the date of the first day of school and began a countdown.

To my dismay, Hassan kept trying to rekindle things between

us. I remember the last time. I was in my room, reading an abbreviated Farsi translation of *Ivanhoe*, when he knocked on my door.

"What is it?"

"I'm going to the baker to buy *naan*," he said from the other side. "I was wondering if you . . . if you wanted to come along."

"I think I'm just going to read," I said, rubbing my temples. Lately, every time Hassan was around, I was getting a headache.

"It's a sunny day," he said.

"I can see that."

"Might be fun to go for a walk."

"You go."

"I wish you'd come along," he said. Paused. Something thumped against the door, maybe his forehead. "I don't know what I've done, Amir agha. I wish you'd tell me. I don't know why we don't play anymore."

"You haven't done anything, Hassan. Just go."

"You can tell me, I'll stop doing it."

I buried my head in my lap, squeezed my temples with my knees, like a vice. "I'll tell you what I want you to stop doing," I said, eyes pressed shut.

"Anything."

"I want you to stop harassing me. I want you to go away," I snapped. I wished he would give it right back to me, break the door open and tell me off—it would have made things easier, better. But he didn't do anything like that, and when I opened the door minutes later, he wasn't there. I fell on my bed, buried my head under the pillow, and cried.

HASSAN MILLED ABOUT the periphery of my life after that. I made sure our paths crossed as little as possible, planned my day that way. Because when he was around, the oxygen seeped out of the room. My chest tightened and I couldn't draw enough air; I'd stand there, gasping in my own little airless bubble of atmosphere. But even when he wasn't around, he was. He was there in the hand-washed and ironed clothes on the cane-seat chair, in the warm slippers left outside my door, in the wood already burning in the stove when I came down for breakfast. Everywhere I turned, I saw signs of his loyalty, his goddamn unwavering loyalty.

Early that spring, a few days before the new school year started, Baba and I were planting tulips in the garden. Most of the snow had melted and the hills in the north were already dotted with patches of green grass. It was a cool, gray morning, and Baba was squatting next to me, digging the soil and planting the bulbs I handed to him. He was telling me how most people thought it was better to plant tulips in the fall and how that wasn't true, when I came right out and said it. "Baba, have you ever thought about getting new servants?"

He dropped the tulip bulb and buried the trowel in the dirt. Took off his gardening gloves. I'd startled him. "*Chi?* What did you say?"

"I was just wondering, that's all."

"Why would I ever want to do that?" Baba said curtly.

"You wouldn't, I guess. It was just a question," I said, my voice fading to a murmur. I was already sorry I'd said it.

"Is this about you and Hassan? I know there's something going on between you two, but whatever it is, you have to deal with it, not me. I'm staying out of it."

"I'm sorry, Baba."

He put on his gloves again. "I grew up with Ali," he said through clenched teeth. "My father took him in, he loved Ali like his own son. Forty years Ali's been with my family. Forty goddamn

years. And you think I'm just going to throw him out?" He turned
to me now, his face as red as a tulip. "I've never laid a hand on you,
Amir, but you ever say that again . . ." He looked away, shaking his
head. "You bring me shame. And Hassan . . . Hassan's not going
anywhere, do you understand?"

I looked down and picked up a fistful of cool soil. Let it pour
between my fingers.

"I said, Do you understand?" Baba roared.

I flinched. "Yes, Baba."

"Hassan's not going anywhere," Baba snapped. He dug a new
hole with the trowel, striking the dirt harder than he had to. "He's
staying right here with us, where he belongs. This is his home and
we're his family. Don't you ever ask me that question again!"

"I won't, Baba. I'm sorry."

We planted the rest of the tulips in silence.

I was relieved when school started that next week. Students
with new notebooks and sharpened pencils in hand ambled about
the courtyard, kicking up dust, chatting in groups, waiting for the
class captains' whistles. Baba drove down the dirt lane that led to
the entrance. The school was an old two-story building with broken windows and dim, cobblestone hallways, patches of its origi-
nal dull yellow paint still showing between sloughing chunks of
plaster. Most of the boys walked to school, and Baba's black Mustang drew more than one envious look. I should have been beaming with pride when he dropped me off—the old me would
have—but all I could muster was a mild form of embarrassment.
That and emptiness. Baba drove away without saying good-bye.

I bypassed the customary comparing of kite-fighting scars and
stood in line. The bell rang and we marched to our assigned class,
filed in in pairs. I sat in the back row. As the Farsi teacher handed
out our textbooks, I prayed for a heavy load of homework.

School gave me an excuse to stay in my room for long hours. And, for a while, it took my mind off what had happened that winter, what I had *let* happen. For a few weeks, I preoccupied myself with gravity and momentum, atoms and cells, the Anglo-Afghan wars, instead of thinking about Hassan and what had happened to him. But, always, my mind returned to the alley. To Hassan's brown corduroy pants lying on the bricks. To the droplets of blood staining the snow dark red, almost black.

One sluggish, hazy afternoon early that summer, I asked Hassan to go up the hill with me. Told him I wanted to read him a new story I'd written. He was hanging clothes to dry in the yard and I saw his eagerness in the harried way he finished the job.

We climbed the hill, making small talk. He asked about school, what I was learning, and I talked about my teachers, especially the mean math teacher who punished talkative students by sticking a metal rod between their fingers and then squeezing them together. Hassan winced at that, said he hoped I'd never have to experience it. I said I'd been lucky so far, knowing that luck had nothing to do with it. I had done my share of talking in class too. But my father was rich and everyone knew him, so I was spared the metal rod treatment.

We sat against the low cemetery wall under the shade thrown by the pomegranate tree. In another month or two, crops of scorched yellow weeds would blanket the hillside, but that year the spring showers had lasted longer than usual, nudging their way into early summer, and the grass was still green, peppered with tangles of wildflowers. Below us, Wazir Akbar Khan's white-walled, flat-topped houses gleamed in the sunshine, the laundry hanging on clotheslines in their yards stirred by the breeze to dance like butterflies.

We had picked a dozen pomegranates from the tree. I

unfolded the story I'd brought along, turned to the first page, then put it down. I stood up and picked up an overripe pomegranate that had fallen to the ground.

"What would you do if I hit you with this?" I said, tossing the fruit up and down.

Hassan's smile wilted. He looked older than I'd remembered. No, not older, *old*. Was that possible? Lines had etched into his tanned face and creases framed his eyes, his mouth. I might as well have taken a knife and carved those lines myself.

"What would you do?" I repeated.

The color fell from his face. Next to him, the stapled pages of the story I'd promised to read him fluttered in the breeze. I hurled the pomegranate at him. It struck him in the chest, exploded in a spray of red pulp. Hassan's cry was pregnant with surprise and pain.

"Hit me back!" I snapped. Hassan looked from the stain on his chest to me.

"Get up! Hit me!" I said. Hassan *did* get up, but he just stood there, looking dazed like a man dragged into the ocean by a riptide when, just a moment ago, he was enjoying a nice stroll on the beach.

I hit him with another pomegranate, in the shoulder this time. The juice splattered his face. "Hit me back!" I spat. "Hit me back, goddamn you!" I wished he would. I wished he'd give me the punishment I craved, so maybe I'd finally sleep at night. Maybe then things could return to how they used to be between us. But Hassan did nothing as I pelted him again and again. "You're a coward!" I said. "Nothing but a goddamn coward!"

I don't know how many times I hit him. All I know is that, when I finally stopped, exhausted and panting, Hassan was smeared in red like he'd been shot by a firing squad. I fell to my knees, tired, spent, frustrated.

Then Hassan *did* pick up a pomegranate. He walked toward me. He opened it and crushed it against his own forehead. "There," he croaked, red dripping down his face like blood. "Are you satisfied? Do you feel better?" He turned around and started down the hill.

I let the tears break free, rocked back and forth on my knees. "What am I going to do with you, Hassan? What am I going to do with you?" But by the time the tears dried up and I trudged down the hill, I knew the answer to that question.

I TURNED THIRTEEN that summer of 1976, Afghanistan's next to last summer of peace and anonymity. Things between Baba and me were already cooling off again. I think what started it was the stupid comment I'd made the day we were planting tulips, about getting new servants. I regretted saying it—I really did—but I think even if I hadn't, our happy little interlude would have come to an end. Maybe not quite so soon, but it would have. By the end of the summer, the scraping of spoon and fork against the plate had replaced dinner table chatter and Baba had resumed retreating to his study after supper. And closing the door. I'd gone back to thumbing through Hãfez and Khayyám, gnawing my nails down to the cuticles, writing stories. I kept the stories in a stack under my bed, keeping them just in case, though I doubted Baba would ever again ask me to read them to him.

Baba's motto about throwing parties was this: Invite the whole world or it's not a party. I remember scanning over the invitation list a week before my birthday party and not recognizing at least three-quarters of the four hundred–plus Kakas and Khalas who were going to bring me gifts and congratulate me for having lived to thirteen. Then I realized they weren't really coming for me. It was my birthday, but I knew who the real star of the show was.

For days, the house was teeming with Baba's hired help. There was Salahuddin the butcher, who showed up with a calf and two sheep in tow, refusing payment for any of the three. He slaughtered the animals himself in the yard by a poplar tree. "Blood is good for the tree," I remember him saying as the grass around the poplar soaked red. Men I didn't know climbed the oak trees with coils of small electric bulbs and meters of extension cords. Others set up dozens of tables in the yard, spread a tablecloth on each. The night before the big party Baba's friend Del-Muhammad, who owned a kabob house in Shar-e-Nau, came to the house with his bags of spices. Like the butcher, Del-Muhammad—or Dello, as Baba called him—refused payment for his services. He said Baba had done enough for his family already. It was Rahim Khan who whispered to me, as Dello marinated the meat, that Baba had lent Dello the money to open his restaurant. Baba had refused repayment until Dello had shown up one day in our driveway in a Benz and insisted he wouldn't leave until Baba took his money.

I guess in most ways, or at least in the ways in which parties are judged, my birthday bash was a huge success. I'd never seen the house so packed. Guests with drinks in hand were chatting in the hallways, smoking on the stairs, leaning against doorways. They sat where they found space, on kitchen counters, in the foyer, even under the stairwell. In the backyard, they mingled under the glow of blue, red, and green lights winking in the trees, their faces illuminated by the light of kerosene torches propped everywhere. Baba had had a stage built on the balcony that overlooked the garden and planted speakers throughout the yard.

Ahmad Zahir was playing an accordion and singing on the stage over masses of dancing bodies.

I had to greet each of the guests personally—Baba made sure of that; no one was going to gossip the next day about how he'd raised a son with no manners. I kissed hundreds of cheeks, hugged total strangers, thanked them for their gifts. My face ached from the strain of my plastered smile.

I was standing with Baba in the yard near the bar when someone said, "Happy birthday, Amir." It was Assef, with his parents. Assef's father, Mahmood, was a short, lanky sort with dark skin and a narrow face. His mother, Tanya, was a small, nervous woman who smiled and blinked a lot. Assef was standing between the two of them now, grinning, looming over both, his arms resting on their shoulders. He led them toward us, like *he* had brought *them* here. Like he was the parent, and they his children. A wave of dizziness rushed through me. Baba thanked them for coming.

"I picked out your present myself," Assef said. Tanya's face twitched and her eyes flicked from Assef to me. She smiled, unconvincingly, and blinked. I wondered if Baba had noticed.

"Still playing soccer, Assef jan?" Baba said. He'd always wanted me to be friends with Assef.

Assef smiled. It was creepy how genuinely sweet he made it look. "Of course, Kaka jan."

"Right wing, as I recall?"

"Actually, I switched to center forward this year," Assef said. "You get to score more that way. We're playing the Mekro-Rayan team next week. Should be a good match. They have some good players."

Baba nodded. "You know, I played center forward too when I was young."

"I'll bet you still could if you wanted to," Assef said. He favored Baba with a good-natured wink.

Baba returned the wink. "I see your father has taught you his world-famous flattering ways." He elbowed Assef's father, almost knocked the little fellow down. Mahmood's laughter was about as convincing as Tanya's smile, and suddenly I wondered if maybe, on some level, their son frightened them. I tried to fake a smile, but all I could manage was a feeble upturning of the corners of my mouth—my stomach was turning at the sight of my father bonding with Assef.

Assef shifted his eyes to me. "Wali and Kamal are here too. They wouldn't miss your birthday for anything," he said, laughter lurking just beneath the surface. I nodded silently.

"We're thinking about playing a little game of volleyball tomorrow at my house," Assef said. "Maybe you'll join us. Bring Hassan if you want to."

"That sounds fun," Baba said, beaming. "What do you think, Amir?"

"I don't really like volleyball," I muttered. I saw the light wink out of Baba's eyes and an uncomfortable silence followed.

"Sorry, Assef jan," Baba said, shrugging. That stung, his apologizing for me.

"Nay, no harm done," Assef said. "But you have an open invitation, Amir jan. Anyway, I heard you like to read so I brought you a book. One of my favorites." He extended a wrapped birthday gift to me. "Happy birthday."

He was dressed in a cotton shirt and blue slacks, a red silk tie and shiny black loafers. He smelled of cologne and his blond hair was neatly combed back. On the surface, he was the embodiment of every parent's dream, a strong, tall, well-dressed and well-mannered boy with talent and striking looks, not to mention the wit to joke with an adult. But to me, his eyes betrayed him. When I looked into them, the facade faltered, revealed a glimpse of the madness hiding behind them.

"Aren't you going to take it, Amir?" Baba was saying.

"Huh?"

"Your present," he said testily. "Assef jan is giving you a present."

"Oh," I said. I took the box from Assef and lowered my gaze. I wished I could be alone in my room, with my books, away from these people.

"Well?" Baba said.

"What?"

Baba spoke in a low voice, the one he took on whenever I embarrassed him in public. "Aren't you going to thank Assef jan? That was very considerate of him."

I wished Baba would stop calling him that. How often did he call me "Amir jan"? "Thanks," I said. Assef's mother looked at me like she wanted to say something, but she didn't, and I realized that neither of Assef's parents had said a word. Before I could embarrass myself and Baba anymore—but mostly to get away from Assef and his grin—I stepped away. "Thanks for coming," I said.

I squirmed my way through the throng of guests and slipped through the wrought-iron gates. Two houses down from our house, there was a large, barren dirt lot. I'd heard Baba tell Rahim Khan that a judge had bought the land and that an architect was working on the design. For now, the lot was bare, save for dirt, stones, and weeds.

I tore the wrapping paper from Assef's present and tilted the book cover in the moonlight. It was a biography of Hitler. I threw it amid a tangle of weeds.

I leaned against the neighbor's wall, slid down to the ground. I just sat in the dark for a while, knees drawn to my chest, looking up at the stars, waiting for the night to be over.

"Shouldn't you be entertaining your guests?" a familiar voice said. Rahim Khan was walking toward me along the wall.

"They don't need me for that. Baba's there, remember?" I said. The ice in Rahim Khan's drink clinked when he sat next to me. "I didn't know you drank."

"Turns out I do," he said. Elbowed me playfully. "But only on the most important occasions."

I smiled. "Thanks."

He tipped his drink to me and took a sip. He lit a cigarette, one of the unfiltered Pakistani cigarettes he and Baba were always smoking. "Did I ever tell you I was almost married once?"

"Really?" I said, smiling a little at the notion of Rahim Khan getting married. I'd always thought of him as Baba's quiet alter ego, my writing mentor, my pal, the one who never forgot to bring me a souvenir, a *saughat,* when he returned from a trip abroad. But a husband? A father?

He nodded. "It's true. I was eighteen. Her name was Homaira. She was a Hazara, the daughter of our neighbor's servants. She was as beautiful as a *pari,* light brown hair, big hazel eyes...she had this laugh...I can still hear it sometimes." He twirled his glass. "We used to meet secretly in my father's apple orchards, always after midnight when everyone had gone to sleep. We'd walk under the trees and I'd hold her hand...Am I embarrassing you, Amir jan?"

"A little," I said.

"It won't kill you," he said, taking another puff. "Anyway, we had this fantasy. We'd have a great, fancy wedding and invite family and friends from Kabul to Kandahar. I would build us a big house, white with a tiled patio and large windows. We would plant fruit trees in the garden and grow all sorts of flowers, have a lawn for our kids to play on. On Fridays, after *namaz* at the mosque, everyone would get together at our house for lunch and we'd eat in the garden, under cherry trees, drink fresh water from the well. Then tea with candy as we watched our kids play with their cousins..."

He took a long gulp of his scotch. Coughed. "You should have seen the look on my father's face when I told him. My mother actually fainted. My sisters splashed her face with water. They fanned her and looked at me as if I had slit her throat. My brother Jalal actually went to fetch his hunting rifle before my father stopped him." Rahim Khan barked a bitter laughter. "It was Homaira and me against the world. And I'll tell you this, Amir jan: In the end, the world always wins. That's just the way of things."

"So what happened?"

"That same day, my father put Homaira and her family on a lorry and sent them off to Hazarajat. I never saw her again."

"I'm sorry," I said.

"Probably for the best, though," Rahim Khan said, shrugging. "She would have suffered. My family would have never accepted her as an equal. You don't order someone to polish your shoes one day and call them 'sister' the next." He looked at me. "You know, you can tell me anything you want, Amir jan. Anytime."

"I know," I said uncertainly. He looked at me for a long time, like he was waiting, his black bottomless eyes hinting at an unspoken secret between us. For a moment, I almost did tell him. Almost told him everything, but then what would he think of me? He'd hate me, and rightfully.

"Here." He handed me something. "I almost forgot. Happy birthday." It was a brown leather-bound notebook. I traced my fingers along the gold-colored stitching on the borders. I smelled the leather. "For your stories," he said. I was going to thank him when something exploded and bursts of fire lit up the sky.

"Fireworks!"

We hurried back to the house and found the guests all standing in the yard, looking up to the sky. Kids hooted and screamed with each *crackle* and *whoosh*. People cheered, burst into applause each time flares sizzled and exploded into bouquets of fire. Every few seconds, the backyard lit up in sudden flashes of red, green, and yellow.

In one of those brief bursts of light, I saw something I'll never forget: Hassan serving drinks to Assef and Wali from a silver platter. The light winked out, a hiss and a crackle, then another flicker of orange light: Assef grinning, kneading Hassan in the chest with a knuckle.

Then, mercifully, darkness.

NINE

Sitting in the middle of my room the next morning, I ripped open box after box of presents. I don't know why I even bothered, since I just gave them a joyless glance and pitched them to the corner of the room. The pile was growing there: a Polaroid camera, a transistor radio, an elaborate electric train set—and several sealed envelopes containing cash. I knew I'd never spend the money or listen to the radio, and the electric train would never trundle down its tracks in my room. I didn't want any of it—it was all blood money; Baba would have never thrown me a party like that if I hadn't won the tournament.

Baba gave me two presents. One was sure to become the envy of every kid in the neighborhood: a brand new Schwinn Stingray, the king of all bicycles. Only a handful of kids in all of Kabul owned a new Stingray and now I was one of them. It had high-rise handlebars with black rubber grips and its famous banana seat. The spokes were gold colored and the steel-frame body red, like a candy apple. Or blood. Any other kid would have hopped on the bike immediately and taken it for a full block skid. I might have done the same a few months ago.

"You like it?" Baba said, leaning in the doorway to my room. I gave him a sheepish grin and a quick "Thank you." I wished I could have mustered more.

"We could go for a ride," Baba said. An invitation, but only a halfhearted one.

"Maybe later. I'm a little tired," I said.

"Sure," Baba said.

"Baba?"

"Yes?"

"Thanks for the fireworks," I said. A thank-you, but only a halfhearted one.

"Get some rest," Baba said, walking toward his room.

The other present Baba gave me—and he didn't wait around for me to open this one—was a wristwatch. It had a blue face with gold hands in the shape of lightning bolts. I didn't even try it on. I tossed it on the pile of toys in the corner. The only gift I didn't toss on that mound was Rahim Khan's leather-bound notebook. That was the only one that didn't feel like blood money.

I sat on the edge of my bed, turned the notebook in my hands, thought about what Rahim Khan had said about Homaira, how his father's dismissing her had been for the best in the end. *She would have suffered.* Like the times Kaka Homayoun's projector got stuck on the same slide, the same image kept flashing in my mind over and over: Hassan, his head downcast, serving drinks to Assef and Wali. Maybe it *would* be for the best. Lessen his suffering. And mine too. Either way, this much had become clear: One of us had to go.

Later that afternoon, I took the Schwinn for its first and last spin. I pedaled around the block a couple of times and came back. I rolled up the driveway to the backyard where Hassan and Ali were cleaning up the mess from last night's party. Paper cups, crumpled napkins, and empty bottles of soda littered the yard. Ali was folding chairs, setting them along the wall. He saw me and waved.

"*Salaam*, Ali," I said, waving back.

He held up a finger, asking me to wait, and walked to his living quarters. A moment later, he emerged with something in his hands. "The opportunity never presented itself last night for Hassan and me to give you this," he said, handing me a box. "It's modest and not worthy of you, Amir agha. But we hope you like it still. Happy birthday."

A lump was rising in my throat. "Thank you, Ali," I said. I wished they hadn't bought me anything. I opened the box and found a brand new *Shahnamah*, a hardback with glossy colored illustrations beneath the passages. Here was Ferangis gazing at her newborn son, Kai Khosrau. There was Afrasiyab riding his horse, sword drawn, leading his army. And, of course, Rostam inflicting a mortal wound onto his son, the warrior Sohrab. "It's beautiful," I said.

"Hassan said your copy was old and ragged, and that some of the pages were missing," Ali said. "All the pictures are hand-drawn in this one with pen and ink," he added proudly, eyeing a book neither he nor his son could read.

"It's lovely," I said. And it was. And, I suspected, not inexpensive either. I wanted to tell Ali it was not the book, but *I* who was unworthy. I hopped back on the bicycle. "Thank Hassan for me," I said.

I ended up tossing the book on the heap of gifts in the corner of my room. But my eyes kept going back to it, so I buried it at the bottom. Before I went to bed that night, I asked Baba if he'd seen my new watch anywhere.

THE NEXT MORNING, I waited in my room for Ali to clear the breakfast table in the kitchen. Waited for him to do the dishes, wipe the counters. I looked out my bedroom window and waited until Ali and Hassan went grocery shopping to the bazaar, pushing the empty wheelbarrows in front of them.

Then I took a couple of the envelopes of cash from the pile of gifts and my watch, and tiptoed out. I paused before Baba's study and listened in. He'd been in there all morning, making phone calls. He was talking to someone now, about a shipment of rugs due to arrive next week. I went downstairs, crossed the yard, and entered Ali and Hassan's living quarters by the loquat tree. I lifted Hassan's mattress and planted my new watch and a handful of Afghani bills under it.

I waited another thirty minutes. Then I knocked on Baba's door and told what I hoped would be the last in a long line of shameful lies.

THROUGH MY BEDROOM WINDOW, I watched Ali and Hassan push the wheelbarrows loaded with meat, *naan,* fruit, and vegetables up the driveway. I saw Baba emerge from the house and walk up to Ali. Their mouths moved over words I couldn't hear. Baba pointed to the house and Ali nodded. They separated. Baba came back to the house; Ali followed Hassan to their hut.

A few moments later, Baba knocked on my door. "Come to my office," he said. "We're all going to sit down and settle this thing."

I went to Baba's study, sat in one of the leather sofas. It was thirty minutes or more before Hassan and Ali joined us.

THEY'D BOTH BEEN CRYING; I could tell from their red, puffed-up eyes. They stood before Baba, hand in hand, and I wondered how and when I'd become capable of causing this kind of pain.

Baba came right out and asked. "Did you steal that money? Did you steal Amir's watch, Hassan?"

Hassan's reply was a single word, delivered in a thin, raspy voice: "Yes."

I flinched, like I'd been slapped. My heart sank and I almost blurted out the truth. Then I understood: This was Hassan's final sacrifice for me. If he'd said no, Baba would have believed him because we all knew Hassan never lied. And if Baba believed him, then I'd be the accused; I would have to explain and I would be revealed for what I really was. Baba would never, ever forgive me. And that led to another understanding: Hassan knew. He knew I'd seen everything in that alley, that I'd stood there and done nothing. He knew I had betrayed him and yet he was rescuing me once again, maybe for the last time. I loved him in that moment, loved him more than I'd ever loved anyone, and I wanted to tell them all that *I* was the snake in the grass, the monster in the lake. I wasn't worthy of this sacrifice; I was a liar, a cheat, and a thief. And I *would* have told, except that a part of me was glad. Glad that this would all be over with soon. Baba would dismiss them, there would be some pain, but life would move on. I wanted that, to move on, to forget, to start with a clean slate. I wanted to be able to breathe again.

Except Baba stunned me by saying, "I forgive you."

Forgive? But theft was the one unforgivable sin, the common denominator of all sins. *When you kill a man, you steal a life. You steal his wife's right to a husband, rob his children of a father. When you tell a lie, you steal someone's right to the truth. When you cheat, you steal the right to fairness. There is no act more wretched than stealing.* Hadn't Baba sat me on his lap and said those words to me? Then how could he just forgive Hassan? And if Baba could forgive that, then why couldn't he forgive me for not being the son he'd always wanted? Why—

"We are leaving, Agha sahib," Ali said.

"What?" Baba said, the color draining from his face.

"We can't live here anymore," Ali said.

"But I forgive him, Ali, didn't you hear?" said Baba.

"Life here is impossible for us now, Agha sahib. We're leaving." Ali drew Hassan to him, curled his arm around his son's shoulder. It was a protective gesture and I knew whom Ali was protecting him from. Ali glanced my way and in his cold, unforgiving look, I saw that Hassan had told him. He had told him everything, about what Assef and his friends had done to him, about the kite, about me. Strangely, I was glad that someone knew me for who I really was; I was tired of pretending.

"I don't care about the money or the watch," Baba said, his arms open, palms up. "I don't understand why you're doing this... what do you mean 'impossible'?"

"I'm sorry, Agha sahib, but our bags are already packed. We have made our decision."

Baba stood up, a sheen of grief across his face. "Ali, haven't I provided well for you? Haven't I been good to you and Hassan? You're the brother I never had, Ali, you know that. Please don't do this."

"Don't make this even more difficult than it already is, Agha sahib," Ali said. His mouth twitched and, for a moment, I thought I saw a grimace. That was when I understood the depth of the pain I had caused, the blackness of the grief I had brought onto everyone, that not even Ali's paralyzed face could mask his sorrow. I forced myself to look at Hassan, but his head was downcast, his shoulders slumped, his finger twirling a loose string on the hem of his shirt.

Baba was pleading now. "At least tell me why. I need to know!"

Ali didn't tell Baba, just as he didn't protest when Hassan confessed to the stealing. I'll never really know why, but I could imagine the two of them in that dim little hut, weeping, Hassan pleading him not to give me away. But I couldn't imagine the restraint it must have taken Ali to keep that promise.

"Will you drive us to the bus station?"

"I forbid you to do this!" Baba bellowed. "Do you hear me? I forbid you!"

"Respectfully, you can't forbid me anything, Agha sahib," Ali said. "We don't work for you anymore."

"Where will you go?" Baba asked. His voice was breaking.

"Hazarajat."

"To your cousin?"

"Yes. Will you take us to the bus station, Agha sahib?"

Then I saw Baba do something I had never seen him do before: He cried. It scared me a little, seeing a grown man sob. Fathers weren't supposed to cry. "Please," Baba was saying, but Ali had already turned to the door, Hassan trailing him. I'll never forget the way Baba said that, the pain in his plea, the fear.

IN KABUL, it rarely rained in the summer. Blue skies stood tall and far, the sun like a branding iron searing the back of your neck.

Creeks where Hassan and I skipped stones all spring turned dry, and rickshaws stirred dust when they sputtered by. People went to mosques for their ten *raka'ts* of noontime prayer and then retreated to whatever shade they could find to nap in, waiting for the cool of early evening. Summer meant long school days sweating in tightly packed, poorly ventilated classrooms learning to recite *ayats* from the Koran, struggling with those tongue-twisting, exotic Arabic words. It meant catching flies in your palm while the mullah droned on and a hot breeze brought with it the smell of shit from the outhouse across the schoolyard, churning dust around the lone rickety basketball hoop.

But it rained the afternoon Baba took Ali and Hassan to the bus station. Thunderheads rolled in, painted the sky iron gray. Within minutes, sheets of rain were sweeping in, the steady hiss of falling water swelling in my ears.

Baba had offered to drive them to Bamiyan himself, but Ali refused. Through the blurry, rain-soaked window of my bedroom, I watched Ali haul the lone suitcase carrying all of their belongings to Baba's car idling outside the gates. Hassan lugged his mattress, rolled tightly and tied with a rope, on his back. He'd left all of his toys behind in the empty shack—I discovered them the next day, piled in a corner just like the birthday presents in my room.

Slithering beads of rain sluiced down my window. I saw Baba slam the trunk shut. Already drenched, he walked to the driver's side. Leaned in and said something to Ali in the backseat, perhaps one last-ditch effort to change his mind. They talked that way awhile, Baba getting soaked, stooping, one arm on the roof of the car. But when he straightened, I saw in his slumping shoulders that the life I had known since I'd been born was over. Baba slid in. The headlights came on and cut twin funnels of light in the rain. If this were one of the Hindi movies Hassan and I used to watch, this was the part where I'd run outside, my bare feet splashing rainwater. I'd chase the car, screaming for it to stop. I'd pull Hassan out of the backseat and tell him I was sorry, so sorry, my tears mixing with rainwater. We'd hug in the downpour. But this was no Hindi movie. I *was* sorry, but I didn't cry and I didn't chase the car. I watched Baba's car pull away from the curb, taking with it the person whose first spoken word had been my name. I caught one final blurry glimpse of Hassan slumped in the backseat before Baba turned left at the street corner where we'd played marbles so many times.

I stepped back and all I saw was rain through windowpanes that looked like melting silver.

TEN

March 1981

A young woman sat across from us. She was dressed in an olive green dress with a black shawl wrapped tightly around her face against the night chill. She burst into prayer every time the truck jerked or stumbled into a pothole, her *"Bismillah!"* peaking with each of the truck's shudders and jolts. Her husband, a burly man in baggy pants and sky blue turban, cradled an infant in one arm and thumbed prayer beads with his free hand. His lips moved in silent prayer. There were others, in all about a dozen, including Baba and me, sitting with our suitcases between our legs, cramped with these strangers in the tarpaulin-covered cab of an old Russian truck.

My innards had been roiling since we'd left Kabul just after two in the morning. Baba never said so, but I knew he saw my car sickness as yet another of my array of weakness—I saw it on his embarrassed face the couple of times my stomach had clenched so badly I had moaned. When the burly guy with the beads—the

praying woman's husband—asked if I was going to get sick, I said
I might. Baba looked away. The man lifted his corner of the tarpaulin cover and rapped on the driver's window, asked him to
stop. But the driver, Karim, a scrawny dark-skinned man with
hawk-boned features and a pencil-thin mustache, shook his head.

"We are too close to Kabul," he shot back. "Tell him to have a
strong stomach."

Baba grumbled something under his breath. I wanted to tell
him I was sorry, but suddenly I was salivating, the back of my
throat tasting bile. I turned around, lifted the tarpaulin, and
threw up over the side of the moving truck. Behind me, Baba was
apologizing to the other passengers. As if car sickness was a crime.
As if you weren't supposed to get sick when you were eighteen. I
threw up two more times before Karim agreed to stop, mostly so I
wouldn't stink up his vehicle, the instrument of his livelihood.
Karim was a people smuggler—it was a pretty lucrative business
then, driving people out of *Shorawi*-occupied Kabul to the relative
safety of Pakistan. He was taking us to Jalalabad, about 170 kilometers southeast of Kabul, where his brother, Toor, who had a bigger truck with a second convoy of refugees, was waiting to drive
us across the Khyber Pass and into Peshawar.

We were a few kilometers west of Mahipar Falls when Karim
pulled to the side of the road. Mahipar—which means "Flying
Fish"—was a high summit with a precipitous drop overlooking the
hydro plant the Germans had built for Afghanistan back in 1967.
Baba and I had driven over the summit countless times on our way
to Jalalabad, the city of cypress trees and sugarcane fields where
Afghans vacationed in the winter.

I hopped down the back of the truck and lurched to the dusty
embankment on the side of the road. My mouth filled with saliva,

a sign of the retching that was yet to come. I stumbled to the edge of the cliff overlooking the deep valley that was shrouded in darkness. I stooped, hands on my kneecaps, and waited for the bile. Somewhere, a branch snapped, an owl hooted. The wind, soft and cold, clicked through tree branches and stirred the bushes that sprinkled the slope. And from below, the faint sound of water tumbling through the valley.

Standing on the shoulder of the road, I thought of the way we'd left the house where I'd lived my entire life, as if we were going out for a bite: dishes smeared with *kofta* piled in the kitchen sink; laundry in the wicker basket in the foyer; beds unmade; Baba's business suits hanging in the closet. Tapestries still hung on the walls of the living room and my mother's books still crowded the shelves in Baba's study. The signs of our elopement were subtle: My parents' wedding picture was gone, as was the grainy photograph of my grandfather and King Nader Shah standing over the dead deer. A few items of clothing were missing from the closets. The leather-bound notebook Rahim Khan had given me five years earlier was gone.

In the morning, Jalaluddin—our seventh servant in five years—would probably think we'd gone out for a stroll or a drive. We hadn't told him. You couldn't trust anyone in Kabul anymore—for a fee or under threat, people told on each other, neighbor on neighbor, child on parent, brother on brother, servant on master, friend on friend. I thought of the singer Ahmad Zahir, who had played the accordion at my thirteenth birthday. He had gone for a drive with some friends, and someone had later found his body on the side of the road, a bullet in the back of his head. The *rafiq*s, the comrades, were everywhere and they'd split Kabul into two groups: those who eavesdropped and those who didn't. The tricky part was that no one knew who belonged to which. A casual remark to the tailor while getting fitted for a suit might land you in the dungeons of Poleh-charkhi. Complain about the curfew to the butcher and next thing you knew, you were behind bars staring at the muzzle end of a Kalashnikov. Even at the dinner table, in the privacy of their home, people had to speak in a calculated manner—the *rafiq*s were in the classrooms too; they'd taught children to spy on their parents, what to listen for, whom to tell.

What was I doing on this road in the middle of the night? I should have been in bed, under my blanket, a book with dog-eared pages at my side. This had to be a dream. Had to be. Tomorrow morning, I'd wake up, peek out the window: No grim-faced Russian soldiers patrolling the sidewalks, no tanks rolling up and down the streets of my city, their turrets swiveling like accusing fingers, no rubble, no curfews, no Russian Army Personnel Carriers weaving through the bazaars. Then, behind me, I heard Baba and Karim discussing the arrangement in Jalalabad over a smoke. Karim was reassuring Baba that his brother had a big truck of "excellent and first-class quality," and that the trek to Peshawar would be very routine. "He could take you there with his eyes closed," Karim said. I overheard him telling Baba how he and his brother knew the Russian and Afghan soldiers who worked the checkpoints, how they had set up a "mutually profitable" arrangement. This was no dream. As if on cue, a MiG suddenly screamed past overhead. Karim tossed his cigarette and produced a handgun from his waist. Pointing it to the sky and making shooting gestures, he spat and cursed at the MiG.

I wondered where Hassan was. Then the inevitable. I vomited on a tangle of weeds, my retching and groaning drowned in the deafening roar of the MiG.

. . .

WE PULLED UP to the checkpoint at Mahipar twenty minutes later. Our driver let the truck idle and hopped down to greet the approaching voices. Feet crushed gravel. Words were exchanged, brief and hushed. A flick of a lighter. *"Spasseba."*

Another flick of the lighter. Someone laughed, a shrill cackling sound that made me jump. Baba's hand clamped down on my thigh. The laughing man broke into song, a slurring, off-key rendition of an old Afghan wedding song, delivered with a thick Russian accent:

> *Ahesta boro, Mah-e-man, ahesta boro.*
> *Go slowly, my lovely moon, go slowly.*

Boot heels clicked on asphalt. Someone flung open the tarpaulin hanging over the back of the truck, and three faces peered in. One was Karim, the other two were soldiers, one Afghan, the other a grinning Russian, face like a bulldog's, cigarette dangling from the side of his mouth. Behind them, a bone-colored moon hung in the sky. Karim and the Afghan soldier had a brief exchange in Pashtu. I caught a little of it—something about Toor and his bad luck. The Russian soldier thrust his face into the rear of the truck. He was humming the wedding song and drumming his finger on the edge of the tailgate. Even in the dim light of the moon, I saw the glazed look in his eyes as they skipped from passenger to passenger. Despite the cold, sweat streamed from his brow. His eyes settled on the young woman wearing the black shawl. He spoke in Russian to Karim without taking his eyes off her. Karim gave a curt reply in Russian, which the soldier returned with an even curter retort. The Afghan soldier said something too, in a low, reasoning voice. But the Russian soldier shouted something that made the other two flinch. I could feel

Baba tightening up next to me. Karim cleared his throat, dropped his head. Said the soldier wanted a half hour with the lady in the back of the truck.

The young woman pulled the shawl down over her face. Burst into tears. The toddler sitting in her husband's lap started crying too. The husband's face had become as pale as the moon hovering above. He told Karim to ask "Mister Soldier Sahib" to show a little mercy, maybe he had a sister or a mother, maybe he had a wife too. The Russian listened to Karim and barked a series of words.

"It's his price for letting us pass," Karim said. He couldn't bring himself to look the husband in the eye.

"But we've paid a fair price already. He's getting paid good money," the husband said.

Karim and the Russian soldier spoke. "He says...he says every price has a tax."

That was when Baba stood up. It was my turn to clamp a hand on his thigh, but Baba pried it loose, snatched his leg away. When he stood, he eclipsed the moonlight. "I want you to ask this man something," Baba said. He said it to Karim, but looked directly at the Russian officer. "Ask him where his shame is."

They spoke. "He says this is war. There is no shame in war."

"Tell him he's wrong. War doesn't negate decency. It *demands* it, even more than in times of peace."

Do you have to always be the hero? I thought, my heart fluttering. *Can't you just let it go for once?* But I knew he couldn't—it wasn't in his nature. The problem was, his nature was going to get us all killed.

The Russian soldier said something to Karim, a smile creasing his lips. "Agha sahib," Karim said, "these *Roussi* are not like us. They understand nothing about respect, honor."

"What did he say?"

"He says he'll enjoy putting a bullet in you almost as much as..." Karim trailed off, but nodded his head toward the young woman who had caught the guard's eye. The soldier flicked his unfinished cigarette and unholstered his handgun. *So this is where Baba dies,* I thought. *This is how it's going to happen.* In my head, I said a prayer I had learned in school.

"Tell him I'll take a thousand of his bullets before I let this indecency take place," Baba said. My mind flashed to that winter day six years ago. Me, peering around the corner in the alley. Kamal and Wali holding Hassan down. Assef's buttock muscles clenching and unclenching, his hips thrusting back and forth. Some hero I had been, fretting about the kite. Sometimes, I too wondered if I was really Baba's son.

The bulldog-faced Russian raised his gun.

"Baba, sit down please," I said, tugging at his sleeve. "I think he really means to shoot you."

Baba slapped my hand away. "Haven't I taught you anything?" he snapped. He turned to the grinning soldier. "Tell him he'd better kill me good with that first shot. Because if I don't go down, I'm tearing him to pieces, goddamn his father!"

The Russian soldier's grin never faltered when he heard the translation. He clicked the safety on the gun. Pointed the barrel to Baba's chest. Heart pounding in my throat, I buried my face in my hands.

The gun roared.

It's done, then. I'm eighteen and alone. I have no one left in the world. Baba's dead and now I have to bury him. Where do I bury him? Where do I go after that?

But the whirlwind of half thoughts spinning in my head came to a halt when I cracked my eyelids, found Baba still standing. I saw a second Russian officer with the others. It was from the muzzle of his upturned gun that smoke swirled. The soldier who had meant to shoot Baba had already holstered his weapon. He was shuffling his feet. I had never felt more like crying and laughing at the same time.

The second Russian officer, gray-haired and heavyset, spoke to us in broken Farsi. He apologized for his comrade's behavior. "Russia sends them here to fight," he said. "But they are just boys, and when they come here, they find the pleasure of drug." He gave the younger officer the rueful look of a father exasperated with his misbehaving son. "This one is attached to drug now. I try to stop him..." He waved us off.

Moments later, we were pulling away. I heard a laugh and then the first soldier's voice, slurry and off-key, singing the old wedding song.

WE RODE IN SILENCE for about fifteen minutes before the young woman's husband suddenly stood and did something I'd seen many others do before him: He kissed Baba's hand.

TOOR'S BAD LUCK. Hadn't I overheard that in a snippet of conversation back at Mahipar?

We rolled into Jalalabad about an hour before sunrise. Karim ushered us quickly from the truck into a one-story house at the intersection of two dirt roads lined with flat one-story homes, acacia trees, and closed shops. I pulled the collar of my coat against the chill as we hurried into the house, dragging our belongings. For some reason, I remember smelling radishes.

Once he had us inside the dimly lit, bare living room, Karim locked the front door, pulled the tattered sheets that passed for curtains. Then he took a deep breath and gave us the bad news: His brother Toor couldn't take us to Peshawar. It seemed his truck's engine had blown the week before and Toor was still waiting for parts.

"*Last* week?" someone exclaimed. "If you knew this, why did you bring us here?"

I caught a flurry of movement out of the corner of my eye. Then a blur of something zipping across the room, and the next thing I saw was Karim slammed against the wall, his sandaled feet dangling two feet above the floor. Wrapped around his neck were Baba's hands.

"I'll tell you why," Baba snapped. "Because he got paid for his leg of the trip. That's all he cared about." Karim was making guttural choking sounds. Spittle dripped from the corner of his mouth.

"Put him down, Agha, you're killing him," one of the passengers said.

"It's what I intend to do," Baba said. What none of the others in the room knew was that Baba wasn't joking. Karim was turning red and kicking his legs. Baba kept choking him until the young mother, the one the Russian officer had fancied, begged him to stop.

Karim collapsed on the floor and rolled around fighting for air when Baba finally let go. The room fell silent. Less than two hours ago, Baba had volunteered to take a bullet for the honor of a woman he didn't even know. Now he'd almost choked a man to death, would have done it cheerfully if not for the pleas of that same woman.

Something thumped next door. No, not next door, below.

"What's that?" someone asked.

"The others," Karim panted between labored breaths. "In the basement."

"How long have they been waiting?" Baba said, standing over Karim.

"Two weeks."

"I thought you said the truck broke down last week."

Karim rubbed his throat. "It might have been the week before," he croaked.

"How long?"

"What?"

"How long for the parts?" Baba roared. Karim flinched but said nothing. I was glad for the darkness. I didn't want to see the murderous look on Baba's face.

THE STENCH OF SOMETHING DANK, like mildew, bludgeoned my nostrils the moment Karim opened the door that led down the creaky steps to the basement. We descended in single file. The steps groaned under Baba's weight. Standing in the cold basement, I felt watched by eyes blinking in the dark. I saw shapes huddled around the room, their silhouettes thrown on the walls by the dim light of a pair of kerosene lamps. A low murmur buzzed through the basement, beneath it the sound of water drops trickling somewhere, and, something else, a scratching sound.

Baba sighed behind me and dropped the bags.

Karim told us it should be a matter of a couple of short days before the truck was fixed. Then we'd be on our way to Peshawar. On to freedom. On to safety.

The basement was our home for the next week and, by the third night, I discovered the source of the scratching sounds. Rats.

. . .

ONCE MY EYES ADJUSTED to the dark, I counted about thirty refugees in that basement. We sat shoulder to shoulder along the walls, ate crackers, bread with dates, apples. That first night, all the men prayed together. One of the refugees asked Baba why he wasn't joining them. "God is going to save us all. Why don't you pray to him?"

Baba snorted a pinch of his snuff. Stretched his legs. "What'll save us is eight cylinders and a good carburetor." That silenced the rest of them for good about the matter of God.

It was later that first night when I discovered that two of the people hiding with us were Kamal and his father. That was shocking enough, seeing Kamal sitting in the basement just a few feet away from me. But when he and his father came over to our side of the room and I saw Kamal's face, *really* saw it...

He had withered—there was simply no other word for it. His eyes gave me a hollow look and no recognition at all registered in them. His shoulders hunched and his cheeks sagged like they were too tired to cling to the bone beneath. His father, who'd owned a movie theater in Kabul, was telling Baba how, three months before, a stray bullet had struck his wife in the temple and killed her. Then he told Baba about Kamal. I caught only snippets of it: *Should have never let him go alone...always so handsome, you know...four of them...tried to fight...God... took him...bleeding down there...his pants...doesn't talk anymore...just stares...*

THERE WOULD BE NO TRUCK, Karim told us after we'd spent a week in the rat-infested basement. The truck was beyond repair.

"There is another option," Karim said, his voice rising amid the groans. His cousin owned a fuel truck and had smuggled people with it a couple of times. He was here in Jalalabad and could probably fit us all.

Everyone except an elderly couple decided to go.

We left that night, Baba and I, Kamal and his father, the others. Karim and his cousin, a square-faced balding man named Aziz, helped us get into the fuel tank. One by one, we mounted the idling truck's rear deck, climbed the rear access ladder, and slid down into the tank. I remember Baba climbed halfway up the ladder, hopped back down and fished the snuffbox from his pocket. He emptied the box and picked up a handful of dirt from the middle of the unpaved road. He kissed the dirt. Poured it into the box. Stowed the box in his breast pocket, next to his heart.

PANIC.

You open your mouth. Open it so wide your jaws creak. You order your lungs to draw air, NOW, you need air, need it NOW. But your airways ignore you. They collapse, tighten, squeeze, and suddenly you're breathing through a drinking straw. Your mouth closes and your lips purse and all you can manage is a strangled croak. Your hands wriggle and shake. Somewhere a dam has cracked open and a flood of cold sweat spills, drenches your body. You want to scream. You would if you could. But you have to breathe to scream.

Panic.

The basement had been dark. The fuel tank was pitch-black. I looked right, left, up, down, waved my hands before my eyes, didn't see so much as a hint of movement. I blinked, blinked again. Nothing at all. The air wasn't right, it was too thick, almost solid. Air wasn't supposed to be solid. I wanted to reach out with my hands, crush the air into little pieces, stuff them down my windpipe. And the stench of gasoline. My eyes stung from the fumes, like someone had peeled my lids back and rubbed a lemon on them. My nose caught fire with each breath. You could die in a place like this, I thought. A scream was coming. Coming, coming...

And then a small miracle. Baba tugged at my sleeve and something glowed green in the dark. Light! Baba's wristwatch. I kept my eyes glued to those fluorescent green hands. I was so afraid I'd lose them, I didn't dare blink.

Slowly I became aware of my surroundings. I heard groans and muttered prayers. I heard a baby cry, its mother's muted soothing. Someone retched. Someone else cursed the *Shorawi*. The truck bounced side to side, up and down. Heads banged against metal.

"Think of something good," Baba said in my ear. "Something happy."

Something good. Something happy. I let my mind wander. I let it come:

Friday afternoon in Paghman. An open field of grass speckled with mulberry trees in blossom. Hassan and I stand ankle-deep in untamed grass, I am tugging on the line, the spool spinning in Hassan's calloused hands, our eyes turned up to the kite in the sky. Not a word passes between us, not because we have nothing to say, but because we don't have to say anything—that's how it is between people who are each other's first memories, people who have fed from the same breast. A breeze stirs the grass and Hassan lets the spool roll. The kite spins, dips, steadies. Our twin shadows dance on the rippling grass. From somewhere over the low brick wall at the other end of the field, we hear chatter and

laughter and the chirping of a water fountain. And music, something old and familiar, I think it's *Ya Mowlah* on *rubab* strings.
Someone calls our names over the wall, says it's time for tea and
cake.

I didn't remember what month that was, or what year even. I
only knew the memory lived in me, a perfectly encapsulated
morsel of a good past, a brushstroke of color on the gray, barren
canvas that our lives had become.

THE REST OF THAT RIDE is scattered bits and pieces of
memory that come and go, most of it sounds and smells: MiGs
roaring past overhead; staccatos of gunfire; a donkey braying
nearby; the jingling of bells and mewling of sheep; gravel crushed
under the truck's tires; a baby wailing in the dark; the stench of
gasoline, vomit, and shit.

What I remember next is the blinding light of early morning as
I climbed out of the fuel tank. I remember turning my face up to
the sky, squinting, breathing like the world was running out of air.
I lay on the side of the dirt road next to a rocky trench, looked up
to the gray morning sky, thankful for air, thankful for light, thankful to be alive.

"We're in Pakistan, Amir," Baba said. He was standing over me.
"Karim says he will call for a bus to take us to Peshawar."

I rolled onto my chest, still lying on the cool dirt, and saw our
suitcases on either side of Baba's feet. Through the upside down V
between his legs, I saw the truck idling on the side of the road, the
other refugees climbing down the rear ladder. Beyond that, the
dirt road unrolled through fields that were like leaden sheets
under the gray sky and disappeared behind a line of bowl-shaped

hills. Along the way, it passed a small village strung out atop a sun-baked slope.

My eyes returned to our suitcases. They made me sad for Baba. After everything he'd built, planned, fought for, fretted over, dreamed of, this was the summation of his life: one disappointing son and two suitcases.

Someone was screaming. No, not screaming. Wailing. I saw the passengers huddled in a circle, heard their urgent voices. Someone said the word "fumes." Someone else said it too. The wail turned into a throat-ripping screech.

Baba and I hurried to the pack of onlookers and pushed our way through them. Kamal's father was sitting cross-legged in the center of the circle, rocking back and forth, kissing his son's ashen face.

"He won't breathe! My boy won't breathe!" he was crying. Kamal's lifeless body lay on his father's lap. His right hand, uncurled and limp, bounced to the rhythm of his father's sobs. "My boy! He won't breathe! Allah, help him breathe!"

Baba knelt beside him and curled an arm around his shoulder. But Kamal's father shoved him away and lunged for Karim who was standing nearby with his cousin. What happened next was too fast and too short to be called a scuffle. Karim uttered a surprised cry and backpedaled. I saw an arm swing, a leg kick. A moment later, Kamal's father was standing with Karim's gun in his hand.

"Don't shoot me!" Karim cried.

But before any of us could say or do a thing, Kamal's father shoved the barrel in his own mouth. I'll never forget the echo of that blast. Or the flash of light and the spray of red.

I doubled over again and dry-heaved on the side of the road.

ELEVEN

Fremont, California. 1980s

Baba loved the *idea* of America.

It was living in America that gave him an ulcer.

I remember the two of us walking through Lake Elizabeth Park in Fremont, a few streets down from our apartment, and watching boys at batting practice, little girls giggling on the swings in the playground. Baba would enlighten me with his politics during those walks with long-winded dissertations. "There are only three real men in this world, Amir," he'd say. He'd count them off on his fingers: America the brash savior, Britain, and Israel. "The rest of them—" he used to wave his hand and make a *phht* sound "—they're like gossiping old women."

The bit about Israel used to draw the ire of Afghans in Fremont who accused him of being pro-Jewish and, de facto, anti-Islam. Baba would meet them for tea and *rowt* cake at the park, drive them crazy with his politics. "What they don't understand," he'd tell me later, "is that religion has nothing to do with it." In Baba's view, Israel was an island of "real men" in a sea of Arabs too busy getting fat off their oil to care for their own. "Israel does this, Israel does that," Baba would say in a mock-Arabic accent. "Then do something about it! Take action. You're Arabs, help the Palestinians, then!"

He loathed Jimmy Carter, whom he called a "big-toothed cretin." In 1980, when we were still in Kabul, the U.S. announced it would be boycotting the Olympic Games in Moscow. *"Wah wah!"* Baba exclaimed with disgust. "Brezhnev is massacring Afghans and all that peanut eater can say is I won't come swim in your pool." Baba believed Carter had unwittingly done more for communism than Leonid Brezhnev. "He's not fit to run this country. It's like putting a boy who can't ride a bike behind the wheel of a brand new Cadillac." What America and the world needed was a hard man. A man to be reckoned with, someone who took action instead of wringing his hands. That someone came in the form of Ronald Reagan. And when Reagan went on TV and called the *Shorawi* "the Evil Empire," Baba went out and bought a picture of the grinning president giving a thumbs up. He framed the picture and hung it in our hallway, nailing it right next to the old black-and-white of himself in his thin necktie shaking hands with King Zahir Shah. Most of our neighbors in Fremont were bus drivers, policemen, gas station attendants, and unwed mothers collecting welfare, exactly the sort of blue-collar people who would soon suffocate under the pillow Reganomics pressed to their faces. Baba was the lone Republican in our building.

But the Bay Area's smog stung his eyes, the traffic noise gave him headaches, and the pollen made him cough. The fruit was never sweet enough, the water never clean enough, and where were all the trees and open fields? For two years, I tried to get Baba to enroll in ESL classes to improve his broken English. But he scoffed at the idea. "Maybe I'll spell 'cat' and the teacher will give me a glittery little star so I can run home and show it off to you," he'd grumble.

One Sunday in the spring of 1983, I walked into a small bookstore that sold used paperbacks, next to the Indian movie theater just west of where Amtrak crossed Fremont Boulevard. I told Baba I'd be out in five minutes and he shrugged. He had been working at a gas station in Fremont and had the day off. I watched him jaywalk across Fremont Boulevard and enter Fast & Easy, a little grocery store run by an elderly Vietnamese couple, Mr. and Mrs. Nguyen. They were gray-haired, friendly people; she had Parkinson's, he'd had his hip replaced. "He's like Six Million Dollar Man now," she always said to me, laughing toothlessly. "Remember Six Million Dollar Man, Amir?" Then Mr. Nguyen would scowl like Lee Majors, pretend he was running in slow motion.

I was flipping through a worn copy of a Mike Hammer mystery when I heard screaming and glass breaking. I dropped the book and hurried across the street. I found the Nguyens behind the counter, all the way against the wall, faces ashen, Mr. Nguyen's arms wrapped around his wife. On the floor: oranges, an overturned magazine rack, a broken jar of beef jerky, and shards of glass at Baba's feet.

It turned out that Baba had had no cash on him for the oranges. He'd written Mr. Nguyen a check and Mr. Nguyen had asked for an ID. "He wants to see my license," Baba bellowed in Farsi. "Almost two years we've bought his damn fruits and put money in his pocket and the son of a dog wants to see my license!"

"Baba, it's not personal," I said, smiling at the Nguyens. "They're supposed to ask for an ID."

"I don't want you here," Mr. Nguyen said, stepping in front of his wife. He was pointing at Baba with his cane. He turned to me.

"You're nice young man but your father, he's crazy. Not welcome anymore."

"Does he think I'm a thief?" Baba said, his voice rising. People had gathered outside. They were staring. "What kind of a country is this? No one trusts anybody!"

"I call police," Mrs. Nguyen said, poking out her face. "You get out or I call police."

"Please, Mrs. Nguyen, don't call the police. I'll take him home. Just don't call the police, okay? Please?"

"Yes, you take him home. Good idea," Mr. Nguyen said. His eyes, behind his wire-rimmed bifocals, never left Baba. I led Baba through the doors. He kicked a magazine on his way out. After I'd made him promise he wouldn't go back in, I returned to the store and apologized to the Nguyens. Told them my father was going through a difficult time. I gave Mrs. Nguyen our telephone number and address, and told her to get an estimate for the damages. "Please call me as soon as you know. I'll pay for everything, Mrs. Nguyen. I'm so sorry." Mrs. Nguyen took the sheet of paper from me and nodded. I saw her hands were shaking more than usual, and that made me angry at Baba, his causing an old woman to shake like that.

"My father is still adjusting to life in America," I said, by way of explanation.

I wanted to tell them that, in Kabul, we snapped a tree branch and used it as a credit card. Hassan and I would take the wooden stick to the bread maker. He'd carve notches on our stick with his knife, one notch for each loaf of *naan* he'd pull for us from the *tandoor*'s roaring flames. At the end of the month, my father paid him for the number of notches on the stick. That was it. No questions. No ID.

But I didn't tell them. I thanked Mr. Nguyen for not calling the cops. Took Baba home. He sulked and smoked on the balcony while I made rice with chicken neck stew. A year and a half since we'd stepped off the Boeing from Peshawar, and Baba was still adjusting.

We ate in silence that night. After two bites, Baba pushed away his plate.

I glanced at him across the table, his nails chipped and black with engine oil, his knuckles scraped, the smells of the gas station—dust, sweat, and gasoline—on his clothes. Baba was like the widower who remarries but can't let go of his dead wife. He missed the sugarcane fields of Jalalabad and the gardens of Paghman. He missed people milling in and out of his house, missed walking down the bustling aisles of Shor Bazaar and greeting people who knew him and his father, knew his grandfather, people who shared ancestors with him, whose pasts intertwined with his.

For me, America was a place to bury my memories.

For Baba, a place to mourn his.

"Maybe we should go back to Peshawar," I said, watching the ice float in my glass of water. We'd spent six months in Peshawar waiting for the INS to issue our visas. Our grimy one-bedroom apartment smelled like dirty socks and cat droppings, but we were surrounded by people we knew—at least people Baba knew. He'd invite the entire corridor of neighbors for dinner, most of them Afghans waiting for visas. Inevitably, someone would bring a set of tabla and someone else a harmonium. Tea would brew, and whoever had a passing singing voice would sing until the sun rose, the mosquitoes stopped buzzing, and clapping hands grew sore.

"You were happier there, Baba. It was more like home," I said.

"Peshawar was good for me. Not good for you."

"You work so hard here."

"It's not so bad now," he said, meaning since he had become

the day manager at the gas station. But I'd seen the way he winced
and rubbed his wrists on damp days. The way sweat erupted on
his forehead as he reached for his bottle of antacids after meals.
"Besides, I didn't bring us here for me, did I?"

I reached across the table and put my hand on his. My student
hand, clean and soft, on his laborer's hand, grubby and calloused.
I thought of all the trucks, train sets, and bikes he'd bought me in
Kabul. Now America. One last gift for Amir.

Just one month after we arrived in the U.S., Baba found a job
off Washington Boulevard as an assistant at a gas station owned
by an Afghan acquaintance—he'd started looking for work the
same week we arrived. Six days a week, Baba pulled twelve-hour
shifts pumping gas, running the register, changing oil, and wash-
ing windshields. I'd bring him lunch sometimes and find him looking for a pack of cigarettes on the shelves, a customer waiting on
the other side of the oil-stained counter, Baba's face drawn and
pale under the bright fluorescent lights. The electronic bell over
the door would *ding-dong* when I walked in, and Baba would look
over his shoulder, wave, and smile, his eyes watering from fatigue.

The same day he was hired, Baba and I went to our eligibility
officer in San Jose, Mrs. Dobbins. She was an overweight black
woman with twinkling eyes and a dimpled smile. She'd told me
once that she sang in church, and I believed her—she had a voice
that made me think of warm milk and honey. Baba dropped the
stack of food stamps on her desk. "Thank you but I don't want,"
Baba said. "I work always. In Afghanistan I work, in America I
work. Thank you very much, Mrs. Dobbins, but I don't like it free
money."

Mrs. Dobbins blinked. Picked up the food stamps, looked
from me to Baba like we were pulling a prank, or "slipping her a
trick" as Hassan used to say. "Fifteen years I been doin' this job

and nobody's ever done this," she said. And that was how Baba ended those humiliating food stamp moments at the cash register and alleviated one of his greatest fears: that an Afghan would see him buying food with charity money. Baba walked out of the welfare office like a man cured of a tumor.

THAT SUMMER OF 1983, I graduated from high school at the age of twenty, by far the oldest senior tossing his mortarboard on the football field that day. I remember losing Baba in the swarm of families, flashing cameras, and blue gowns. I found him near the twenty-yard line, hands shoved in his pockets, camera dangling on his chest. He disappeared and reappeared behind the people moving between us: squealing blue-clad girls hugging, crying, boys high-fiving their fathers, each other. Baba's beard was graying, his hair thinning at the temples, and hadn't he been taller in Kabul? He was wearing his brown suit—his only suit, the same one he wore to Afghan weddings and funerals—and the red tie I had bought for his fiftieth birthday that year. Then he saw me and waved. Smiled. He motioned for me to wear my mortarboard, and took a picture of me with the school's clock tower in the background. I smiled for him—in a way, this was his day more than mine. He walked to me, curled his arm around my neck, and gave my brow a single kiss. "I am *moftakhir*, Amir," he said. Proud. His eyes gleamed when he said that and I liked being on the receiving end of that look.

He took me to an Afghan kabob house in Hayward that night and ordered far too much food. He told the owner that his son was going to college in the fall. I had debated him briefly about that just before graduation, and told him I wanted to get a job. Help out, save some money, maybe go to college the following year. But he had shot me one of his smoldering Baba looks, and the words had vaporized on my tongue.

After dinner, Baba took me to a bar across the street from the restaurant. The place was dim, and the acrid smell of beer I'd always disliked permeated the walls. Men in baseball caps and tank tops played pool, clouds of cigarette smoke hovering over the green tables, swirling in the fluorescent light. We drew looks, Baba in his brown suit and me in pleated slacks and sports jacket. We took a seat at the bar, next to an old man, his leathery face sickly in the blue glow of the Michelob sign overhead. Baba lit a cigarette and ordered us beers. "Tonight I am too much happy," he announced to no one and everyone. "Tonight I drinking with my son. And one, please, for my friend," he said, patting the old man on the back. The old fellow tipped his hat and smiled. He had no upper teeth.

Baba finished his beer in three gulps and ordered another. He had three before I forced myself to drink a quarter of mine. By then he had bought the old man a scotch and treated a foursome of pool players to a pitcher of Budweiser. Men shook his hand and clapped him on the back. They drank to him. Someone lit his cigarette. Baba loosened his tie and gave the old man a handful of quarters. He pointed to the jukebox. "Tell him to play his favorite songs," he said to me. The old man nodded and gave Baba a salute. Soon, country music was blaring, and, just like that, Baba had started a party.

At one point, Baba stood, raised his beer, spilling it on the sawdust floor, and yelled, "Fuck the Russia!" The bar's laughter, then its full-throated echo followed. Baba bought another round of pitchers for everyone.

When we left, everyone was sad to see him go. Kabul, Peshawar, Hayward. Same old Baba, I thought, smiling.

I drove us home in Baba's old, ochre yellow Buick Century. Baba dozed off on the way, snoring like a jackhammer. I smelled tobacco on him and alcohol, sweet and pungent. But he sat up when I stopped the car and said in a hoarse voice, "Keep driving to the end of the block."

"Why, Baba?"

"Just go." He had me park at the south end of the street. He reached in his coat pocket and handed me a set of keys. "There," he said, pointing to the car in front of us. It was an old model Ford, long and wide, a dark color I couldn't discern in the moonlight. "It needs painting, and I'll have one of the guys at the station put in new shocks, but it runs."

I took the keys, stunned. I looked from him to the car.

"You'll need it to go to college," he said.

I took his hand in mine. Squeezed it. My eyes were tearing over and I was glad for the shadows that hid our faces. "Thank you, Baba."

We got out and sat inside the Ford. It was a Grand Torino. Navy blue, Baba said. I drove it around the block, testing the brakes, the radio, the turn signals. I parked it in the lot of our apartment building and shut off the engine. "*Tashakor*, Baba jan," I said. I wanted to say more, tell him how touched I was by his act of kindness, how much I appreciated all that he had done for me, all that he was still doing. But I knew I'd embarrass him. "*Tashakor*," I repeated instead.

He smiled and leaned back against the headrest, his forehead almost touching the ceiling. We didn't say anything. Just sat in the dark, listened to the *tink-tink* of the engine cooling, the wail of a siren in the distance. Then Baba rolled his head toward me. "I wish Hassan had been with us today," he said.

A pair of steel hands closed around my windpipe at the sound of Hassan's name. I rolled down the window. Waited for the steel hands to loosen their grip.

I WOULD ENROLL in junior college classes in the fall, I told Baba the day after graduation. He was drinking cold black tea and chewing cardamom seeds, his personal trusted antidote for hangover headaches.

"I think I'll major in English," I said. I winced inside, waiting for his reply.

"English?"

"Creative writing."

He considered this. Sipped his tea. "Stories, you mean. You'll make up stories." I looked down at my feet.

"They pay for that, making up stories?"

"If you're good," I said. "And if you get discovered."

"How likely is that, getting discovered?"

"It happens," I said.

He nodded. "And what will you do while you wait to get good and get discovered? How will you earn money? If you marry, how will you support your *khanum*?"

I couldn't lift my eyes to meet his. "I'll...find a job."

"Oh," he said. "*Wah wah!* So, if I understand, you'll study several years to earn a degree, then you'll get a *chatti* job like mine, one you could just as easily land today, on the small chance that your degree might someday help you get...discovered." He took a deep breath and sipped his tea. Grunted something about medical school, law school, and "real work."

My cheeks burned and guilt coursed through me, the guilt of

indulging myself at the expense of his ulcer, his black fingernails and aching wrists. But I would stand my ground, I decided. I didn't want to sacrifice for Baba anymore. The last time I had done that, I had damned myself.

Baba sighed and, this time, tossed a whole handful of cardamom seeds in his mouth.

SOMETIMES, I GOT BEHIND the wheel of my Ford, rolled down the windows, and drove for hours, from the East Bay to the South Bay, up the Peninsula and back. I drove through the grids of cottonwood-lined streets in our Fremont neighborhood, where people who'd never shaken hands with kings lived in shabby, flat one-story houses with barred windows, where old cars like mine dripped oil on blacktop driveways. Pencil gray chain-link fences closed off the backyards in our neighborhood. Toys, bald tires, and beer bottles with peeling labels littered unkempt front lawns. I drove past tree-shaded parks that smelled like bark, past strip malls big enough to hold five simultaneous *Buzkashi* tournaments. I drove the Torino up the hills of Los Altos, idling past estates with picture windows and silver lions guarding the wrought-iron gates, homes with cherub fountains lining the manicured walkways and no Ford Torinos in the driveways. Homes that made Baba's house in Wazir Akbar Khan look like a servant's hut.

I'd get up early some Saturday mornings and drive south on Highway 17, push the Ford up the winding road through the mountains to Santa Cruz. I would park by the old lighthouse and wait for sunrise, sit in my car and watch the fog rolling in from the sea. In Afghanistan, I had only seen the ocean at the cinema. Sitting in the dark next to Hassan, I had always wondered if it was true what I'd read, that sea air smelled like salt. I used to tell Hassan that someday we'd walk on a strip of seaweed-strewn beach, sink our feet in the sand, and watch the water recede from our toes. The first time I saw the Pacific, I almost cried. It was as vast and blue as the oceans on the movie screens of my childhood.

Sometimes in the early evening, I parked the car and walked up a freeway overpass. My face pressed against the fence, I'd try to count the blinking red taillights inching along, stretching as far as my eyes could see. BMWs. Saabs. Porsches. Cars I'd never seen in Kabul, where most people drove Russian Volgas, old Opels, or Iranian Paikans.

Almost two years had passed since we had arrived in the U.S., and I was still marveling at the size of this country, its vastness. Beyond every freeway lay another freeway, beyond every city another city, hills beyond mountains and mountains beyond hills, and, beyond those, more cities and more people.

Long before the *Roussi* army marched into Afghanistan, long before villages were burned and schools destroyed, long before mines were planted like seeds of death and children buried in rock-piled graves, Kabul had become a city of ghosts for me. A city of harelipped ghosts.

America was different. America was a river, roaring along, unmindful of the past. I could wade into this river, let my sins drown to the bottom, let the waters carry me someplace far. Someplace with no ghosts, no memories, and no sins.

If for nothing else, for that, I embraced America.

THE FOLLOWING SUMMER, the summer of 1984—the summer I turned twenty-one—Baba sold his Buick and bought a dilap-

idated '71 Volkswagen bus for $550 from an old Afghan acquain-
tance who'd been a high-school science teacher in Kabul. The
neighbors' heads turned the afternoon the bus sputtered up the
street and farted its way across our lot. Baba killed the engine and
let the bus roll silently into our designated spot. We sank in our
seats, laughed until tears rolled down our cheeks, and, more
important, until we were sure the neighbors weren't watching
anymore. The bus was a sad carcass of rusted metal, shattered
windows replaced with black garbage bags, balding tires, and
upholstery shredded down to the springs. But the old teacher had
reassured Baba that the engine and transmission were sound and,
on that account, the man hadn't lied.

On Saturdays, Baba woke me up at dawn. As he dressed, I
scanned the classifieds in the local papers and circled the garage
sale ads. We mapped our route—Fremont, Union City, Newark,
and Hayward first, then San Jose, Milpitas, Sunnyvale, and
Campbell if time permitted. Baba drove the bus, sipping hot tea
from the thermos, and I navigated. We stopped at garage sales
and bought knickknacks that people no longer wanted. We haggled over old sewing machines, one-eyed Barbie dolls, wooden
tennis rackets, guitars with missing strings, and old Electrolux
vacuum cleaners. By midafternoon, we'd filled the back of the
VW bus with used goods. Then early Sunday mornings, we drove
to the San Jose flea market off Berryessa, rented a spot, and sold
the junk for a small profit: a Chicago record that we'd bought for
a quarter the day before might go for $1, or $4 for a set of five; a
ramshackle Singer sewing machine purchased for $10 might,
after some bargaining, bring in $25.

By that summer, Afghan families were working an entire section of the San Jose flea market. Afghan music played in the aisles
of the Used Goods section. There was an unspoken code of

behavior among Afghans at the flea market: You greeted the guy across the aisle, you invited him for a bite of potato *bolani* or a little *qabuli,* and you chatted. You offered *tassali,* condolences, for the death of a parent, congratulated the birth of children, and shook your head mournfully when the conversation turned to Afghanistan and the *Roussis*—which it inevitably did. But you avoided the topic of Saturday. Because it might turn out that the fellow across the isle was the guy you'd nearly blindsided at the freeway exit yesterday in order to beat him to a promising garage sale.

The only thing that flowed more than tea in those aisles was Afghan gossip. The flea market was where you sipped green tea with almond *kolcha*s, and learned whose daughter had broken off an engagement and run off with her American boyfriend, who used to be *Parchami*—a communist—in Kabul, and who had bought a house with under-the-table money while still on welfare. Tea, Politics, and Scandal, the ingredients of an Afghan Sunday at the flea market.

I ran the stand sometimes as Baba sauntered down the aisle, hands respectfully pressed to his chest, greeting people he knew from Kabul: mechanics and tailors selling hand-me-down wool coats and scraped bicycle helmets, alongside former ambassadors, out-of-work surgeons, and university professors.

One early Sunday morning in July 1984, while Baba set up, I bought two cups of coffee from the concession stand and returned to find Baba talking to an older, distinguished-looking man. I put the cups on the rear bumper of the bus, next to the REAGAN/BUSH FOR '84 sticker.

"Amir," Baba said, motioning me over, "this is General Sahib, Mr. Iqbal Taheri. He was a decorated general in Kabul. He worked for the Ministry of Defense."

Taheri. Why did the name sound familiar?

The general laughed like a man used to attending formal parties where he'd laughed on cue at the minor jokes of important people. He had wispy silver-gray hair combed back from his smooth, tanned forehead, and tufts of white in his bushy eyebrows. He smelled like cologne and wore an iron-gray three-piece suit, shiny from too many pressings; the gold chain of a pocket watch dangled from his vest.

"Such a lofty introduction," he said, his voice deep and cultured. *"Salaam, bachem."* Hello, my child.

"Salaam, General Sahib," I said, shaking his hand. His thin hands belied a firm grip, as if steel hid beneath the moisturized skin.

"Amir is going to be a great writer," Baba said. I did a double take at this. "He has finished his first year of college and earned A's in all of his courses."

"Junior college," I corrected him.

"Mashallah," General Taheri said. "Will you be writing about our country, history perhaps? Economics?"

"I write fiction," I said, thinking of the dozen or so short stories I had written in the leather-bound notebook Rahim Khan had given me, wondering why I was suddenly embarrassed by them in this man's presence.

"Ah, a storyteller," the general said. "Well, people need stories to divert them at difficult times like this." He put his hand on Baba's shoulder and turned to me. "Speaking of stories, your father and I hunted pheasant together one summer day in Jalalabad," he said. "It was a marvelous time. If I recall correctly, your father's eye proved as keen in the hunt as it had in business."

Baba kicked a wooden tennis racket on our tarpaulin spread with the toe of his boot. "Some business."

General Taheri managed a simultaneously sad and polite

smile, heaved a sigh, and gently patted Baba's shoulder. *"Zendagi migzara,"* he said. Life goes on. He turned his eyes to me. "We Afghans are prone to a considerable degree of exaggeration, *bachem,* and I have heard many men foolishly labeled great. But your father has the distinction of belonging to the minority who truly deserves the label." This little speech sounded to me the way his suit looked: often used and unnaturally shiny.

"You're flattering me," Baba said.

"I am not," the general said, tilting his head sideways and pressing his hand to his chest to convey humility. "Boys and girls must know the legacy of their fathers." He turned to me. "Do you appreciate your father, *bachem?* Do you really appreciate him?"

"Balay, General Sahib, I do," I said, wishing he'd not call me "my child."

"Then congratulations, you are already halfway to being a man," he said with no trace of humor, no irony, the compliment of the casually arrogant.

"Padar jan, you forgot your tea." A young woman's voice. She was standing behind us, a slim-hipped beauty with velvety coal black hair, an open thermos and Styrofoam cup in her hand. I blinked, my heart quickening. She had thick black eyebrows that touched in the middle like the arched wings of a flying bird, and the gracefully hooked nose of a princess from old Persia—maybe that of Tahmineh, Rostam's wife and Sohrab's mother from the *Shahnamah.* Her eyes, walnut brown and shaded by fanned lashes, met mine. Held for a moment. Flew away.

"You are so kind, my dear," General Taheri said. He took the cup from her. Before she turned to go, I saw she had a brown, sickle-shaped birthmark on the smooth skin just above her left jawline. She walked to a dull gray van two aisles away and put the thermos inside. Her hair spilled to one side when she kneeled amid boxes of old records and paperbacks.

"My daughter, Soraya jan," General Taheri said. He took a deep breath like a man eager to change the subject and checked his gold pocket watch. "Well, time to go and set up." He and Baba kissed on the cheek and he shook my hand with both of his. "Best of luck with the writing," he said, looking me in the eye. His pale blue eyes revealed nothing of the thoughts behind them.

For the rest of that day, I fought the urge to look toward the gray van.

IT CAME TO ME on our way home. Taheri. I knew I'd heard that name before.

"Wasn't there some story floating around about Taheri's daughter?" I said to Baba, trying to sound casual.

"You know me," Baba said, inching the bus along the queue exiting the flea market. "Talk turns to gossip and I walk away."

"But there was, wasn't there?" I said.

"Why do you ask?" He was looking at me coyly.

I shrugged and fought back a smile. "Just curious, Baba."

"Really? Is that all?" he said, his eyes playful, lingering on mine. "Has she made an impression on you?"

I rolled my eyes. "Please, Baba."

He smiled, and swung the bus out of the flea market. We headed for Highway 680. We drove in silence for a while. "All I've heard is that there was a man once and things...didn't go well." He said this gravely, like he'd disclosed to me that she had breast cancer.

"Oh."

"I hear she is a decent girl, hardworking and kind. But no *khastegar*s, no suitors, have knocked on the general's door since." Baba sighed. "It may be unfair, but what happens in a few days, sometimes even a single day, can change the course of a whole lifetime, Amir," he said.

LYING AWAKE IN BED that night, I thought of Soraya Taheri's sickle-shaped birthmark, her gently hooked nose, and the way her luminous eyes had fleetingly held mine. My heart stuttered at the thought of her. Soraya Taheri. My Swap Meet Princess.

TWELVE

In Afghanistan, *yelda* is the first night of the month of *Jadi*, the first night of winter, and the longest night of the year. As was the tradition, Hassan and I used to stay up late, our feet tucked under the *kursi*, while Ali tossed apple skin into the stove and told us ancient tales of sultans and thieves to pass that longest of nights. It was from Ali that I learned the lore of *yelda*, that bedeviled moths flung themselves at candle flames, and wolves climbed mountains looking for the sun. Ali swore that if you ate watermelon the night of *yelda*, you wouldn't get thirsty the coming summer.

When I was older, I read in my poetry books that *yelda* was the starless night tormented lovers kept vigil, enduring the endless dark, waiting for the sun to rise and bring with it their loved one. After I met Soraya Taheri, every night of the week became a *yelda* for me. And when Sunday mornings came, I rose from bed, Soraya Taheri's brown-eyed face already in my head. In Baba's bus, I counted the miles until I'd see her sitting barefoot, arranging cardboard boxes of yellowed encyclopedias, her heels white against the asphalt, silver bracelets jingling around her slender wrists. I'd think of the shadow her hair cast on the ground when it slid off her back and hung down like a velvet curtain. Soraya. Swap Meet Princess. The morning sun to my *yelda*.

I invented excuses to stroll down the aisle—which Baba acknowledged with a playful smirk—and pass the Taheris' stand. I would wave at the general, perpetually dressed in his shiny over-pressed gray suit, and he would wave back. Sometimes he'd get up from his director's chair and we'd make small talk about my writing, the war, the day's bargains. And I'd have to will my eyes not to peel away, not to wander to where Soraya sat reading a paperback. The general and I would say our good-byes and I'd try not to slouch as I walked away.

Sometimes she sat alone, the general off to some other row to socialize, and I would walk by, pretending not to know her, but dying to. Sometimes she was there with a portly middle-aged woman with pale skin and dyed red hair. I promised myself that I would talk to her before the summer was over, but schools reopened, the leaves reddened, yellowed, and fell, the rains of winter swept in and wakened Baba's joints, baby leaves sprouted once more, and I still hadn't had the heart, the *dil*, to even look her in the eye.

The spring quarter ended in late May 1985. I aced all of my general education classes, which was a minor miracle given how I'd sit in lectures and think of the soft hook of Soraya's nose.

Then, one sweltering Sunday that summer, Baba and I were at the flea market, sitting at our booth, fanning our faces with newspapers. Despite the sun bearing down like a branding iron, the market was crowded that day and sales had been strong—it was only 12:30 but we'd already made $160. I got up, stretched, and asked Baba if he wanted a Coke. He said he'd love one.

"Be careful, Amir," he said as I began to walk.

"Of what, Baba?"

"I am not an *ahmaq*, so don't play stupid with me."

"I don't know what you're talking about."

"Remember this," Baba said, pointing at me, "The man is a Pashtun to the root. He has *nang* and *namoos*." Nang. Namoos. Honor and pride. The tenets of Pashtun men. Especially when it came to the chastity of a wife. Or a daughter.

"I'm only going to get us drinks."

"Just don't embarrass me, that's all I ask."

"I won't. God, Baba."

Baba lit a cigarette and started fanning himself again.

I walked toward the concession booth initially, then turned left at the T-shirt stand—where, for $5, you could have the face of Jesus, Elvis, Jim Morrison, or all three, pressed on a white nylon T-shirt. Mariachi music played overhead, and I smelled pickles and grilled meat.

I spotted the Taheris' gray van two rows from ours, next to a kiosk selling mango-on-a-stick. She was alone, reading. White ankle-length summer dress today. Open-toed sandals. Hair pulled back and crowned with a tulip-shaped bun. I meant to simply walk by again and I thought I had, except suddenly I was standing at the edge of the Taheris' white tablecloth, staring at Soraya across curling irons and old neckties. She looked up.

"*Salaam*," I said. "I'm sorry to be *mozahem*, I didn't mean to disturb you."

"*Salaam*."

"Is General Sahib here today?" I said. My ears were burning. I couldn't bring myself to look her in the eye.

"He went that way," she said. Pointed to her right. The bracelet slipped down to her elbow, silver against olive.

"Will you tell him I stopped by to pay my respects?" I said.

"I will."

"Thank you," I said. "Oh, and my name is Amir. In case you need to know. So you can tell him. That I stopped by. To . . . pay my respects."

"Yes."

I shifted on my feet, cleared my throat. "I'll go now. Sorry to have disturbed you."

"Nay, you didn't," she said.

"Oh. Good." I tipped my head and gave her a half smile. "I'll go now." Hadn't I already said that? *Khoda hafez.*

"Khoda hafez."

I began to walk. Stopped and turned. I said it before I had a chance to lose my nerve: "Can I ask what you're reading?"

She blinked.

I held my breath. Suddenly, I felt the collective eyes of the flea market Afghans shift to us. I imagined a hush falling. Lips stopping in midsentence. Heads turning. Eyes narrowing with keen interest.

What was *this*?

Up to that point, our encounter could have been interpreted as a respectful inquiry, one man asking for the whereabouts of another man. But I'd asked her a question and if she answered, we'd be . . . well, we'd be chatting. Me a *mojarad*, a single young man, and she an unwed young woman. One with a *history*, no less. This was teetering dangerously on the verge of gossip material, and the best kind of it. Poison tongues would flap. And she would bear the brunt of that poison, not me—I was fully aware of the Afghan double standard that favored my gender. Not *Did you see him chatting with her?* but *Wooooy! Did you see how she wouldn't let him go? What a* lochak!

By Afghan standards, my question had been bold. With it, I had bared myself, and left little doubt as to my interest in her. But I was a man, and all I had risked was a bruised ego. Bruises healed. Reputations did not. Would she take my dare?

She turned the book so the cover faced me. *Wuthering Heights*. "Have you read it?" she said.

I nodded. I could feel the pulsating beat of my heart behind my eyes. "It's a sad story."

"Sad stories make good books," she said.

"They do."

"I heard you write."

How did she know? I wondered if her father had told her, maybe she had asked him. I immediately dismissed both scenarios as absurd. Fathers and sons could talk freely about women. But no Afghan girl—no decent and *mohtaram* Afghan girl, at least— queried her father about a young man. And no father, especially a Pashtun with *nang* and *namoos,* would discuss a *mojarad* with his daughter, not unless the fellow in question was a *khastegar,* a suitor, who had done the honorable thing and sent his father to knock on the door.

Incredibly, I heard myself say, "Would you like to read one of my stories?"

"I would like that," she said. I sensed an unease in her now, saw it in the way her eyes began to flick side to side. Maybe checking for the general. I wondered what he would say if he found me speaking for such an inappropriate length of time with his daughter.

"Maybe I'll bring you one someday," I said. I was about to say more when the woman I'd seen on occasion with Soraya came walking up the aisle. She was carrying a plastic bag full of fruit. When she saw us, her eyes bounced from Soraya to me and back. She smiled.

"Amir jan, good to see you," she said, unloading the bag on the tablecloth. Her brow glistened with a sheen of sweat. Her red hair, coiffed like a helmet, glittered in the sunlight—I could see bits of her scalp where the hair had thinned. She had small green eyes buried in a cabbage-round face, capped teeth, and little fingers like sausages. A golden Allah rested on her chest, the chain burrowed under the skin tags and folds of her neck. "I am Jamila, Soraya jan's mother."

"*Salaam*, Khala jan," I said, embarrassed, as I often was around Afghans, that she knew me and I had no idea who she was.

"How is your father?" she said.

"He's well, thank you."

"You know, your grandfather, Ghazi Sahib, the judge? Now, his uncle and my grandfather were cousins," she said. "So you see, we're related." She smiled a cap-toothed smile, and I noticed the right side of her mouth drooping a little. Her eyes moved between Soraya and me again.

I'd asked Baba once why General Taheri's daughter hadn't married yet. No suitors, Baba said. No suitable suitors, he amended. But he wouldn't say more—Baba knew how lethal idle talk could prove to a young woman's prospects of marrying well. Afghan men, especially those from reputable families, were fickle creatures. A whisper here, an insinuation there, and they fled like startled birds. So weddings had come and gone and no one had sung *ahesta boro* for Soraya, no one had painted her palms with henna, no one had held a Koran over her headdress, and it had been General Taheri who'd danced with her at every wedding.

And now, this woman, this mother, with her heartbreakingly eager, crooked smile and the barely veiled hope in her eyes. I cringed a little at the position of power I'd been granted, and all because I had won at the genetic lottery that had determined my sex.

I could never read the thoughts in the general's eyes, but I knew this much about his wife: If I was going to have an adversary in this—whatever *this* was—it would not be her.

"Sit down, Amir jan," she said. "Soraya, get him a chair, *bachem*. And wash one of those peaches. They're sweet and fresh."

"Nay, thank you," I said. "I should get going. My father's waiting."

"Oh?" Khanum Taheri said, clearly impressed that I'd done the polite thing and declined the offer. "Then here, at least have this." She threw a handful of kiwis and a few peaches into a paper bag and insisted I take them. "Carry my *Salaam* to your father. And come back to see us again."

"I will. Thank you, Khala jan," I said. Out of the corner of my eye, I saw Soraya looking away.

"I THOUGHT YOU WERE GETTING COKES," Baba said, taking the bag of peaches from me. He was looking at me in a simultaneously serious and playful way. I began to make something up, but he bit into a peach and waved his hand. "Don't bother, Amir. Just remember what I said."

THAT NIGHT IN BED, I thought of the way dappled sunlight had danced in Soraya's eyes, and of the delicate hollows above her collarbone. I replayed our conversation over and over in my head. Had she said *I heard you write* or *I heard you're a writer*? Which was it? I tossed in my sheets and stared at the ceiling, dismayed at the thought of six laborious, interminable nights of *yelda* until I saw her again.

IT WENT ON LIKE THAT for a few weeks. I'd wait until the general went for a stroll, then I'd walk past the Taheris' stand. If Khanum Taheri was there, she'd offer me tea and a *kolcha* and we'd chat about Kabul in the old days, the people we knew, her arthritis. Undoubtedly, she had noticed that my appearances always coincided with her husband's absences, but she never let on. "Oh you just missed your Kaka," she'd say. I actually liked it when Khanum Taheri was there, and not just because of her amiable ways; Soraya was more relaxed, more talkative with her mother around. As if her presence legitimized whatever was happening between us—though certainly not to the same degree that the general's would have. Khanum Taheri's chaperoning made our meetings, if not gossip-proof, then less gossip-worthy, even if her borderline fawning on me clearly embarrassed Soraya.

One day, Soraya and I were alone at their booth, talking. She was telling me about school, how she too was working on her general education classes, at Ohlone Junior College in Fremont.

"What will you major in?"

"I want to be a teacher," she said.

"Really? Why?"

"I've always wanted to. When we lived in Virginia, I became ESL certified and now I teach at the public library one night a week. My mother was a teacher too, she taught Farsi and history at Zarghoona High School for girls in Kabul."

A potbellied man in a deerstalker hat offered three dollars for a five-dollar set of candlesticks and Soraya let him have it. She dropped the money in a little candy box by her feet. She looked at me shyly. "I want to tell you a story," she said, "but I'm a little embarrassed about it."

"Tell me."

"It's kind of silly."

"Please tell me."

She laughed. "Well, when I was in fourth grade in Kabul, my father hired a woman named Ziba to help around the house. She had a sister in Iran, in Mashad, and, since Ziba was illiterate, she'd ask me to write her sister letters once in a while. And when the sister replied, I'd read her letter to Ziba. One day, I asked her if she'd like to learn to read and write. She gave me this big smile, crinkling her eyes, and said she'd like that very much. So we'd sit at the kitchen table after I was done with my own schoolwork and I'd teach her *Alef-beh*. I remember looking up sometimes in the middle of homework and seeing Ziba in the kitchen, stirring meat in the pressure cooker, then sitting down with a pencil to do the alphabet homework I'd assigned to her the night before.

"Anyway, within a year, Ziba could read children's books. We sat in the yard and she read me the tales of Dara and Sara—slowly but correctly. She started calling me *Moalem* Soraya, Teacher Soraya." She laughed again. "I know it sounds childish, but the first time Ziba wrote her own letter, I knew there was nothing else I'd ever want to be but a teacher. I was so proud of her and I felt I'd done something really worthwhile, you know?"

"Yes," I lied. I thought of how I had used my literacy to ridicule Hassan. How I had teased him about big words he didn't know.

"My father wants me to go to law school, my mother's always throwing hints about medical school, but I'm going to be a teacher. Doesn't pay much here, but it's what I want."

"My mother was a teacher too," I said.

"I know," she said. "My mother told me." Then her face reddened with a blush at what she had blurted, at the implication of her answer, that "Amir Conversations" took place between them when I wasn't there. It took an enormous effort to stop myself from smiling.

"I brought you something." I fished the roll of stapled pages from my back pocket. "As promised." I handed her one of my short stories.

"Oh, you remembered," she said, actually beaming. "Thank you!" I barely had time to register that she'd addressed me with *"tu"* for the first time and not the formal *"shoma,"* because suddenly her smile vanished. The color dropped from her face, and her eyes fixed on something behind me. I turned around. Came face-to-face with General Taheri.

"Amir jan. Our aspiring storyteller. What a pleasure," he said. He was smiling thinly.

"*Salaam,* General Sahib," I said through heavy lips.

He moved past me, toward the booth. "What a beautiful day it is, nay?" he said, thumb hooked in the breast pocket of his vest, the other hand extended toward Soraya. She gave him the pages.

"They say it will rain this week. Hard to believe, isn't it?" He dropped the rolled pages in the garbage can. Turned to me and gently put a hand on my shoulder. We took a few steps together.

"You know, *bachem,* I have grown rather fond of you. You are a decent boy, I really believe that, but—" he sighed and waved a hand "—even decent boys need reminding sometimes. So it's my duty to remind you that you are among peers in this flea market." He stopped. His expressionless eyes bore into mine. "You see, *everyone* here is a storyteller." He smiled, revealing perfectly even teeth. "Do pass my respects to your father, Amir jan."

He dropped his hand. Smiled again.

. . .

"WHAT'S WRONG?" Baba said. He was taking an elderly woman's money for a rocking horse.

"Nothing," I said. I sat down on an old TV set. Then I told him anyway.

"Akh, Amir," he sighed.

As it turned out, I didn't get to brood too much over what had happened.

Because later that week, Baba caught a cold.

IT STARTED WITH A HACKING COUGH and the sniffles. He got over the sniffles, but the cough persisted. He'd hack into his handkerchief, stow it in his pocket. I kept after him to get it checked, but he'd wave me away. He hated doctors and hospitals. To my knowledge, the only time Baba had ever gone to a doctor was the time he'd caught malaria in India.

Then, two weeks later, I caught him coughing a wad of blood-stained phlegm into the toilet.

"How long have you been doing that?" I said.

"What's for dinner?" he said.

"I'm taking you to the doctor."

Even though Baba was a manager at the gas station, the owner hadn't offered him health insurance, and Baba, in his reckless-ness, hadn't insisted. So I took him to the county hospital in San Jose. The sallow, puffy-eyed doctor who saw us introduced himself as a second-year resident. "He looks younger than you and sicker than me," Baba grumbled. The resident sent us down for a chest X ray. When the nurse called us back in, the resident was filling out a form.

"Take this to the front desk," he said, scribbling quickly.

"What is it?" I asked.

"A referral." *Scribble scribble.*

"For what?"

"Pulmonary clinic."

"What's that?"

He gave me a quick glance. Pushed up his glasses. Began scribbling again. "He's got a spot on his right lung. I want them to check it out."

"A spot?" I said, the room suddenly too small.

"Cancer?" Baba added casually.

"Possible. It's suspicious, anyway," the doctor muttered.

"Can't you tell us more?" I asked.

"Not really. Need a CAT scan first, then see the lung doctor." He handed me the referral form. "You said your father smokes, right?"

"Yes."

He nodded. Looked from me to Baba and back again. "They'll call you within two weeks."

I wanted to ask him how I was supposed to live with that word, "suspicious," for two whole weeks. How was I supposed eat, work, study? How could he send me home with that word?

I took the form and turned it in. That night, I waited until Baba fell asleep, and then folded a blanket. I used it as a prayer rug. Bowing my head to the ground, I recited half-forgotten verses from the Koran—verses the mullah had made us commit to memory in Kabul—and asked for kindness from a God I wasn't sure existed. I envied the mullah now, envied his faith and certainty.

Two weeks passed and no one called. And when I called them, they told me they'd lost the referral. Was I sure I had turned it in? They said they would call in another three weeks. I raised hell and bargained the three weeks down to one for the CAT scan, two to see the doctor.

The visit with the pulmonologist, Dr. Schneider, was going well until Baba asked him where he was from. Dr. Schneider said Russia. Baba lost it.

"Excuse us, Doctor," I said, pulling Baba aside. Dr. Schneider smiled and stood back, stethoscope still in hand.

"Baba, I read Dr. Schneider's biography in the waiting room. He was born in Michigan. *Michigan!* He's American, a lot more American than you and I will ever be."

"I don't care where he was born, he's *Roussi*," Baba said, grimacing like it was a dirty word. "His parents were *Roussi*, his grandparents were *Roussi*. I swear on your mother's face I'll break his arm if he tries to touch me."

"Dr. Schneider's parents fled from *Shorawi*, don't you see? They escaped!"

But Baba would hear none of it. Sometimes I think the only thing he loved as much as his late wife was Afghanistan, his late country. I almost screamed with frustration. Instead, I sighed and turned to Dr. Schneider. "I'm sorry, Doctor. This isn't going to work out."

The next pulmonologist, Dr. Amani, was Iranian and Baba approved. Dr. Amani, a soft-spoken man with a crooked mustache and a mane of gray hair, told us he had reviewed the CAT scan results and that he would have to perform a procedure called a bronchoscopy to get a piece of the lung mass for pathology. He scheduled it for the following week. I thanked him as I helped Baba out of the office, thinking that now I had to live a whole week with this new word, "mass," an even more ominous word than "suspicious." I wished Soraya were there with me.

It turned out that, like Satan, cancer had many names. Baba's was called "Oat Cell Carcinoma." Advanced. Inoperable. Baba asked Dr. Amani for a prognosis. Dr. Amani bit his lip, used the word "grave." "There is chemotherapy, of course," he said. "But it would only be palliative."

"What does that mean?" Baba asked.

Dr. Amani sighed. "It means it wouldn't change the outcome, just prolong it."

"That's a clear answer, Dr. Amani. Thank you for that," Baba said. "But no chemo medication for me." He had the same resolved look on his face as the day he'd dropped the stack of food stamps on Mrs. Dobbins's desk.

"But Baba—"

"Don't you challenge me in public, Amir. Ever. Who do you think you are?"

THE RAIN General Taheri had spoken about at the flea market was a few weeks late, but when we stepped out of Dr. Amani's office, passing cars sprayed grimy water onto the sidewalks. Baba lit a cigarette. He smoked all the way to the car and all the way home.

As he was slipping the key into the lobby door, I said, "I wish you'd give the chemo a chance, Baba."

Baba pocketed the keys, pulled me out of the rain and under the building's striped awning. He kneaded me on the chest with the hand holding the cigarette. "*Bas!* I've made my decision."

"What about me, Baba? What am I supposed to do?" I said, my eyes welling up.

A look of disgust swept across his rain-soaked face. It was the same look he'd give me when, as a kid, I'd fall, scrape my knees, and cry. It was the crying that brought it on then, the crying that brought it on now. "You're twenty-two years old, Amir! A grown man! You..." he opened his mouth, closed it, opened it again, reconsidered. Above us, rain drummed on the canvas awning. "What's going to happen to you, you say? All those years, that's what I was trying to teach you, how to never have to ask that question."

He opened the door. Turned back to me. "And one more thing. No one finds out about this, you hear me? No one. I don't want anybody's sympathy." Then he disappeared into the dim lobby. He chain-smoked the rest of that day in front of the TV. I didn't know what or whom he was defying. Me? Dr. Amani? Or maybe the God he had never believed in.

FOR A WHILE, even cancer couldn't keep Baba from the flea market. We made our garage sale treks on Saturdays, Baba the driver and me the navigator, and set up our display on Sundays. Brass lamps. Baseball gloves. Ski jackets with broken zippers. Baba greeted acquaintances from the old country and I haggled with buyers over a dollar or two. Like any of it mattered. Like the day I would become an orphan wasn't inching closer with each closing of shop.

Sometimes, General Taheri and his wife strolled by. The general, ever the diplomat, greeted me with a smile and his two-handed shake. But there was a new reticence to Khanum Taheri's demeanor. A reticence broken only by her secret, droopy smiles and the furtive, apologetic looks she cast my way when the general's attention was engaged elsewhere.

I remember that period as a time of many "firsts": The first time I heard Baba moan in the bathroom. The first time I found blood on his pillow. In over three years running the gas station, Baba had never called in sick. Another first.

By Halloween of that year, Baba was getting so tired by mid–Saturday afternoon that he'd wait behind the wheel while I got out and bargained for junk. By Thanksgiving, he wore out before noon. When sleighs appeared on front lawns and fake snow on Douglas firs, Baba stayed home and I drove the VW bus alone up and down the peninsula.

Sometimes at the flea market, Afghan acquaintances made remarks about Baba's weight loss. At first, they were complimentary. They even asked the secret to his diet. But the queries and compliments stopped when the weight loss didn't. When the pounds kept shedding. And shedding. When his cheeks hollowed. And his temples melted. And his eyes receded in their sockets.

Then, one cool Sunday shortly after New Year's Day, Baba was selling a lampshade to a stocky Filipino man while I rummaged in the VW for a blanket to cover his legs with.

"Hey, man, this guy needs help!" the Filipino man said with alarm. I turned around and found Baba on the ground. His arms and legs were jerking.

"*Komak!*" I cried. "Somebody help!" I ran to Baba. He was frothing at the mouth, the foamy spittle soaking his beard. His upturned eyes showed nothing but white.

People were rushing to us. I heard someone say seizure. Someone else yelling, "Call 911!" I heard running footsteps. The sky darkened as a crowd gathered around us.

Baba's spittle turned red. He was biting his tongue. I kneeled beside him and grabbed his arms and said I'm here Baba, I'm here, you'll be all right, I'm right here. As if I could soothe the convulsions out of him. Talk them into leaving my Baba alone. I felt a wetness on my knees. Saw Baba's bladder had let go. *Shhh, Baba jan, I'm here. Your son is right here.*

THE DOCTOR, white-bearded and perfectly bald, pulled me out of the room. "I want to go over your father's CAT scans with you," he said. He put the films up on a viewing box in the hall-way and pointed with the eraser end of his pencil to the pictures of Baba's cancer, like a cop showing mug shots of the killer to the victim's family. Baba's brain on those pictures looked like cross sections of a big walnut, riddled with tennis ball–shaped gray things.

"As you can see, the cancer's metastasized," he said. "He'll have to take steroids to reduce the swelling in his brain and anti-seizure medications. And I'd recommend palliative radiation. Do you know what that means?"

I said I did. I'd become conversant in cancer talk.

"All right, then," he said. He checked his beeper. "I have to go, but you can have me paged if you have any questions."

"Thank you."

I spent the night sitting on a chair next to Baba's bed.

THE NEXT MORNING, the waiting room down the hall was jammed with Afghans. The butcher from Newark. An engineer who'd worked with Baba on his orphanage. They filed in and paid Baba their respects in hushed tones. Wished him a swift recovery. Baba was awake then, groggy and tired, but awake.

Midmorning, General Taheri and his wife came. Soraya followed. We glanced at each other, looked away at the same time. "How are you, my friend?" General Taheri said, taking Baba's hand.

Baba motioned to the IV hanging from his arm. Smiled thinly. The general smiled back.

"You shouldn't have burdened yourselves. All of you," Baba croaked.

"It's no burden," Khanum Taheri said.

"No burden at all. More importantly, do you need anything?" General Taheri said. "Anything at all? Ask me like you'd ask a brother."

I remembered something Baba had said about Pashtuns once. *We may be hardheaded and I know we're far too proud, but, in the hour of need, believe me that there's no one you'd rather have at your side than a Pashtun.*

Baba shook his head on the pillow. "Your coming here has brightened my eyes." The general smiled and squeezed Baba's hand. "How are you, Amir jan? Do you need anything?"

The way he was looking at me, the kindness in his eyes... "Nay thank you, General Sahib. I'm..." A lump shot up in my throat and my eyes teared over. I bolted out of the room.

I wept in the hallway, by the viewing box where, the night before, I'd seen the killer's face.

Baba's door opened and Soraya walked out of his room. She stood near me. She was wearing a gray sweatshirt and jeans. Her hair was down. I wanted to find comfort in her arms.

"I'm so sorry, Amir," she said. "We all knew something was wrong, but we had no idea it was this."

I blotted my eyes with my sleeve. "He didn't want anyone to know."

"Do you need anything?"

"No." I tried to smile. She put her hand on mine. Our first

touch. I took it. Brought it to my face. My eyes. I let it go. "You'd better go back inside. Or your father will come after me."

She smiled and nodded. "I should." She turned to go.

"Soraya?"

"Yes?"

"I'm happy you came. It means... the world to me."

THEY DISCHARGED BABA two days later. They brought in a specialist called a radiation oncologist to talk Baba into getting radiation treatment. Baba refused. They tried to talk me into talking him into it. But I'd seen the look on Baba's face. I thanked them, signed their forms, and took Baba home in my Ford Torino.

That night, Baba was lying on the couch, a wool blanket covering him. I brought him hot tea and roasted almonds. Wrapped my arms around his back and pulled him up much too easily. His shoulder blade felt like a bird's wing under my fingers. I pulled the blanket back up to his chest where ribs stretched his thin, sallow skin.

"Can I do anything else for you, Baba?"

"Nay, *bachem*. Thank you."

I sat beside him. "Then I wonder if you'll do something for me. If you're not too exhausted."

"What?"

"I want you to go *khastegari*. I want you to ask General Taheri for his daughter's hand."

Baba's dry lips stretched into a smile. A spot of green on a wilted leaf. "Are you sure?"

"More sure than I've ever been about anything."

"You've thought it over?"

"*Balay*, Baba."

"Then give me the phone. And my little notebook."

I blinked. "Now?"

"Then when?"

I smiled. "Okay." I gave him the phone and the little black notebook where Baba had scribbled his Afghan friends' numbers. He looked up the Taheris. Dialed. Brought the receiver to his ear. My heart was doing pirouettes in my chest.

"Jamila jan? *Salaam alaykum,*" he said. He introduced himself. Paused. "Much better, thank you. It was so gracious of you to come." He listened for a while. Nodded. "I'll remember that, thank you. Is General Sahib home?" Pause. "Thank you."

His eyes flicked to me. I wanted to laugh for some reason. Or scream. I brought the ball of my hand to my mouth and bit on it. Baba laughed softly through his nose.

"General Sahib, *Salaam alaykum* . . . Yes, much much better . . . *Balay* . . . You're so kind. General Sahib, I'm calling to ask if I may pay you and Khanum Taheri a visit tomorrow morning. It's an honorable matter . . . Yes . . . Eleven o'clock is just fine. Until then. *Khoda hafez.*"

He hung up. We looked at each other. I burst into giggles. Baba joined in.

BABA WET HIS HAIR and combed it back. I helped him into a clean white shirt and knotted his tie for him, noting the two inches of empty space between the collar button and Baba's neck. I thought of all the empty spaces Baba would leave behind when he was gone, and I made myself think of something else. He wasn't gone. Not yet. And this was a day for good thoughts. The jacket of his brown suit, the one he'd worn to my graduation, hung over him—too much of Baba had melted away to fill it any-

more. I had to roll up the sleeves. I stooped and tied his shoelaces
for him.

The Taheris lived in a flat, one-story house in one of the residential areas in Fremont known for housing a large number of
Afghans. It had bay windows, a pitched roof, and an enclosed
front porch on which I saw potted geraniums. The general's gray
van was parked in the driveway.

I helped Baba out of the Ford and slipped back behind the
wheel. He leaned in the passenger window. "Be home, I'll call you
in an hour."

"Okay, Baba," I said. "Good luck."

He smiled.

I drove away. In the rearview mirror, Baba was hobbling up the
Taheris' driveway for one last fatherly duty.

I PACED THE LIVING ROOM of our apartment waiting for
Baba's call. Fifteen paces long. Ten and a half paces wide. What if
the general said no? What if he hated me? I kept going to the
kitchen, checking the oven clock.

The phone rang just before noon. It was Baba.

"Well?"

"The general accepted."

I let out a burst of air. Sat down. My hands were shaking.
"He did?"

"Yes, but Soraya jan is upstairs in her room. She wants to talk
to you first."

"Okay."

Baba said something to someone and there was a double click
as he hung up.

"Amir?" Soraya's voice.

"*Salaam.*"

"My father said yes."

"I know," I said. I switched hands. I was smiling. "I'm so happy I don't know what to say."

"I'm happy too, Amir. I . . . can't believe this is happening."

I laughed. "I know."

"Listen," she said, "I want to tell you something. Something you have to know before . . ."

"I don't care what it is."

"You need to know. I don't want us to start with secrets. And I'd rather you hear it from me."

"If it will make you feel better, tell me. But it won't change anything."

There was a long pause at the other end. "When we lived in Virginia, I ran away with an Afghan man. I was eighteen at the time . . . rebellious . . . stupid, and . . . he was into drugs . . . We lived together for almost a month. All the Afghans in Virginia were talking about it.

"Padar eventually found us. He showed up at the door and . . . made me come home. I was hysterical. Yelling. Screaming. Saying I hated him . . .

"Anyway, I came home and—" She was crying. "Excuse me." I heard her put the phone down. Blow her nose. "Sorry," she came back on, sounding hoarse. "When I came home, I saw my mother had had a stroke, the right side of her face was paralyzed and . . . I felt so guilty. She didn't deserve that.

"Padar moved us to California shortly after." A silence followed.

"How are you and your father now?" I said.

"We've always had our differences, we still do, but I'm grateful he came for me that day. I really believe he saved me." She paused. "So, does what I told you bother you?"

"A little," I said. I owed her the truth on this one. I couldn't lie to her and say that my pride, my *iftikhar,* wasn't stung at all that she had been with a man, whereas I had never taken a woman to bed. It did bother me a bit, but I had pondered this quite a lot in the weeks before I asked Baba to go *khastegari.* And in the end the question that always came back to me was this: How could I, of all people, chastise someone for their past?

"Does it bother you enough to change your mind?"

"No, Soraya. Not even close," I said. "Nothing you said changes anything. I want us to marry."

She broke into fresh tears.

I envied her. Her secret was out. Spoken. Dealt with. I opened my mouth and almost told her how I'd betrayed Hassan, lied, driven him out, and destroyed a forty-year relationship between Baba and Ali. But I didn't. I suspected there were many ways in which Soraya Taheri was a better person than me. Courage was just one of them.

THIRTEEN

When we arrived at the Taheris' home the next evening—for *lafz*, the ceremony of "giving word"—I had to park the Ford across the street. Their driveway was already jammed with cars. I wore a navy blue suit I had bought the previous day, after I had brought Baba home from *khastegari*. I checked my tie in the rearview mirror.

"You look *khoshteep*," Baba said. Handsome.

"Thank you, Baba. Are you all right? Do you feel up to this?"

"Up to this? It's the happiest day of my life, Amir," he said, smiling tiredly.

I COULD HEAR CHATTER from the other side of the door, laughter, and Afghan music playing softly—it sounded like a classical *ghazal* by Ustad Sarahang. I rang the bell. A face peeked through the curtains of the foyer window and disappeared. "They're here!" I heard a woman's voice say. The chatter stopped. Someone turned off the music.

Khanum Taheri opened the door. *"Salaam alaykum,"* she said, beaming. She'd permed her hair, I saw, and wore an elegant, ankle-length black dress. When I stepped into the foyer, her eyes moistened. "You're barely in the house and I'm crying already, Amir jan," she said. I planted a kiss on her hand, just as Baba had instructed me to do the night before.

She led us through a brightly lit hallway to the living room. On the wood-paneled walls, I saw pictures of the people who would become my new family: A young bouffant-haired Khanum Taheri and the general—Niagara Falls in the background; Khanum Taheri in a seamless dress, the general in a narrow-lapelled jacket and thin tie, his hair full and black; Soraya, about to board a wooden roller coaster, waving and smiling, the sun glinting off the silver wires in her teeth. A photo of the general, dashing in full military outfit, shaking hands with King Hussein of Jordan. A portrait of Zahir Shah.

The living room was packed with about two dozen guests seated on chairs placed along the walls. When Baba entered, everybody stood up. We went around the room, Baba leading slowly, me behind him, shaking hands and greeting the guests. The general—still in his gray suit—and Baba embraced, gently tapping each other on the back. They said their *Salaam*s in respectful hushed tones.

The general held me at arm's length and smiled knowingly, as if saying, "Now, this is the right way—the Afghan way—to do it, *bachem.*" We kissed three times on the cheek.

We sat in the crowded room, Baba and I next to each other, across from the general and his wife. Baba's breathing had grown a little ragged, and he kept wiping sweat off his forehead and scalp with his handkerchief. He saw me looking at him and managed a strained grin. "I'm all right," he mouthed.

In keeping with tradition, Soraya was not present.

A few moments of small talk and idle chatter followed until the general cleared his throat. The room became quiet and everyone looked down at their hands in respect. The general nodded toward Baba.

Baba cleared his own throat. When he began, he couldn't speak in complete sentences without stopping to breathe. "General Sahib, Khanum Jamila jan . . . it's with great humility that my son and I . . . have come to your home today. You are . . . honorable people . . . from distinguished and reputable families and . . . proud lineage. I come with nothing but the utmost *ihtiram* . . . and the highest regards for you, your family names, and the memory . . . of your ancestors." He stopped. Caught his breath. Wiped his brow. "Amir jan is my only son . . . my only child, and he has been a good son to me. I hope he proves . . . worthy of your kindness. I ask that you honor Amir jan and me . . . and accept my son into your family."

The general nodded politely.

"We are honored to welcome the son of a man such as yourself into our family," he said. "Your reputation precedes you. I was your humble admirer in Kabul and remain so today. We are honored that your family and ours will be joined.

"Amir jan, as for you, I welcome you to my home as a son, as the husband of my daughter who is the *noor* of my eye. Your pain will be our pain, your joy our joy. I hope that you will come to see your Khala Jamila and me as a second set of parents, and I pray for your and our lovely Soraya jan's happiness. You both have our blessings."

Everyone applauded, and with that signal, heads turned toward the hallway. The moment I'd waited for.

Soraya appeared at the end. Dressed in a stunning wine-colored traditional Afghan dress with long sleeves and gold trim-

mings. Baba's hand took mine and tightened. Khanum Taheri
burst into fresh tears. Slowly, Soraya came to us, tailed by a procession of young female relatives.

She kissed my father's hands. Sat beside me at last, her eyes
downcast.

The applause swelled.

ACCORDING TO TRADITION, Soraya's family would have
thrown the engagement party, the *Shirini-khori*—or "Eating of the
Sweets" ceremony. Then an engagement period would have followed which would have lasted a few months. Then the wedding,
which would be paid for by Baba.

We all agreed that Soraya and I would forgo the *Shirini-khori*.
Everyone knew the reason, so no one had to actually say it: that
Baba didn't have months to live.

Soraya and I never went out alone together while preparations
for the wedding proceeded—since we weren't married yet, hadn't
even had a *Shirini-khori*, it was considered improper. So I had to
make do with going over to the Taheris with Baba for dinner. Sit
across from Soraya at the dinner table. Imagine what it would be
like to feel her head on my chest, smell her hair. Kiss her. Make
love to her.

Baba spent $35,000, nearly the balance of his life savings, on
the *awroussi*, the wedding ceremony. He rented a large Afghan
banquet hall in Fremont—the man who owned it knew him from
Kabul and gave him a substantial discount. Baba paid for the *chila*s, our matching wedding bands, and for the diamond ring I
picked out. He bought my tuxedo, and my traditional green suit
for the *nika*—the swearing ceremony.

For all the frenzied preparations that went into the wedding night—most of it, blessedly, by Khanum Taheri and her friends— I remember only a handful of moments from it.

I remember our *nika*. We were seated around a table, Soraya and I dressed in green—the color of Islam, but also the color of spring and new beginnings. I wore a suit, Soraya (the only woman at the table) a veiled long-sleeved dress. Baba, General Taheri (in a tuxedo this time), and several of Soraya's uncles were also present at the table. Soraya and I looked down, solemnly respectful, casting only sideway glances at each other. The mullah questioned the witnesses and read from the Koran. We said our oaths. Signed the certificates. One of Soraya's uncles from Virginia, Sharif jan, Khanum Taheri's brother, stood up and cleared his throat. Soraya had told me that he had lived in the U.S. for more than twenty years. He worked for the INS and had an American wife. He was also a poet. A small man with a birdlike face and fluffy hair, he read a lengthy poem dedicated to Soraya, jotted down on hotel stationery paper. "*Wah wah*, Sharif jan!" everyone exclaimed when he finished.

I remember walking toward the stage, now in my tuxedo, Soraya a veiled *pari* in white, our hands locked. Baba hobbled next to me, the general and his wife beside their daughter. A procession of uncles, aunts, and cousins followed as we made our way through the hall, parting a sea of applauding guests, blinking at flashing cameras. One of Soraya's cousins, Sharif jan's son, held a Koran over our heads as we inched along. The wedding song, *ahesta boro*, blared from the speakers, the same song the Russian soldier at the Mahipar checkpoint had sung the night Baba and I left Kabul:

Make morning into a key and throw it into the well,
Go slowly, my lovely moon, go slowly.

Let the morning sun forget to rise in the east,
Go slowly, my lovely moon, go slowly.

I remember sitting on the sofa, set on the stage like a throne, Soraya's hand in mine, as three hundred or so faces looked on. We did *Ayena Masshaf*, where they gave us a mirror and threw a veil over our heads, so we'd be alone to gaze at each other's reflection. Looking at Soraya's smiling face in that mirror, in the momentary privacy of the veil, I whispered to her for the first time that I loved her. A blush, red like henna, bloomed on her cheeks.

I picture colorful platters of *chopan* kabob, *sholeh-goshti*, and wild-orange rice. I see Baba between us on the sofa, smiling. I remember sweat-drenched men dancing the traditional *attan* in a circle, bouncing, spinning faster and faster with the feverish tempo of the tabla, until all but a few dropped out of the ring with exhaustion. I remember wishing Rahim Khan were there.

And I remember wondering if Hassan too had married. And if so, whose face he had seen in the mirror under the veil? Whose henna-painted hands had he held?

AROUND 2 A.M., the party moved from the banquet hall to Baba's apartment. Tea flowed once more and music played until the neighbors called the cops. Later that night, the sun less than an hour from rising and the guests finally gone, Soraya and I lay together for the first time. All my life, I'd been around men. That night, I discovered the tenderness of a woman.

. . .

IT WAS SORAYA who suggested that she move in with Baba and me.

"I thought you might want us to have our own place," I said.

"With Kaka jan as sick as he is?" she replied. Her eyes told me that was no way to start a marriage. I kissed her. "Thank you."

Soraya dedicated herself to taking care of my father. She made his toast and tea in the morning, and helped him in and out of bed. She gave him his pain pills, washed his clothes, read him the international section of the newspaper every afternoon. She cooked his favorite dish, potato *shorwa,* though he could scarcely eat more than a few spoonfuls, and took him out every day for a brief walk around the block. And when he became bedridden, she turned him on his side every hour so he wouldn't get a bedsore.

One day, I came home from the pharmacy with Baba's morphine pills. Just as I shut the door, I caught a glimpse of Soraya quickly sliding something under Baba's blanket. "Hey, I saw that! What were you two doing?" I said.

"Nothing," Soraya said, smiling.

"Liar." I lifted Baba's blanket. "What's this?" I said, though as soon as I picked up the leather-bound book, I knew. I traced my fingers along the gold-stitched borders. I remembered the fireworks the night Rahim Khan had given it to me, the night of my thirteenth birthday, flares sizzling and exploding into bouquets of red, green, and yellow.

"I can't believe you can write like this," Soraya said.

Baba dragged his head off the pillow. "I put her up to it. I hope you don't mind."

I gave the notebook back to Soraya and left the room. Baba hated it when I cried.

. . .

A MONTH AFTER THE WEDDING, the Taheris, Sharif, his wife Suzy, and several of Soraya's aunts came over to our apartment for dinner. Soraya made *sabzi challow*—white rice with spinach and lamb. After dinner, we all had green tea and played cards in groups of four. Soraya and I played with Sharif and Suzy on the coffee table, next to the couch where Baba lay under a wool blanket. He watched me joking with Sharif, watched Soraya and me lacing our fingers together, watched me push back a loose curl of her hair. I could see his internal smile, as wide as the skies of Kabul on nights when the poplars shivered and the sound of crickets swelled in the gardens.

Just before midnight, Baba asked us to help him into bed. Soraya and I placed his arms on our shoulders and wrapped ours around his back. When we lowered him, he had Soraya turn off the bedside lamp. He asked us to lean in, gave us each a kiss.

"I'll come back with your morphine and a glass of water, Kaka jan," Soraya said.

"Not tonight," he said. "There is no pain tonight."

"Okay," she said. She pulled up his blanket. We closed the door. Baba never woke up.

THEY FILLED THE PARKING SPOTS at the mosque in Hayward. On the balding grass field behind the building, cars and SUVs parked in crowded makeshift rows. People had to drive three or four blocks north of the mosque to find a spot.

The men's section of the mosque was a large square room, covered with Afghan rugs and thin mattresses placed in parallel lines. Men filed into the room, leaving their shoes at the entrance, and sat cross-legged on the mattresses. A mullah chanted *surrah*s from the Koran into a microphone. I sat by the door, the customary position for the family of the deceased. General Taheri was seated next to me.

Through the open door, I could see lines of cars pulling in, sunlight winking in their windshields. They dropped off passengers, men dressed in dark suits, women clad in black dresses, their heads covered with traditional white *hijab*s.

As words from the Koran reverberated through the room, I thought of the old story of Baba wrestling a black bear in Baluchistan. Baba had wrestled bears his whole life. Losing his young wife. Raising a son by himself. Leaving his beloved homeland, his *watan*. Poverty. Indignity. In the end, a bear had come that he couldn't best. But even then, he had lost on his own terms.

After each round of prayers, groups of mourners lined up and greeted me on their way out. Dutifully, I shook their hands. Many of them I barely knew. I smiled politely, thanked them for their wishes, listened to whatever they had to say about Baba.

"...helped me build the house in Taimani..."

"...bless him..."

"...no one else to turn to and he lent me..."

"...found me a job...barely knew me..."

"...like a brother to me..."

Listening to them, I realized how much of who I was, what I was, had been defined by Baba and the marks he had left on people's lives. My whole life, I had been "Baba's son." Now he was gone. Baba couldn't show me the way anymore; I'd have to find it on my own.

The thought of it terrified me.

Earlier, at the gravesite in the small Muslim section of the cemetery, I had watched them lower Baba into the hole. The mullah and another man got into an argument over which was the correct *ayat* of the Koran to recite at the gravesite. It might have turned ugly had General Taheri not intervened. The mullah chose an *ayat* and recited it, casting the other fellow nasty glances. I watched them toss the first shovelful of dirt into the grave. Then I left. Walked to the other side of the cemetery. Sat in the shade of a red maple.

Now the last of the mourners had paid their respects and the mosque was empty, save for the mullah unplugging the microphone and wrapping his Koran in green cloth. The general and I stepped out into a late-afternoon sun. We walked down the steps, past men smoking in clusters. I heard snippets of their conversations, a soccer game in Union City next weekend, a new Afghan restaurant in Santa Clara. Life moving on already, leaving Baba behind.

"How are you, *bachem*?" General Taheri said.

I gritted my teeth. Bit back the tears that had threatened all day. "I'm going to find Soraya," I said.

"Okay."

I walked to the women's side of the mosque. Soraya was standing on the steps with her mother and a couple of ladies I recognized vaguely from the wedding. I motioned to Soraya. She said something to her mother and came to me.

"Can we walk?" I said.

"Sure." She took my hand.

We walked in silence down a winding gravel path lined by a row of low hedges. We sat on a bench and watched an elderly couple kneeling beside a grave a few rows away and placing a bouquet of daisies by the headstone. "Soraya?"

"Yes?"

"I'm going to miss him."

She put her hand on my lap. Baba's *chila* glinted on her ring finger. Behind her, I could see Baba's mourners driving away on Mission Boulevard. Soon we'd leave too, and for the first time ever, Baba would be all alone.

Soraya pulled me to her and the tears finally came.

BECAUSE SORAYA AND I never had an engagement period, much of what I learned about the Taheris I learned after I married into their family. For example, I learned that, once a month, the general suffered from blinding migraines that lasted almost a week. When the headaches struck, the general went to his room, undressed, turned off the light, locked the door, and didn't come out until the pain subsided. No one was allowed to go in, no one was allowed to knock. Eventually, he would emerge, dressed in his gray suit once more, smelling of sleep and bedsheets, his eyes puffy and bloodshot. I learned from Soraya that he and Khanum Taheri had slept in separate rooms for as long as she could remember. I learned that he could be petty, such as when he'd take a bite of the *qurma* his wife placed before him, sigh, and push it away. "I'll make you something else," Khanum Taheri would say, but he'd ignore her, sulk, and eat bread and onion. This made Soraya angry and her mother cry. Soraya told me he took antidepressants. I learned that he had kept his family on welfare and had never held a job in the U.S., preferring to cash government-issued checks than degrading himself with work unsuitable for a man of his stature—he saw the flea market only as a hobby, a way to socialize with his fellow Afghans. The general believed that, sooner or later, Afghanistan would be freed, the monarchy restored, and his services would once again be called upon. So every day, he donned his gray suit, wound his pocket watch, and waited.

I learned that Khanum Taheri—whom I called Khala Jamila now—had once been famous in Kabul for her enchanting singing voice. Though she had never sung professionally, she had had the talent to—I learned she could sing folk songs, *ghazal*s, even raga, which was usually a man's domain. But as much as the general appreciated listening to music—he owned, in fact, a considerable collection of classical *ghazal* tapes by Afghan and Hindi singers— he believed the performing of it best left to those with lesser repu- tations. That she never sing in public had been one of the general's conditions when they had married. Soraya told me that her mother had wanted to sing at our wedding, only one song, but the general gave her one of his looks and the matter was buried. Khala Jamila played the lotto once a week and watched Johnny Carson every night. She spent her days in the garden, tending to her roses, geraniums, potato vines, and orchids.

When I married Soraya, the flowers and Johnny Carson took a backseat. I was the new delight in Khala Jamila's life. Unlike the general's guarded and diplomatic manners—he didn't correct me when I continued to call him "General Sahib"—Khala Jamila made no secret of how much she adored me. For one thing, I lis- tened to her impressive list of maladies, something the general had long turned a deaf ear to. Soraya told me that, ever since her mother's stroke, every flutter in her chest was a heart attack, every aching joint the onset of rheumatoid arthritis, and every twitch of the eye another stroke. I remember the first time Khala Jamila mentioned a lump in her neck to me. "I'll skip school tomorrow and take you to the doctor," I said, to which the general smiled and said, "Then you might as well turn in your books for good, *bachem*. Your khala's medical charts are like the works of Rumi: They come in volumes."

But it wasn't just that she'd found an audience for her monologues of illness. I firmly believed that if I had picked up a rifle and gone on a murdering rampage, I would have still had the benefit of her unblinking love. Because I had rid her heart of its gravest malady. I had relieved her of the greatest fear of every Afghan mother: that no honorable *khastegar* would ask for her daughter's hand. That her daughter would age alone, husbandless, childless. Every woman needed a husband. Even if he did silence the song in her.

And, from Soraya, I learned the details of what had happened in Virginia.

We were at a wedding. Soraya's uncle, Sharif, the one who worked for the INS, was marrying his son to an Afghan girl from Newark. The wedding was at the same hall where, six months prior, Soraya and I had had our *awroussi*. We were standing in a crowd of guests, watching the bride accept rings from the groom's family, when we overheard two middle-aged women talking, their backs to us.

"What a lovely bride," one of them said, "Just look at her. So *maghbool*, like the moon."

"Yes," the other said. "And pure too. Virtuous. No boyfriends."

"I know. I tell you that boy did well not to marry his cousin."

Soraya broke down on the way home. I pulled the Ford off to the curb, parked under a streetlight on Fremont Boulevard.

"It's all right," I said, pushing back her hair. "Who cares?"

"It's so fucking unfair," she barked.

"Just forget it."

"Their sons go out to nightclubs looking for meat and get their girlfriends pregnant, they have kids out of wedlock and no one says a goddamn thing. Oh, they're just men having fun! I make one mistake and suddenly everyone is talking *nang* and *namoos*, and I have to have my face rubbed in it for the rest of my life."

I wiped a tear from her jawline, just above her birthmark, with the pad of my thumb.

"I didn't tell you," Soraya said, dabbing at her eyes, "but my father showed up with a gun that night. He told...him...that he had two bullets in the chamber, one for him and one for himself if I didn't come home. I was screaming, calling my father all kinds of names, saying he couldn't keep me locked up forever, that I wished he were dead." Fresh tears squeezed out between her lids. "I actually said that to him, that I wished he were dead.

"When he brought me home, my mother threw her arms around me and she was crying too. She was saying things but I couldn't understand any of it because she was slurring her words so badly. So my father took me up to my bedroom and sat me in front of the dresser mirror. He handed me a pair of scissors and calmly told me to cut off all my hair. He watched while I did it.

"I didn't step out of the house for weeks. And when I did, I heard whispers or imagined them everywhere I went. That was four years ago and three thousand miles away and I'm still hearing them."

"Fuck 'em," I said.

She made a sound that was half sob, half laugh. "When I told you about this on the phone the night of *khastegari*, I was sure you'd change your mind."

"No chance of that, Soraya."

She smiled and took my hand. "I'm so lucky to have found you. You're so different from every Afghan guy I've met."

"Let's never talk about this again, okay?"

"Okay."

I kissed her cheek and pulled away from the curb. As I drove, I wondered why I was different. Maybe it was because I had been raised by men; I hadn't grown up around women and had never been exposed firsthand to the double standard with which Afghan society sometimes treated them. Maybe it was because Baba had been such an unusual Afghan father, a liberal who had lived by his own rules, a maverick who had disregarded or embraced societal customs as he had seen fit.

But I think a big part of the reason I didn't care about Soraya's past was that I had one of my own. I knew all about regret.

SHORTLY AFTER BABA'S DEATH, Soraya and I moved into a one-bedroom apartment in Fremont, just a few blocks away from the general and Khala Jamila's house. Soraya's parents bought us a brown leather couch and a set of Mikasa dishes as housewarming presents. The general gave me an additional present, a brand-new IBM typewriter. In the box, he had slipped a note written in Farsi:

Amir jan,
I hope you discover many tales on these keys.
General Iqbal Taheri

I sold Baba's VW bus and, to this day, I have not gone back to the flea market. I would drive to his gravesite every Friday, and, sometimes, I'd find a fresh bouquet of freesias by the headstone and know Soraya had been there too.

Soraya and I settled into the routines—and minor wonders— of married life. We shared toothbrushes and socks, passed each other the morning paper. She slept on the right side of the bed, I preferred the left. She liked fluffy pillows, I liked the hard ones. She ate her cereal dry, like a snack, and chased it with milk.

I got my acceptance at San Jose State that summer and declared an English major. I took on a security job, swing shift at a furniture warehouse in Sunnyvale. The job was dreadfully bor- ing, but its saving grace was a considerable one: When everyone left at 6 P.M. and shadows began to crawl between aisles of plastic- covered sofas piled to the ceiling, I took out my books and studied. It was in the Pine-Sol-scented office of that furniture warehouse that I began my first novel.

Soraya joined me at San Jose State the following year and enrolled, to her father's chagrin, in the teaching track.

"I don't know why you're wasting your talents like this," the general said one night over dinner. "Did you know, Amir jan, that she earned nothing but A's in high school?" He turned to her. "An intelligent girl like you could become a lawyer, a political scientist. And, *Inshallah*, when Afghanistan is free, you could help write the new constitution. There would be a need for young talented Afghans like you. They might even offer you a ministry position, given your family name."

I could see Soraya holding back, her face tightening. "I'm not a girl, Padar. I'm a married woman. Besides, they'd need teachers too."

"Anyone can teach."

"Is there any more rice, *Madar*?" Soraya said.

After the general excused himself to meet some friends in Hayward, Khala Jamila tried to console Soraya. "He means well," she said. "He just wants you to be successful."

"So he can boast about his attorney daughter to his friends. Another medal for the general," Soraya said.

"Such nonsense you speak!"

"Successful," Soraya hissed. "At least I'm not like him, sitting around while other people fight the *Shorawi*, waiting for when the dust settles so he can move in and reclaim his posh little government position. Teaching may not pay much, but it's what I want to do! It's what I love, and it's a whole lot better than collecting welfare, by the way."

Khala Jamila bit her tongue. "If he ever hears you saying that, he will never speak to you again."

"Don't worry," Soraya snapped, tossing her napkin on the plate. "I won't bruise his precious ego."

IN THE SUMMER of 1988, about six months before the Soviets withdrew from Afghanistan, I finished my first novel, a father-son story set in Kabul, written mostly with the typewriter the general had given me. I sent query letters to a dozen agencies and was stunned one August day when I opened our mailbox and found a request from a New York agency for the completed manuscript. I mailed it the next day. Soraya kissed the carefully wrapped manuscript and Khala Jamila insisted we pass it under the Koran. She told me that she was going to do *nazr* for me, a vow to have a sheep slaughtered and the meat given to the poor if my book was accepted.

"Please, no *nazr*, Khala jan," I said, kissing her face. "Just do *zakat,* give the money to someone in need, okay? No sheep kill-ing."

Six weeks later, a man named Martin Greenwalt called from New York and offered to represent me. I only told Soraya about it. "But just because I have an agent doesn't mean I'll get published. If Martin sells the novel, then we'll celebrate."

A month later, Martin called and informed me I was going to be a published novelist. When I told Soraya, she screamed.

We had a celebration dinner with Soraya's parents that night. Khala Jamila made *kofta*—meatballs and white rice—and white *ferni.* The general, a sheen of moisture in his eyes, said that he was proud of me. After General Taheri and his wife left, Soraya and I celebrated with an expensive bottle of Merlot I had bought on the way home—the general did not approve of women drinking alcohol, and Soraya didn't drink in his presence.

"I am so proud of you," she said, raising her glass to mine. "Kaka would have been proud too."

"I know," I said, thinking of Baba, wishing he could have seen me.

Later that night, after Soraya fell asleep—wine always made her sleepy—I stood on the balcony and breathed in the cool sum-mer air. I thought of Rahim Khan and the little note of support he had written me after he'd read my first story. And I thought of Hassan. *Some day,* Inshallah, *you will be a great writer,* he had said once, *and people all over the world will read your stories.* There was so much goodness in my life. So much happiness. I wondered whether I deserved any of it.

The novel was released in the summer of that following year, 1989, and the publisher sent me on a five-city book tour. I became a minor celebrity in the Afghan community. That was the year that the *Shorawi* completed their withdrawal from Afghanistan. It should have been a time of glory for Afghans. Instead, the war raged on, this time between Afghans, the *Mujahedin,* against the Soviet puppet government of Najibullah, and Afghan refugees kept flocking to Pakistan. That was the year that the cold war ended, the year the Berlin Wall came down. It was the year of Tiananmen Square. In the midst of it all, Afghanistan was forgotten. And General Taheri, whose hopes had stirred awake after the Soviets pulled out, went back to winding his pocket watch.

That was also the year that Soraya and I began trying to have a child.

THE IDEA OF FATHERHOOD unleashed a swirl of emotions in me. I found it frightening, invigorating, daunting, and exhilarating all at the same time. What sort of father would I make, I wondered. I wanted to be just like Baba and I wanted to be nothing like him.

But a year passed and nothing happened. With each cycle of blood, Soraya grew more frustrated, more impatient, more irritable. By then, Khala Jamila's initially subtle hints had become overt, as in *"Kho dega!"* So! "When am I going to sing *alahoo* for my little *nawasa?*" The general, ever the Pashtun, never made any queries—doing so meant alluding to a sexual act between his daughter and a man, even if the man in question had been married to her for over four years. But his eyes perked up when Khala Jamila teased us about a baby.

"Sometimes, it takes a while," I told Soraya one night.

"A year isn't a while, Amir!" she said, in a terse voice so unlike her. "Something's wrong, I know it."

"Then let's see a doctor."

.   .   .

DR. ROSEN, a round-bellied man with a plump face and small, even teeth, spoke with a faint Eastern European accent, something remotely Slavic. He had a passion for trains—his office was littered with books about the history of railroads, model locomotives, paintings of trains trundling on tracks through green hills and over bridges. A sign above his desk read, LIFE IS A TRAIN. GET ON BOARD.

He laid out the plan for us. I'd get checked first. "Men are easy," he said, fingers tapping on his mahogany desk. "A man's plumbing is like his mind: simple, very few surprises. You ladies, on the other hand...well, God put a lot of thought into making you." I wondered if he fed that bit about the plumbing to all of his couples.

"Lucky us," Soraya said.

Dr. Rosen laughed. It fell a few notches short of genuine. He gave me a lab slip and a plastic jar, handed Soraya a request for some routine blood tests. We shook hands. "Welcome aboard," he said, as he showed us out.

I PASSED WITH FLYING COLORS.

The next few months were a blur of tests on Soraya: Basal body temperatures, blood tests for every conceivable hormone, urine tests, something called a "Cervical Mucus Test," ultrasounds, more blood tests, and more urine tests. Soraya underwent a procedure called a hysteroscopy—Dr. Rosen inserted a telescope into Soraya's uterus and took a look around. He found nothing. "The plumbing's clear," he announced, snapping off his latex gloves. I wished he'd stop calling it that—we weren't bathrooms. When the tests were over, he explained that he couldn't explain why we couldn't have kids. And, apparently, that wasn't so unusual. It was called "Unexplained Infertility."

Then came the treatment phase. We tried a drug called Clomiphene, and hMG, a series of shots which Soraya gave to herself. When these failed, Dr. Rosen advised in vitro fertilization. We received a polite letter from our HMO, wishing us the best of luck, regretting they couldn't cover the cost.

We used the advance I had received for my novel to pay for it. IVF proved lengthy, meticulous, frustrating, and ultimately unsuccessful. After months of sitting in waiting rooms reading magazines like *Good Housekeeping* and *Reader's Digest,* after endless paper gowns and cold, sterile exam rooms lit by fluorescent lights, the repeated humiliation of discussing every detail of our sex life with a total stranger, the injections and probes and specimen collections, we went back to Dr. Rosen and his trains.

He sat across from us, tapped his desk with his fingers, and used the word "adoption" for the first time. Soraya cried all the way home.

Soraya broke the news to her parents the weekend after our last visit with Dr. Rosen. We were sitting on picnic chairs in the Taheris' backyard, grilling trout and sipping yogurt *dogh.* It was an early evening in March 1991. Khala Jamila had watered the roses and her new honeysuckles, and their fragrance mixed with the smell of cooking fish. Twice already, she had reached across her chair to caress Soraya's hair and say, "God knows best, *bachem.* Maybe it wasn't meant to be."

Soraya kept looking down at her hands. She was tired, I knew, tired of it all. "The doctor said we could adopt," she murmured.

General Taheri's head snapped up at this. He closed the barbecue lid. "He did?"

"He said it was an option," Soraya said.

We'd talked at home about adoption. Soraya was ambivalent at best. "I know it's silly and maybe vain," she said to me on the way to her parents' house, "but I can't help it. I've always dreamed that I'd hold it in my arms and know my blood had fed it for nine months, that I'd look in its eyes one day and be startled to see you or me, that the baby would grow up and have your smile or mine. Without that . . . Is that wrong?"

"No," I had said.

"Am I being selfish?"

"No, Soraya."

"Because if you really want to do it . . ."

"No," I said. "If we're going to do it, we shouldn't have any doubts at all about it, and we should both be in agreement. It wouldn't be fair to the baby otherwise."

She rested her head on the window and said nothing else the rest of the way.

Now the general sat beside her. "*Bachem,* this adoption . . . thing, I'm not so sure it's for us Afghans." Soraya looked at me tiredly and sighed.

"For one thing, they grow up and want to know who their natural parents are," he said. "Nor can you blame them. Sometimes, they leave the home in which you labored for years to provide for them so they can find the people who gave them life. Blood is a powerful thing, *bachem,* never forget that."

"I don't want to talk about this anymore," Soraya said.

"I'll say one more thing," he said. I could tell he was getting revved up; we were about to get one of the general's little speeches. "Take Amir jan, here. We all knew his father, I know who his grandfather was in Kabul and his great-grandfather before him, I could sit here and trace generations of his ancestors for you if you asked. That's why when his father—God give him peace—came *khastegari,* I didn't hesitate. And believe me, his father wouldn't have agreed to ask for your hand if he didn't know whose descendant you were. Blood is a powerful thing, *bachem,* and when you adopt, you don't know whose blood you're bringing into your house.

"Now, if you were American, it wouldn't matter. People here marry for love, family name and ancestry never even come into the equation. They adopt that way too, as long as the baby is healthy, everyone is happy. But we are Afghans, *bachem.*"

"Is the fish almost ready?" Soraya said. General Taheri's eyes lingered on her. He patted her knee. "Just be happy you have your health and a good husband."

"What do you think, Amir jan?" Khala Jamila said.

I put my glass on the ledge, where a row of her potted geraniums were dripping water. "I think I agree with General Sahib."

Reassured, the general nodded and went back to the grill.

We all had our reasons for not adopting. Soraya had hers, the general his, and I had this: that perhaps something, someone, somewhere, had decided to deny me fatherhood for the things I had done. Maybe this was my punishment, and perhaps justly so. *It wasn't meant to be,* Khala Jamila had said. Or, maybe, it was meant not to be.

A FEW MONTHS LATER, we used the advance for my second novel and placed a down payment on a pretty, two-bedroom Victorian house in San Francisco's Bernal Heights. It had a peaked roof, hardwood floors, and a tiny backyard which ended in a sun deck and a fire pit. The general helped me refinish the deck and paint the walls. Khala Jamila bemoaned us moving almost an hour away, especially since she thought Soraya needed all the love and support she could get—oblivious to the fact that her well-intended but overbearing sympathy was precisely what was driving Soraya to move.

SOMETIMES, SORAYA SLEEPING NEXT TO ME, I lay in bed and listened to the screen door swinging open and shut with the breeze, to the crickets chirping in the yard. And I could almost feel the emptiness in Soraya's womb, like it was a living, breathing thing. It had seeped into our marriage, that emptiness, into our laughs, and our lovemaking. And late at night, in the darkness of our room, I'd feel it rising from Soraya and settling between us. Sleeping between us. Like a newborn child.

FOURTEEN

June 2001

I lowered the phone into the cradle and stared at it for a long time. It wasn't until Aflatoon startled me with a bark that I realized how quiet the room had become. Soraya had muted the television.

"You look pale, Amir," she said from the couch, the same one her parents had given us as a housewarming gift for our first apartment. She'd been lying on it with Aflatoon's head nestled on her chest, her legs buried under the worn pillows. She was half-watching a PBS special on the plight of wolves in Minnesota, half-correcting essays from her summer-school class—she'd been teaching at the same school now for six years. She sat up, and Aflatoon leapt down from the couch. It was the general who had given our cocker spaniel his name, Farsi for "Plato," because, he said, if you looked hard enough and long enough into the dog's filmy black eyes, you'd swear he was thinking wise thoughts.

There was a sliver of fat, just a hint of it, beneath Soraya's chin now. The past ten years had padded the curves of her hips some, and combed into her coal black hair a few streaks of cinder gray. But she still had the face of a Grand Ball princess, with her bird-in-flight eyebrows and nose, elegantly curved like a letter from ancient Arabic writings.

"You look pale," Soraya repeated, placing the stack of papers on the table.

"I have to go to Pakistan."

She stood up now. "Pakistan?"

"Rahim Khan is very sick." A fist clenched inside me with those words.

"Kaka's old business partner?" She'd never met Rahim Khan, but I had told her about him. I nodded.

"Oh," she said. "I'm so sorry, Amir."

"We used to be close," I said. "When I was a kid, he was the first grown-up I ever thought of as a friend." I pictured him and Baba drinking tea in Baba's study, then smoking near the window, a sweetbrier-scented breeze blowing from the garden and bending the twin columns of smoke.

"I remember you telling me that," Soraya said. She paused. "How long will you be gone?"

"I don't know. He wants to see me."

"Is it..."

"Yes, it's safe. I'll be all right, Soraya." It was the question she'd wanted to ask all along—fifteen years of marriage had turned us into mind readers. "I'm going to go for a walk."

"Should I go with you?"

"Nay, I'd rather be alone."

I DROVE TO GOLDEN GATE PARK and walked along Spreckels Lake on the northern edge of the park. It was a beautiful Sunday afternoon; the sun sparkled on the water where dozens of miniature boats sailed, propelled by a crisp San Francisco breeze. I sat on a park bench, watched a man toss a football to his son, telling him to not sidearm the ball, to throw over the shoulder. I glanced up and saw a pair of kites, red with long blue tails. They floated high above the trees on the west end of the park, over the windmills.

I thought about a comment Rahim Khan had made just before we hung up. Made it in passing, almost as an afterthought. I closed my eyes and saw him at the other end of the scratchy long-distance line, saw him with his lips slightly parted, head tilted to one side. And again, something in his bottomless black eyes hinted at an unspoken secret between us. Except now I knew he knew. My suspicions had been right all those years. He knew about Assef, the kite, the money, the watch with the lightning bolt hands. He had always known.

Come. There is a way to be good again, Rahim Khan had said on the phone just before hanging up. Said it in passing, almost as an afterthought.

A way to be good again.

WHEN I CAME HOME, Soraya was on the phone with her mother. "Won't be long, Madar jan. A week, maybe two . . . Yes, you and Padar can stay with me . . ."

Two years earlier, the general had broken his right hip. He'd had one of his migraines again, and emerging from his room, bleary-eyed and dazed, he had tripped on a loose carpet edge. His scream had brought Khala Jamila running from the kitchen. "It sounded like a *jaroo,* a broomstick, snapping in half," she was always fond of saying, though the doctor had said it was unlikely she'd heard anything of the sort. The general's shattered hip—and all of the ensuing complications, the pneumonia, blood poisoning, the protracted stay at the nursing home—ended Khala Jamila's long-running soliloquies about her own health. And started new ones about the general's. She'd tell anyone who would listen that the doctors had told them his kidneys were failing. "But then they had never seen Afghan kidneys, had they?" she'd say proudly. What I remember most about the general's hospital stay is how Khala Jamila would wait until he fell asleep, and then sing to him, songs I remembered from Kabul, playing on Baba's scratchy old transistor radio.

The general's frailty—and time—had softened things between him and Soraya too. They took walks together, went to lunch on Saturdays, and, sometimes, the general sat in on some of her classes. He'd sit in the back of the room, dressed in his shiny old gray suit, wooden cane across his lap, smiling. Sometimes he even took notes.

THAT NIGHT, Soraya and I lay in bed, her back pressed to my chest, my face buried in her hair. I remembered when we used to lay forehead to forehead, sharing afterglow kisses and whispering until our eyes drifted closed, whispering about tiny, curled toes, first smiles, first words, first steps. We still did sometimes, but the whispers were about school, my new book, a giggle over someone's ridiculous dress at a party. Our lovemaking was still good, at times better than good, but some nights all I'd feel was a relief to be done with it, to be free to drift away and forget, at least for a while, about the futility of what we'd just done. She never said so, but I knew sometimes Soraya felt it too. On those nights, we'd each roll to our side of the bed and let our own savior take us away. Soraya's was sleep. Mine, as always, was a book.

I lay in the dark the night Rahim Khan called and traced with my eyes the parallel silver lines on the wall made by moonlight pouring through the blinds. At some point, maybe just before dawn, I drifted to sleep. And dreamed of Hassan running in the snow, the hem of his green *chapan* dragging behind him, snow crunching under his black rubber boots. He was yelling over his shoulder: *For you, a thousand times over!*

A WEEK LATER, I sat on a window seat aboard a Pakistani International Airlines flight, watching a pair of uniformed airline workers remove the wheel chocks. The plane taxied out of the terminal and, soon, we were airborne, cutting through the clouds. I rested my head against the window. Waited, in vain, for sleep.

FIFTEEN

Three hours after my flight landed in Peshawar, I was sitting on shredded upholstery in the backseat of a smoke-filled taxicab. My driver, a chain-smoking, sweaty little man who introduced himself as Gholam, drove nonchalantly and recklessly, averting collisions by the thinnest of margins, all without so much as a pause in the incessant stream of words spewing from his mouth:

"... terrible what is happening in your country, *yar*. Afghani people and Pakistani people they are like brothers, I tell you. Muslims have to help Muslims so ..."

I tuned him out, switched to a polite nodding mode. I remembered Peshawar pretty well from the few months Baba and I had spent there in 1981. We were heading west now on Jamrud road, past the Cantonment and its lavish, high-walled homes. The bustle of the city blurring past me reminded me of a busier, more crowded version of the Kabul I knew, particularly of the *Kocheh-Morgha,* or Chicken Bazaar, where Hassan and I used to buy chutney-dipped potatoes and cherry water. The streets were clogged with bicycle riders, milling pedestrians, and rickshaws popping blue smoke, all weaving through a maze of narrow lanes and alleys. Bearded vendors draped in thin blankets sold animal-skin lampshades, carpets, embroidered shawls, and copper goods from rows of small, tightly jammed stalls. The city was bursting with sounds; the shouts of vendors rang in my ears mingled with the blare of Hindi music, the sputtering of rickshaws, and the jin-gling bells of horse-drawn carts. Rich scents, both pleasant and not so pleasant, drifted to me through the passenger window, the spicy aroma of *pakora* and the *nihari* Baba had loved so much blended with the sting of diesel fumes, the stench of rot, garbage, and feces.

A little past the redbrick buildings of Peshawar University, we entered an area my garrulous driver referred to as "Afghan Town." I saw sweetshops and carpet vendors, kabob stalls, kids with dirt-caked hands selling cigarettes, tiny restaurants—maps of Afghanistan painted on their windows—all interlaced with back-street aid agencies. "Many of your brothers in this area, *yar*. They are opening businesses, but most of them are very poor." He *tsk*'ed his tongue and sighed. "Anyway, we're getting close now."

I thought about the last time I had seen Rahim Khan, in 1981. He had come to say good-bye the night Baba and I had fled Kabul. I remember Baba and him embracing in the foyer, crying softly. When Baba and I arrived in the U.S., he and Rahim Khan kept in touch. They would speak four or five times a year and, sometimes, Baba would pass me the receiver. The last time I had spoken to Rahim Khan had been shortly after Baba's death. The news had reached Kabul and he had called. We'd only spoken for a few minutes and lost the connection.

The driver pulled up to a narrow building at a busy corner where two winding streets intersected. I paid the driver, took my lone suitcase, and walked up to the intricately carved door. The building had wooden balconies with open shutters—from many of them, laundry was hanging to dry in the sun. I walked up the creaky stairs to the second floor, down a dim hallway to the last door on the right. Checked the address on the piece of stationery paper in my palm. Knocked.

Then, a thing made of skin and bones pretending to be Rahim Khan opened the door.

A CREATIVE WRITING TEACHER at San Jose State used to say about clichés: "Avoid them like the plague." Then he'd laugh at his own joke. The class laughed along with him, but I always thought clichés got a bum rap. Because, often, they're dead-on. But the aptness of the clichéd saying is overshadowed by the nature of the saying as a cliché. For example, the "elephant in the room" saying. Nothing could more correctly describe the initial moments of my reunion with Rahim Khan.

We sat on a wispy mattress set along the wall, across the window overlooking the noisy street below. Sunlight slanted in and cast a triangular wedge of light onto the Afghan rug on the floor. Two folding chairs rested against one wall and a small copper samovar sat in the opposite corner. I poured us tea from it.

"How did you find me?" I asked.

"It's not difficult to find people in America. I bought a map of the U.S., and called up information for cities in Northern California," he said. "It's wonderfully strange to see you as a grown man."

I smiled and dropped three sugar cubes in my tea. He liked his black and bitter, I remembered. "Baba didn't get the chance to tell you but I got married fifteen years ago." The truth was, by then, the cancer in Baba's brain had made him forgetful, negligent.

"You are married? To whom?"

"Her name is Soraya Taheri." I thought of her back home, worrying about me. I was glad she wasn't alone.

"Taheri . . . whose daughter is she?"

I told him. His eyes brightened. "Oh, yes, I remember now. Isn't General Taheri married to Sharif jan's sister? What was her name . . ."

"Jamila jan."

"*Balay!*" he said, smiling. "I knew Sharif jan in Kabul, long time ago, before he moved to America."

"He's been working for the INS for years, handles a lot of Afghan cases."

"*Haiiii,*" he sighed. "Do you and Soraya jan have children?"

"Nay."

"Oh." He slurped his tea and didn't ask more; Rahim Khan had always been one of the most instinctive people I'd ever met.

I told him a lot about Baba, his job, the flea market, and how, at the end, he'd died happy. I told him about my schooling, my books—four published novels to my credit now. He smiled at this, said he had never had any doubt. I told him I had written short stories in the leather-bound notebook he'd given me, but he didn't remember the notebook.

The conversation inevitably turned to the Taliban.

"Is it as bad as I hear?" I said.

"Nay, it's worse. Much worse," he said. "They don't let you be human." He pointed to a scar above his right eye cutting a crooked path through his bushy eyebrow. "I was at a soccer game in Ghazi Stadium in 1998. Kabul against Mazar-i-Sharif, I think, and by the way the players weren't allowed to wear shorts. Indecent exposure, I guess." He gave a tired laugh. "Anyway, Kabul

scored a goal and the man next to me cheered loudly. Suddenly
this young bearded fellow who was patrolling the aisles, eighteen
years old at most by the look of him, he walked up to me and
struck me on the forehead with the butt of his Kalashnikov. 'Do
that again and I'll cut out your tongue, you old donkey!' he said."
Rahim Khan rubbed the scar with a gnarled finger. "I was old
enough to be his grandfather and I was sitting there, blood gushing down my face, apologizing to that son of a dog."

I poured him more tea. Rahim Khan talked some more.
Much of it I knew already, some not. He told me that, as
arranged between Baba and him, he had lived in Baba's house
since 1981—this I knew about. Baba had "sold" the house to
Rahim Khan shortly before he and I fled Kabul. The way Baba
had seen it those days, Afghanistan's troubles were only a tempo-
rary interruption of our way of life—the days of parties at the
Wazir Akbar Khan house and picnics in Paghman would surely
return. So he'd given the house to Rahim Khan to keep watch
over until that day.

Rahim Khan told me how, when the Northern Alliance took
over Kabul between 1992 and 1996, different factions claimed
different parts of Kabul. "If you went from the Shar-e-Nau section to Kerteh-Parwan to buy a carpet, you risked getting shot by a
sniper or getting blown up by a rocket—if you got past all the
checkpoints, that was. You practically needed a visa to go from
one neighborhood to the other. So people just stayed put, prayed
the next rocket wouldn't hit their home." He told me how people
knocked holes in the walls of their homes so they could bypass the
dangerous streets and would move down the block from hole to
hole. In other parts, people moved about in underground tunnels.

"Why didn't you leave?" I said.

"Kabul was my home. It still is." He snickered. "Remember the street that went from your house to the *Qishla*, the military barracks next to Istiqlal School?"

"Yes." It was the shortcut to school. I remembered the day Hassan and I crossed it and the soldiers had teased Hassan about his mother. Hassan had cried in the cinema later, and I'd put an arm around him.

"When the Taliban rolled in and kicked the Alliance out of Kabul, I actually danced on that street," Rahim Khan said. "And, believe me, I wasn't alone. People were celebrating at *Chaman*, at *Deh-Mazang*, greeting the Taliban in the streets, climbing their tanks and posing for pictures with them. People were so tired of the constant fighting, tired of the rockets, the gunfire, the explosions, tired of watching Gulbuddin and his cohorts firing on anything that moved. The Alliance did more damage to Kabul than the *Shorawi*. They destroyed your father's orphanage, did you know that?"

"Why?" I said. "Why would they destroy an orphanage?" I remembered sitting behind Baba the day they opened the orphanage. The wind had knocked off his caracul hat and everyone had laughed, then stood and clapped when he'd delivered his speech. And now it was just another pile of rubble. All the money Baba had spent, all those nights he'd sweated over the blueprints, all the visits to the construction site to make sure every brick, every beam, and every block was laid just right . . .

"Collateral damage," Rahim Khan said. "You don't want to know, Amir jan, what it was like sifting through the rubble of that orphanage. There were body parts of children . . ."

"So when the Taliban came . . ."

"They were heroes," Rahim Khan said.

"Peace at last."

"Yes, hope is a strange thing. Peace at last. But at what price?" A violent coughing fit gripped Rahim Khan and rocked his gaunt body back and forth. When he spat into his handkerchief, it immediately stained red. I thought that was as good a time as any to address the elephant sweating with us in the tiny room.

"How are you?" I asked. "I mean *really*, how are you?"

"Dying, actually," he said in a gurgling voice. Another round of coughing. More blood on the handkerchief. He wiped his mouth, blotted his sweaty brow from one wasted temple to the other with his sleeve, and gave me a quick glance. When he nodded, I knew he had read the next question on my face. "Not long," he breathed.

"How long?"

He shrugged. Coughed again. "I don't think I'll see the end of this summer," he said.

"Let me take you home with me. I can find you a good doctor. They're coming up with new treatments all the time. There are new drugs and experimental treatments, we could enroll you in one..." I was rambling and I knew it. But it was better than crying, which I was probably going to do anyway.

He let out a chuff of laughter, revealed missing lower incisors. It was the most tired laughter I'd ever heard. "I see America has infused you with the optimism that has made her so great. That's very good. We're a melancholic people, we Afghans, aren't we? Often, we wallow too much in *ghamkhori* and self-pity. We give in to loss, to suffering, accept it as a fact of life, even see it as necessary. *Zendagi migzara,* we say, life goes on. But I am not surrendering to fate here, I am being pragmatic. I have seen several good doctors here and they have given the same answer. I trust them and believe them. There is such a thing as God's will."

"There is only what you do and what you don't do," I said.

Rahim Khan laughed. "You sounded like your father just now. I miss him so much. But it *is* God's will, Amir jan. It really is." He paused. "Besides, there's another reason I asked you to come here. I wanted to see you before I go, yes, but something else too."

"Anything."

"You know all those years I lived in your father's house after you left?"

"Yes."

"I wasn't alone for all of them. Hassan lived there with me."

"Hassan," I said. When was the last time I had spoken his name? Those thorny old barbs of guilt bore into me once more, as if speaking his name had broken a spell, set them free to torment me anew. Suddenly the air in Rahim Khan's little flat was too thick, too hot, too rich with the smell of the street.

"I thought about writing you and telling you before, but I wasn't sure you wanted to know. Was I wrong?"

The truth was no. The lie was yes. I settled for something in between. "I don't know."

He coughed another patch of blood into the handkerchief. When he bent his head to spit, I saw honey-crusted sores on his scalp. "I brought you here because I am going to ask something of you. I'm going to ask you to do something for me. But before I do, I want to tell you about Hassan. Do you understand?"

"Yes," I murmured.

"I want to tell you about him. I want to tell you everything. You will listen?"

I nodded.

Then Rahim Khan sipped some more tea. Rested his head against the wall and spoke.

SIXTEEN

There were a lot of reasons why I went to Hazarajat to find Hassan in 1986. The biggest one, Allah forgive me, was that I was lonely. By then, most of my friends and relatives had either been killed or had escaped the country to Pakistan or Iran. I barely knew anyone in Kabul anymore, the city where I had lived my entire life. Everybody had fled. I would take a walk in the Karteh-Parwan section—where the melon vendors used to hang out in the old days, you remember that spot?—and I wouldn't recognize anyone there. No one to greet, no one to sit down with for *chai*, no one to share stories with, just *Roussi* soldiers patrolling the streets. So eventually, I stopped going out to the city. I would spend my days in your father's house, up in the study, reading your mother's old books, listening to the news, watching the communist propaganda on television. Then I would pray *namaz*, cook something, eat, read some more, pray again, and go to bed. I would rise in the morning, pray, do it all over again.

And with my arthritis, it was getting harder for me to maintain the house. My knees and back were always aching—I would get up in the morning and it would take me at least an hour to shake the stiffness from my joints, especially in the wintertime. I did not want to let your father's house go to rot; we had all had many good times in that house, so many memories, Amir jan. It was not right—your father had designed that house himself; it had meant so much to him, and besides, I had promised him I would care for it when he and you left for Pakistan. Now it was just me and the house and...I did my best. I tried to water the trees every few days, cut the lawn, tend to the flowers, fix things that needed fixing, but, even then, I was not a young man anymore.

But even so, I might have been able to manage. At least for a while longer. But when news of your father's death reached me... for the first time, I felt a terrible loneliness in that house. An unbearable emptiness.

So one day, I fueled up the Buick and drove up to Hazarajat. I remembered that, after Ali dismissed himself from the house, your father told me he and Hassan had moved to a small village just outside Bamiyan. Ali had a cousin there as I recalled. I had no idea if Hassan would still be there, if anyone would even know of him or his whereabouts. After all, it had been ten years since Ali and Hassan had left your father's house. Hassan would have been a grown man in 1986, twenty-two, twenty-three years old. If he was even alive, that is—the *Shorawi*, may they rot in hell for what they did to our *watan*, killed so many of our young men. I don't have to tell you that.

But, with the grace of God, I found him there. It took very little searching—all I had to do was ask a few questions in Bamiyan and people pointed me to his village. I do not even recall its name, or whether it even had one. But I remember it was a scorching summer day and I was driving up a rutted dirt road, nothing on either side but sunbaked bushes, gnarled, spiny tree trunks, and dried grass like pale straw. I passed a dead donkey rotting on the side of the road. And then I turned a corner and, right in the middle of that barren land, I saw a cluster of mud houses, beyond them nothing but broad sky and mountains like jagged teeth.

The people in Bamiyan had told me I would find him easily—he lived in the only house in the village that had a walled garden. The mud wall, short and pocked with holes, enclosed the tiny house—which was really not much more than a glorified hut. Barefoot children were playing on the street, kicking a ragged tennis ball with a stick, and they stared when I pulled up and killed the engine. I knocked on the wooden door and stepped through into a yard that had very little in it save for a parched strawberry patch and a bare lemon tree. There was a *tandoor* in the corner in the shadow of an acacia tree and I saw a man squatting beside it. He was placing dough on a large wooden spatula and slapping it against the walls of the *tandoor*. He dropped the dough when he saw me. I had to make him stop kissing my hands.

"Let me look at you," I said. He stepped away. He was so tall now—I stood on my toes and still just came up to his chin. The Bamiyan sun had toughened his skin, and turned it several shades darker than I remembered, and he had lost a few of his front teeth. There were sparse strands of hair on his chin. Other than that, he had those same narrow green eyes, that scar on his upper lip, that round face, that affable smile. You would have recognized him, Amir jan. I am sure of it.

We went inside. There was a young light-skinned Hazara woman sewing a shawl in a corner of the room. She was visibly expecting. "This is my wife, Rahim Khan," Hassan said proudly. "Her name is Farzana jan." She was a shy woman, so courteous she spoke in a voice barely higher than a whisper and she would not raise her pretty hazel eyes to meet my gaze. But the way she was looking at Hassan, he might as well have been sitting on the throne at the *Arg*.

"When is the baby coming?" I said after we all settled around the adobe room. There was nothing in the room, just a frayed rug, a few dishes, a pair of mattresses, and a lantern.

"*Inshallah,* this winter," Hassan said. "I am praying for a boy to carry on my father's name."

"Speaking of Ali, where is he?"

Hassan dropped his gaze. He told me that Ali and his cousin— who had owned the house—had been killed by a land mine two years before, just outside of Bamiyan. A land mine. Is there a more Afghan way of dying, Amir jan? And for some crazy reason, I became absolutely certain that it had been Ali's right leg—his twisted polio leg—that had finally betrayed him and stepped on that land mine. I was deeply saddened to hear Ali had died. Your father and I grew up together, as you know, and Ali had been with him as long as I could remember. I remember when we were all little, the year Ali got polio and almost died. Your father would walk around the house all day crying.

Farzana made us *shorwa* with beans, turnips, and potatoes. We washed our hands and dipped fresh *naan* from the *tandoor* into the *shorwa*—it was the best meal I had had in months. It was then that I asked Hassan to move to Kabul with me. I told him about the house, how I could not care for it by myself anymore. I told him I would pay him well, that he and his *khanum* would be comfortable. They looked to each other and did not say anything. Later, after we had washed our hands and Farzana had served us grapes, Hassan said the village was his home now; he and Farzana had made a life for themselves there.

"And Bamiyan is so close. We know people there. Forgive me, Rahim Khan. I pray you understand."

"Of course," I said. "You have nothing to apologize for. I understand."

It was midway through tea after *shorwa* that Hassan asked about you. I told him you were in America, but that I did not know much more. Hassan had so many questions about you. Had you married? Did you have children? How tall were you? Did you still fly kites and go to the cinema? Were you happy? He said he had befriended an old Farsi teacher in Bamiyan who had taught him to read and write. If he wrote you a letter, would I pass it on to you? And did I think you would write back? I told him what I knew of you from the few phone conversations I had had with your father, but mostly I did not know how to answer him. Then he asked me about your father. When I told him, Hassan buried his face in his hands and broke into tears. He wept like a child for the rest of that night.

They insisted that I spend the night there. Farzana fixed a cot for me and left me a glass of well water in case I got thirsty. All night, I heard her whispering to Hassan, and heard him sobbing.

In the morning, Hassan told me he and Farzana had decided to move to Kabul with me.

"I should not have come here," I said. "You were right, Hassan jan. You have a *zendagi*, a life here. It was presumptuous of me to just show up and ask you to drop everything. It is me who needs to be forgiven."

"We don't have that much to drop, Rahim Khan," Hassan said. His eyes were still red and puffy. "We'll go with you. We'll help you take care of the house."

"Are you absolutely sure?"

He nodded and dropped his head. "Agha sahib was like my second father...God give him peace."

They piled their things in the center of a few worn rags and tied the corners together. We loaded the bundle into the Buick. Hassan stood in the threshold of the house and held the Koran as we all kissed it and passed under it. Then we left for Kabul. I remember as I was pulling away, Hassan turned to take a last look at their home.

When we got to Kabul, I discovered that Hassan had no intention of moving *into* the house. "But all these rooms are empty, Hassan jan. No one is going to live in them," I said.

But he would not. He said it was a matter of *ihtiram*, a matter of respect. He and Farzana moved their things into the hut in the backyard, where he was born. I pleaded for them to move into one of the guest bedrooms upstairs, but Hassan would hear nothing of it. "What will Amir agha think?" he said to me. "What will he think when he comes back to Kabul after the war and finds that I have assumed his place in the house?" Then, in mourning for your father, Hassan wore black for the next forty days.

I did not want them to, but the two of them did all the cooking, all the cleaning. Hassan tended to the flowers in the garden, soaked the roots, picked off yellowing leaves, and planted rosebushes. He painted the walls. In the house, he swept rooms no one had slept in for years, and cleaned bathrooms no one had bathed in. Like he was preparing the house for someone's return. Do you remember the wall behind the row of corn your father had planted, Amir jan? What did you and Hassan call it, "the Wall of Ailing Corn"? A rocket destroyed a whole section of that wall in the middle of the night early that fall. Hassan rebuilt the wall with his own hands, brick by brick, until it stood whole again. I do not know what I would have done if he had not been there.

Then late that fall, Farzana gave birth to a stillborn baby girl. Hassan kissed the baby's lifeless face, and we buried her in the backyard, near the sweetbrier bushes. We covered the little mound with leaves from the poplar trees. I said a prayer for her. Farzana stayed in the hut all day and wailed—it is a heartbreaking sound, Amir jan, the wailing of a mother. I pray to Allah you never hear it.

Outside the walls of that house, there was a war raging. But the three of us, in your father's house, we made our own little haven from it. My vision started going by the late 1980s, so I had Hassan read me your mother's books. We would sit in the foyer, by the stove, and Hassan would read me from Masnawi or Khayyám, as Farzana cooked in the kitchen. And every morning, Hassan placed a flower on the little mound by the sweetbrier bushes.

In early 1990, Farzana became pregnant again. It was that same year, in the middle of the summer, that a woman covered in a sky blue *burqa* knocked on the front gates one morning. When I walked up to the gates, she was swaying on her feet, like she was too weak to even stand. I asked her what she wanted, but she would not answer.

"Who are you?" I said. But she just collapsed right there in the driveway. I yelled for Hassan and he helped me carry her into the house, to the living room. We lay her on the sofa and took off her *burqa*. Beneath it, we found a toothless woman with stringy graying hair and sores on her arms. She looked like she had not eaten for days. But the worst of it by far was her face. Someone had taken a knife to it and...Amir jan, the slashes cut this way and that way. One of the cuts went from cheekbone to hairline and it had not spared her left eye on the way. It was grotesque. I patted her brow with a wet cloth and she opened her eyes. "Where is Hassan?" she whispered.

"I'm right here," Hassan said. He took her hand and squeezed it.

Her good eye rolled to him. "I have walked long and far to see if you are as beautiful in the flesh as you are in my dreams. And you are. Even more." She pulled his hand to her scarred face. "Smile for me. Please."

Hassan did and the old woman wept. "You smiled coming out of me, did anyone ever tell you? And I wouldn't even hold you. Allah forgive me, I wouldn't even hold you."

None of us had seen Sanaubar since she had eloped with a band of singers and dancers in 1964, just after she had given birth to Hassan. You never saw her, Amir, but in her youth, she was a vision. She had a dimpled smile and a walk that drove men crazy. No one who passed her on the street, be it a man or a woman, could look at her only once. And now...

Hassan dropped her hand and bolted out of the house. I went after him, but he was too fast. I saw him running up the hill where you two used to play, his feet kicking up plumes of dust. I let him go. I sat with Sanaubar all day as the sky went from bright blue to purple. Hassan still had not come back when night fell and moonlight bathed the clouds. Sanaubar cried that coming back had been a mistake, maybe even a worse one than leaving. But I made her stay. Hassan would return, I knew.

He came back the next morning, looking tired and weary, like he had not slept all night. He took Sanaubar's hand in both of his and told her she could cry if she wanted to but she needn't, she was home now, he said, home with her family. He touched the scars on her face, and ran his hand through her hair.

Hassan and Farzana nursed her back to health. They fed her and washed her clothes. I gave her one of the guest rooms upstairs. Sometimes, I would look out the window into the yard and watch Hassan and his mother kneeling together, picking tomatoes or trimming a rosebush, talking. They were catching up on all the lost years, I suppose. As far as I know, he never asked where she had been or why she had left and she never told. I guess some stories do not need telling.

It was Sanaubar who delivered Hassan's son that winter of 1990. It had not started snowing yet, but the winter winds were blowing through the yards, bending the flowerbeds and rustling the leaves. I remember Sanaubar came out of the hut holding her grandson, had him wrapped in a wool blanket. She stood beaming under a dull gray sky, tears streaming down her cheeks, the needle-cold wind blowing her hair, and clutching that baby in her arms like she never wanted to let go. Not this time. She handed him to Hassan and he handed him to me and I sang the prayer of *Ayat-ul-kursi* in that little boy's ear.

They named him Sohrab, after Hassan's favorite hero from the *Shahnamah*, as you know, Amir jan. He was a beautiful little boy, sweet as sugar, and had the same temperament as his father. You should have seen Sanaubar with that baby, Amir jan. He became the center of her existence. She sewed clothes for him, built him toys from scraps of wood, rags, and dried grass. When he caught a fever, she stayed up all night, and fasted for three days. She burned *isfand* for him on a skillet to cast out *nazar*, the evil eye. By the time Sohrab was two, he was calling her *Sasa*. The two of them were inseparable.

She lived to see him turn four, and then, one morning, she just did not wake up. She looked calm, at peace, like she did not mind dying now. We buried her in the cemetery on the hill, the one by the pomegranate tree, and I said a prayer for her too. The loss was hard on Hassan—it always hurts more to have and lose than to not have in the first place. But it was even harder on little Sohrab.

He kept walking around the house, looking for *Sasa,* but you know how children are, they forget so quickly.

By then—that would have been 1995—the *Shorawi* were defeated and long gone and Kabul belonged to Massoud, Rabbani, and the *Mujahedin.* The infighting between the factions was fierce and no one knew if they would live to see the end of the day. Our ears became accustomed to the whistle of falling shells, to the rumble of gunfire, our eyes familiar with the sight of men digging bodies out of piles of rubble. Kabul in those days, Amir jan, was as close as you could get to that proverbial hell on earth. Allah was kind to us, though. The Wazir Akbar Khan area was not attacked as much, so we did not have it as bad as some of the other neighborhoods.

On those days when the rocket fire eased up a bit and the gunfighting was light, Hassan would take Sohrab to the zoo to see Marjan the lion, or to the cinema. Hassan taught him how to shoot the slingshot, and, later, by the time he was eight, Sohrab had become deadly with that thing: He could stand on the terrace and hit a pinecone propped on a pail halfway across the yard. Hassan taught him to read and write—his son was not going to grow up illiterate like he had. I grew very attached to that little boy—I had seen him take his first step, heard him utter his first word. I bought children's books for Sohrab from the bookstore by Cinema Park—they have destroyed that too now—and Sohrab read them as quickly as I could get them to him. He reminded me of you, how you loved to read when you were little, Amir jan. Sometimes, I read to him at night, played riddles with him, taught him card tricks. I miss him terribly.

In the wintertime, Hassan took his son kite running. There were not nearly as many kite tournaments as in the old days—no one felt safe outside for too long—but there were still a few scattered tournaments. Hassan would prop Sohrab on his shoulders and they would go trotting through the streets, running kites, climbing trees where kites had dropped. You remember, Amir jan, what a good kite runner Hassan was? He was still just as good. At the end of winter, Hassan and Sohrab would hang the kites they had run all winter on the walls of the main hallway. They would put them up like paintings.

I told you how we all celebrated in 1996 when the Taliban rolled in and put an end to the daily fighting. I remember coming home that night and finding Hassan in the kitchen, listening to the radio. He had a sober look in his eyes. I asked him what was wrong, and he just shook his head. "God help the Hazaras now, Rahim Khan sahib," he said.

"The war is over, Hassan," I said. "There's going to be peace, *Inshallah,* and happiness and calm. No more rockets, no more killing, no more funerals!" But he just turned off the radio and asked if he could get me anything before he went to bed.

A few weeks later, the Taliban banned kite fighting. And two years later, in 1998, they massacred the Hazaras in Mazar-i-Sharif.

SEVENTEEN

Rahim Khan slowly uncrossed his legs and leaned against the bare wall in the wary, deliberate way of a man whose every movement triggers spikes of pain. Outside, a donkey was braying and someone was shouting something in Urdu. The sun was beginning to set, glittering red through the cracks between the ramshackle buildings.

It hit me again, the enormity of what I had done that winter and that following summer. The names rang in my head: Hassan, Sohrab, Ali, Farzana, and Sanaubar. Hearing Rahim Khan speak Ali's name was like finding an old dusty music box that hadn't been opened in years; the melody began to play immediately: *Who did you eat today, Babalu? Who did you eat, you slant-eyed Babalu?* I tried to conjure Ali's frozen face, to *really* see his tranquil eyes, but time can be a greedy thing—sometimes it steals all the details for itself.

"Is Hassan still in that house now?" I asked.

Rahim Khan raised the teacup to his parched lips and took a

sip. He then fished an envelope from the breast pocket of his vest and handed it to me. "For you."

I tore the sealed envelope. Inside, I found a Polaroid photograph and a folded letter. I stared at the photograph for a full minute.

A tall man dressed in a white turban and a green-striped *chapan* stood with a little boy in front of a set of wrought-iron gates. Sunlight slanted in from the left, casting a shadow on half of his rotund face. He was squinting and smiling at the camera, showing a pair of missing front teeth. Even in this blurry Polaroid, the man in the *chapan* exuded a sense of self-assuredness, of ease. It was in the way he stood, his feet slightly apart, his arms comfortably crossed on his chest, his head titled a little toward the sun. Mostly, it was in the way he smiled. Looking at the photo, one might have concluded that this was a man who thought the world had been good to him. Rahim Khan was right: I would have recognized him if I had bumped into him on the street. The little boy stood barefoot, one arm wrapped around the man's thigh, his shaved head resting against his father's hip. He too was grinning and squinting.

I unfolded the letter. It was written in Farsi. No dots were omitted, no crosses forgotten, no words blurred together—the handwriting was almost childlike in its neatness. I began to read:

In the name of Allah the most beneficent,
the most merciful,
Amir agha, with my deepest respects,
    Farzana jan, Sohrab, and I pray that this latest letter finds you in good health and in the light of Allah's good graces. Please offer my warmest thanks to Rahim Khan sahib for carrying it to you. I am hopeful that one day I will

hold one of your letters in my hands and read of your life in America. Perhaps a photograph of you will even grace our eyes. I have told much about you to Farzana jan and Sohrab, about us growing up together and playing games and running in the streets. They laugh at the stories of all the mischief you and I used to cause!

Amir agha,

Alas the Afghanistan of our youth is long dead. Kindness is gone from the land and you cannot escape the killings. Always the killings. In Kabul, fear is everywhere, in the streets, in the stadium, in the markets, it is a part of our lives here, Amir agha. The savages who rule our *watan* don't care about human decency. The other day, I accompanied Farzana jan to the bazaar to buy some potatoes and *naan*. She asked the vendor how much the potatoes cost, but he did not hear her, I think he had a deaf ear. So she asked louder and suddenly a young Talib ran over and hit her on the thighs with his wooden stick. He struck her so hard she fell down. He was screaming at her and cursing and saying the Ministry of Vice and Virtue does not allow women to speak loudly. She had a large purple bruise on her leg for days but what could I do except stand and watch my wife get beaten? If I fought, that dog would have surely put a bullet in me, and gladly! Then what would happen to my Sohrab? The streets are full enough already of hungry orphans and every day I thank Allah that I am alive, not because I fear death, but because my wife has a husband and my son is not an orphan.

I wish you could see Sohrab. He is a good boy. Rahim Khan sahib and I have taught him to read and write so he

does not grow up stupid like his father. And can he shoot
with that slingshot! I take Sohrab around Kabul sometimes
and buy him candy. There is still a monkey man in Shar-e-
Nau and if we run into him, I pay him to make his monkey
dance for Sohrab. You should see how he laughs! The two
of us often walk up to the cemetery on the hill. Do you
remember how we used to sit under the pomegranate tree
there and read from the *Shahnamah*? The droughts have
dried the hill and the tree hasn't borne fruit in years, but
Sohrab and I still sit under its shade and I read to him
from the *Shahnamah*. It is not necessary to tell you that
his favorite part is the one with his namesake, Rostam and
Sohrab. Soon he will be able to read from the book himself. I am a very proud and very lucky father.

Amir agha,

   Rahim Khan sahib is quite ill. He coughs all day and I
see blood on his sleeve when he wipes his mouth. He has
lost much weight and I wish he would eat a little of the
shorwa and rice that Farzana jan cooks for him. But he
only takes a bite or two and even that I think is out of
courtesy to Farzana jan. I am so worried about this dear
man I pray for him every day. He is leaving for Pakistan in
a few days to consult some doctors there and, *Inshallah*,
he will return with good news. But in my heart I fear for
him. Farzana jan and I have told little Sohrab that Rahim
Khan sahib is going to be well. What can we do? He is
only ten and he adores Rahim Khan sahib. They have
grown so close to each other. Rahim Khan sahib used to
take him to the bazaar for balloons and biscuits but he is
too weak for that now.

I have been dreaming a lot lately, Amir agha. Some of them are nightmares, like hanged corpses rotting in soccer fields with bloodred grass. I wake up from those short of breath and sweaty. Mostly, though, I dream of good things, and praise Allah for that. I dream that Rahim Khan sahib will be well. I dream that my son will grow up to be a good person, a free person, and an important person. I dream that *lawla* flowers will bloom in the streets of Kabul again and *rubab* music will play in the samovar houses and kites will fly in the skies. And I dream that someday you will return to Kabul to revisit the land of our childhood. If you do, you will find an old faithful friend waiting for you.

May Allah be with you always.

Hassan

I read the letter twice. I folded the note and looked at the photograph for another minute. I pocketed both. "How is he?" I asked.

"That letter was written six months ago, a few days before I left for Peshawar," Rahim Khan said. "I took the Polaroid the day before I left. A month after I arrived in Peshawar, I received a telephone call from one of my neighbors in Kabul. He told me this story: Soon after I took my leave, a rumor spread that a Hazara family was living alone in the big house in Wazir Akbar Khan, or so the Taliban claim. A pair of Talib officials came to investigate and interrogated Hassan. They accused him of lying when Hassan told them he was living with me even though many of the neighbors, including the one who called me, supported Hassan's story. The Talibs said he was a liar and a thief like all Hazaras and ordered him to get his family out of the house by sundown. Hassan protested. But my neighbor said the Talibs were looking at the big house like—how did he say it?—yes, like 'wolves looking at a flock of sheep.' They told Hassan they would be moving in to supposedly keep it safe until I return. Hassan protested again. So they took him to the street—"

"No," I breathed.

"—and order him to kneel—"

"No. God, no."

"—and shot him in the back of the head."

"No."

"—Farzana came screaming and attacked them—"

"No."

"—shot her too. Self-defense, they claimed later—"

But all I could manage was to whisper "No. No. No" over and over again.

I KEPT THINKING OF THAT DAY in 1974, in the hospital room, just after Hassan's harelip surgery. Baba, Rahim Khan, Ali, and I had huddled around Hassan's bed, watched him examine his new lip in a handheld mirror. Now everyone in that room was either dead or dying. Except for me.

Then I saw something else: a man dressed in a herringbone vest pressing the muzzle of his Kalashnikov to the back of Hassan's head. The blast echoes through the street of my father's house. Hassan slumps to the asphalt, his life of unrequited loyalty drifting from him like the windblown kites he used to chase.

"The Taliban moved into the house," Rahim Khan said. "The pretext was that they had evicted a trespasser. Hassan's and Farzana's murders were dismissed as a case of self-defense. No one said a word about it. Most of it was fear of the Taliban, I think. But no one was going to risk anything for a pair of Hazara servants."

"What did they do with Sohrab?" I asked. I felt tired, drained. A coughing fit gripped Rahim Khan and went on for a long time. When he finally looked up, his face was flushed and his eyes bloodshot. "I heard he's in an orphanage somewhere in Karteh-Seh. Amir jan—" then he was coughing again. When he stopped, he looked older than a few moments before, like he was aging with each coughing fit. "Amir jan, I summoned you here because I wanted to see you before I die, but that's not all."

I said nothing. I think I already knew what he was going to say.

"I want you to go to Kabul. I want you to bring Sohrab here," he said.

I struggled to find the right words. I'd barely had time to deal with the fact that Hassan was dead.

"Please hear me. I know an American pair here in Peshawar, a husband and wife named Thomas and Betty Caldwell. They are Christians and they run a small charity organization that they manage with private donations. Mostly they house and feed Afghan children who have lost their parents. I have seen the place. It's clean and safe, the children are well cared for, and Mr. and Mrs. Caldwell are kind people. They have already told me that Sohrab would be welcome to their home and—"

"Rahim Khan, you can't be serious."

"Children are fragile, Amir jan. Kabul is already full of broken children and I don't want Sohrab to become another."

"Rahim Khan, I don't want to go to Kabul. I can't!" I said.

"Sohrab is a gifted little boy. We can give him a new life here, new hope, with people who would love him. Thomas agha is a good man and Betty khanum is so kind, you should see how she treats those orphans."

"Why me? Why can't you pay someone here to go? I'll pay for it if it's a matter of money."

"It isn't about money, Amir!" Rahim Khan roared. "I'm a dying man and I will not be insulted! It has *never* been about money with me, you know that. And why you? I think we both know why it has to be you, don't we?"

I didn't want to understand that comment, but I did. I understood it all too well. "I have a wife in America, a home, a career, and a family. Kabul is a dangerous place, you know that, and you'd have me risk everything for..." I stopped.

"You know," Rahim Khan said, "one time, when you weren't around, your father and I were talking. And you know how he always worried about you in those days. I remember he said to me, 'Rahim, a boy who won't stand up for himself becomes a man who can't stand up to anything.' I wonder, is that what you've become?"

I dropped my eyes.

"What I'm asking from you is to grant an old man his dying wish," he said gravely.

He had gambled with that comment. Played his best card. Or so I thought then. His words hung in limbo between us, but at least he'd known what to say. I was still searching for the right words, and I was the writer in the room. Finally, I settled for this: "Maybe Baba was right."

"I'm sorry you think that, Amir."

I couldn't look at him. "And you don't?"

"If I did, I would not have asked you to come here."

I toyed with my wedding ring. "You've always thought too highly of me, Rahim Khan."

"And you've always been far too hard on yourself." He hesitated. "But there's something else. Something you don't know."

"Please, Rahim Khan—"

"Sanaubar wasn't Ali's first wife."

Now I looked up.

"He was married once before, to a Hazara woman from the Jaghori area. This was long before you were born. They were married for three years."

"What does this have to do with anything?"

"She left him childless after three years and married a man in Khost. She bore *him* three daughters. That's what I am trying to tell you."

I began to see where he was going. But I didn't want to hear the rest of it. I had a good life in California, pretty Victorian home with a peaked roof, a good marriage, a promising writing career, in-laws who loved me. I didn't need any of this shit.

"Ali was sterile," Rahim Khan said.

"No he wasn't. He and Sanaubar had Hassan, didn't they? They had Hassan—"

"No they didn't," Rahim Khan said.

"Yes they did!"

"No they didn't, Amir."

"Then who—"

"I think you know who."

I felt like a man sliding down a steep cliff, clutching at shrubs and tangles of brambles and coming up empty-handed. The room was swooping up and down, swaying side to side. "Did Hassan know?" I said through lips that didn't feel like my own. Rahim Khan closed his eyes. Shook his head.

"You bastards," I muttered. Stood up. "You goddamn bastards!" I screamed. "All of you, you bunch of lying goddamn bastards!"

"Please sit down," Rahim Khan said.

"How could you hide this from me? From *him*?" I bellowed.

"Please think, Amir jan. It was a shameful situation. People would talk. All that a man had back then, all that he was, was his honor, his name, and if people talked...We couldn't tell anyone, surely you can see that." He reached for me, but I shed his hand. Headed for the door.

"Amir jan, please don't leave."

I opened the door and turned to him. "Why? What can you possibly say to me? I'm thirty-eight years old and I've just found out my whole life is one big fucking lie! What can you possibly say to make things better? Nothing. Not a goddamn thing!"

And with that, I stormed out of the apartment.

EIGHTEEN

The sun had almost set and left the sky swathed in smothers of purple and red. I walked down the busy, narrow street that led away from Rahim Khan's building. The street was a noisy lane in a maze of alleyways choked with pedestrians, bicycles, and rickshaws. Billboards hung at its corners, advertising Coca-Cola and cigarettes; Lollywood movie posters displayed sultry actresses dancing with handsome, brown-skinned men in fields of marigolds.

I walked into a smoky little samovar house and ordered a cup of tea. I tilted back on the folding chair's rear legs and rubbed my face. That feeling of sliding toward a fall was fading. But in its stead, I felt like a man who awakens in his own house and finds all the furniture rearranged, so that every familiar nook and cranny looks foreign now. Disoriented, he has to reevaluate his surroundings, reorient himself.

How could I have been so blind? The signs had been there for me to see all along; they came flying back at me now: Baba hiring

Dr. Kumar to fix Hassan's harelip. Baba never missing Hassan's birthday. I remembered the day we were planting tulips, when I had asked Baba if he'd ever consider getting new servants. *Hassan's not going anywhere,* he'd barked. *He's staying right here with us, where he belongs. This is his home and we're his family.* He had wept, *wept,* when Ali announced he and Hassan were leaving us.

The waiter placed a teacup on the table before me. Where the table's legs crossed like an X, there was a ring of brass balls, each walnut-sized. One of the balls had come unscrewed. I stooped and tightened it. I wished I could fix my own life as easily. I took a gulp of the blackest tea I'd had in years and tried to think of Soraya, of the general and Khala Jamila, of the novel that needed finishing. I tried to watch the traffic bolting by on the street, the people milling in and out of the little sweetshops. Tried to listen to the *Qawali* music playing on the transistor radio at the next table. Anything. But I kept seeing Baba on the night of my graduation, sitting in the Ford he'd just given me, smelling of beer and saying, *I wish Hassan had been with us today.*

How could he have lied to me all those years? To Hassan? He had sat me on his lap when I was little, looked me straight in the eyes, and said, *There is only one sin. And that is theft... When you tell a lie, you steal someone's right to the truth.* Hadn't he said those words to me? And now, fifteen years after I'd buried him, I was learning that Baba had been a thief. And a thief of the worst kind, because the things he'd stolen had been sacred: from me the right to know I had a brother, from Hassan his identity, and from Ali his honor. His *nang.* His *namoos.*

The questions kept coming at me: How had Baba brought himself to look Ali in the eye? How had Ali lived in that house, day in and day out, knowing he had been dishonored by his master in the single worst way an Afghan man can be dishonored?

And how was I going to reconcile this new image of Baba with the one that had been imprinted on my mind for so long, that of him in his old brown suit, hobbling up the Taheris' driveway to ask for Soraya's hand?

Here is another cliché my creative writing teacher would have scoffed at; like father, like son. But it was true, wasn't it? As it turned out, Baba and I were more alike than I'd ever known. We had both betrayed the people who would have given their lives for us. And with that came this realization: that Rahim Khan had summoned me here to atone not just for my sins but for Baba's too.

Rahim Khan said I'd always been too hard on myself. But I wondered. True, I hadn't made Ali step on the land mine, and I hadn't brought the Taliban to the house to shoot Hassan. But I had driven Hassan and Ali out of the house. Was it too far-fetched to imagine that things might have turned out differently if I hadn't? Maybe Baba would have brought them along to America. Maybe Hassan would have had a home of his own now, a job, a family, a life in a country where no one cared that he was a Hazara, where most people didn't even know what a Hazara was. Maybe not. But maybe so.

I can't go to Kabul, I had said to Rahim Khan. *I have a wife in America, a home, a career, and a family.* But how could I pack up and go back home when my actions may have cost Hassan a chance at those very same things?

I wished Rahim Khan hadn't called me. I wished he had let me live on in my oblivion. But he had called me. And what Rahim Khan revealed to me changed things. Made me see how my entire life, long before the winter of 1975, dating back to when that singing Hazara woman was still nursing me, had been a cycle of lies, betrayals, and secrets.

There is a way to be good again, he'd said.

A way to end the cycle.

With a little boy. An orphan. Hassan's son. Somewhere in Kabul.

ON THE RICKSHAW RIDE back to Rahim Khan's apartment, I remembered Baba saying that my problem was that someone had always done my fighting for me. I was thirty-eight now. My hair was receding and streaked with gray, and lately I'd traced little crow's-feet etched around the corners of my eyes. I was older now, but maybe not yet too old to start doing my own fighting. Baba had lied about a lot of things as it turned out but he hadn't lied about that.

I looked at the round face in the Polaroid again, the way the sun fell on it. My brother's face. Hassan had loved me once, loved me in a way that no one ever had or ever would again. He was gone now, but a little part of him lived on. It was in Kabul.

Waiting.

I FOUND RAHIM KHAN praying *namaz* in a corner of the room. He was just a dark silhouette bowing eastward against a bloodred sky. I waited for him to finish.

Then I told him I was going to Kabul. Told him to call the Caldwells in the morning.

"I'll pray for you, Amir jan," he said.

NINETEEN

Again, the car sickness. By the time we drove past the bullet-riddled sign that read THE KHYBER PASS WELCOMES YOU, my mouth had begun to water. Something inside my stomach churned and twisted. Farid, my driver, threw me a cold glance. There was no empathy in his eyes.

"Can we roll down the window?" I asked.

He lit a cigarette and tucked it between the remaining two fingers of his left hand, the one resting on the steering wheel. Keeping his black eyes on the road, he stooped forward, picked up the screwdriver lying between his feet, and handed it to me. I stuck it in the small hole in the door where the handle belonged and turned it to roll down my window.

Farid gave me another dismissive look, this one with a hint of barely suppressed animosity, and went back to smoking his cigarette. He hadn't said more than a dozen words since we'd departed from Jamrud Fort.

"*Tashakor,*" I muttered. I leaned my head out of the window and let the cold midafternoon air rush past my face. The drive through the tribal lands of the Khyber Pass, winding between cliffs of shale and limestone, was just as I remembered it—Baba and I had driven through the broken terrain back in 1974. The arid, imposing mountains sat along deep gorges and soared to jagged peaks. Old fortresses, adobe-walled and crumbling, topped the crags. I tried to keep my eyes glued to the snowcapped Hindu Kush on the north side, but each time my stomach settled even a bit, the truck skidded around yet another turn, rousing a fresh wave of nausea.

"Try a lemon."

"What?"

"Lemon. Good for the sickness," Farid said. "I always bring one for this drive."

"Nay, thank you," I said. The mere thought of adding acidity to my stomach stirred more nausea. Farid snickered. "It's not fancy like American medicine, I know, just an old remedy my mother taught me."

I regretted blowing my chance to warm up to him. "In that case, maybe you should give me some."

He grabbed a paper bag from the backseat and plucked a half lemon out of it. I bit down on it, waited a few minutes. "You were right. I feel better," I lied. As an Afghan, I knew it was better to be miserable than rude. I forced a weak smile.

"Old *watani* trick, no need for fancy medicine," he said. His tone bordered on the surly. He flicked the ash off his cigarette and gave himself a self-satisfied look in the rearview mirror. He was a Tajik, a lanky, dark man with a weather-beaten face, narrow shoulders, and a long neck punctuated by a protruding Adam's apple that only peeked from behind his beard when he turned his head. He was dressed much as I was, though I suppose it was really the other way around: a rough-woven wool blanket wrapped over a gray *pirhan-tumban* and a vest. On his head, he wore a brown *pakol*, tilted slightly to one side, like the Tajik hero Ahmad Shah Massoud—referred to by Tajiks as "the Lion of Panjsher."

It was Rahim Khan who had introduced me to Farid in Peshawar. He told me Farid was twenty-nine, though he had the wary, lined face of a man twenty years older. He was born in Mazar-i-Sharif and lived there until his father moved the family to Jalalabad when Farid was ten. At fourteen, he and his father had joined the jihad against the *Shorawi*. They had fought in the Panjsher Valley for two years until helicopter gunfire had torn the older man to pieces. Farid had two wives and five children. "He used to have seven," Rahim Khan said with a rueful look, but he'd lost his two youngest girls a few years earlier in a land mine blast just outside Jalalabad, the same explosion that had severed toes from his feet and three fingers from his left hand. After that, he had moved his wives and children to Peshawar.

"Checkpoint," Farid grumbled. I slumped a little in my seat, arms folded across my chest, forgetting for a moment about the nausea. But I needn't have worried. Two Pakistani militia approached our dilapidated Land Cruiser, took a cursory glance inside, and waved us on.

Farid was first on the list of preparations Rahim Khan and I made, a list that included exchanging dollars for Kaldar and Afghani bills, my garment and *pakol*—ironically, I'd never worn either when I'd actually lived in Afghanistan—the Polaroid of Hassan and Sohrab, and, finally, perhaps the most important item: an artificial beard, black and chest length, *Shari'a*-friendly—or at least the Taliban version of *Shari'a*. Rahim Khan knew of a fellow in Peshawar who specialized in weaving them, sometimes for Western journalists who covered the war.

Rahim Khan had wanted me to stay with him a few more days, to plan more thoroughly. But I knew I had to leave as soon as possible. I was afraid I'd change my mind. I was afraid I'd deliberate, ruminate, agonize, rationalize, and talk myself into not going. I was afraid the appeal of my life in America would draw me back, that I would wade back into that great, big river and let myself forget, let the things I had learned these last few days sink to the bottom. I was afraid that I'd let the waters carry me away from what I had to do. From Hassan. From the past that had come calling. And from this one last chance at redemption. So I left before there was any possibility of that happening. As for Soraya, telling her I was going back to Afghanistan wasn't an option. If I had, she would have booked herself on the next flight to Pakistan.

We had crossed the border and the signs of poverty were everywhere. On either side of the road, I saw chains of little villages sprouting here and there, like discarded toys among the rocks, broken mud houses and huts consisting of little more than four wooden poles and a tattered cloth as a roof. I saw children dressed in rags chasing a soccer ball outside the huts. A few miles later, I spotted a cluster of men sitting on their haunches, like a row of crows, on the carcass of an old burned-out Soviet tank, the wind fluttering the edges of the blankets thrown around them. Behind them, a woman in a brown *burqa* carried a large clay pot on her shoulder, down a rutted path toward a string of mud houses.

"Strange," I said.

"What?"

"I feel like a tourist in my own country," I said, taking in a goatherd leading a half-dozen emaciated goats along the side of the road.

Farid snickered. Tossed his cigarette. "You still think of this place as your country?"

"I think a part of me always will," I said, more defensively than I had intended.

"After twenty years of living in America," he said, swerving the truck to avoid a pothole the size of a beach ball.

I nodded. "I grew up in Afghanistan."

Farid snickered again.

"Why do you do that?"

"Never mind," he murmured.

"No, I want to know. Why do you do that?"

In his rearview mirror, I saw something flash in his eyes. "You want to know?" he sneered. "Let me imagine, Agha sahib. You probably lived in a big two- or three-story house with a nice back-yard that your gardener filled with flowers and fruit trees. All gated, of course. Your father drove an American car. You had ser-vants, probably Hazaras. Your parents hired workers to decorate the house for the fancy *mehmani*s they threw, so their friends would come over to drink and boast about their travels to Europe or America. And I would bet my first son's eyes that this is the first time you've ever worn a *pakol*." He grinned at me, revealing a mouthful of prematurely rotting teeth. "Am I close?"

"Why are you saying these things?" I said.

"Because you wanted to know," he spat. He pointed to an old man dressed in ragged clothes trudging down a dirt path, a large burlap pack filled with scrub grass tied to his back. "That's the real Afghanistan, Agha sahib. That's the Afghanistan I know. You? You've *always* been a tourist here, you just didn't know it."

Rahim Khan had warned me not to expect a warm welcome in Afghanistan from those who had stayed behind and fought the wars. "I'm sorry about your father," I said. "I'm sorry about your daughters, and I'm sorry about your hand."

"That means nothing to me," he said. He shook his head. "Why are you coming back here anyway? Sell off your Baba's land? Pocket the money and run back to your mother in America?"

"My mother died giving birth to me," I said.

He sighed and lit another cigarette. Said nothing.

"Pull over."

"What?"

"Pull over, goddamn it!" I said. "I'm going to be sick." I tumbled out of the truck as it was coming to a rest on the gravel alongside the road.

BY LATE AFTERNOON, the terrain had changed from one of sun-beaten peaks and barren cliffs to a greener, more rural landscape. The main pass had descended from Landi Kotal through Shinwari territory to Landi Khana. We'd entered Afghanistan at Torkham. Pine trees flanked the road, fewer than I remembered and many of them bare, but it was good to see trees again after the arduous drive through the Khyber Pass. We were getting closer to Jalalabad, where Farid had a brother who would take us in for the night.

The sun hadn't quite set when we drove into Jalalabad, capital of the state of Nangarhar, a city once renowned for its fruit and warm climate. Farid drove past the buildings and stone houses of the city's central district. There weren't as many palm trees there as I remembered, and some of the homes had been reduced to roofless walls and piles of twisted clay.

Farid turned onto a narrow unpaved road and parked the Land Cruiser along a dried-up gutter. I slid out of the truck, stretched, and took a deep breath. In the old days, the winds swept through

the irrigated plains around Jalalabad where farmers grew sugarcane, and impregnated the city's air with a sweet scent. I closed
my eyes and searched for the sweetness. I didn't find it.

"Let's go," Farid said impatiently. We walked up the dirt road
past a few leafless poplars along a row of broken mud walls. Farid
led me to a dilapidated one-story house and knocked on the wood-
plank door.

A young woman with ocean-green eyes and a white scarf
draped around her face peeked out. She saw me first, flinched,
spotted Farid and her eyes lit up. "*Salaam alaykum,* Kaka
Farid!"

"*Salaam,* Maryam jan," Farid replied and gave her something
he'd denied me all day: a warm smile. He planted a kiss on the
top of her head. The young woman stepped out of the way, eyeing me a little apprehensively as I followed Farid into the small
house.

The adobe ceiling was low, the dirt walls entirely bare, and the
only light came from a pair of lanterns set in a corner. We took off
our shoes and stepped on the straw mat that covered the floor.
Along one of the walls sat three young boys, cross-legged, on a
mattress covered with a blanket with shredded borders. A tall
bearded man with broad shoulders stood up to greet us. Farid and
he hugged and kissed on the cheek. Farid introduced him to me as
Wahid, his older brother. "He's from America," he said to Wahid,
flicking his thumb toward me. He left us alone and went to greet
the boys.

Wahid sat with me against the wall across from the boys, who
had ambushed Farid and climbed his shoulders. Despite my
protests, Wahid ordered one of the boys to fetch another blanket
so I'd be more comfortable on the floor, and asked Maryam to

bring me some tea. He asked about the ride from Peshawar, the drive over the Khyber Pass.

"I hope you didn't come across any *dozd*s," he said. The Khyber Pass was as famous for its terrain as for the bandits who used that terrain to rob travelers. Before I could answer, he winked and said in a loud voice, "Of course no *dozd* would waste his time on a car as ugly as my brother's."

Farid wrestled the smallest of the three boys to the floor and tickled him on the ribs with his good hand. The kid giggled and kicked. "At least I have a car," Farid panted. "How is your donkey these days?"

"My donkey is a better ride than your car."

"*Khar khara mishnassah,*" Farid shot back. *Takes a donkey to know a donkey.* They all laughed and I joined in. I heard female voices from the adjoining room. I could see half of the room from where I sat. Maryam and an older woman wearing a brown *hijab*—presumably her mother—were speaking in low voices and pouring tea from a kettle into a pot.

"So what do you do in America, Amir agha?" Wahid asked.

"I'm a writer," I said. I thought I heard Farid chuckle at that.

"A writer?" Wahid said, clearly impressed. "Do you write about Afghanistan?"

"Well, I have. But not currently," I said. My last novel, *A Season for Ashes,* had been about a university professor who joins a clan of gypsies after he finds his wife in bed with one of his students. It wasn't a bad book. Some reviewers had called it a "good" book, and one had even used the word "riveting." But suddenly I was embarrassed by it. I hoped Wahid wouldn't ask what it was about.

"Maybe you should write about Afghanistan again," Wahid

said. "Tell the rest of the world what the Taliban are doing to our country."

"Well, I'm not . . . I'm not quite that kind of writer."

"Oh," Wahid said, nodding and blushing a bit. "You know best, of course. It's not for me to suggest . . ."

Just then, Maryam and the other woman came into the room with a pair of cups and a teapot on a small platter. I stood up in respect, pressed my hand to my chest, and bowed my head. *"Salaam alaykum,"* I said.

The woman, who had now wrapped her *hijab* to conceal her lower face, bowed her head too. *"Salaam,"* she replied in a barely audible voice. We never made eye contact. She poured the tea while I stood.

The woman placed the steaming cup of tea before me and exited the room, her bare feet making no sound at all as she disappeared. I sat down and sipped the strong black tea. Wahid finally broke the uneasy silence that followed.

"So what brings you back to Afghanistan?"

"What brings them *all* back to Afghanistan, dear brother?" Farid said, speaking to Wahid but fixing me with a contemptuous gaze.

"Bas!" Wahid snapped.

"It's always the same thing," Farid said. "Sell this land, sell that house, collect the money, and run away like a mouse. Go back to America, spend the money on a family vacation to Mexico."

"Farid!" Wahid roared. His children, and even Farid, flinched. "Have you forgotten your manners? This is *my* house! Amir agha is my guest tonight and I will not allow you to dishonor me like this!"

Farid opened his mouth, almost said something, reconsidered

and said nothing. He slumped against the wall, muttered something under his breath, and crossed his mutilated foot over the good one. His accusing eyes never left me.

"Forgive us, Amir agha," Wahid said. "Since childhood, my brother's mouth has been two steps ahead of his head."

"It's my fault, really," I said, trying to smile under Farid's intense gaze. "I am not offended. I should have explained to him my business here in Afghanistan. I am not here to sell property. I'm going to Kabul to find a boy."

"A boy," Wahid repeated.

"Yes." I fished the Polaroid from the pocket of my shirt. Seeing Hassan's picture again tore the fresh scab off his death. I had to turn my eyes away from it. I handed it to Wahid. He studied the photo. Looked from me to the photo and back again. "This boy?"

I nodded.

"This Hazara boy."

"Yes."

"What does he mean to you?"

"His father meant a lot to me. He is the man in the photo. He's dead now."

Wahid blinked. "He was a friend of yours?"

My instinct was to say yes, as if, on some deep level, I too wanted to protect Baba's secret. But there had been enough lies already. "He was my half-brother." I swallowed. Added, "My illegitimate half brother." I turned the teacup. Toyed with the handle.

"I didn't mean to pry."

"You're not prying," I said.

"What will you do with him?"

"Take him back to Peshawar. There are people there who will take care of him."

Wahid handed the photo back and rested his thick hand on my shoulder. "You are an honorable man, Amir agha. A true Afghan."

I cringed inside.

"I am proud to have you in our home tonight," Wahid said. I thanked him and chanced a glance over to Farid. He was looking down now, playing with the frayed edges of the straw mat.

A SHORT WHILE LATER, Maryam and her mother brought two steaming bowls of vegetable *shorwa* and two loaves of bread. "I'm sorry we can't offer you meat," Wahid said. "Only the Taliban can afford meat now."

"This looks wonderful," I said. It did too. I offered some to him, to the kids, but Wahid said the family had eaten before we arrived. Farid and I rolled up our sleeves, dipped our bread in the *shorwa,* and ate with our hands.

As I ate, I noticed Wahid's boys, all three thin with dirt-caked faces and short-cropped brown hair under their skullcaps, stealing furtive glances at my digital wristwatch. The youngest whispered something in his brother's ear. The brother nodded, didn't take his eyes off my watch. The oldest of the boys—I guessed his age at about twelve—rocked back and forth, his gaze glued to my wrist. After dinner, after I'd washed my hands with the water Maryam poured from a clay pot, I asked for Wahid's permission to give his boys a *hadia,* a gift. He said no, but, when I insisted, he reluctantly agreed. I unsnapped the wristwatch and gave it to the youngest of the three boys. He muttered a sheepish *"Tashakor."*

"It tells you the time in any city in the world," I told him. The boys nodded politely, passing the watch between them, taking turns trying it on. But they lost interest and, soon, the watch sat abandoned on the straw mat.

"You could have told me," Farid said later. The two of us were lying next to each other on the straw mats Wahid's wife had spread for us.

"Told you what?"

"Why you've come to Afghanistan." His voice had lost the rough edge I'd heard in it since the moment I had met him.

"You didn't ask," I said.

"You should have told me."

"You didn't ask."

He rolled to face me. Curled his arm under his head. "Maybe I will help you find this boy."

"Thank you, Farid," I said.

"It was wrong of me to assume."

I sighed. "Don't worry. You were more right than you know."

His hands are tied behind him with roughly woven rope cutting through the flesh of his wrists. He is blindfolded with black cloth. He is kneeling on the street, on the edge of a gutter filled with still water, his head drooping between his shoulders. His knees roll on the hard ground and bleed through his pants as he rocks in prayer. It is late afternoon and his long shadow sways back and forth on the gravel. He is muttering something under his breath. I step closer. A thousand times over, he mutters. For you a thousand times over. Back and forth he rocks. He lifts his face. I see a faint scar above his upper lip.

We are not alone.

I see the barrel first. Then the man standing behind him. He is tall, dressed in a herringbone vest and a black turban. He looks down at the blindfolded man before him with eyes that show nothing but a vast, cavernous emptiness. He takes a step back and raises the barrel. Places it on the back of the kneeling man's head. For a moment, fading sunlight catches in the metal and twinkles.

The rifle roars with a deafening crack.

I follow the barrel on its upward arc. I see the face behind the plume of smoke swirling from the muzzle. I am the man in the herringbone vest.

I woke up with a scream trapped in my throat.

I STEPPED OUTSIDE. Stood in the silver tarnish of a half-moon and glanced up to a sky riddled with stars. Crickets chirped in the shuttered darkness and a wind wafted through the trees. The ground was cool under my bare feet and suddenly, for the first time since we had crossed the border, I felt like I was back. After all these years, I was home again, standing on the soil of my ancestors. This was the soil on which my great-grandfather had married his third wife a year before dying in the cholera epidemic that hit Kabul in 1915. She'd borne him what his first two wives had failed to, a son at last. It was on this soil that my grandfather had gone on a hunting trip with King Nadir Shah and shot a deer. My mother had died on this soil. And on this soil, I had fought for my father's love.

I sat against one of the house's clay walls. The kinship I felt suddenly for the old land...it surprised me. I'd been gone long enough to forget and be forgotten. I had a home in a land that might as well be in another galaxy to the people sleeping on the other side of the wall I leaned against. I thought I had forgotten about this land. But I hadn't. And, under the bony glow of a half-moon, I sensed Afghanistan humming under my feet. Maybe Afghanistan hadn't forgotten me either.

I looked westward and marveled that, somewhere over those mountains, Kabul still existed. It really existed, not just as an old memory, or as the heading of an AP story on page 15 of the *San Francisco Chronicle*. Somewhere over those mountains in the west slept the city where my harelipped brother and I had run kites. Somewhere over there, the blindfolded man from my dream had died a needless death. Once, over those mountains, I had made a choice. And now, a quarter of a century later, that choice had landed me right back on this soil.

I was about to go back inside when I heard voices coming from the house. I recognized one as Wahid's.

"—nothing left for the children."

"We're hungry but we're not savages! He is a guest! What was I supposed to do?" he said in a strained voice.

"—to find something tomorrow." She sounded near tears. "What do I feed—"

I tiptoed away. I understood now why the boys hadn't shown any interest in the watch. They hadn't been staring at the watch at all. They'd been staring at my food.

WE SAID OUR GOOD-BYES early the next morning. Just before I climbed into the Land Cruiser, I thanked Wahid for his hospitality. He pointed to the little house behind him. "This is your home," he said. His three sons were standing in the doorway watching us. The little one was wearing the watch—it dangled around his twiggy wrist.

I glanced in the side-view mirror as we pulled away. Wahid stood surrounded by his boys in a cloud of dust whipped up by the truck. It occurred to me that, in a different world, those boys wouldn't have been too hungry to chase after the car.

Earlier that morning, when I was certain no one was looking, I did something I had done twenty-six years earlier: I planted a fistful of crumpled money under a mattress.

TWENTY

Farid had warned me. He had. But, as it turned out, he had wasted his breath.

We were driving down the cratered road that winds from Jalalabad to Kabul. The last time I'd traveled that road was in a tarpaulin-covered truck going the other way. Baba had nearly gotten himself shot by a singing, stoned *Roussi* officer—Baba had made me so mad that night, so scared, and, ultimately, so proud. The trek between Kabul and Jalalabad, a bone-jarring ride down a teetering pass snaking through the rocks, had become a relic now, a relic of two wars. Twenty years earlier, I had seen some of the first war with my own eyes. Grim reminders of it were strewn along the road: burned carcasses of old Soviet tanks, overturned military trucks gone to rust, a crushed Russian jeep that had plunged over the mountainside. The second war, I had watched on my TV screen. And now I was seeing it through Farid's eyes.

Swerving effortlessly around potholes in the middle of the broken road, Farid was a man in his element. He had become much chattier since our overnight stay at Wahid's house. He had me sit in the passenger seat and looked at me when he spoke. He even smiled once or twice. Maneuvering the steering wheel with his mangled hand, he pointed to mud-hut villages along the way where he'd known people years before. Most of those people, he said, were either dead or in refugee camps in Pakistan. "And sometimes the dead are luckier," he said.

He pointed to the crumbled, charred remains of a tiny village. It was just a tuft of blackened, roofless walls now. I saw a dog sleeping along one of the walls. "I had a friend there once," Farid said. "He was a very good bicycle repairman. He played the tabla well too. The Taliban killed him and his family and burned the village."

We drove past the burned village, and the dog didn't move.

IN THE OLD DAYS, the drive from Jalalabad to Kabul took two hours, maybe a little more. It took Farid and me over four hours to reach Kabul. And when we did... Farid warned me just after we passed the Mahipar dam.

"Kabul is not the way you remember it," he said.

"So I hear."

Farid gave me a look that said hearing is not the same as seeing. And he was right. Because when Kabul finally did unroll before us, I was certain, absolutely certain, that he had taken a wrong turn somewhere. Farid must have seen my stupefied expression; shuttling people back and forth to Kabul, he would have become familiar with that expression on the faces of those who hadn't seen Kabul for a long time.

He patted me on the shoulder. "Welcome back," he said morosely.

. . .

RUBBLE AND BEGGARS. Everywhere I looked, that was what
I saw. I remembered beggars in the old days too—Baba always carried an extra handful of Afghani bills in his pocket just for them;
I'd never seen him deny a peddler. Now, though, they squatted at
every street corner, dressed in shredded burlap rags, mud-caked
hands held out for a coin. And the beggars were mostly children
now, thin and grim-faced, some no older than five or six. They sat
in the laps of their *burqa*-clad mothers alongside gutters at busy
street corners and chanted *"Bakhshesh, bakhshesh!"* And something else, something I hadn't noticed right away: Hardly any of
them sat with an adult male—the wars had made fathers a rare
commodity in Afghanistan.

We were driving westbound toward the Karteh-Seh district on
what I remembered as a major thoroughfare in the seventies:
Jadeh Maywand. Just north of us was the bone-dry Kabul River.
On the hills to the south stood the broken old city wall. Just east
of it was the Bala Hissar Fort—the ancient citadel that the war-
lord Dostum had occupied in 1992—on the Shirdarwaza mountain range, the same mountains from which *Mujahedin* forces
had showered Kabul with rockets between 1992 and 1996,
inflicting much of the damage I was witnessing now. The Shirdarwaza range stretched all the way west. It was from those
mountains that I remember the firing of the *Topeh chasht*, the
"noon cannon." It went off every day to announce noontime, and
also to signal the end of daylight fasting during the month of
Ramadan. You'd hear the roar of that cannon all through the city
in those days.

"I used to come here to Jadeh Maywand when I was a kid," I
mumbled. "There used to be shops here and hotels. Neon lights

and restaurants. I used to buy kites from an old man named Saifo. He ran a little kite shop by the old police headquarters."

"The police headquarters is still there," Farid said. "No shortage of police in this city. But you won't find kites or kite shops on Jadeh Maywand or anywhere else in Kabul. Those days are over."

Jadeh Maywand had turned into a giant sand castle. The buildings that hadn't entirely collapsed barely stood, with caved in roofs and walls pierced with rockets shells. Entire blocks had been obliterated to rubble. I saw a bullet-pocked sign half buried at an angle in a heap of debris. It read DRINK COCA CO—. I saw children playing in the ruins of a windowless building amid jagged stumps of brick and stone. Bicycle riders and mule-drawn carts swerved around kids, stray dogs, and piles of debris. A haze of dust hovered over the city and, across the river, a single plume of smoke rose to the sky.

"Where are the trees?" I said.

"People cut them down for firewood in the winter," Farid said. "The *Shorawi* cut a lot of them down too."

"Why?"

"Snipers used to hide in them."

A sadness came over me. Returning to Kabul was like running into an old, forgotten friend and seeing that life hadn't been good to him, that he'd become homeless and destitute.

"My father built an orphanage in Shar-e-Kohna, the old city, south of here," I said.

"I remember it," Farid said. "It was destroyed a few years ago."

"Can you pull over?" I said. "I want to take a quick walk here."

Farid parked along the curb on a small backstreet next to a ramshackle, abandoned building with no door. "That used to be a pharmacy," Farid muttered as we exited the truck. We walked back to Jadeh Maywand and turned right, heading west. "What's that smell?" I said. Something was making my eyes water.

"Diesel," Farid replied. "The city's generators are always going down, so electricity is unreliable, and people use diesel fuel."

"Diesel. Remember what this street smelled like in the old days?"

Farid smiled. "Kabob."

"Lamb kabob," I said.

"Lamb," Farid said, tasting the word in his mouth. "The only people in Kabul who get to eat lamb now are the Taliban." He pulled on my sleeve. "Speaking of which..."

A vehicle was approaching us. "Beard Patrol," Farid murmured.

That was the first time I saw the Taliban. I'd seen them on TV, on the Internet, on the cover of magazines, and in newspapers. But here I was now, less than fifty feet from them, telling myself that the sudden taste in my mouth wasn't unadulterated, naked fear. Telling myself my flesh hadn't suddenly shrunk against my bones and my heart wasn't battering. Here they came. In all their glory.

The red Toyota pickup truck idled past us. A handful of stern-faced young men sat on their haunches in the cab, Kalashnikovs slung on their shoulders. They all wore beards and black turbans. One of them, a dark-skinned man in his early twenties with thick, knitted eyebrows twirled a whip in his hand and rhythmically swatted the side of the truck with it. His roaming eyes fell on me. Held my gaze. I'd never felt so naked in my entire life. Then the Talib spat tobacco-stained spittle and looked away. I found I could breathe again. The truck rolled down Jadeh Maywand, leaving in its trail a cloud of dust.

"What is the matter with you?" Farid hissed.

"What?"

"Don't ever stare at them! Do you understand me? Never!"

"I didn't mean to," I said.

"Your friend is quite right, Agha. You might as well poke a rabid dog with a stick," someone said. This new voice belonged to an old beggar sitting barefoot on the steps of a bullet-scarred building. He wore a threadbare *chapan* worn to frayed shreds and a dirt-crusted turban. His left eyelid drooped over an empty socket. With an arthritic hand, he pointed to the direction the red truck had gone. "They drive around looking. Looking and hoping that someone will provoke them. Sooner or later, someone always obliges. Then the dogs feast and the day's boredom is broken at last and everyone says *'Allah-u-akbar!'* And on those days when no one offends, well, there is always random violence, isn't there?"

"Keep your eyes on your feet when the Talibs are near," Farid said.

"Your friend dispenses good advice," the old beggar chimed in. He barked a wet cough and spat in a soiled handkerchief. "Forgive me, but could you spare a few Afghanis?" he breathed.

"*Bas.* Let's go," Farid said, pulling me by the arm.

I handed the old man a hundred thousand Afghanis, or the equivalent of about three dollars. When he leaned forward to take the money, his stench—like sour milk and feet that hadn't been washed in weeks—flooded my nostrils and made my gorge rise. He hurriedly slipped the money in his waist, his lone eye darting side to side. "A world of thanks for your benevolence, Agha sahib."

"Do you know where the orphanage is in Karteh-Seh?" I said.

"It's not hard to find, it's just west of Darulaman Boulevard," he said. "The children were moved from here to Karteh-Seh after the rockets hit the old orphanage. Which is like saving someone from the lion's cage and throwing them in the tiger's."

"Thank you, Agha," I said. I turned to go.

"That was your first time, nay?"

"I'm sorry?"

"The first time you saw a Talib."

I said nothing. The old beggar nodded and smiled. Revealed a handful of remaining teeth, all crooked and yellow. "I remember the first time I saw them rolling into Kabul. What a joyous day that was!" he said. "An end to the killing! *Wah wah!* But like the poet says: 'How seamless seemed love and then came trouble!'"

A smile sprouted on my face. "I know that *ghazal*. That's Hafez."

"Yes it is. Indeed," the old man replied. "I should know. I used to teach it at the university."

"You did?"

The old man coughed. "From 1958 to 1996. I taught Hãfez, Khayyám, Rumi, Beydel, Jami, Saadi. Once, I was even a guest lecturer in Tehran, 1971 that was. I gave a lecture on the mystic Beydel. I remember how they all stood and clapped. Ha!" He shook his head. "But you saw those young men in the truck. What value do you think they see in Sufism?"

"My mother taught at the university," I said.

"And what was her name?"

"Sofia Akrami."

His eye managed to twinkle through the veil of cataracts. "'The desert weed lives on, but the flower of spring blooms and wilts.' Such grace, such dignity, such a tragedy."

"You knew my mother?" I asked, kneeling before the old man.

"Yes indeed," the old beggar said. "We used to sit and talk after class. The last time was on a rainy day just before final exams when we shared a marvelous slice of almond cake together. Almond cake with hot tea and honey. She was rather obviously pregnant by then, and all the more beautiful for it. I will never forget what she said to me that day."

"What? Please tell me." Baba had always described my mother to me in broad strokes, like, "She was a great woman." But what I had always thirsted for were the details: the way her hair glinted in the sunlight, her favorite ice cream flavor, the songs she liked to hum, did she bite her nails? Baba took his memories of her to the grave with him. Maybe speaking her name would have reminded him of his guilt, of what he had done so soon after she had died. Or maybe his loss had been so great, his pain so deep, he couldn't bear to talk about her. Maybe both.

"She said, 'I'm so afraid.' And I said, 'Why?,' and she said, 'Because I'm so profoundly happy, Dr. Rasul. Happiness like this is frightening.' I asked her why and she said, 'They only let you be this happy if they're preparing to take something from you,' and I said, 'Hush up, now. Enough of this silliness.'"

Farid took my arm. "We should go, Amir agha," he said softly. I snatched my arm away. "What else? What else did she say?"

The old man's features softened. "I wish I remembered for you. But I don't. Your mother passed away a long time ago and my memory is as shattered as these buildings. I am sorry."

"But even a small thing, anything at all."

The old man smiled. "I'll try to remember and that's a promise. Come back and find me."

"Thank you," I said. "Thank you so much." And I meant it. Now I knew my mother had liked almond cake with honey and hot tea, that she'd once used the word "profoundly," that she'd fretted about her happiness. I had just learned more about my mother from this old man on the street than I ever did from Baba.

Walking back to the truck, neither one of us commented about what most non-Afghans would have seen as an improbable coincidence, that a beggar on the street would happen to know my mother. Because we both knew that in Afghanistan, and particularly in Kabul, such absurdity was commonplace. Baba used to say, "Take two Afghans who've never met, put them in a room for ten minutes, and they'll figure out how they're related."

We left the old man on the steps of that building. I meant to take him up on his offer, come back and see if he'd unearthed any more stories about my mother. But I never saw him again.

WE FOUND THE NEW ORPHANAGE in the northern part of Karteh-Seh, along the banks of the dried-up Kabul River. It was a flat, barracks-style building with splintered walls and windows boarded with planks of wood. Farid had told me on the way there that Karteh-Seh had been one of the most war-ravaged neighborhoods in Kabul, and, as we stepped out of the truck, the evidence was overwhelming. The cratered streets were flanked by little more than ruins of shelled buildings and abandoned homes. We passed the rusted skeleton of an overturned car, a TV set with no screen half-buried in rubble, a wall with the words ZENDA BAD TAL-IBAN! (Long live the Taliban!) sprayed in black.

A short, thin, balding man with a shaggy gray beard opened the door. He wore a ragged tweed jacket, a skullcap, and a pair of eyeglasses with one chipped lens resting on the tip of his nose. Behind the glasses, tiny eyes like black peas flitted from me to Farid. "*Salaam alaykum,*" he said.

"*Salaam alaykum,*" I said. I showed him the Polaroid. "We're searching for this boy."

He gave the photo a cursory glance. "I am sorry. I have never seen him."

"You barely looked at the picture, my friend," Farid said. "Why not take a closer look?"

"*Lotfan,*" I added. Please.

The man behind the door took the picture. Studied it. Handed it back to me. "Nay, sorry. I know just about every single child in this institution and that one doesn't look familiar. Now, if you'll permit me, I have work to do." He closed the door. Locked the bolt.

I rapped on the door with my knuckles. "Agha! Agha, please open the door. We don't mean him any harm."

"I told you. He's not here," his voice came from the other side. "Now, please go away."

Farid stepped up to the door, rested his forehead on it. "Friend, we are not with the Taliban," he said in a low, cautious voice. "The man who is with me wants to take this boy to a safe place."

"I come from Peshawar," I said. "A good friend of mine knows an American couple there who run a charity home for children." I felt the man's presence on the other side of the door. Sensed him standing there, listening, hesitating, caught between suspicion and hope. "Look, I knew Sohrab's father," I said. "His name was Hassan. His mother's name was Farzana. He called his grandmother *Sasa*. He knows how to read and write. And he's good with the slingshot. There's hope for this boy, Agha, a way out. Please open the door."

From the other side, only silence.

"I'm his half uncle," I said.

A moment passed. Then a key rattled in the lock. The man's

narrow face reappeared in the crack. He looked from me to Farid and back. "You were wrong about one thing."

"What?"

"He's *great* with the slingshot."

I smiled.

"He's inseparable from that thing. He tucks it in the waist of his pants everywhere he goes."

THE MAN WHO LET US IN introduced himself as Zaman, the director of the orphanage. "I'll take you to my office," he said.

We followed him through dim, grimy hallways where barefoot children dressed in frayed sweaters ambled around. We walked past rooms with no floor covering but matted carpets and windows shuttered with sheets of plastic. Skeleton frames of steel beds, most with no mattress, filled the rooms.

"How many orphans live here?" Farid asked.

"More than we have room for. About two hundred and fifty," Zaman said over his shoulder. "But they're not all *yateem*. Many of them have lost their fathers in the war, and their mothers can't feed them because the Taliban don't allow them to work. So they bring their children here." He made a sweeping gesture with his hand and added ruefully, "This place is better than the street, but not that much better. This building was never meant to be lived in—it used to be a storage warehouse for a carpet manufacturer. So there's no water heater and they've let the well go dry." He dropped his voice. "I've asked the Taliban for money to dig a new well more times than I remember and they just twirl their rosaries and tell me there is no money. No money." He snickered.

He pointed to a row of beds along the wall. "We don't have

enough beds, and not enough mattresses for the beds we do have. Worse, we don't have enough blankets." He showed us a little girl skipping rope with two other kids. "You see that girl? This past winter, the children had to share blankets. Her brother died of exposure." He walked on. "The last time I checked, we have less than a month's supply of rice left in the warehouse, and, when that runs out, the children will have to eat bread and tea for breakfast *and* dinner." I noticed he made no mention of lunch.

He stopped and turned to me. "There is very little shelter here, almost no food, no clothes, no clean water. What I have in ample supply here is children who've lost their childhood. But the tragedy is that these are the lucky ones. We're filled beyond capacity and every day I turn away mothers who bring their children." He took a step toward me. "You say there is hope for Sohrab? I pray you don't lie, Agha. But...you may well be too late."

"What do you mean?"

Zaman's eyes shifted. "Follow me."

WHAT PASSED FOR THE DIRECTOR'S OFFICE was four bare, cracked walls, a mat on the floor, a table, and two folding chairs. As Zaman and I sat down, I saw a gray rat poke its head from a burrow in the wall and flit across the room. I cringed when it sniffed at my shoes, then Zaman's, and scurried through the open door.

"What did you mean it may be too late?" I said.

"Would you like some *chai*? I could make some."

"Nay, thank you. I'd rather we talk."

Zaman tilted back in his chair and crossed his arms on his chest. "What I have to tell you is not pleasant. Not to mention that it may be very dangerous."

"For whom?"

"You. Me. And, of course, for Sohrab, if it's not too late already."

"I need to know," I said.

He nodded. "So you say. But first I want to ask you a question: How badly do you want to find your nephew?"

I thought of the street fights we'd get into when we were kids, all the times Hassan used to take them on for me, two against one, sometimes three against one. I'd wince and watch, tempted to step in, but always stopping short, always held back by something.

I looked at the hallway, saw a group of kids dancing in a circle. A little girl, her left leg amputated below the knee, sat on a ratty mattress and watched, smiling and clapping along with the other children. I saw Farid watching the children too, his own mangled hand hanging at his side. I remembered Wahid's boys and . . . I realized something: I would not leave Afghanistan without finding Sohrab. "Tell me where he is," I said.

Zaman's gaze lingered on me. Then he nodded, picked up a pencil, and twirled it between his fingers. "Keep my name out of it."

"I promise."

He tapped the table with the pencil. "Despite your promise, I think I'll live to regret this, but perhaps it's just as well. I'm damned anyway. But if something can be done for Sohrab . . . I'll tell you because I believe you. You have the look of a desperate man." He was quiet for a long time. "There is a Talib official," he muttered. "He visits once every month or two. He brings cash with him, not a lot, but better than nothing at all." His shifty eyes fell on me, rolled away. "Usually he'll take a girl. But not always."

"And you allow this?" Farid said behind me. He was going around the table, closing in on Zaman.

"What choice do I have?" Zaman shot back. He pushed himself away from the desk.

"You're the director here," Farid said. "Your job is watch over these children."

"There's nothing I can do to stop it."

"You're selling children!" Farid barked.

"Farid, sit down! Let it go!" I said. But I was too late. Because suddenly Farid was leaping over the table. Zaman's chair went flying as Farid fell on him and pinned him to the floor. The director thrashed beneath Farid and made muffled screaming sounds. His legs kicked a desk drawer free and sheets of paper spilled to the floor.

I ran around the desk and saw why Zaman's screaming was muffled: Farid was strangling him. I grasped Farid's shoulders with both hands and pulled hard. He snatched away from me. "That's enough!" I barked. But Farid's face had flushed red, his lips pulled back in a snarl. "I'm killing him! You can't stop me! I'm killing him," he sneered.

"Get off him!"

"I'm killing him!" Something in his voice told me that if I didn't do something quickly I'd witness my first murder.

"The children are watching, Farid. They're watching," I said. His shoulder muscles tightened under my grip and, for a moment, I thought he'd keep squeezing Zaman's neck anyway. Then he turned around, saw the children. They were standing silently by the door, holding hands, some of them crying. I felt Farid's muscles slacken. He dropped his hands, rose to his feet. He looked down on Zaman and dropped a mouthful of spit on his face. Then he walked to the door and closed it.

Zaman struggled to his feet, blotted his bloody lips with his sleeve, wiped the spit off his cheek. Coughing and wheezing, he put on his skullcap, his glasses, saw both lenses had cracked, and took them off. He buried his face in his hands. None of us said anything for a long time.

"He took Sohrab a month ago," Zaman finally croaked, hands still shielding his face.

"You call yourself a director?" Farid said.

Zaman dropped his hands. "I haven't been paid in over six months. I'm broke because I've spent my life's savings on this orphanage. Everything I ever owned or inherited I sold to run this godforsaken place. You think I don't have family in Pakistan and Iran? I could have run like everyone else. But I didn't. I stayed. I stayed because of *them*." He pointed to the door. "If I deny him one child, he takes ten. So I let him take one and leave the judging to Allah. I swallow my pride and take his goddamn filthy...dirty money. Then I go to the bazaar and buy food for the children."

Farid dropped his eyes.

"What happens to the children he takes?" I asked.

Zaman rubbed his eyes with his forefinger and thumb. "Sometimes they come back."

"Who is he? How do we find him?" I said.

"Go to Ghazi Stadium tomorrow. You'll see him at halftime. He'll be the one wearing black sunglasses." He picked up his broken glasses and turned them in his hands. "I want you to go now. The children are frightened."

He escorted us out.

As the truck pulled away, I saw Zaman in the side-view mirror, standing in the doorway. A group of children surrounded him, clutching the hem of his loose shirt. I saw he had put on his broken glasses.

TWENTY-ONE

We crossed the river and drove north through the crowded Pashtunistan Square. Baba used to take me to Khyber Restaurant there for kabob. The building was still standing, but its doors were padlocked, the windows shattered, and the letters *K* and *R* missing from its name.

I saw a dead body near the restaurant. There had been a hanging. A young man dangled from the end of a rope tied to a beam, his face puffy and blue, the clothes he'd worn on the last day of his life shredded, bloody. Hardly anyone seemed to notice him.

We rode silently through the square and headed toward the Wazir Akbar Khan district. Everywhere I looked, a haze of dust covered the city and its sun-dried brick buildings. A few blocks north of Pashtunistan Square, Farid pointed to two men talking animatedly at a busy street corner. One of them was hobbling on one leg, his other leg amputated below the knee. He cradled an artificial leg in his arms. "You know what they're doing? Haggling over the leg."

"He's selling his leg?"

Farid nodded. "You can get good money for it on the black market. Feed your kids for a couple of weeks."

TO MY SURPRISE, most of the houses in the Wazir Akbar Khan district still had roofs and standing walls. In fact, they were in pretty good shape. Trees still peeked over the walls, and the streets weren't nearly as rubble-strewn as the ones in Karteh-Seh. Faded streets signs, some twisted and bullet-pocked, still pointed the way.

"This isn't so bad," I remarked.

"No surprise. Most of the important people live here now."

"Taliban?"

"Them too," Farid said.

"Who else?"

He drove us into a wide street with fairly clean sidewalks and walled homes on either side. "The people behind the Taliban. The real brains of this government, if you can call it that: Arabs, Chechens, Pakistanis," Farid said. He pointed northwest. "Street 15, that way, is called Sarak-e-Mehmana." Street of the Guests. "That's what they call them here, guests. I think someday these guests are going to pee all over the carpet."

"I think that's it!" I said. "Over there!" I pointed to the landmark that used to serve as a guide for me when I was a kid. *If you ever get lost,* Baba used to say, *remember that our street is the one with the pink house at the end of it.* The pink house with the steeply pitched roof had been the neighborhood's only house of that color in the old days. It still was.

Farid turned onto the street. I saw Baba's house right away.

.   .   .

WE FIND THE LITTLE TURTLE behind tangles of sweetbrier in the yard. We don't know how it got there and we're too excited to care. We paint its shell a bright red, Hassan's idea, and a good one: This way, we'll never lose it in the bushes. We pretend we're a pair of daredevil explorers who've discovered a giant prehistoric monster in some distant jungle and we've brought it back for the world to see. We set it down in the wooden wagon Ali built Hassan last winter for his birthday, pretend it's a giant steel cage. Behold the fire-breathing monstrosity! We march on the grass and pull the wagon behind us, around apple and cherry trees, which become skyscrapers soaring into clouds, heads poking out of thousands of windows to watch the spectacle passing below. We walk over the little semilunar bridge Baba has built near a cluster of fig trees; it becomes a great suspension bridge joining cities, and the little pond below, a foamy sea. Fireworks explode above the bridge's massive pylons and armed soldiers salute us on both sides as gigantic steel cables shoot to the sky. The little turtle bouncing around in the cab, we drag the wagon around the circular redbrick driveway outside the wrought-iron gates and return the salutes of the world's leaders as they stand and applaud. We are Hassan and Amir, famed adventurers and the world's greatest explorers, about to receive a medal of honor for our courageous feat...

GINGERLY, I WALKED up the driveway where tufts of weed now grew between the sun-faded bricks. I stood outside the gates of my father's house, feeling like a stranger. I set my hands on the rusty bars, remembering how I'd run through these same gates thousands of times as a child, for things that mattered not at all now and yet had seemed so important then. I peered in.

The driveway extension that led from the gates to the yard,

where Hassan and I took turns falling the summer we learned to ride a bike, didn't look as wide or as long as I remembered it. The asphalt had split in a lightning-streak pattern, and more tangles of weed sprouted through the fissures. Most of the poplar trees had been chopped down—the trees Hassan and I used to climb to shine our mirrors into the neighbors' homes. The ones still standing were nearly leafless. The Wall of Ailing Corn was still there, though I saw no corn, ailing or otherwise, along that wall now. The paint had begun to peel and sections of it had sloughed off altogether. The lawn had turned the same brown as the haze of dust hovering over the city, dotted by bald patches of dirt where nothing grew at all.

A jeep was parked in the driveway and that looked all wrong: Baba's black Mustang belonged there. For years, the Mustang's eight cylinders roared to life every morning, rousing me from sleep. I saw that oil had spilled under the jeep and stained the driveway like a big Rorschach inkblot. Beyond the jeep, an empty wheelbarrow lay on its side. I saw no sign of the rosebushes that Baba and Ali had planted on the left side of the driveway, only dirt that spilled onto the asphalt. And weeds.

Farid honked twice behind me. "We should go, Agha. We'll draw attention," he called.

"Just give me one more minute," I said.

The house itself was far from the sprawling white mansion I remembered from my childhood. It looked smaller. The roof sagged and the plaster was cracked. The windows to the living room, the foyer, and the upstairs guest bathroom were broken, patched haphazardly with sheets of clear plastic or wooden boards nailed across the frames. The paint, once sparkling white, had faded to ghostly gray and eroded in parts, revealing the layered bricks beneath. The front steps had crumbled. Like so much else in Kabul, my father's house was the picture of fallen splendor.

I found the window to my old bedroom, second floor, third window south of the main steps to the house. I stood on tiptoes, saw nothing behind the window but shadows. Twenty-five years earlier, I had stood behind that same window, thick rain dripping down the panes and my breath fogging up the glass. I had watched Hassan and Ali load their belongings into the trunk of my father's car.

"Amir agha," Farid called again.

"I'm coming," I shot back.

Insanely, I wanted to go in. Wanted to walk up the front steps where Ali used to make Hassan and me take off our snow boots. I wanted to step into the foyer, smell the orange peel Ali always tossed into the stove to burn with sawdust. Sit at the kitchen table, have tea with a slice of *naan*, listen to Hassan sing old Hazara songs.

Another honk. I walked back to the Land Cruiser parked along the sidewalk. Farid sat smoking behind the wheel.

"I have to look at one more thing," I told him.

"Can you hurry?"

"Give me ten minutes."

"Go, then." Then, just as I was turning to go: "Just forget it all. Makes it easier."

"To what?"

"To go on," Farid said. He flicked his cigarette out of the window. "How much more do you need to see? Let me save you the trouble: Nothing that you remember has survived. Best to forget."

"I don't want to forget anymore," I said. "Give me ten minutes."

WE HARDLY BROKE A SWEAT, Hassan and I, when we hiked up the hill just north of Baba's house. We scampered about the hilltop chasing each other or sat on a sloped ridge where there was a good view of the airport in the distance. We'd watch airplanes take off and land. Go running again.

Now, by the time I reached the top of the craggy hill, each ragged breath felt like inhaling fire. Sweat trickled down my face. I stood wheezing for a while, a stitch in my side. Then I went looking for the abandoned cemetery. It didn't take me long to find it. It was still there, and so was the old pomegranate tree.

I leaned against the gray stone gateway to the cemetery where Hassan had buried his mother. The old metal gates hanging off the hinges were gone, and the headstones were barely visible through the thick tangles of weeds that had claimed the plot. A pair of crows sat on the low wall that enclosed the cemetery.

Hassan had said in his letter that the pomegranate tree hadn't borne fruit in years. Looking at the wilted, leafless tree, I doubted it ever would again. I stood under it, remembered all the times we'd climbed it, straddled its branches, our legs swinging, dappled sunlight flickering through the leaves and casting on our faces a mosaic of light and shadow. The tangy taste of pomegranate crept into my mouth.

I hunkered down on my knees and brushed my hands against the trunk. I found what I was looking for. The carving had dulled, almost faded altogether, but it was still there: "Amir and Hassan. The Sultans of Kabul." I traced the curve of each letter with my fingers. Picked small bits of bark from the tiny crevasses.

I sat cross-legged at the foot of the tree and looked south on the city of my childhood. In those days, treetops poked behind the walls of every house. The sky stretched wide and blue, and laundry drying on clotheslines glimmered in the sun. If you listened hard, you might even have heard the call of the fruit seller passing through Wazir Akbar Khan with his donkey: *Cherries! Apricots!*

Grapes! In the early evening, you would have heard *azan,* the *mueszzin*'s call to prayer from the mosque in Shar-e-Nau.

I heard a honk and saw Farid waving at me. It was time to go.

WE DROVE SOUTH AGAIN, back toward Pashtunistan Square. We passed several more red pickup trucks with armed, bearded young men crammed into the cabs. Farid cursed under his breath every time we passed one.

I paid for a room at a small hotel near Pashtunistan Square. Three little girls dressed in identical black dresses and white scarves clung to the slight, bespectacled man behind the counter. He charged me $75, an unthinkable price given the run-down appearance of the place, but I didn't mind. Exploitation to finance a beach house in Hawaii was one thing. Doing it to feed your kids was another.

There was no hot running water and the cracked toilet didn't flush. Just a single steel-frame bed with a worn mattress, a ragged blanket, and a wooden chair in the corner. The window overlooking the square had broken, hadn't been replaced. As I lowered my suitcase, I noticed a dried bloodstain on the wall behind the bed.

I gave Farid some money and he went out to get food. He returned with four sizzling skewers of kabob, fresh *naan,* and a bowl of white rice. We sat on the bed and all but devoured the food. There *was* one thing that hadn't changed in Kabul after all: The kabob was as succulent and delicious as I remembered.

That night, I took the bed and Farid lay on the floor, wrapped himself with an extra blanket for which the hotel owner charged me an additional fee. No light came into the room except for the moonbeams streaming through the broken window. Farid said the owner had told him that Kabul had been without electricity for two days now and his generator needed fixing. We talked for a while. He told me about growing up in Mazar-i-Sharif, in Jalal-abad. He told me about a time shortly after he and his father joined the jihad and fought the *Shorawi* in the Panjsher Valley. They were stranded without food and ate locust to survive. He told me of the day helicopter gunfire killed his father, of the day the land mine took his two daughters. He asked me about America. I told him that in America you could step into a grocery store and buy any of fifteen or twenty different types of cereal. The lamb was always fresh and the milk cold, the fruit plentiful and the water clear. Every home had a TV, and every TV a remote, and you could get a satellite dish if you wanted. Receive over five hundred channels.

"Five hundred?" Farid exclaimed.

"Five hundred."

We fell silent for a while. Just when I thought he had fallen asleep, Farid chuckled. "Agha, did you hear what Mullah Nasruddin did when his daughter came home and complained that her husband had beaten her?" I could feel him smiling in the dark and a smile of my own formed on my face. There wasn't an Afghan in the world who didn't know at least a few jokes about the bumbling mullah.

"What?"

"He beat her too, then sent her back to tell the husband that Mullah was no fool: If the bastard was going to beat his daughter, then Mullah would beat his wife in return."

I laughed. Partly at the joke, partly at how Afghan humor never changed. Wars were waged, the Internet was invented, and a robot had rolled on the surface of Mars, and in Afghanistan we were still telling Mullah Nasruddin jokes. "Did you hear about the time Mullah had placed a heavy bag on his shoulders and was riding his donkey?" I said.

"No."

"Someone on the street said why don't you put the bag on the donkey? And he said, 'That would be cruel, I'm heavy enough already for the poor thing.'"

We exchanged Mullah Nasruddin jokes until we ran out of them and we fell silent again.

"Amir agha?" Farid said, startling me from near sleep.

"Yes?"

"Why are you here? I mean, why are you *really* here?"

"I told you."

"For the boy?"

"For the boy."

Farid shifted on the ground. "It's hard to believe."

"Sometimes I myself can hardly believe I'm here."

"No...What I mean to ask is why *that* boy? You come all the way from America for...a Shi'a?"

That killed all the laughter in me. And the sleep. "I am tired," I said. "Let's just get some sleep."

Farid's snoring soon echoed through the empty room. I stayed awake, hands crossed on my chest, staring into the starlit night through the broken window, and thinking that maybe what people said about Afghanistan was true. Maybe it *was* a hopeless place.

A BUSTLING CROWD was filling Ghazi Stadium when we walked through the entrance tunnels. Thousands of people milled about the tightly packed concrete terraces. Children played in the aisles and chased each other up and down the steps. The scent of garbanzo beans in spicy sauce hung in the air, mixed with the smell of dung and sweat. Farid and I walked past street peddlers selling cigarettes, pine nuts, and biscuits.

A scrawny boy in a tweed jacket grabbed my elbow and spoke into my ear. Asked me if I wanted to buy some "sexy pictures."

"Very sexy, Agha," he said, his alert eyes darting side to side—reminding me of a girl who, a few years earlier, had tried to sell me crack in the Tenderloin district in San Francisco. The kid peeled one side of his jacket open and gave me a fleeting glance of his sexy pictures: postcards of Hindi movies showing doe-eyed sultry actresses, fully dressed, in the arms of their leading men. "So sexy," he repeated.

"Nay, thanks," I said, pushing past him.

"He gets caught, they'll give him a flogging that will waken his father in the grave," Farid muttered.

There was no assigned seating, of course. No one to show us politely to our section, aisle, row, and seat. There never had been, even in the old days of the monarchy. We found a decent spot to sit, just left of midfield, though it took some shoving and elbowing on Farid's part.

I remembered how green the playing field grass had been in the '70s when Baba used to bring me to soccer games here. Now the pitch was a mess. There were holes and craters everywhere, most notably a pair of deep holes in the ground behind the south-end goalposts. And there was no grass at all, just dirt. When the two teams finally took the field—all wearing long pants despite the heat—and play began, it became difficult to follow the ball in the clouds of dust kicked up by the players. Young, whip-toting Talibs roamed the aisles, striking anyone who cheered too loudly.

They brought them out shortly after the halftime whistle blew. A pair of dusty red pickup trucks, like the ones I'd seen around town since I'd arrived, rode into the stadium through the gates. The crowd rose to its feet. A woman dressed in a green *burqa* sat in the cab of one truck, a blindfolded man in the other. The trucks drove around the track, slowly, as if to let the crowd get a long look. It had the desired effect: People craned their necks, pointed, stood on tiptoes. Next to me, Farid's Adam's apple bobbed up and down as he mumbled a prayer under his breath.

The red trucks entered the playing field, rode toward one end in twin clouds of dust, sunlight reflecting off their hubcaps. A third truck met them at the end of the field. This one's cab was filled with something and I suddenly understood the purpose of those two holes behind the goalposts. They unloaded the third truck. The crowd murmured in anticipation.

"Do you want to stay?" Farid said gravely.

"No," I said. I had never in my life wanted to be away from a place as badly as I did now. "But we have to stay."

Two Talibs with Kalashnikovs slung across their shoulders helped the blindfolded man from the first truck and two others helped the *burqa*-clad woman. The woman's knees buckled under her and she slumped to the ground. The soldiers pulled her up and she slumped again. When they tried to lift her again, she screamed and kicked. I will never, as long as I draw breath, forget the sound of that scream. It was the cry of a wild animal trying to pry its mangled leg free from the bear trap. Two more Talibs joined in and helped force her into one of the chest-deep holes. The blindfolded man, on the other hand, quietly allowed them to lower him into the hole dug for him. Now only the accused pair's torsos protruded from the ground.

A chubby, white-bearded cleric dressed in gray garments stood near the goalposts and cleared his throat into a handheld microphone. Behind him the woman in the hole was still screaming. He recited a lengthy prayer from the Koran, his nasal voice undulating through the sudden hush of the stadium's crowd. I remembered something Baba had said to me a long time ago: *Piss on the beards of all those self-righteous monkeys. They do nothing but thumb their rosaries and recite a book written in a tongue they don't even understand. God help us all if Afghanistan ever falls into their hands.*

When the prayer was done, the cleric cleared his throat. "Brothers and sisters!" he called, speaking in Farsi, his voice booming through the stadium. "We are here today to carry out *Shari'a*. We are here today to carry out justice. We are here today because the will of Allah and the word of the Prophet Muhammad, peace be upon him, are alive and well here in Afghanistan, our beloved homeland. We listen to what God says and we obey because we are nothing but humble, powerless creatures before God's greatness. And what does God say? I ask you! WHAT DOES GOD SAY? God says that every sinner must be punished in a manner befitting his sin. Those are not my words, nor the words of my brothers. Those are the words of GOD!" He pointed with his free hand to the sky. My head was pounding and the sun felt much too hot.

"Every sinner must be punished in a manner befitting his sin!" the cleric repeated into the mike, lowering his voice, enunciating each word slowly, dramatically. "And what manner of punishment, brothers and sisters, befits the adulterer? How shall we punish those who dishonor the sanctity of marriage? How shall we deal with those who spit in the face of God? How shall we answer those who throw stones at the windows of God's house? WE SHALL THROW THE STONES BACK!" He shut off the microphone. A low-pitched murmur spread through the crowd.

Next to me, Farid was shaking his head. "And they call themselves Muslims," he whispered.

Then a tall, broad-shouldered man stepped out of the pickup truck. The sight of him drew cheers from a few spectators. This time, no one was struck with a whip for cheering too loudly. The tall man's sparkling white garment glimmered in the afternoon sun. The hem of his loose shirt fluttered in the breeze, his arms spread like those of Jesus on the cross. He greeted the crowd by turning slowly in a full circle. When he faced our section, I saw he was wearing dark round sunglasses like the ones John Lennon wore.

"That must be our man," Farid said.

The tall Talib with the black sunglasses walked to the pile of stones they had unloaded from the third truck. He picked up a rock and showed it to the crowd. The noise fell, replaced by a buzzing sound that rippled through the stadium. I looked around me and saw that everyone was *tsk*'ing. The Talib, looking absurdly like a baseball pitcher on the mound, hurled the stone at the blindfolded man in the hole. It struck the side of his head. The woman screamed again. The crowd made a startled "OH!" sound. I closed my eyes and covered my face with my hands. The spectators' "OH!" rhymed with each flinging of the stone, and that went on for a while. When they stopped, I asked Farid if it was over. He said no. I guessed the people's throats had tired. I don't know how much longer I sat with my face in my hands. I know that I reopened my eyes when I heard people around me asking, *"Mord? Mord? Is he dead?"*

The man in the hole was now a mangled mess of blood and shredded rags. His head slumped forward, chin on chest. The Talib in the John Lennon sunglasses was looking down at another man squatting next to the hole, tossing a rock up and down in his hand. The squatting man had one end of a stethoscope to his ears and the other pressed on the chest of the man in the hole. He removed the stethoscope from his ears and shook his head no at the Talib in the sunglasses. The crowd moaned.

John Lennon walked back to the mound.

When it was all over, when the bloodied corpses had been unceremoniously tossed into the backs of red pickup trucks—separate ones—a few men with shovels hurriedly filled the holes. One of them made a passing attempt at covering up the large blood-stains by kicking dirt over them. A few minutes later, the teams took the field. Second half was under way.

Our meeting was arranged for three o'clock that afternoon. The swiftness with which the appointment was set surprised me. I'd expected delays, a round of questioning at least, perhaps a check of our papers. But I was reminded of how unofficial even official matters still were in Afghanistan: all Farid had to do was tell one of the whip-carrying Talibs that we had personal business to discuss with the man in white. Farid and he exchanged words. The guy with the whip then nodded and shouted something in Pashtu to a young man on the field, who ran to the south-end goalposts where the Talib in the sunglasses was chatting with the plump cleric who'd given the sermon. The three spoke. I saw the guy in the sunglasses look up. He nodded. Said something in the messenger's ear. The young man relayed the message back to us.

It was set, then. Three o'clock.

TWENTY-TWO

Farid eased the Land Cruiser up the driveway of a big house in Wazir Akbar Khan. He parked in the shadows of willow trees that spilled over the walls of the compound located on Street 15, Sarak-e-Mehmana, Street of the Guests. He killed the engine and we sat for a minute, listening to the *tink-tink* of the engine cooling off, neither one of us saying anything. Farid shifted on his seat and toyed with the keys still hanging from the ignition switch. I could tell he was readying himself to tell me something.

"I guess I'll wait in the car for you," he said finally, his tone a little apologetic. He wouldn't look at me. "This is your business now. I—"

I patted his arm. "You've done much more than I've paid you for. I don't expect you to go with me." But I wished I didn't have to go in alone. Despite what I had learned about Baba, I wished he were standing alongside me now. Baba would have busted through the front doors and demanded to be taken to the man in charge, piss on the beard of anyone who stood in his way. But Baba was long dead, buried in the Afghan section of a little cemetery in Hayward. Just last month, Soraya and I had placed a bouquet of daisies and freesias beside his headstone. I was on my own.

I stepped out of the car and walked to the tall, wooden front gates of the house. I rang the bell but no buzz came—still no electricity—and I had to pound on the doors. A moment later, I heard terse voices from the other side and a pair of men toting Kalashnikovs answered the door.

I glanced at Farid sitting in the car and mouthed, *I'll be back,* not so sure at all that I would be.

The armed men frisked me head to toe, patted my legs, felt my crotch. One of them said something in Pashtu and they both chuckled. We stepped through the front gates. The two guards escorted me across a well-manicured lawn, past a row of geraniums and stubby bushes lined along the wall. An old hand-pump water well stood at the far end of the yard. I remembered how Kaka Homayoun's house in Jalalabad had had a water well like that—the twins, Fazila and Karima, and I used to drop pebbles in it, listen for the *plink.*

We climbed a few steps and entered a large, sparsely decorated house. We crossed the foyer—a large Afghan flag draped one of the walls—and the men took me upstairs to a room with twin mint green sofas and a big-screen TV in the far corner. A prayer rug showing a slightly oblong Mecca was nailed to one of the walls. The older of the two men motioned toward the sofa with the barrel of his weapon. I sat down. They left the room.

I crossed my legs. Uncrossed them. Sat with my sweaty hands on my knees. Did that make me look nervous? I clasped them together, decided that was worse and just crossed my arms on my chest. Blood thudded in my temples. I felt utterly alone. Thoughts were flying around in my head, but I didn't want to think at all, because a sober part of me knew that what I had managed to get myself into was insanity. I was thousands of miles from my wife, sitting in a room that felt like a holding cell, waiting for a man I had seen murder two people that same day. It *was* insanity. Worse yet, it was irresponsible. There was a very realistic chance that I was going to render Soraya a *biwa*, a widow, at the age of thirty-six. *This isn't you, Amir,* part of me said. *You're gutless. It's how you were made. And that's not such a bad thing because your saving grace is that you've never lied to yourself about it. Not about that. Nothing wrong with cowardice as long as it comes with prudence. But when a coward stops remembering who he is . . . God help him.*

There was a coffee table by the sofa. The base was X-shaped, walnut-sized brass balls studding the ring where the metallic legs crossed. I'd seen a table like that before. Where? And then it came to me: at the crowded tea shop in Peshawar, that night I'd gone for a walk. On the table sat a bowl of red grapes. I plucked one and tossed it in my mouth. I had to preoccupy myself with something, anything, to silence the voice in my head. The grape was sweet. I popped another one in, unaware that it would be the last bit of solid food I would eat for a long time.

The door opened and the two armed men returned, between them the tall Talib in white, still wearing his dark John Lennon glasses, looking like some broad-shouldered, New Age mystic guru.

He took a seat across from me and lowered his hands on the armrests. For a long time, he said nothing. Just sat there, watching me, one hand drumming the upholstery, the other twirling turquoise blue prayer beads. He wore a black vest over the white shirt now, and a gold watch. I saw a splotch of dried blood on his left sleeve. I found it morbidly fascinating that he hadn't changed clothes after the executions earlier that day.

Periodically, his free hand floated up and his thick fingers batted at something in the air. They made slow stroking motions, up and down, side to side, as if he were caressing an invisible pet. One of his sleeves retracted and I saw marks on his forearm—I'd seen those same tracks on homeless people living in grimy alleys in San Francisco.

His skin was much paler than the other two men's, almost sallow, and a crop of tiny sweat beads gleamed on his forehead just below the edge of his black turban. His beard, chest-length like the others, was lighter in color too.

"*Salaam alaykum,*" he said.

"*Salaam.*"

"You can do away with that now, you know," he said.

"Pardon?"

He turned his palm to one of the armed men and motioned. *Rrrriiiip.* Suddenly my cheeks were stinging and the guard was tossing my beard up and down in his hand, giggling. The Talib grinned. "One of the better ones I've seen in a while. But it really is so much better this way, I think. Don't you?" He twirled his fingers, snapped them, fist opening and closing. "So, *Inshallah,* you enjoyed the show today?"

"Was that what it was?" I said, rubbing my cheeks, hoping my voice didn't betray the explosion of terror I felt inside.

"Public justice is the greatest kind of show, my brother. Drama. Suspense. And, best of all, education en masse." He snapped his fingers. The younger of the two guards lit him a cigarette. The Talib laughed. Mumbled to himself. His hands were shaking and he almost dropped the cigarette. "But you want a real show, you should have been with me in Mazar. August 1998, that was."

"I'm sorry?"

"We left them out for the dogs, you know."

I saw what he was getting at.

He stood up, paced around the sofa once, twice. Sat down again. He spoke rapidly. "Door to door we went, calling for the men and the boys. We'd shoot them right there in front of their families. Let them see. Let them remember who they were, where they belonged." He was almost panting now. "Sometimes, we broke down their doors and went inside their homes. And . . . I'd . . . I'd sweep the barrel of my machine gun around the room and fire and fire until the smoke blinded me." He leaned toward me, like a man about to share a great secret. "You don't know the meaning of the word 'liberating' until you've done that, stood in a roomful of targets, let the bullets fly, free of guilt and remorse, knowing you are virtuous, good, and decent. Knowing you're doing God's work. It's breathtaking." He kissed the prayer beads, tilted his head. "You remember that, Javid?"

"Yes, Agha sahib," the younger of the guards replied. "How could I forget?"

I had read about the Hazara massacre in Mazar-i-Sharif in the papers. It had happened just after the Taliban took over Mazar, one of the last cities to fall. I remembered Soraya handing me the article over breakfast, her face bloodless.

"Door-to-door. We only rested for food and prayer," the Talib said. He said it fondly, like a man telling of a great party he'd attended. "We left the bodies in the streets, and if their families tried to sneak out to drag them back into their homes, we'd shoot them too. We left them in the streets for days. We left them for the dogs. Dog meat for dogs." He crushed his cigarette. Rubbed his eyes with tremulous hands. "You come from America?"

"Yes."

"How is that whore these days?"

I had a sudden urge to urinate. I prayed it would pass. "I'm looking for a boy."

"Isn't everyone?" he said. The men with the Kalashnikovs laughed. Their teeth were stained green with *naswar*.

"I understand he is here, with you," I said. "His name is Sohrab."

"I'll ask you something: What are you doing with that whore? Why aren't you here, with your Muslim brothers, serving your country?"

"I've been away a long time," was all I could think of saying. My head felt so hot. I pressed my knees together, held my bladder.

The Talib turned to the two men standing by the door. "That's an answer?" he asked them.

"Nay, Agha sahib," they said in unison, smiling.

He turned his eyes to me. Shrugged. "Not an answer, they say." He took a drag of his cigarette. "There are those in my circle who believe that abandoning *watan* when it needs you the most is the same as treason. I could have you arrested for treason, have you shot for it even. Does that frighten you?"

"I'm only here for the boy."

"Does that frighten you?"

"Yes."

"It should," he said. He leaned back in the sofa. Crushed the cigarette.

I thought about Soraya. It calmed me. I thought of her sickle-shaped birthmark, the elegant curve of her neck, her luminous eyes. I thought of our wedding night, gazing at each other's reflection in the mirror under the green veil, and how her cheeks blushed when I whispered that I loved her. I remembered the two of us dancing to an old Afghan song, round and round, everyone watching and clapping, the world a blur of flowers, dresses, tuxedos, and smiling faces.

The Talib was saying something.

"Pardon?"

"I said would you like to see him? Would you like to see my boy?" His upper lip curled up in a sneer when he said those last two words.

"Yes."

The guard left the room. I heard the creak of a door swinging open. Heard the guard say something in Pashtu, in a hard voice. Then, footfalls, and the jingle of bells with each step. It reminded me of the Monkey Man Hassan and I used to chase down in Share-Nau. We used to pay him a *rupia* of our allowance for a dance. The bell around his monkey's neck had made that same jingling sound.

Then the door opened and the guard walked in. He carried a stereo—a boom box—on his shoulder. Behind him, a boy dressed in a loose, sapphire blue *pirhan-tumban* followed.

The resemblance was breathtaking. Disorienting. Rahim Khan's Polaroid hadn't done justice to it.

The boy had his father's round moon face, his pointy stub of a chin, his twisted, seashell ears, and the same slight frame. It was the Chinese doll face of my childhood, the face peering above fanned-out playing cards all those winter days, the face behind the mosquito net when we slept on the roof of my father's house in the summer. His head was shaved, his eyes darkened with mascara, and his cheeks glowed with an unnatural red. When he stopped in the middle of the room, the bells strapped around his anklets stopped jingling.

His eyes fell on me. Lingered. Then he looked away. Looked down at his naked feet.

One of the guards pressed a button and Pashtu music filled the room. Tabla, harmonium, the whine of a *dil-roba*. I guessed music wasn't sinful as long as it played to Taliban ears. The three men began to clap.

"*Wah wah! Mashallah!*" they cheered.

Sohrab raised his arms and turned slowly. He stood on tiptoes, spun gracefully, dipped to his knees, straightened, and spun again. His little hands swiveled at the wrists, his fingers snapped, and his head swung side to side like a pendulum. His feet pounded the floor, the bells jingling in perfect harmony with the beat of the tabla. He kept his eyes closed.

"*Mashallah!*" they cheered. "*Shahbas!* Bravo!" The two guards whistled and laughed. The Talib in white was tilting his head back and forth with the music, his mouth half-open in a leer.

Sohrab danced in a circle, eyes closed, danced until the music stopped. The bells jingled one final time when he stomped his foot with the song's last note. He froze in midspin.

"*Bia, bia,* my boy," the Talib said, calling Sohrab to him. Sohrab went to him, head down, stood between his thighs. The Talib wrapped his arms around the boy. "How talented he is, nay, my Hazara boy!" he said. His hands slid down the child's back, then up, felt under his armpits. One of the guards elbowed the other and snickered. The Talib told them to leave us alone.

"Yes, Agha sahib," they said as they exited.

The Talib spun the boy around so he faced me. He locked his arms around Sohrab's belly, rested his chin on the boy's shoulder. Sohrab looked down at his feet, but kept stealing shy, furtive glances at me. The man's hand slid up and down the boy's belly. Up and down, slowly, gently.

"I've been wondering," the Talib said, his bloodshot eyes peering at me over Sohrab's shoulder. "Whatever happened to old *Babalu,* anyway?"

The question hit me like a hammer between the eyes. I felt the color drain from my face. My legs went cold. Numb.

He laughed. "What did you think? That you'd put on a fake beard and I wouldn't recognize you? Here's something I'll bet you never knew about me: I never forget a face. Not ever." He brushed his lips against Sohrab's ear, kept his eye on me. "I heard your father died. *Tsk-tsk.* I always did want to take him on. Looks like I'll have to settle for his weakling of a son." Then he took off his sunglasses and locked his bloodshot blue eyes on mine.

I tried to take a breath and couldn't. I tried to blink and couldn't. The moment felt surreal—no, not surreal, *absurd*—it had knocked the breath out of me, brought the world around me to a standstill. My face was burning. What was the old saying about the bad penny? My past was like that, always turning up. His name rose from the deep and I didn't want to say it, as if uttering it might conjure him. But he was already here, in the flesh, sitting less than ten feet from me, after all these years. His name escaped my lips: "Assef."

"Amir jan."

"What are you doing here?" I said, knowing how utterly foolish the question sounded, yet unable to think of anything else to say.

"Me?" Assef arched an eyebrow. "I'm in my element. The question is what are you doing here?"

"I already told you," I said. My voice was trembling. I wished it wouldn't do that, wished my flesh wasn't shrinking against my bones.

"The boy?"

"Yes."

"Why?"

"I'll pay you for him," I said. "I can have money wired."

"Money?" Assef said. He tittered. "Have you ever heard of Rockingham? Western Australia, a slice of heaven. You should see it, miles and miles of beach. Green water, blue skies. My parents live there, in a beachfront villa. There's a golf course behind the villa and a little lake. Father plays golf every day. Mother, she prefers tennis—Father says she has a wicked backhand. They own an Afghan restaurant and two jewelry stores; both businesses are doing spectacularly." He plucked a red grape. Put it, lovingly, in Sohrab's mouth. "So if I need money, I'll have *them* wire it to me." He kissed the side of Sohrab's neck. The boy flinched a little, closed his eyes again. "Besides, I didn't fight the *Shorawi* for money. Didn't join the Taliban for money either. Do you want to know why I joined them?"

My lips had gone dry. I licked them and found my tongue had dried too.

"Are you thirsty?" Assef said, smirking.

"No."

"I think you're thirsty."

"I'm fine," I said. The truth was, the room felt too hot suddenly—sweat was bursting from my pores, prickling my skin. And was this really happening? Was I really sitting across from Assef?

"As you wish," he said. "Anyway, where was I? Oh yes, how I joined the Taliban. Well, as you may remember, I wasn't much of a religious type. But one day I had an epiphany. I had it in jail. Do you want to hear?"

I said nothing.

"Good. I'll tell you," he said. "I spent some time in jail, at Poleh-Charkhi, just after Babrak Karmal took over in 1980. I ended up there one night, when a group of *Parchami* soldiers marched into our house and ordered my father and me at gunpoint to follow them. The bastards didn't give a reason, and they wouldn't answer my mother's questions. Not that it was a mystery; everyone knew the communists had no class. They came from poor families with no name. The same dogs who weren't fit to lick my shoes before the *Shorawi* came were now ordering me at gunpoint, *Parchami* flag on their lapels, making their little point about the fall of the bourgeoisie and acting like they were the ones with class. It was happening all over: Round up the rich, throw them in jail, make an example for the comrades.

"Anyway, we were crammed in groups of six in these tiny cells each the size of a refrigerator. Every night the commandant, a half-Hazara, half-Uzbek thing who smelled like a rotting donkey, would have one of the prisoners dragged out of the cell and he'd beat him until sweat poured from his fat face. Then he'd light a cigarette, crack his joints, and leave. The next night, he'd pick someone else. One night, he picked me. It couldn't have come at a worse time. I'd been peeing blood for three days. Kidney stones. And if you've never had one, believe me when I say it's the worst imaginable pain. My mother used to get them too, and I remember she told me once she'd rather give birth than pass a kidney stone. Anyway, what could I do? They dragged me out and he started kicking me. He had knee-high boots with steel toes that he wore every night for his little kicking game, and he used them on me. I was screaming and screaming and he kept kicking me and then, suddenly, he kicked me on the left kidney and the stone passed. Just like that! Oh, the relief!" Assef laughed. "And I yelled '*Allah-u-akbar*' and he kicked me even harder and I started laughing. He got mad and hit me harder, and the harder he kicked me, the harder I laughed. They threw me back in the cell laughing. I kept laughing and laughing because suddenly I knew that had been a message from God: He was on *my* side. He wanted me to live for a reason.

"You know, I ran into that commandant on the battlefield a few years later—funny how God works. I found him in a trench just outside Meymanah, bleeding from a piece of shrapnel in his chest. He was still wearing those same boots. I asked him if he remembered me. He said no. I told him the same thing I just told you, that I never forget a face. Then I shot him in the balls. I've been on a mission since."

"What mission is that?" I heard myself say. "Stoning adulterers? Raping children? Flogging women for wearing high heels? Massacring Hazaras? All in the name of Islam?" The words spilled suddenly and unexpectedly, came out before I could yank the leash. I wished I could take them back. Swallow them. But they were out. I had crossed a line, and whatever little hope I had of getting out alive had vanished with those words.

A look of surprise passed across Assef's face, briefly, and disappeared. "I see this may turn out to be enjoyable after all," he said, snickering. "But there are things traitors like you don't understand."

"Like what?"

Assef's brow twitched. "Like pride in your people, your customs, your language. Afghanistan is like a beautiful mansion littered with garbage, and someone has to take out the garbage."

"That's what you were doing in Mazar, going door-to-door? Taking out the garbage?"

"Precisely."

"In the west, they have an expression for that," I said. "They call it ethnic cleansing."

"Do they?" Assef's face brightened. "Ethnic cleansing. I like it. I like the sound of it."

"All I want is the boy."

"Ethnic cleansing," Assef murmured, tasting the words.

"I want the boy," I said again. Sohrab's eyes flicked to me. They were slaughter sheep's eyes. They even had the mascara—I remembered how, on the day of *Eid* of *qorban*, the mullah in our backyard used to apply mascara to the eyes of the sheep and feed it a cube of sugar before slicing its throat. I thought I saw pleading in Sohrab's eyes.

"Tell me why," Assef said. He pinched Sohrab's earlobe between his teeth. Let go. Sweat beads rolled down his brow.

"That's my business."

"What do you want to do with him?" he said. Then a coy smile. "Or *to* him."

"That's disgusting," I said.

"How would you know? Have you tried it?"

"I want to take him to a better place."

"Tell me why."

"That's my business," I said. I didn't know what had emboldened me to be so curt, maybe the fact that I thought I was going to die anyway.

"I wonder," Assef said. "I wonder why you've come all this way, Amir, come all this way for a Hazara? Why are you here? Why are you *really* here?"

"I have my reasons," I said.

"Very well then," Assef said, sneering. He shoved Sohrab in the back, pushed him right into the table. Sohrab's hips struck the table, knocking it upside down and spilling the grapes. He fell on them, face first, and stained his shirt purple with grape juice. The table's legs, crossing through the ring of brass balls, were now pointing to the ceiling.

"Take him, then," Assef said. I helped Sohrab to his feet, swatted the bits of crushed grape that had stuck to his pants like barnacles to a pier.

"Go, take him," Assef said, pointing to the door.

I took Sohrab's hand. It was small, the skin dry and calloused. His fingers moved, laced themselves with mine. I saw Sohrab in that Polaroid again, the way his arm was wrapped around Hassan's leg, his head resting against his father's hip. They'd both been smiling. The bells jingled as we crossed the room.

We made it as far as the door.

"Of course," Assef said behind us, "I didn't say you could take him for free."

I turned. "What do you want?"

"You have to earn him."

"What do you want?"

"We have some unfinished business, you and I," Assef said. "You remember, don't you?"

He needn't have worried. I would never forget the day after Daoud Khan overthrew the king. My entire adult life, whenever I heard Daoud Khan's name, what I saw was Hassan with his slingshot pointed at Assef's face, Hassan saying that they'd have to start calling him One-Eyed Assef instead of Assef *Goshkhor*. I remember how envious I'd been of Hassan's bravery. Assef had backed down, promised that in the end he'd get us both. He'd kept that promise with Hassan. Now it was my turn.

"All right," I said, not knowing what else there was to say. I wasn't about to beg; that would have only sweetened the moment for him.

Assef called the guards back into the room. "I want you to listen to me," he said to them. "In a moment, I'm going to close the door. Then he and I are going to finish an old bit of business. No matter what you hear, don't come in! Do you hear me? Don't come in!"

The guards nodded. Looked from Assef to me. "Yes, Agha sahib."

"When it's all done, only one of us will walk out of this room alive," Assef said. "If it's him, then he's earned his freedom and you let him pass, do you understand?"

The older guard shifted on his feet. "But Agha sahib—"

"If it's him, you let him pass!" Assef screamed. The two men flinched but nodded again. They turned to go. One of them reached for Sohrab.

"Let him stay," Assef said. He grinned. "Let him watch. Lessons are good things for boys."

The guards left. Assef put down his prayer beads. Reached in the breast pocket of his black vest. What he fished out of that pocket didn't surprise me one bit: stainless-steel brass knuckles.

HE HAS GEL IN HIS HAIR and a Clark Gable mustache above his thick lips. The gel has soaked through the green paper surgical cap, made a dark stain the shape of Africa. I remember that about him. That, and the gold Allah chain around his dark neck. He is peering down at me, speaking rapidly in a language I don't understand, Urdu, I think. My eyes keep going to his Adam's apple bobbing up and down, up and down, and I want to ask him how old he is anyway—he looks far too young, like an actor from some foreign soap opera—but all I can mutter is, I think I gave him a good fight. I think I gave him a good fight.

. . .

I DON'T KNOW if I gave Assef a good fight. I don't think I did. How could I have? That was the first time I'd fought anyone. I had never so much as thrown a punch in my entire life.

My memory of the fight with Assef is amazingly vivid in stretches: I remember Assef turning on the music before slipping on his brass knuckles. The prayer rug, the one with the oblong, woven Mecca, came loose from the wall at one point and landed on my head; the dust from it made me sneeze. I remember Assef shoving grapes in my face, his snarl all spit-shining teeth, his bloodshot eyes rolling. His turban fell at some point, let loose curls of shoulder-length blond hair.

And the end, of course. That, I still see with perfect clarity. I always will.

Mostly, I remember this: His brass knuckles flashing in the afternoon light; how cold they felt with the first few blows and how quickly they warmed with my blood. Getting thrown against the wall, a nail where a framed picture may have hung once jabbing at my back. Sohrab screaming. Tabla, harmonium, a *dil-roba.* Getting hurled against the wall. The knuckles shattering my jaw. Choking on my own teeth, swallowing them, thinking about all the countless hours I'd spent flossing and brushing. Getting hurled against the wall. Lying on the floor, blood from my split upper lip staining the mauve carpet, pain ripping through my belly, and wondering when I'd be able to breathe again. The sound of my ribs snapping like the tree branches Hassan and I used to break to swordfight like Sinbad in those old movies. Sohrab screaming. The side of my face slamming against the corner of the television stand. That snapping sound again, this time just under my left eye. Music. Sohrab screaming. Fingers grasping my hair, pulling my head back, the twinkle of stainless steel. Here they come. That snapping sound yet again, now my nose. Biting down in pain, noticing how my teeth didn't align like they used to. Getting kicked. Sohrab screaming.

I don't know at what point I started laughing, but I did. It hurt to laugh, hurt my jaws, my ribs, my throat. But I was laughing and laughing. And the harder I laughed, the harder he kicked me, punched me, scratched me.

"WHAT'S SO FUNNY?" Assef kept roaring with each blow. His spittle landed in my eye. Sohrab screamed.

"WHAT'S SO FUNNY?" Assef bellowed. Another rib snapped, this time left lower. What was so funny was that, for the first time since the winter of 1975, I felt at peace. I laughed because I saw that, in some hidden nook in a corner of my mind, I'd even been looking forward to this. I remembered the day on the hill I had pelted Hassan with pomegranates and tried to provoke him. He'd just stood there, doing nothing, red juice soaking through his shirt like blood. Then he'd taken the pomegranate from my hand, crushed it against his forehead. *Are you satisfied now?* he'd hissed. *Do you feel better?* I hadn't been happy and I hadn't felt better, not at all. But I did now. My body was broken—just how badly I wouldn't find out until later—but I felt *healed*. Healed at last. I laughed.

Then the end. That, I'll take to my grave:

I was on the ground laughing, Assef straddling my chest, his face a mask of lunacy, framed by snarls of his hair swaying inches from my face. His free hand was locked around my throat. The other, the one with the brass knuckles, cocked above his shoulder. He raised his fist higher, raised it for another blow.

Then: *"Bas."* A thin voice.

We both looked.

"Please, no more."

I remembered something the orphanage director had said when he'd opened the door to me and Farid. What had been his name? Zaman? *He's inseparable from that thing,* he had said. *He tucks it in the waist of his pants everywhere he goes.*

"No more."

Twin trails of black mascara, mixed with tears, had rolled down his cheeks, smeared the rouge. His lower lip trembled. Mucus seeped from his nose. *"Bas,"* he croaked.

His hand was cocked above his shoulder, holding the cup of the slingshot at the end of the elastic band which was pulled all the way back. There was something in the cup, something shiny and yellow. I blinked the blood from my eyes and saw it was one of the brass balls from the ring in the table base. Sohrab had the slingshot pointed to Assef's face.

"No more, Agha. Please," he said, his voice husky and trembling. "Stop hurting him."

Assef's mouth moved wordlessly. He began to say something, stopped. "What do you think you're you doing?" he finally said.

"Please stop," Sohrab said, fresh tears pooling in his green eyes, mixing with mascara.

"Put it down, Hazara," Assef hissed. "Put it down or what I'm doing to him will be a gentle ear twisting compared to what I'll do to you."

The tears broke free. Sohrab shook his head. "Please, Agha," he said. "Stop."

"Put it down."

"Don't hurt him anymore."

"Put it down."

"Please."

"PUT IT DOWN!"

"Bas."

"PUT IT DOWN!" Assef let go of my throat. Lunged at Sohrab.

The slingshot made a *thwiiiiit* sound when Sohrab released the cup. Then Assef was screaming. He put his hand where his left eye had been just a moment ago. Blood oozed between his fingers. Blood and something else, something white and gel-like. *That's called vitreous fluid,* I thought with clarity. *I've read that somewhere. Vitreous fluid.*

Assef rolled on the carpet. Rolled side to side, shrieking, his hand still cupped over the bloody socket.

"Let's go!" Sohrab said. He took my hand. Helped me to my feet. Every inch of my battered body wailed with pain. Behind us, Assef kept shrieking.

"OUT! GET IT OUT!" he screamed.

Teetering, I opened the door. The guards' eyes widened when they saw me and I wondered what I looked like. My stomach hurt with each breath. One of the guards said something in Pashtu and then they blew past us, running into the room where Assef was still screaming. "OUT!"

"Bia," Sohrab said, pulling my hand. "Let's go!"

I stumbled down the hallway, Sohrab's little hand in mine. I took a final look over my shoulder. The guards were huddled over Assef, doing something to his face. Then I understood: The brass ball was still stuck in his empty eye socket.

The whole world rocking up and down, swooping side to side, I hobbled down the steps, leaning on Sohrab. From above, Assef's screams went on and on, the cries of a wounded animal. We made it outside, into daylight, my arm around Sohrab's shoulder, and I saw Farid running toward us.

"Bismillah! Bismillah!" he said, eyes bulging at the sight of me.

He slung my arm around his shoulder and lifted me. Carried me
to the truck, running. I think I screamed. I watched the way his
sandals pounded the pavement, slapped his black, calloused heels.
It hurt to breathe. Then I was looking up at the roof of the Land
Cruiser, in the backseat, the upholstery beige and ripped, listening to the *ding-ding-ding* signaling an open door. Running footsteps around the truck. Farid and Sohrab exchanging quick words.
The truck's doors slammed shut and the engine roared to life. The
car jerked forward and I felt a tiny hand on my forehead. I heard
voices on the street, some shouting, and saw trees blurring past in
the window. Sohrab was sobbing. Farid was still repeating, *"Bismillah! Bismillah!"*

It was about then that I passed out.

TWENTY-THREE

Faces poke through the haze, linger, fade away. They peer down, ask me questions. They all ask questions. Do I know who I am? Do I hurt anywhere? I know who I am and I hurt everywhere. I want to tell them this but talking hurts. I know this because some time ago, maybe a year ago, maybe two, maybe ten, I tried to talk to a child with rouge on his cheeks and eyes smeared black. The child. Yes, I see him now. We are in a car of sorts, the child and I, and I don't think Soraya's driving because Soraya never drives this fast. I want to say something to this child—it seems very important that I do. But I don't remember what I want to say, or why it might have been important. Maybe I want to tell him to stop crying, that everything will be all right now. Maybe not. For some reason I can't think of, I want to thank the child.

Faces. They're all wearing green hats. They slip in and out of view. They talk rapidly, use words I don't understand. I hear other voices, other noises, beeps and alarms. And always more faces. Peering down. I don't remember any of them, except for the one with the gel in his hair and the Clark Gable mustache, the one with the Africa stain on his cap. Mister Soap Opera Star. That's funny. I want to laugh now. But laughing hurts too.

I fade out.

SHE SAYS HER NAME IS AISHA, "like the prophet's wife." Her graying hair is parted in the middle and tied in a ponytail, her nose pierced with a stud shaped like the sun. She wears bifocals that make her eyes bug out. She wears green too and her hands are soft. She sees me looking at her and smiles. Says something in English. Something is jabbing at the side of my chest.

I fade out.

A MAN IS STANDING at my bedside. I know him. He is dark and lanky, has a long beard. He wears a hat—what are those hats called? *Pakols?* Wears it tilted to one side like a famous person whose name escapes me now. I know this man. He drove me somewhere a few years ago. I know him. There is something wrong with my mouth. I hear a bubbling sound.

I fade out.

MY RIGHT ARM BURNS. The woman with the bifocals and sun-shaped stud is hunched over my arm, attaching a clear plastic tubing to it. She says it's "the Potassium." "It stings like a bee, no?" she says. It does. What's her name? Something to do with a prophet. I know her too from a few years ago. She used to wear her hair in a ponytail. Now it's pulled back, tied in a bun. Soraya wore her hair like that the first time we spoke. When was that? Last week?

Aisha! Yes.

There is something wrong with my mouth. And that thing jabbing at my chest.

I fade out.

WE ARE IN THE SULAIMAN MOUNTAINS of Baluchistan and Baba is wrestling the black bear. He is the Baba of my childhood, *Toophan agha*, the towering specimen of Pashtun might, not the withered man under the blankets, the man with the sunken cheeks and hollow eyes. They roll over a patch of green grass, man and beast, Baba's curly brown hair flying. The bear roars, or maybe it's Baba. Spittle and blood fly; claw and hand swipe. They fall to the ground with a loud thud and Baba is sitting on the bear's chest, his fingers digging in its snout. He looks up at me and I see. He's me. I am wrestling the bear.

I wake up. The lanky, dark man is back at my bedside. His name is Farid, I remember now. And with him is the child from the car. His face reminds me of the sound of bells. I am thirsty.

I fade out.

I keep fading in and out.

THE NAME OF THE MAN with the Clark Gable mustache turned out to be Dr. Faruqi. He wasn't a soap opera star at all, but a head-and-neck surgeon, though I kept thinking of him as someone named Armand in some steamy soap set on a tropical island.

Where am I? I wanted to ask. But my mouth wouldn't open. I frowned. Grunted. Armand smiled; his teeth were blinding white.

"Not yet, Amir," he said, "but soon. When the wires are out."
He spoke English with a thick, rolling Urdu accent.

Wires?

Armand crossed his arms; he had hairy forearms and wore a
gold wedding band. "You must be wondering where you are, what
happened to you. That's perfectly normal, the postsurgical state is
always disorienting. So I'll tell you what I know."

I wanted to ask him about the wires. Postsurgical? Where was
Aisha? I wanted her to smile at me, wanted her soft hands in mine.

Armand frowned, cocked one eyebrow in a slightly self-
important way. "You are in a hospital in Peshawar. You've been
here two days. You have suffered some very significant injuries,
Amir, I should tell you. I would say you're very lucky to be alive, my
friend." He swayed his index finger back and forth like a pendulum when he said this. "Your spleen had ruptured, probably—and
fortunately for you—a delayed rupture, because you had signs of
early hemorrhage into your abdominal cavity. My colleagues from
the general surgery unit had to perform an emergency splenec-
tomy. If it had ruptured earlier, you would have bled to death." He
patted me on the arm, the one with the IV, and smiled. "You also
suffered seven broken ribs. One of them caused a pneumothorax."

I frowned. Tried to open my mouth. Remembered about the
wires.

"That means a punctured lung," Armand explained. He tugged
at a clear plastic tubing on my left side. I felt the jabbing again in
my chest. "We sealed the leak with this chest tube." I followed the
tube poking through bandages on my chest to a container half-
filled with columns of water. The bubbling sound came from there.

"You had also suffered various lacerations. That means 'cuts.' "

I wanted to tell him I knew what the word meant; I was a writer. I went to open my mouth. Forgot about the wires again.

"The worst laceration was on your upper lip," Armand said. "The impact had cut your upper lip in two, clean down the middle. But not to worry, the plastics guys sewed it back together and they think you will have an excellent result, though there will be a scar. That is unavoidable.

"There was also an orbital fracture on the left side; that's the eye socket bone, and we had to fix that too. The wires in your jaws will come out in about six weeks," Armand said. "Until then it's liquids and shakes. You will lose some weight and you will be talking like Al Pacino from the first *Godfather* movie for a little while." He laughed. "But you have a job to do today. Do you know what it is?"

I shook my head.

"Your job today is to pass gas. You do that and we can start feeding you liquids. No fart, no food." He laughed again.

Later, after Aisha changed the IV tubing and raised the head of the bed like I'd asked, I thought about what had happened to me. Ruptured spleen. Broken teeth. Punctured lung. Busted eye socket. But as I watched a pigeon peck at a bread crumb on the windowsill, I kept thinking of something else Armand/Dr. Faruqi had said: *The impact had cut your upper lip in two,* he had said, *clean down the middle.* Clean down the middle. Like a harelip.

FARID AND SOHRAB came to visit the next day. "Do you know who we are today? Do you remember?" Farid said, only half-jokingly. I nodded.

"*Al hamdullellah!*" he said, beaming. "No more talking nonsense."

"Thank you, Farid," I said through jaws wired shut. Armand was right—I did sound like Al Pacino from *The Godfather.* And my tongue surprised me every time it poked in one of the empty spaces left by the teeth I had swallowed. "I mean, thank you. For everything."

He waved a hand, blushed a little. "*Bas,* it's not worthy of thanks," he said. I turned to Sohrab. He was wearing a new outfit, light brown *pirhan-tumban* that looked a bit big for him, and a black skullcap. He was looking down at his feet, toying with the IV line coiled on the bed.

"We were never properly introduced," I said. I offered him my hand. "I am Amir."

He looked at my hand, then to me. "You are the Amir agha Father told me about?" he said.

"Yes." I remembered the words from Hassan's letter. *I have told much about you to Farzana jan and Sohrab, about us growing up together and playing games and running in the streets. They laugh at the stories of all the mischief you and I used to cause!* "I owe you thanks too, Sohrab jan," I said. "You saved my life."

He didn't say anything. I dropped my hand when he didn't take it. "I like your new clothes," I mumbled.

"They're my son's," Farid said. "He has outgrown them. They fit Sohrab pretty well, I would say." Sohrab could stay with him, he said, until we found a place for him. "We don't have a lot of room, but what can I do? I can't leave him to the streets. Besides, my children have taken a liking to him. *Ha,* Sohrab?" But the boy just kept looking down, twirling the line with his finger.

"I've been meaning to ask," Farid said, a little hesitantly. "What happened in that house? What happened between you and the Talib?"

"Let's just say we both got what we deserved," I said.

Farid nodded, didn't push it. It occurred to me that somewhere between the time we had left Peshawar for Afghanistan and now, we had become friends. "I've been meaning to ask something too."

"What?"

I didn't want to ask. I was afraid of the answer. "Rahim Khan," I said.

"He's gone."

My heart skipped. "Is he—"

"No, just . . . gone." He handed me a folded piece of paper and a small key. "The landlord gave me this when I went looking for him. He said Rahim Khan left the day after we did."

"Where did he go?"

Farid shrugged. "The landlord didn't know. He said Rahim Khan left the letter and the key for you and took his leave." He checked his watch. "I'd better go. *Bia*, Sohrab."

"Could you leave him here for a while?" I said. "Pick him up later?" I turned to Sohrab. "Do you want to stay here with me for a little while?"

He shrugged and said nothing.

"Of course," Farid said. "I'll pick him up just before evening *namaz*."

THERE WERE THREE OTHER PATIENTS in my room. Two older men, one with a cast on his leg, the other wheezing with asthma, and a young man of fifteen or sixteen who'd had appendix surgery. The old guy in the cast stared at us without blinking, his eyes switching from me to the Hazara boy sitting on a stool. My roommates' families—old women in bright *shalwar-kameez*es, children, men wearing skullcaps—shuffled noisily in and out of the room. They brought with them *pakora*s, *naan, samosa*s, *biryani.* Sometimes people just wandered into the room, like the tall, bearded man who walked in just before Farid and Sohrab arrived. He wore a brown blanket wrapped around him. Aisha asked him something in Urdu. He paid her no attention and scanned the room with his eyes. I thought he looked at me a little longer than necessary. When the nurse spoke to him again, he just spun around and left.

"How are you?" I asked Sohrab. He shrugged, looked at his hands.

"Are you hungry? That lady there gave me a plate of *biryani,* but I can't eat it," I said. I didn't know what else to say to him. "You want it?"

He shook his head.

"Do you want to talk?"

He shook his head again.

We sat there like that for a while, silent, me propped up in bed, two pillows behind my back, Sohrab on the three-legged stool next to the bed. I fell asleep at some point, and, when I woke up, daylight had dimmed a bit, the shadows had stretched, and Sohrab was still sitting next to me. He was still looking down at his hands.

THAT NIGHT, after Farid picked up Sohrab, I unfolded Rahim Khan's letter. I had delayed reading it as long as possible. It read:

> Amir jan,
> *Inshallah,* you have reached this letter safely. I pray that I have not put you in harm's way and that Afghanistan has not been too unkind to you. You have been in my prayers since the day you left.

You were right all those years to suspect that I knew. I did know. Hassan told me shortly after it happened. What you did was wrong, Amir jan, but do not forget that you were a boy when it happened. A troubled little boy. You were too hard on yourself then, and you still are—I saw it in your eyes in Peshawar. But I hope you will heed this: A man who has no conscience, no goodness, does not suffer. I hope your suffering comes to an end with this journey to Afghanistan.

Amir jan, I am ashamed for the lies we told you all those years. You were right to be angry in Peshawar. You had a right to know. So did Hassan. I know it doesn't absolve anyone of anything, but the Kabul we lived in in those days was a strange world, one in which some things mattered more than the truth.

Amir jan, I know how hard your father was on you when you were growing up. I saw how you suffered and yearned for his affections, and my heart bled for you. But your father was a man torn between two halves, Amir jan: you and Hassan. He loved you both, but he could not love Hassan the way he longed to, openly, and as a father. So he took it out on you instead—Amir, the socially legitimate half, the half that represented the riches he had inherited and the sin-with-impunity privileges that came with them. When he saw you, he saw himself. And his guilt. You are still angry and I realize it is far too early to expect you to accept this, but maybe someday you will see that when your father was hard on you, he was also being hard on himself. Your father, like you, was a tortured soul, Amir jan.

I cannot describe to you the depth and blackness of the sorrow that came over me when I learned of his passing. I loved him because he was my friend, but also because he was a good man, maybe even a great man. And this is what I want you to understand, that good, *real* good, was born out of your father's remorse. Sometimes, I think everything he did, feeding the poor on the streets, building the orphanage, giving money to friends in need, it was all his way of redeeming himself. And that, I believe, is what true redemption is, Amir jan, when guilt leads to good.

I know that in the end, God will forgive. He will forgive your father, me, and you too. I hope you can do the same. Forgive your father if you can. Forgive me if you wish. But, most important, forgive yourself.

I have left you some money, most of what I have left, in fact. I think you may have some expenses when you return here, and the money should be enough to cover them. There is a bank in Peshawar; Farid knows the location. The money is in a safe-deposit box. I have given you the key.

As for me, it is time to go. I have little time left and I wish to spend it alone. Please do not look for me. That is my final request of you.

I leave you in the hands of God.

Your friend always,
Rahim

I dragged the hospital gown sleeve across my eyes. I folded the letter and put it under my mattress.

Amir, the socially legitimate half, the half that represented the riches he had inherited and the sin-with-impunity privileges that came with them. Maybe that was why Baba and I had been on such better terms in the U.S., I wondered. Selling junk for petty cash, our menial jobs, our grimy apartment—the American version of a hut; maybe in America, when Baba looked at me, he saw a little bit of Hassan.

Your father, like you, was a tortured soul, Rahim Khan had written. Maybe so. We had both sinned and betrayed. But Baba had found a way to create good out of his remorse. What had I done, other than take my guilt out on the very same people I had betrayed, and then try to forget it all? What had I done, other than become an insomniac?

What had I ever done to right things?

When the nurse—not Aisha but a red-haired woman whose name escapes me—walked in with a syringe in hand and asked me if I needed a morphine injection, I said yes.

THEY REMOVED THE CHEST TUBE early the next morning, and Armand gave the staff the go-ahead to let me sip apple juice. I asked Aisha for a mirror when she placed the cup of juice on the dresser next to my bed. She lifted her bifocals to her forehead as she pulled the curtain open and let the morning sun flood the room. "Remember, now," she said over her shoulder, "it will look better in a few days. My son-in-law was in a moped accident last year. His handsome face was dragged on the asphalt and became purple like an eggplant. Now he is beautiful again, like a Lolly-wood movie star."

Despite her reassurances, looking in the mirror and seeing the thing that insisted it was my face left me a little breathless. It looked like someone had stuck an air pump nozzle under my skin and had pumped away. My eyes were puffy and blue. The worst of it was my mouth, a grotesque blob of purple and red, all bruise and stitches. I tried to smile and a bolt of pain ripped through my lips. I wouldn't be doing that for a while. There were stitches

across my left cheek, just under the chin, on the forehead just
below the hairline.

The old guy with the leg cast said something in Urdu. I gave
him a shrug and shook my head. He pointed to his face, patted it,
and grinned a wide, toothless grin. "Very good," he said in English. *"Inshallah."*

"Thank you," I whispered.

Farid and Sohrab came in just as I put the mirror away.
Sohrab took his seat on the stool, rested his head on the bed's
side rail.

"You know, the sooner we get you out of here the better,"
Farid said.

"Dr. Faruqi says—"

"I don't mean the hospital. I mean Peshawar."

"Why?"

"I don't think you'll be safe here for long," Farid said. He lowered his voice. "The Taliban have friends here. They will start
looking for you."

"I think they already may have," I murmured. I thought suddenly of the bearded man who'd wandered into the room and just
stood there staring at me.

Farid leaned in. "As soon as you can walk, I'll take you to
Islamabad. Not entirely safe there either, no place in Pakistan is,
but it's better than here. At least it will buy you some time."

"Farid jan, this can't be safe for you either. Maybe you
shouldn't be seen with me. You have a family to take care of."

Farid made a waving gesture. "My boys are young, but they are
very shrewd. They know how to take care of their mothers and sisters." He smiled. "Besides, I didn't say I'd do it for free."

"I wouldn't let you if you offered," I said. I forgot I couldn't smile and tried. A tiny streak of blood trickled down my chin. "Can I ask you for one more favor?"

"For you a thousand times over," Farid said.

And, just like that, I was crying. I hitched gusts of air, tears gushing down my cheeks, stinging the raw flesh of my lips.

"What's the matter?" Farid said, alarmed.

I buried my face in one hand and held up the other. I knew the whole room was watching me. After, I felt tired, hollow. "I'm sorry," I said. Sohrab was looking at me with a frown creasing his brow.

When I could talk again, I told Farid what I needed. "Rahim Khan said they live here in Peshawar."

"Maybe you should write down their names," Farid said, eyeing me cautiously, as if wondering what might set me off next. I scribbled their names on a scrap of paper towel. "John and Betty Caldwell."

Farid pocketed the folded piece of paper. "I will look for them as soon as I can," he said. He turned to Sohrab. "As for you, I'll pick you up this evening. Don't tire Amir agha too much."

But Sohrab had wandered to the window, where a half-dozen pigeons strutted back and forth on the sill, pecking at wood and scraps of old bread.

IN THE MIDDLE DRAWER of the dresser beside my bed, I had found an old *National Geographic* magazine, a chewed-up pencil, a comb with missing teeth, and what I was reaching for now, sweat pouring down my face from the effort: a deck of cards. I had counted them earlier and, surprisingly, found the deck complete. I asked Sohrab if he wanted to play. I didn't expect him to answer, let alone play. He'd been quiet since we had fled Kabul.

But he turned from the window and said, "The only game I know is panjpar."

"I feel sorry for you already, because I am a grand master at panjpar. World renowned."

He took his seat on the stool next to me. I dealt him his five cards. "When your father and I were your age, we used to play this game. Especially in the winter, when it snowed and we couldn't go outside. We used to play until the sun went down."

He played me a card and picked one up from the pile. I stole looks at him as he pondered his cards. He was his father in so many ways: the way he fanned out his cards with both hands, the way he squinted while reading them, the way he rarely looked a person in the eye.

We played in silence. I won the first game, let him win the next one, and lost the next five fair and square. "You're as good as your father, maybe even better," I said, after my last loss. "I used to beat him sometimes, but I think he let me win." I paused before saying, "Your father and I were nursed by the same woman."

"I know."

"What . . . what did he tell you about us?"

"That you were the best friend he ever had," he said.

I twirled the jack of diamonds in my fingers, flipped it back and forth. "I wasn't such a good friend, I'm afraid," I said. "But I'd like to be your friend. I think I could be a good friend to you. Would that be all right? Would you like that?" I put my hand on his arm, gingerly, but he flinched. He dropped his cards and pushed away on the stool. He walked back to the window. The sky was awash with streaks of red and purple as the sun set on Peshawar. From the street below came a succession of honks and the braying of a donkey, the whistle of a policeman. Sohrab stood

in that crimson light, forehead pressed to the glass, fists buried in
his armpits.

AISHA HAD A MALE ASSISTANT help me take my first steps
that night. I only walked around the room once, one hand clutching the wheeled IV stand, the other clasping the assistant's forearm. It took me ten minutes to make it back to bed, and, by then,
the incision on my stomach throbbed and I'd broken out in a
drenching sweat. I lay in bed, gasping, my heart hammering in my
ears, thinking how much I missed my wife.

Sohrab and I played panjpar most of the next day, again in
silence. And the day after that. We hardly spoke, just played panjpar, me propped in bed, he on the three-legged stool, our routine
broken only by my taking a walk around the room, or going to the
bathroom down the hall. I had a dream later that night. I dreamed
Assef was standing in the doorway of my hospital room, brass ball
still in his eye socket. "We're the same, you and I," he was saying.
"You nursed with him, but you're *my* twin."

I TOLD ARMAND early that next day that I was leaving.

"It's still early for discharge," Armand protested. He wasn't
dressed in surgical scrubs that day, instead in a button-down navy
blue suit and yellow tie. The gel was back in the hair. "You are still
in intravenous antibiotics and—"

"I have to go," I said. "I appreciate everything you've done for
me, all of you. Really. But I have to leave."

"Where will you go?" Armand said.

"I'd rather not say."

"You can hardly walk."

"I can walk to the end of the hall and back," I said. "I'll be fine." The plan was this: Leave the hospital. Get the money from the safe-deposit box and pay my medical bills. Drive to the orphanage and drop Sohrab off with John and Betty Caldwell. Then get a ride to Islamabad and change travel plans. Give myself a few more days to get better. Fly home.

That was the plan, anyway. Until Farid and Sohrab arrived that morning. "Your friends, this John and Betty Caldwell, they aren't in Peshawar," Farid said.

It had taken me ten minutes just to slip into my *pirhan-tumban*. My chest, where they'd cut me to insert the chest tube, hurt when I raised my arm, and my stomach throbbed every time I leaned over. I was drawing ragged breaths just from the effort of packing a few of my belongings into a brown paper bag. But I'd managed to get ready and was sitting on the edge of the bed when Farid came in with the news. Sohrab sat on the bed next to me.

"Where did they go?" I asked.

Farid shook his head. "You don't understand—"

"Because Rahim Khan said—"

"I went to the U.S. consulate," Farid said, picking up my bag. "There never was a John and Betty Caldwell in Peshawar. According to the people at the consulate, they never existed. Not here in Peshawar, anyhow."

Next to me, Sohrab was flipping through the pages of the old *National Geographic*.

WE GOT THE MONEY from the bank. The manager, a paunchy man with sweat patches under his arms, kept flashing smiles and telling me that no one in the bank had touched the money.

"Absolutely nobody," he said gravely, swinging his index finger the same way Armand had.

Driving through Peshawar with so much money in a paper bag was a slightly frightening experience. Plus, I suspected every bearded man who stared at me to be a Talib killer, sent by Assef. Two things compounded my fears: There are a lot of bearded men in Peshawar, and everybody stares.

"What do we do with him?" Farid said, walking me slowly from the hospital accounting office back to the car. Sohrab was in the backseat of the Land Cruiser, looking at traffic through the rolled-down window, chin resting on his palms.

"He can't stay in Peshawar," I said, panting.

"Nay, Amir agha, he can't," Farid said. He'd read the question in my words. "I'm sorry. I wish I—"

"That's all right, Farid," I said. I managed a tired smile. "You have mouths to feed." A dog was standing next to the truck now, propped on its rear legs, paws on the truck's door, tail wagging. Sohrab was petting the dog. "I guess he goes to Islamabad for now," I said.

I SLEPT THROUGH almost the entire four-hour ride to Islamabad. I dreamed a lot, and most of it I only remember as a hodge-podge of images, snippets of visual memory flashing in my head like cards in a Rolodex: Baba marinating lamb for my thirteenth birthday party. Soraya and I making love for the first time, the sun rising in the east, our ears still ringing from the wedding music, her henna-painted hands laced in mine. The time Baba had taken Hassan and me to a strawberry field in Jalalabad—the owner had told us we could eat as much as we wanted to as long as we bought at least four kilos—and how we'd both ended up with bellyaches. How dark, almost black, Hassan's blood had looked on the snow, dropping from the seat of his pants. *Blood is a powerful thing,* bachem. Khala Jamila patting Soraya's knee and saying, *God knows best, maybe it wasn't meant to be.* Sleeping on the roof of my father's house. Baba saying that the only sin that mattered was theft. *When you tell a lie, you steal a man's right to the truth.* Rahim Khan on the phone, telling me there was a way to be good again. *A way to be good again . . .*

TWENTY-FOUR

If Peshawar was the city that reminded me of what Kabul used to be, then Islamabad was the city Kabul could have become someday. The streets were wider than Peshawar's, cleaner, and lined with rows of hibiscus and flame trees. The bazaars were more organized and not nearly as clogged with rickshaws and pedestrians. The architecture was more elegant too, more modern, and I saw parks where roses and jasmine bloomed in the shadows of trees.

Farid found a small hotel on a side street running along the foot of the Margalla Hills. We passed the famous Shah Faisal Mosque on the way there, reputedly the biggest mosque in the world, with its giant concrete girders and soaring minarets. Sohrab perked up at the sight of the mosque, leaned out of the window and looked at it until Farid turned a corner.

THE HOTEL ROOM was a vast improvement over the one in Kabul where Farid and I had stayed. The sheets were clean, the carpet vacuumed, and the bathroom spotless. There was shampoo, soap, razors for shaving, a bathtub, and towels that smelled like lemon. And no bloodstains on the walls. One other thing: a television set sat on the dresser across from the two single beds.

"Look!" I said to Sohrab. I turned it on manually—no remote—and turned the dial. I found a children's show with two fluffy sheep puppets singing in Urdu. Sohrab sat on one of the beds and drew his knees to his chest. Images from the TV reflected in his green eyes as he watched, stone-faced, rocking back and forth. I remembered the time I'd promised Hassan I'd buy his family a color TV when we both grew up.

"I'll get going, Amir agha," Farid said.

"Stay the night," I said. "It's a long drive. Leave tomorrow."

"Tashakor," he said. "But I want to get back tonight. I miss my children." On his way out of the room, he paused in the doorway. "Good-bye, Sohrab jan," he said. He waited for a reply, but Sohrab paid him no attention. Just rocked back and forth, his face lit by the silver glow of the images flickering across the screen.

Outside, I gave him an envelope. When he tore it, his mouth opened.

"I didn't know how to thank you," I said. "You've done so much for me."

"How much is in here?" Farid said, slightly dazed.

"A little over two thousand dollars."

"Two thou—" he began. His lower lip was quivering a little. Later, when he pulled away from the curb, he honked twice and waved. I waved back. I never saw him again.

I returned to the hotel room and found Sohrab lying on the bed, curled up in a big *C*. His eyes were closed but I couldn't tell if he was sleeping. He had shut off the television. I sat on my bed and grimaced with pain, wiped the cool sweat off my brow. I wondered how much longer it would hurt to get up, sit down, roll over in bed. I wondered when I'd be able to eat solid food. I wondered what I'd do with the wounded little boy lying on the bed, though a part of me already knew.

There was a carafe of water on the dresser. I poured a glass and took two of Armand's pain pills. The water was warm and bitter. I pulled the curtains, eased myself back on the bed, and lay down. I thought my chest would rip open. When the pain dropped a notch and I could breathe again, I pulled the blanket to my chest and waited for Armand's pills to work.

WHEN I WOKE UP, the room was darker. The slice of sky peeking between the curtains was the purple of twilight turning into night. The sheets were soaked and my head pounded. I'd been dreaming again, but I couldn't remember what it had been about.

My heart gave a sick lurch when I looked to Sohrab's bed and found it empty. I called his name. The sound of my voice startled me. It was disorienting, sitting in a dark hotel room, thousands of miles from home, my body broken, calling the name of a boy I'd only met a few days ago. I called his name again and heard nothing. I struggled out of bed, checked the bathroom, looked in the narrow hallway outside the room. He was gone.

I locked the door and hobbled to the manager's office in the lobby, one hand clutching the rail along the walkway for support. There was a fake, dusty palm tree in the corner of the lobby and flying pink flamingos on the wallpaper. I found the hotel manager reading a newspaper behind the Formica-topped check-in counter. I described Sohrab to him, asked if he'd seen him. He put down his paper and took off his reading glasses. He had greasy hair and a square-shaped little mustache speckled with gray. He smelled vaguely of some tropical fruit I couldn't quite recognize.

"Boys, they like to run around," he said, sighing. "I have three of them. All day they are running around, troubling their mother." He fanned his face with the newspaper, staring at my jaws.

"I don't think he's out running around," I said. "And we're not from here. I'm afraid he might get lost."

He bobbed his head from side to side. "Then you should have kept an eye on the boy, mister."

"I know," I said. "But I fell asleep and when I woke up, he was gone."

"Boys must be tended to, you know."

"Yes," I said, my pulse quickening. How could he be so oblivious to my apprehension? He shifted the newspaper to his other hand, resumed the fanning. "They want bicycles now."

"Who?"

"My boys," he said. "They're saying, 'Daddy, Daddy, please buy us bicycles and we'll not trouble you. Please, Daddy!'" He gave a short laugh through his nose. "Bicycles. Their mother will kill me, I swear to you."

I imagined Sohrab lying in a ditch. Or in the trunk of some car, bound and gagged. I didn't want his blood on my hands. Not his too. "Please..." I said. I squinted. Read his name tag on the lapel of his short-sleeve blue cotton shirt. "Mr. Fayyaz, have you seen him?"

"The boy?"

I bit down. "Yes, the boy! The boy who came with me. Have you seen him or not, for God's sake?"

The fanning stopped. His eyes narrowed. "No getting smart with me, my friend. I am not the one who lost him."

That he had a point did not stop the blood from rushing to my face. "You're right. I'm wrong. My fault. Now, have you seen him?"

"Sorry," he said curtly. He put his glasses back on. Snapped his newspaper open. "I have seen no such boy."

I stood at the counter for a minute, trying not to scream. As I was exiting the lobby, he said, "Any idea where he might have wandered to?"

"No," I said. I felt tired. Tired and scared.

"Does he have any interests?" he said. I saw he had folded the paper. "My boys, for example, they will do anything for American action films, especially with that Arnold Whatsanegger—"

"The mosque!" I said. "The big mosque." I remembered the way the mosque had jolted Sohrab from his stupor when we'd driven by it, how he'd leaned out of the window looking at it.

"Shah Faisal?"

"Yes. Can you take me there?"

"Did you know it's the biggest mosque in the world?" he asked.

"No, but—"

"The courtyard alone can fit forty thousand people."

"Can you take me there?"

"It's only a kilometer from here," he said. But he was already pushing away from the counter.

"I'll pay you for the ride," I said.

He sighed and shook his head. "Wait here." He disappeared into the back room, returned wearing another pair of eyeglasses, a set of keys in hand, and with a short, chubby woman in an orange sari trailing him. She took his seat behind the counter. "I don't take your money," he said, blowing by me. "I will drive you because I am a father like you."

I THOUGHT WE'D END UP DRIVING around the city until night fell. I saw myself calling the police, describing Sohrab to them under Fayyaz's reproachful glare. I heard the officer, his voice tired and uninterested, asking his obligatory questions. And beneath the official questions, an unofficial one: Who the hell cared about another dead Afghan kid?

But we found him about a hundred yards from the mosque, sitting in the half-full parking lot, on an island of grass. Fayyaz pulled up to the island and let me out. "I have to get back," he said.

"That's fine. We'll walk back," I said. "Thank you, Mr. Fayyaz. Really."

He leaned across the front seat when I got out. "Can I say something to you?"

"Sure."

In the dark of twilight, his face was just a pair of eyeglasses reflecting the fading light. "The thing about you Afghanis is that . . . well, you people are a little reckless."

I was tired and in pain. My jaws throbbed. And those damn wounds on my chest and stomach felt like barbed wire under my skin. But I started to laugh anyway.

"What . . . what did I . . ." Fayyaz was saying, but I was cackling by then, full-throated bursts of laughter spilling through my wired mouth.

"Crazy people," he said. His tires screeched when he peeled away, his taillights blinking red in the dimming light.

"You gave me a good scare," I said. I sat beside him, wincing with pain as I bent.

He was looking at the mosque. Shah Faisal Mosque was shaped like a giant tent. Cars came and went; worshipers dressed in white streamed in and out. We sat in silence, me leaning against the tree, Sohrab next to me, knees to his chest. We listened to the call to prayer, watched the building's hundreds of lights come on as daylight faded. The mosque sparkled like a diamond in the dark. It lit up the sky, Sohrab's face.

"Have you ever been to Mazar-i-Sharif?" Sohrab said, his chin resting on his kneecaps.

"A long time ago. I don't remember it much."

"Father took me there when I was little. Mother and Sasa came along too. Father bought me a monkey from the bazaar. Not a real one but the kind you have to blow up. It was brown and had a bow tie."

"I might have had one of those when I was a kid."

"Father took me to the Blue Mosque," Sohrab said. "I remember there were so many pigeons outside the *masjid*, and they weren't afraid of people. They came right up to us. Sasa gave me little pieces of *naan* and I fed the birds. Soon, there were pigeons cooing all around me. That was fun."

"You must miss your parents very much," I said. I wondered if he'd seen the Taliban drag his parents out into the street. I hoped he hadn't.

"Do you miss your parents?" he aked, resting his cheek on his knees, looking up at me.

"Do I miss my parents? Well, I never met my mother. My father died a few years ago, and, yes, I do miss him. Sometimes a lot."

"Do you remember what he looked like?"

I thought of Baba's thick neck, his black eyes, his unruly brown hair. Sitting on his lap had been like sitting on a pair of tree trunks. "I remember what he looked like," I said. "What he smelled like too."

"I'm starting to forget their faces," Sohrab said. "Is that bad?"

"No," I said. "Time does that." I thought of something. I

looked in the front pocket of my coat. Found the Polaroid snap-shot of Hassan and Sohrab. "Here," I said.

He brought the photo to within an inch of his face, turned it so the light from the mosque fell on it. He looked at it for a long time. I thought he might cry, but he didn't. He just held it in both hands, traced his thumb over its surface. I thought of a line I'd read somewhere, or maybe I'd heard someone say it: There are a lot of children in Afghanistan, but little childhood. He stretched his hand to give it back to me.

"Keep it," I said. "It's yours."

"Thank you." He looked at the photo again and stowed it in the pocket of his vest. A horse-drawn cart *clip-clopped* by in the parking lot. Little bells dangled from the horse's neck and jingled with each step.

"I've been thinking a lot about mosques lately," Sohrab said.

"You have? What about them?"

He shrugged. "Just thinking about them." He lifted his face, looked straight at me. Now he was crying, softly, silently. "Can I ask you something, Amir agha?"

"Of course."

"Will God..." he began, and choked a little. "Will God put me in hell for what I did to that man?"

I reached for him and he flinched. I pulled back. "Nay. Of course not," I said. I wanted to pull him close, hold him, tell him the world had been unkind to *him*, not the other way around.

His face twisted and strained to stay composed. "Father used to say it's wrong to hurt even bad people. Because they don't know any better, and because bad people sometimes become good."

"Not always, Sohrab."

He looked at me questioningly.

"The man who hurt you, I knew him from many years ago," I

said. "I guess you figured that out that from the conversation he and I had. He...he tried to hurt me once when I was your age, but your father saved me. Your father was very brave and he was always rescuing me from trouble, standing up for me. So one day the bad man hurt your father instead. He hurt him in a very bad way, and I...I couldn't save your father the way he had saved me."

"Why did people want to hurt my father?" Sohrab said in a wheezy little voice. "He was never mean to anyone."

"You're right. Your father was a good man. But that's what I'm trying to tell you, Sohrab jan. That there are bad people in this world, and sometimes bad people stay bad. Sometimes you have to stand up to them. What you did to that man is what I should have done to him all those years ago. You gave him what he deserved, and he deserved even more."

"Do you think Father is disappointed in me?"

"I know he's not," I said. "You saved my life in Kabul. I know he is very proud of you for that."

He wiped his face with the sleeve of his shirt. It burst a bubble of spittle that had formed on his lips. He buried his face in his hands and wept a long time before he spoke again. "I miss Father, and Mother too," he croaked. "And I miss Sasa and Rahim Khan sahib. But sometimes I'm glad they're not ...they're not here anymore."

"Why?" I touched his arm. He drew back.

"Because—" he said, gasping and hitching between sobs, "because I don't want them to see me...I'm so dirty." He sucked in his breath and let it out in a long, wheezy cry. "I'm so dirty and full of sin."

"You're not dirty, Sohrab," I said.

"Those men—"

"You're not dirty at all."

"—they did things...the bad man and the other two...they did things...did things to me."

"You're not dirty, and you're not full of sin." I touched his arm again and he drew away. I reached again, gently, and pulled him to me. "I won't hurt you," I whispered. "I promise." He resisted a little. Slackened. He let me draw him to me and rested his head on my chest. His little body convulsed in my arms with each sob.

A kinship exists between people who've fed from the same breast. Now, as the boy's pain soaked through my shirt, I saw that a kinship had taken root between us too. What had happened in that room with Assef had irrevocably bound us.

I'd been looking for the right time, the right moment, to ask the question that had been buzzing around in my head and keeping me up at night. I decided the moment was now, right here, right now, with the bright lights of the house of God shining on us.

"Would you like to come live in America with me and my wife?"

He didn't answer. He sobbed into my shirt and I let him.

FOR A WEEK, neither one of us mentioned what I had asked him, as if the question hadn't been posed at all. Then one day, Sohrab and I took a taxicab to the Daman-e-Koh Viewpoint—or "the hem of the mountain." Perched midway up the Margalla Hills, it gives a panoramic view of Islamabad, its rows of clean, tree-lined avenues and white houses. The driver told us we could see the presidential palace from up there. "If it has rained and the air is clear, you can even see past Rawalpindi," he said. I saw his eyes in his rearview mirror, skipping from Sohrab to me, back and forth, back and forth. I saw my own face too. It wasn't as swollen as before, but it had taken on a yellow tint from my assortment of fading bruises.

We sat on a bench in one of the picnic areas, in the shade of a gum tree. It was a warm day, the sun perched high in a topaz blue sky. On benches nearby, families snacked on *samosa*s and *pakora*s. Somewhere, a radio played a Hindi song I thought I remembered from an old movie, maybe *Pakeeza*. Kids, many of them Sohrab's age, chased soccer balls, giggling, yelling. I thought about the orphanage in Karteh-Seh, thought about the rat that had scurried between my feet in Zaman's office. My chest tightened with a surge of unexpected anger at the way my countrymen were destroying their own land.

"What?" Sohrab asked. I forced a smile and told him it wasn't important.

We unrolled one of the hotel's bathroom towels on the picnic table and played panjpar on it. It felt good being there, with my half brother's son, playing cards, the warmth of the sun patting the back of my neck. The song ended and another one started, one I didn't recognize.

"Look," Sohrab said. He was pointing to the sky with his cards. I looked up, saw a hawk circling in the broad seamless sky. "Didn't know there were hawks in Islamabad," I said.

"Me neither," he said, his eyes tracing the bird's circular flight. "Do they have them where you live?"

"San Francisco? I guess so. I can't say I've seen too many, though."

"Oh," he said. I was hoping he'd ask more, but he dealt another hand and asked if we could eat. I opened the paper bag and gave him his meatball sandwich. My lunch consisted of yet another cup of blended bananas and oranges—I'd rented Mrs.

Fayyaz's blender for the week. I sucked through the straw and my mouth filled with the sweet, blended fruit. Some of it dripped from the corner of my lips. Sohrab handed me a napkin and watched me dab at my lips. I smiled and he smiled back.

"Your father and I were brothers," I said. It just came out. I had wanted to tell him the night we had sat by the mosque, but I hadn't. But he had a right to know; I didn't want to hide anything anymore. "Half brothers, really. We had the same father."

Sohrab stopped chewing. Put the sandwich down. "Father never said he had a brother."

"That's because he didn't know."

"Why didn't he know?"

"No one told him," I said. "No one told me either. I just found out recently."

Sohrab blinked. Like he was looking at me, *really* looking at me, for the very first time. "But why did people hide it from Father and you?"

"You know, I asked myself that same question the other day. And there's an answer, but not a good one. Let's just say they didn't tell us because your father and I . . . we weren't supposed to be brothers."

"Because he was a Hazara?"

I willed my eyes to stay on him. "Yes."

"Did your father," he began, eyeing his food, "did your father love you and my father equally?"

I thought of a long ago day at Ghargha Lake, when Baba had allowed himself to pat Hassan on the back when Hassan's stone had outskipped mine. I pictured Baba in the hospital room, beaming as they removed the bandages from Hassan's lips. "I think he loved us equally but differently."

"Was he ashamed of my father?"

"No," I said. "I think he was ashamed of himself."

He picked up his sandwich and nibbled at it silently.

WE LEFT LATE THAT AFTERNOON, tired from the heat, but tired in a pleasant way. All the way back, I felt Sohrab watching me. I had the driver pull over at a store that sold calling cards. I gave him the money and a tip for running in and buying me one.

That night, we were lying on our beds, watching a talk show on TV. Two clerics with pepper gray long beards and white turbans were taking calls from the faithful all over the world. One caller from Finland, a guy named Ayub, asked if his teenaged son could go to hell for wearing his baggy pants so low the seam of his underwear showed.

"I saw a picture of San Francisco once," Sohrab said.

"Really?"

"There was a red bridge and a building with a pointy top."

"You should see the streets," I said.

"What about them?" He was looking at me now. On the TV screen, the two mullahs were consulting each other.

"They're so steep, when you drive up all you see is the hood of your car and the sky," I said.

"It sounds scary," he said. He rolled to his side, facing me, his back to the TV.

"It is the first few times," I said. "But you get used to it."

"Does it snow there?"

"No, but we get a lot of fog. You know that red bridge you saw?"

"Yes."

"Sometimes the fog is so thick in the morning, all you see is the tip of the two towers poking through."

There was wonder in his smile. "Oh."

"Sohrab?"

"Yes."

"Have you given any thought to what I asked you before?"

His smiled faded. He rolled to his back. Laced his hands under his head. The mullahs decided that Ayub's son would go to hell after all for wearing his pants the way he did. They claimed it was in the *Haddith*. "I've thought about it," Sohrab said.

"And?"

"It scares me."

"I know it's a little scary," I said, grabbing onto that loose thread of hope. "But you'll learn English so fast and you'll get used to—"

"That's not what I mean. That scares me too, but..."

"But what?"

He rolled toward me again. Drew his knees up. "What if you get tired of me? What if your wife doesn't like me?"

I struggled out of bed and crossed the space between us. I sat beside him. "I won't ever get tired of you, Sohrab," I said. "Not ever. That's a promise. You're my nephew, remember? And Soraya jan, she's a very kind woman. Trust me, she's going to love you. I promise that too." I chanced something. Reached down and took his hand. He tightened up a little but let me hold it.

"I don't want to go to another orphanage," he said.

"I won't ever let that happen. I promise you that." I cupped his hand in both of mine. "Come home with me."

His tears were soaking the pillow. He didn't say anything for a long time. Then his hand squeezed mine back. And he nodded. He nodded.

THE CONNECTION WENT THROUGH on the fourth try. The phone rang three times before she picked it up. "Hello?" It was

7:30 in the evening in Islamabad, roughly about the same time in the morning in California. That meant Soraya had been up for an hour, getting ready for school.

"It's me," I said. I was sitting on my bed, watching Sohrab sleep.

"Amir!" she almost screamed. "Are you okay? Where are you?"

"I'm in Pakistan."

"Why didn't you call earlier? I've been sick with *tashweesh!* My mother's praying and doing *nazr* every day."

"I'm sorry I didn't call. I'm fine now." I had told her I'd be away a week, two at the most. I'd been gone for nearly a month. I smiled. "And tell Khala Jamila to stop killing sheep."

"What do you mean 'fine now'? And what's wrong with your voice?"

"Don't worry about that for now. I'm fine. Really. Soraya, I have a story to tell you, a story I should have told you a long time ago, but first I need to tell you one thing."

"What is it?" she said, her voice lower now, more cautious.

"I'm not coming home alone. I'm bringing a little boy with me." I paused. "I want us to adopt him."

"*What?*"

I checked my watch. "I have fifty-seven minutes left on this stupid calling card and I have so much to tell you. Sit somewhere." I heard the legs of a chair dragged hurriedly across the wooden floor.

"Go ahead," she said.

Then I did what I hadn't done in fifteen years of marriage: I told my wife everything. Everything. I had pictured this moment so many times, dreaded it, but, as I spoke, I felt something lifting off my chest. I imagined Soraya had experienced something very similar the night of our *khastegari,* when she'd told me about her past.

By the time I was done with my story, she was weeping.

"What do you think?" I said.

"I don't know what to think, Amir. You've told me so much all at once."

"I realize that."

I heard her blowing her nose. "But I know this much: You have to bring him home. I want you to."

"Are you sure?" I said, closing my eyes and smiling.

"Am I sure?" she said. "Amir, he's your *qaom*, your family, so he's my *qaom* too. Of course I'm sure. You can't leave him to the streets." There was a short pause. "What's he like?"

I looked over at Sohrab sleeping on the bed. "He's sweet, in a solemn kind of way."

"Who can blame him?" she said. "I want to see him, Amir. I really do."

"Soraya?"

"Yeah."

"*Dostet darum.*" I love you.

"I love you back," she said. I could hear the smile in her words. "And be careful."

"I will. And one more thing. Don't tell your parents who he is. If they need to know, it should come from me."

"Okay."

We hung up.

THE LAWN OUTSIDE the American embassy in Islamabad was neatly mowed, dotted with circular clusters of flowers, bordered by razor-straight hedges. The building itself was like a lot of buildings in Islamabad: flat and white. We passed through several road-blocks to get there and three different security officials conducted a body search on me after the wires in my jaws set off the metal detectors. When we finally stepped in from the heat, the air-conditioning hit my face like a splash of ice water. The secretary in the lobby, a fifty-something, lean-faced blond woman, smiled when I gave her my name. She wore a beige blouse and black slacks—the first woman I'd seen in weeks dressed in something other than a *burqa* or a *shalwar-kameez*. She looked me up on the appointment list, tapping the eraser end of her pencil on the desk. She found my name and asked me to take a seat.

"Would you like some lemonade?" she asked.

"None for me, thanks," I said.

"How about your son?"

"Excuse me?"

"The handsome young gentleman," she said, smiling at Sohrab.

"Oh. That'd be nice, thank you."

Sohrab and I sat on the black leather sofa across the reception desk, next to a tall American flag. Sohrab picked up a magazine from the glass-top coffee table. He flipped the pages, not really looking at the pictures.

"What?" Sohrab said.

"Sorry?"

"You're smiling."

"I was thinking about you," I said.

He gave a nervous smile. Picked up another magazine and flipped through it in under thirty seconds.

"Don't be afraid," I said, touching his arm. "These people are friendly. Relax." I could have used my own advice. I kept shifting in my seat, untying and retying my shoelaces. The secretary placed a tall glass of lemonade with ice on the coffee table. "There you go."

Sohrab smiled shyly. "Thank you very much," he said in English. It came out as "Tank you wery match." It was the only English he knew, he'd told me, that and "Have a nice day."

She laughed. "You're most welcome." She walked back to her desk, high heels clicking on the floor.

"Have a nice day," Sohrab said.

RAYMOND ANDREWS was a short fellow with small hands, nails perfectly trimmed, wedding band on the ring finger. He gave me a curt little shake; it felt like squeezing a sparrow. *Those are the hands that hold our fates,* I thought as Sohrab and I seated ourselves across from his desk. A *Les Misérables* poster was nailed to the wall behind Andrews next to a topographical map of the U.S. A pot of tomato plants basked in the sun on the windowsill.

"Smoke?" he asked, his voice a deep baritone that was at odds with his slight stature.

"No thanks," I said, not caring at all for the way Andrews's eyes barely gave Sohrab a glance, or the way he didn't look at me when he spoke. He pulled open a desk drawer and lit a cigarette from a half-empty pack. He also produced a bottle of lotion from the same drawer. He looked at his tomato plants as he rubbed lotion into his hands, cigarette dangling from the corner of his mouth. Then he closed the drawer, put his elbows on the desktop, and exhaled. "So," he said, crinkling his gray eyes against the smoke, "tell me your story."

I felt like Jean Valjean sitting across from Javert. I reminded myself that I was on American soil now, that this guy was on my side, that he got paid for helping people like me. "I want to adopt this boy, take him back to the States with me," I said.

"Tell me your story," he repeated, crushing a flake of ash on the neatly arranged desk with his index finger, flicking it into the trash can.

I gave him the version I had worked out in my head since I'd hung up with Soraya. I had gone into Afghanistan to bring back my half brother's son. I had found the boy in squalid conditions, wasting away in an orphanage. I had paid the orphanage director a sum of money and withdrawn the boy. Then I had brought him to Pakistan.

"You are the boy's half uncle?"

"Yes."

He checked his watch. Leaned and turned the tomato plants on the sill. "Know anyone who can attest to that?"

"Yes, but I don't know where he is now."

He turned to me and nodded. I tried to read his face and couldn't. I wondered if he'd ever tried those little hands of his at poker.

"I assume getting your jaws wired isn't the latest fashion statement," he said. We were in trouble, Sohrab and I, and I knew it then. I told him I'd gotten mugged in Peshawar.

"Of course," he said. Cleared his throat. "Are you Muslim?"

"Yes."

"Practicing?"

"Yes." In truth, I didn't remember the last time I had laid my forehead to the ground in prayer. Then I did remember: the day Dr. Amani gave Baba his prognosis. I had kneeled on the prayer rug, remembering only fragments of verses I had learned in school.

"Helps your case some, but not much," he said, scratching a spot on the flawless part in his sandy hair.

"What do you mean?" I asked. I reached for Sohrab's hand, intertwined my fingers with his. Sohrab looked uncertainly from me to Andrews.

"There's a long answer and I'm sure I'll end up giving it to you. You want the short one first?"

"I guess," I said.

Andrews crushed his cigarette, his lips pursed. "Give it up."

"I'm sorry?"

"Your petition to adopt this young fellow. Give it up. That's my advice to you."

"Duly noted," I said. "Now, perhaps you'll tell me why."

"That means you want the long answer," he said, his voice impassive, not reacting at all to my curt tone. He pressed his hands palm to palm, as if he were kneeling before the Virgin Mary. "Let's assume the story you gave me is true, though I'd bet my pension a good deal of it is either fabricated or omitted. Not that I care, mind you. You're here, he's here, that's all that matters. Even so, your petition faces significant obstacles, not the least of which is that this child is not an orphan."

"Of course he is."

"Not legally he isn't."

"His parents were executed in the street. The neighbors saw it," I said, glad we were speaking in English.

"You have death certificates?"

"*Death certificates?* This is Afghanistan we're talking about. Most people there don't have *birth* certificates."

His glassy eyes didn't so much as blink. "I don't make the laws, sir. Your outrage notwithstanding, you still need to prove the parents are deceased. The boy has to be declared a legal orphan."

"But—"

"You wanted the long answer and I'm giving it to you. Your next problem is that you need the cooperation of the child's country of origin. Now, that's difficult under the best of circumstances, and, to quote you, this *is* Afghanistan we're talking about. We don't have an American embassy in Kabul. That makes things extremely complicated. Just about impossible."

"What are you saying, that I should throw him back on the streets?" I said.

"I didn't say that."

"He was sexually abused," I said, thinking of the bells around Sohrab's ankles, the mascara on his eyes.

"I'm sorry to hear that," Andrews's mouth said. The way he was looking at me, though, we might as well have been talking about the weather. "But that is not going to make the INS issue this young fellow a visa."

"What are you saying?"

"I'm saying that if you want to help, send money to a reputable relief organization. Volunteer at a refugee camp. But at this point in time, we strongly discourage U.S. citizens from attempting to adopt Afghan children."

I got up. "Come on, Sohrab," I said in Farsi. Sohrab slid next to me, rested his head on my hip. I remembered the Polaroid of him and Hassan standing that same way. "Can I ask you something, Mr. Andrews?"

"Yes."

"Do you have children?"

For the first time, he blinked.

"Well, do you? It's a simple question."

He was silent.

"I thought so," I said, taking Sohrab's hand. "They ought to put someone in your chair who knows what it's like to want a child." I turned to go, Sohrab trailing me.

"Can I ask *you* a question?" Andrews called.

"Go ahead."

"Have you promised this child you'll take him with you?"

"What if I have?"

He shook his head. "It's a dangerous business, making promises to kids." He sighed and opened his desk drawer again. "You mean to pursue this?" he said, rummaging through papers.

"I mean to pursue this."

He produced a business card. "Then I advise you to get a good immigration lawyer. Omar Faisal works here in Islamabad. You can tell him I sent you."

I took the card from him. "Thanks," I muttered.

"Good luck," he said. As we exited the room, I glanced over my shoulder. Andrews was standing in a rectangle of sunlight, absently staring out the window, his hands turning the potted tomato plants toward the sun, petting them lovingly.

"TAKE CARE," the secretary said as we passed her desk.

"Your boss could use some manners," I said. I expected her to roll her eyes, maybe nod in that "I know, everybody says that," kind of way. Instead, she lowered her voice. "Poor Ray. He hasn't been the same since his daughter died."

I raised an eyebrow.

"Suicide," she whispered.

ON THE TAXI RIDE back to the hotel, Sohrab rested his head on the window, kept staring at the passing buildings, the rows of gum trees. His breath fogged the glass, cleared, fogged it again. I waited for him to ask me about the meeting but he didn't.

. . .

ON THE OTHER SIDE of the closed bathroom door the water was running. Since the day we'd checked into the hotel, Sohrab took a long bath every night before bed. In Kabul, hot running water had been like fathers, a rare commodity. Now Sohrab spent almost an hour a night in the bath, soaking in the soapy water, scrubbing. Sitting on the edge of the bed, I called Soraya. I glanced at the thin line of light under the bathroom door. *Do you feel clean yet, Sohrab?*

I passed on to Soraya what Raymond Andrews had told me. "So what do you think?" I said.

"We have to think he's wrong." She told me she had called a few adoption agencies that arranged international adoptions. She hadn't yet found one that would consider doing an Afghan adoption, but she was still looking.

"How are your parents taking the news?"

"Madar is happy for us. You know how she feels about you, Amir, you can do no wrong in her eyes. Padar...well, as always, he's a little harder to read. He's not saying much."

"And you? Are you happy?"

I heard her shifting the receiver to her other hand. "I think we'll be good for your nephew, but maybe that little boy will be good for us too."

"I was thinking the same thing."

"I know it sounds crazy, but I find myself wondering what his favorite *qurma* will be, or his favorite subject in school. I picture myself helping him with homework..." She laughed. In the bathroom, the water had stopped running. I could hear Sohrab in there, shifting in the tub, spilling water over the sides.

"You're going to be great," I said.

"Oh, I almost forgot! I called Kaka Sharif."

I remembered him reciting a poem at our *nika* from a scrap of hotel stationery paper. His son had held the Koran over our heads as Soraya and I had walked toward the stage, smiling at the flashing cameras. "What did he say?"

"Well, he's going to stir the pot for us. He'll call some of his INS buddies," she said.

"That's really great news," I said. "I can't wait for you to see Sohrab."

"I can't wait to see you," she said.

I hung up smiling.

Sohrab emerged from the bathroom a few minutes later. He had barely said a dozen words since the meeting with Raymond Andrews and my attempts at conversation had only met with a nod or a monosyllabic reply. He climbed into bed, pulled the blanket to his chin. Within minutes, he was snoring.

I wiped a circle on the fogged-up mirror and shaved with one of the hotel's old-fashioned razors, the type that opened and you slid the blade in. Then I took my own bath, lay there until the steaming hot water turned cold and my skin shriveled up. I lay there drifting, wondering, imagining...

OMAR FAISAL WAS CHUBBY, dark, had dimpled cheeks, black button eyes, and an affable, gap-toothed smile. His thinning gray hair was tied back in a ponytail. He wore a brown corduroy suit with leather elbow patches and carried a worn, overstuffed briefcase. The handle was missing, so he clutched the briefcase to his chest. He was the sort of fellow who started a lot of sentences with a laugh and an unnecessary apology, like *I'm sorry, I'll be there at five.* Laugh. When I had called him, he had insisted on coming out to meet us. "I'm sorry, the cabbies in this town are sharks," he said in perfect English, without a trace of an accent. "They smell a foreigner, they triple their fares."

He pushed through the door, all smiles and apologies, wheezing a little and sweating. He wiped his brow with a handkerchief and opened his briefcase, rummaged in it for a notepad and apologized for the sheets of paper that spilled on the bed. Sitting cross-legged on his bed, Sohrab kept one eye on the muted television, the other on the harried lawyer. I had told him in the morning that Faisal would be coming and he had nodded, almost asked something, and had just gone on watching a show with talking animals.

"Here we are," Faisal said, flipping open a yellow legal notepad. "I hope my children take after their mother when it comes to organization. I'm sorry, probably not the sort of thing you want to hear from your prospective lawyer, heh?" He laughed.

"Well, Raymond Andrews thinks highly of you."

"Mr. Andrews. Yes, yes. Decent fellow. Actually, he rang me and told me about you."

"He did?"

"Oh yes."

"So you're familiar with my situation."

Faisal dabbed at the sweat beads above his lips. "I'm familiar with the version of the situation you gave Mr. Andrews," he said. His cheeks dimpled with a coy smile. He turned to Sohrab. "This must be the young man who's causing all the trouble," he said in Farsi.

"This is Sohrab," I said. "Sohrab, this is Mr. Faisal, the lawyer I told you about."

Sohrab slid down the side of his bed and shook hands with Omar Faisal. *"Salaam alaykum,"* he said in a low voice.

"Alaykum salaam, Sohrab," Faisal said. "Did you know you are named after a great warrior?"

Sohrab nodded. Climbed back onto his bed and lay on his side to watch TV.

"I didn't know you spoke Farsi so well," I said in English. "Did you grow up in Kabul?"

"No, I was born in Karachi. But I did live in Kabul for a number of years. Shar-e-Nau, near the Haji Yaghoub Mosque," Faisal said. "I grew up in Berkeley, actually. My father opened a music store there in the late sixties. Free love, headbands, tie-dyed shirts, you name it." He leaned forward. "I was at Woodstock."

"Groovy," I said, and Faisal laughed so hard he started sweating all over again. "Anyway," I continued, "what I told Mr. Andrews was pretty much it, save for a thing or two. Or maybe three. I'll give you the uncensored version."

He licked a finger and flipped to a blank page, uncapped his pen. "I'd appreciate that, Amir. And why don't we just keep it in English from here on out?"

"Fine."

I told him everything that had happened. Told him about my meeting with Rahim Khan, the trek to Kabul, the orphanage, the stoning at Ghazi Stadium.

"God," he whispered. "I'm sorry, I have such fond memories of Kabul. Hard to believe it's the same place you're telling me about."

"Have you been there lately?"

"God no."

"It's not Berkeley, I'll tell you that," I said.

"Go on."

I told him the rest, the meeting with Assef, the fight, Sohrab and his slingshot, our escape back to Pakistan. When I was done, he scribbled a few notes, breathed in deeply, and gave me a sober look. "Well, Amir, you've got a tough battle ahead of you."

"One I can win?"

He capped his pen. "At the risk of sounding like Raymond Andrews, it's not likely. Not impossible, but hardly likely." Gone was the affable smile, the playful look in his eyes.

"But it's kids like Sohrab who need a home the most," I said. "These rules and regulations don't make any sense to me."

"You're preaching to the choir, Amir," he said. "But the fact is, take current immigration laws, adoption agency policies, and the political situation in Afghanistan, and the deck is stacked against you."

"I don't get it," I said. I wanted to hit something. "I mean, I get it but I don't get it."

Omar nodded, his brow furrowed. "Well, it's like this. In the aftermath of a disaster, whether it be natural or man-made—and the Taliban are a disaster, Amir, believe me—it's always difficult to ascertain that a child is an orphan. Kids get displaced in refugee camps, or parents just abandon them because they can't take care of them. Happens all the time. So the INS won't grant a visa unless it's clear the child meets the definition of an eligible orphan. I'm sorry, I know it sounds ridiculous, but you need death certificates."

"You've been to Afghanistan," I said. "You know how improbable that is."

"I know," he said. "But let's suppose it's clear that the child has no surviving parent. Even then, the INS thinks it's good adoption practice to place the child with someone in his own country so his heritage can be preserved."

"What heritage?" I said. "The Taliban have destroyed what heritage Afghans had. You saw what they did to the giant Buddhas in Bamiyan."

"I'm sorry, I'm telling you how the INS works, Amir," Omar said, touching my arm. He glanced at Sohrab and smiled. Turned back to me. "Now, a child has to be legally adopted according to the laws and regulations of his own country. But when you have a country in turmoil, say a country like Afghanistan, government offices are busy with emergencies, and processing adoptions won't be a top priority."

I sighed and rubbed my eyes. A pounding headache was settling in just behind them.

"But let's suppose that somehow Afghanistan gets its act together," Omar said, crossing his arms on his protruding belly. "It still may not permit this adoption. In fact, even the more moderate Muslim nations are hesitant with adoptions because in many of those countries, Islamic law, *Shari'a*, doesn't recognize adoption."

"You're telling me to give it up?" I asked, pressing my palm to my forehead.

"I grew up in the U.S., Amir. If America taught me anything, it's that quitting is right up there with pissing in the Girl Scouts' lemonade jar. But, as your lawyer, I have to give you the facts," he said. "Finally, adoption agencies routinely send staff members to evaluate the child's milieu, and no reasonable agency is going to send an agent to Afghanistan."

I looked at Sohrab sitting on the bed, watching TV, watching us. He was sitting the way his father used to, chin resting on one knee.

"I'm his half uncle, does that count for anything?"

"It does if you can prove it. I'm sorry, do you have any papers or anyone who can support you?"

"No papers," I said, in a tired voice. "No one knew about it. Sohrab didn't know until I told him, and I myself didn't find out until recently. The only other person who knows is gone, maybe dead."

"Hmm."

"What are my options, Omar?"

"I'll be frank. You don't have a lot of them."

"Well, Jesus, what can I do?"

Omar breathed in, tapped his chin with the pen, let his breath out. "You could still file an orphan petition, hope for the best. You could do an independent adoption. That means you'd have to live with Sohrab here in Pakistan, day in and day out, for the next two years. You could seek asylum on his behalf. That's a lengthy process and you'd have to prove political persecution. You could request a humanitarian visa. That's at the discretion of the attorney general and it's not easily given." He paused. "There is another option, probably your best shot."

"What?" I said, leaning forward.

"You could relinquish him to an orphanage here, then file an orphan petition. Start your I-600 form and your home study while he's in a safe place."

"What are those?"

"I'm sorry, the I-600 is an INS formality. The home study is done by the adoption agency you choose," Omar said. "It's, you know, to make sure you and your wife aren't raving lunatics."

"I don't want to do that," I said, looking again at Sohrab. "I promised him I wouldn't send him back to an orphanage."

"Like I said, it may be your best shot."

We talked a while longer. Then I walked him out to his car, an old VW Bug. The sun was setting on Islamabad by then, a flaming red nimbus in the west. I watched the car tilt under Omar's weight as he somehow managed to slide in behind the wheel. He rolled down the window. "Amir?"

"Yes."

"I meant to tell you in there, about what you're trying to do? I think it's pretty great."

He waved as he pulled away. Standing outside the hotel room and waving back, I wished Soraya could be there with me.

SOHRAB HAD TURNED OFF THE TV when I went back into the room. I sat on the edge of my bed, asked him to sit next to me. "Mr. Faisal thinks there is a way I can take you to America with me," I said.

"He does?" Sohrab said, smiling faintly for the first time in days. "When can we go?"

"Well, that's the thing. It might take a little while. But he said it can be done and he's going to help us." I put my hand on the back of his neck. From outside, the call to prayer blared through the streets.

"How long?" Sohrab asked.

"I don't know. A while."

Sohrab shrugged and smiled, wider this time. "I don't mind. I can wait. It's like the sour apples."

"Sour apples?"

"One time, when I was really little, I climbed a tree and ate these green, sour apples. My stomach swelled and became hard like a drum, it hurt a lot. Mother said that if I'd just waited for the apples to ripen, I wouldn't have become sick. So now, whenever I really want something, I try to remember what she said about the apples."

"Sour apples," I said. "*Mashallah,* you're just about the smartest little guy I've ever met, Sohrab jan." His ears reddened with a blush.

"Will you take me to that red bridge? The one with the fog?" he said.

"Absolutely," I said. "Absolutely."

"And we'll drive up those streets, the ones where all you see is the hood of the car and the sky?"

"Every single one of them," I said. My eyes stung with tears and I blinked them away.

"Is English hard to learn?"

"I say, within a year, you'll speak it as well as Farsi."

"Really?"

"Yes." I placed a finger under his chin, turned his face up to mine. "There *is* one other thing, Sohrab."

"What?"

"Well, Mr. Faisal thinks that it would really help if we could . . . if we could ask you to stay in a home for kids for a while."

"Home for kids?" he said, his smile fading. "You mean an orphanage?"

"It would only be for a little while."

"No," he said. "No, please."

"Sohrab, it would be for just a little while. I promise."

"You promised you'd never put me in one of those places, Amir agha," he said. His voice was breaking, tears pooling in his eyes. I felt like a prick.

"This is different. It would be here, in Islamabad, not in Kabul. And I'd visit you all the time until we can get you out and take you to America."

"Please! Please, no!" he croaked. "I'm scared of that place. They'll hurt me! I don't want to go."

"No one is going to hurt you. Not ever again."

"Yes they will! They always say they won't but they lie. They lie! Please, God!"

I wiped the tear streaking down his cheek with my thumb. "Sour apples, remember? It's just like the sour apples," I said softly.

"No it's not. Not that place. God, oh God. Please, no!" He was trembling, snot and tears mixing on his face.

"*Shhh.*" I pulled him close, wrapped my arms around his shaking little body. "*Shhh.* It'll be all right. We'll go home together. You'll see, it'll be all right."

His voice was muffled against my chest, but I heard the panic in it. "Please promise you won't! Oh God, Amir agha! Please promise you won't!"

How could I promise? I held him against me, held him tightly, and rocked back and forth. He wept into my shirt until his tears dried, until his shaking stopped and his frantic pleas dwindled to indecipherable mumbles. I waited, rocked him until his breathing slowed and his body slackened. I remembered something I had read somewhere a long time ago: *That's how children deal with terror. They fall asleep.*

I carried him to his bed, set him down. Then I lay in my own bed, looking out the window at the purple sky over Islamabad.

THE SKY WAS A DEEP BLACK when the phone jolted me from sleep. I rubbed my eyes and turned on the bedside lamp. It was a little past 10:30 P.M.; I'd been sleeping for almost three hours. I picked up the phone. "Hello?"

"Call from America." Mr. Fayyaz's bored voice.

"Thank you," I said. The bathroom light was on; Sohrab was taking his nightly bath. A couple of clicks and then Soraya: "*Salaam!*" She sounded excited.

"Hi."

"How did the meeting go with the lawyer?"

I told her what Omar Faisal had suggested. "Well, you can forget about it," she said. "We won't have to do that."

I sat up. "*Rawsti?* Why, what's up?"

"I heard back from Kaka Sharif. He said the key was getting Sohrab into the country. Once he's in, there are ways of keeping him here. So he made a few calls to his INS friends. He called me back tonight and said he was almost certain he could get Sohrab a humanitarian visa."

"No kidding?" I said. "Oh thank God! Good ol' Sharif jan!"

"I know. Anyway, we'll serve as the sponsors. It should all happen pretty quickly. He said the visa would be good for a year, plenty of time to apply for an adoption petition."

"It's really going to happen, Soraya, huh?"

"It looks like it," she said. She sounded happy. I told her I loved her and she said she loved me back. I hung up.

"Sohrab!" I called, rising from my bed. "I have great news." I knocked on the bathroom door. "Sohrab! Soraya jan just called from California. We won't have to put you in the orphanage, Sohrab. We're going to America, you and I. Did you hear me? We're going to America!"

I pushed the door open. Stepped into the bathroom.

Suddenly I was on my knees, screaming. Screaming through my clenched teeth. Screaming until I thought my throat would rip and my chest explode.

Later, they said I was still screaming when the ambulance arrived.

TWENTY-FIVE

They won't let me in.

I see them wheel him through a set of double doors and I follow. I burst through the doors, the smell of iodine and peroxide hits me, but all I have time to see is two men wearing surgical caps and a woman in green huddling over a gurney. A white sheet spills over the side of the gurney and brushes against grimy checkered tiles. A pair of small, bloody feet poke out from under the sheet and I see that the big toenail on the left foot is chipped. Then a tall, thickset man in blue presses his palm against my chest and he's pushing me back out through the doors, his wedding band cold on my skin. I shove forward and I curse him, but he says you cannot be here, he says it in English, his voice polite but firm. "You must wait," he says, leading me back to the waiting area, and now the double doors swing shut behind him with a sigh and all I see is the top of the men's surgical caps through the doors' narrow rectangular windows.

He leaves me in a wide, windowless corridor crammed with

people sitting on metallic folding chairs set along the walls, others on the thin frayed carpet. I want to scream again, and I remember the last time I felt this way, riding with Baba in the tank of the fuel truck, buried in the dark with the other refugees. I want to tear myself from this place, from this reality, rise up like a cloud and float away, melt into this humid summer night and dissolve somewhere far, over the hills. But I am here, my legs blocks of concrete, my lungs empty of air, my throat burning. There will be no floating away. There will be no other reality tonight. I close my eyes and my nostrils fill with the smells of the corridor, sweat and ammonia, rubbing alcohol and curry. On the ceiling, moths fling themselves at the dull gray light tubes running the length of the corridor and I hear the papery flapping of their wings. I hear chatter, muted sobbing, sniffling, someone moaning, someone else sighing, elevator doors opening with a *bing*, the operator paging someone in Urdu.

I open my eyes again and I know what I have to do. I look around, my heart a jackhammer in my chest, blood thudding in my ears. There is a dark little supply room to my left. In it, I find what I need. It will do. I grab a white bedsheet from the pile of folded linens and carry it back to the corridor. I see a nurse talking to a policeman near the restroom. I take the nurse's elbow and pull, I want to know which way is west. She doesn't understand and the lines on her face deepen when she frowns. My throat aches and my eyes sting with sweat, each breath is like inhaling fire, and I think I am weeping. I ask again. I beg. The policeman is the one who points.

I throw my makeshift *jai-namaz*, my prayer rug, on the floor and I get on my knees, lower my forehead to the ground, my tears soaking through the sheet. I bow to the west. Then I remember I haven't prayed for over fifteen years. I have long forgotten the words. But it doesn't matter, I will utter those few words I still remember: *La illaha il Allah, Muhammad u rasul ullah.* There is no God but Allah and Muhammad is His messenger. I see now that Baba was wrong, there is a God, there always had been. I see Him here, in the eyes of the people in this corridor of desperation. This is the real house of God, this is where those who have lost God will find Him, not the white *masjid* with its bright diamond lights and towering minarets. There is a God, there has to be, and now I will pray, I will pray that He forgive that I have neglected Him all of these years, forgive that I have betrayed, lied, and sinned with impunity only to turn to Him now in my hour of need, I pray that He is as merciful, benevolent, and gracious as His book says He is. I bow to the west and kiss the ground and promise that I will do *zakat,* I will do *namaz,* I will fast during Ramadan and when Ramadan has passed I will go on fasting, I will commit to memory every last word of His holy book, and I will set on a pilgrimage to that sweltering city in the desert and bow before the Ka'bah too. I will do all of this and I will think of Him every day from this day on if He only grants me this one wish: My hands are stained with Hassan's blood; I pray God doesn't let them get stained with the blood of his boy too.

I hear a whimpering and realize it is mine, my lips are salty with the tears trickling down my face. I feel the eyes of everyone in this corridor on me and still I bow to the west. I pray. I pray that my sins have not caught up with me the way I'd always feared they would.

A STARLESS, BLACK NIGHT falls over Islamabad. It's a few hours later and I am sitting now on the floor of a tiny lounge off the corridor that leads to the emergency ward. Before me is a dull brown coffee table cluttered with newspapers and dog-eared mag-

azines—an April 1996 issue of *Time;* a Pakistani newspaper showing the face of a young boy who was hit and killed by a train the
week before; an entertainment magazine with smiling Lollywood
actors on its glossy cover. There is an old woman wearing a jade
green *shalwar-kameez* and a crocheted shawl nodding off in a
wheelchair across from me. Every once in a while, she stirs awake
and mutters a prayer in Arabic. I wonder tiredly whose prayers will
be heard tonight, hers or mine. I picture Sohrab's face, the
pointed meaty chin, his small seashell ears, his slanting bamboo-
leaf eyes so much like his father's. A sorrow as black as the night
outside invades me, and I feel my throat clamping.

I need air.

I get up and open the windows. The air coming through the
screen is musty and hot—it smells of overripe dates and dung. I
force it into my lungs in big heaps, but it doesn't clear the clamping feeling in my chest. I drop back on the floor. I pick up the
Time magazine and flip through the pages. But I can't read, can't
focus on anything. So I toss it on the table and go back to staring
at the zigzagging pattern of the cracks on the cement floor, at the
cobwebs on the ceiling where the walls meet, at the dead flies lit-
tering the windowsill. Mostly, I stare at the clock on the wall. It's
just past 4 A.M. and I have been shut out of the room with the
swinging double doors for over five hours now. I still haven't heard
any news.

The floor beneath me begins to feel like part of my body, and
my breathing is growing heavier, slower. I want to sleep, shut my
eyes and lie my head down on this cold, dusty floor. Drift off.
When I wake up, maybe I will discover that everything I saw in the
hotel bathroom was part of a dream: the water drops dripping
from the faucet and landing with a *plink* into the bloody bathwa-
ter; the left arm dangling over the side of the tub, the blood-

soaked razor sitting on the toilet tank—the same razor I had
shaved with the day before—and his eyes, still half open but lightless. That more than anything. I want to forget the eyes.

Soon, sleep comes and I let it take me. I dream of things I
can't remember later.

SOMEONE IS TAPPING ME on the shoulder. I open my eyes.
There is a man kneeling beside me. He is wearing a cap like the
men behind the swinging double doors and a paper surgical mask
over his mouth—my heart sinks when I see a drop of blood on the
mask. He has taped a picture of a doe-eyed little girl to his beeper.
He unsnaps his mask and I'm glad I don't have to look at Sohrab's
blood anymore. His skin is dark like the imported Swiss chocolate
Hassan and I used to buy from the bazaar in Shar-e-Nau; he has
thinning hair and hazel eyes topped with curved eyelashes. In a
British accent, he tells me his name is Dr. Nawaz, and suddenly I
want to be away from this man, because I don't think I can bear to
hear what he has come to tell me. He says the boy had cut himself
deeply and had lost a great deal of blood and my mouth begins to
mutter that prayer again:

La illaha il Allah, Muhammad u rasul ullah.

They had to transfuse several units of red cells—

How will I tell Soraya?

Twice, they had to revive him—

I will do namaz, I will do zakat.

They would have lost him if his heart hadn't been young and
strong—

I will fast.

He is alive.

Dr. Nawaz smiles. It takes me a moment to register what he
has just said. Then he says more but I don't hear him. Because I

have taken his hands and I have brought them up to my face. I weep my relief into this stranger's small, meaty hands and he says nothing now. He waits.

THE INTENSIVE CARE UNIT is L-shaped and dim, a jumble of bleeping monitors and whirring machines. Dr. Nawaz leads me between two rows of beds separated by white plastic curtains. Sohrab's bed is the last one around the corner, the one nearest the nurses' station where two nurses in green surgical scrubs are jotting notes on clipboards, chatting in low voices. On the silent ride up the elevator with Dr. Nawaz, I had thought I'd weep again when I saw Sohrab. But when I sit on the chair at the foot of his bed, looking at his white face through the tangle of gleaming plastic tubes and IV lines, I am dry-eyed. Watching his chest rise and fall to the rhythm of the hissing ventilator, a curious numbness washes over me, the same numbness a man might feel seconds after he has swerved his car and barely avoided a head-on collision.

I doze off, and, when I wake up, I see the sun rising in a buttermilk sky through the window next to the nurses' station. The light slants into the room, aims my shadow toward Sohrab. He hasn't moved.

"You'd do well to get some sleep," a nurse says to me. I don't recognize her—there must have been a shift change while I'd napped. She takes me to another lounge, this one just outside the ICU. It's empty. She hands me a pillow and a hospital-issue blanket. I thank her and lie on the vinyl sofa in the corner of the lounge. I fall asleep almost immediately.

I dream I am back in the lounge downstairs. Dr. Nawaz walks in and I rise to meet him. He takes off his paper mask, his hands suddenly whiter than I remembered, his nails manicured, he has neatly parted hair, and I see he is not Dr. Nawaz at all but Raymond Andrews, the little embassy man with the potted tomatoes. Andrews cocks his head. Narrows his eyes.

IN THE DAYTIME, the hospital was a maze of teeming, angled hallways, a blur of blazing-white overhead fluorescence. I came to know its layout, came to know that the fourth-floor button in the east wing elevator didn't light up, that the door to the men's room on that same floor was jammed and you had to ram your shoulder into it to open it. I came to know that hospital life has a rhythm, the flurry of activity just before the morning shift change, the midday hustle, the stillness and quiet of the late-night hours interrupted occasionally by a blur of doctors and nurses rushing to revive someone. I kept vigil at Sohrab's bedside in the daytime and wandered through the hospital's serpentine corridors at night, listening to my shoe heels clicking on the tiles, thinking of what I would say to Sohrab when he woke up. I'd end up back in the ICU, by the whooshing ventilator beside his bed, and I'd be no closer to knowing.

After three days in the ICU, they withdrew the breathing tube and transferred him to a ground-level bed. I wasn't there when they moved him. I had gone back to the hotel that night to get some sleep and ended up tossing around in bed all night. In the morning, I tried to not look at the bathtub. It was clean now, someone had wiped off the blood, spread new floor mats on the floor, and scrubbed the walls. But I couldn't stop myself from sitting on its cool, porcelain edge. I pictured Sohrab filling it with warm water. Saw him undressing. Saw him twisting the razor handle and opening the twin safety latches on the head, sliding the blade out, holding it between his thumb and forefinger. I pictured him lowering himself into the water, lying there for a while, his eyes closed. I wondered what his last thought had been as he had raised the blade and brought it down.

I was exiting the lobby when the hotel manager, Mr. Fayyaz, caught up with me. "I am very sorry for you," he said, "but I am asking for you to leave my hotel, please. This is bad for my business, very bad."

I told him I understood and I checked out. He didn't charge me for the three days I'd spent at the hospital. Waiting for a cab outside the hotel lobby, I thought about what Mr. Fayyaz had said to me that night we'd gone looking for Sohrab: *The thing about you Afghanis is that...well, you people are a little reckless.* I had laughed at him, but now I wondered. Had I actually gone to sleep after I had given Sohrab the news he feared most?

When I got in the cab, I asked the driver if he knew any Persian bookstores. He said there was one a couple of kilometers south. We stopped there on the way to the hospital.

SOHRAB'S NEW ROOM had cream-colored walls, chipped, dark gray moldings, and glazed tiles that might have once been white. He shared the room with a teenaged Punjabi boy who, I later learned from one of the nurses, had broken his leg when he had slipped off the roof of a moving bus. His leg was in a cast, raised and held by tongs strapped to several weights.

Sohrab's bed was next to the window, the lower half lit by the late-morning sunlight streaming through the rectangular panes. A uniformed security guard was standing at the window, munching on cooked watermelon seeds—Sohrab was under twenty-four-hours-a-day suicide watch. Hospital protocol, Dr. Nawaz had informed me. The guard tipped his hat when he saw me and left the room.

Sohrab was wearing short-sleeved hospital pajamas and lying

on his back, blanket pulled to his chest, face turned to the window. I thought he was sleeping, but when I scooted a chair up to his bed his eyelids fluttered and opened. He looked at me, then looked away. He was so pale, even with all the blood they had given him, and there was a large purple bruise in the crease of his right arm.

"How are you?" I said.

He didn't answer. He was looking through the window at a fenced-in sandbox and swing set in the hospital garden. There was an arch-shaped trellis near the playground, in the shadow of a row of hibiscus trees, a few green vines climbing up the timber lattice. A handful of kids were playing with buckets and pails in the sandbox. The sky was a cloudless blue that day, and I saw a tiny jet leaving behind twin white trails. I turned back to Sohrab. "I spoke to Dr. Nawaz a few minutes ago and he thinks you'll be discharged in a couple of days. That's good news, *nay*?"

Again I was met by silence. The Punjabi boy at the other end of the room stirred in his sleep and moaned something. "I like your room," I said, trying not to look at Sohrab's bandaged wrists. "It's bright, and you have a view." Silence. A few more awkward minutes passed, and a light sweat formed on my brow, my upper lip. I pointed to the untouched bowl of green pea *aush* on his nightstand, the unused plastic spoon. "You should try to eat something. Gain your *quwat* back, your strength. Do you want me to help you?"

He held my glance, then looked away, his face set like stone. His eyes were still lightless, I saw, vacant, the way I had found them when I had pulled him out of the bathtub. I reached into the paper bag between my feet and took out the used copy of the *Shahnamah* I had bought at the Persian bookstore. I turned the cover so it faced Sohrab. "I used to read this to your father when we were children. We'd go up the hill by our house and sit beneath the pomegranate..." I trailed off. Sohrab was looking through the window again. I forced a smile. "Your father's favorite was the story of Rostam and Sohrab and that's how you got your name, I know you know that." I paused, feeling a bit like an idiot. "Anyway, he said in his letter that it was your favorite too, so I thought I'd read you some of it. Would you like that?"

Sohrab closed his eyes. Covered them with his arm, the one with the bruise.

I flipped to the page I had bent in the taxicab. "Here we go," I said, wondering for the first time what thoughts had passed through Hassan's head when he had finally read the *Shahnamah* for himself and discovered that I had deceived him all those times. I cleared my throat and read. "'Give ear unto the combat of Sohrab against Rostam, though it be a tale replete with tears,'" I began. "'It came about that on a certain day Rostam rose from his couch and his mind was filled with forebodings. He bethought him...'" I read him most of chapter 1, up to the part where the young warrior Sohrab comes to his mother, Tahmineh, the princess of Samengan, and demands to know the identity of his father. I closed the book. "Do you want me to go on? There are battles coming up, remember? Sohrab leading his army to the White Castle in Iran? Should I read on?"

He shook his head slowly. I dropped the book back in the paper bag. "That's fine," I said, encouraged that he had responded at all. "Maybe we can continue tomorrow. How do you feel?"

Sohrab's mouth opened and a hoarse sound came out. Dr. Nawaz had told me that would happen, on account of the breathing tube they had slid through his vocal cords. He licked his lips and tried again. "Tired."

"I know. Dr. Nawaz said that was to be expected—"

He was shaking his head.

"What, Sohrab?"

He winced when he spoke again in that husky voice, barely above a whisper. "Tired of everything."

I sighed and slumped in my chair. There was a band of sunlight on the bed between us, and, for just a moment, the ashen gray face looking at me from the other side of it was a dead ringer for Hassan's, not the Hassan I played marbles with until the mullah belted out the evening *azan* and Ali called us home, not the Hassan I chased down our hill as the sun dipped behind clay rooftops in the west, but the Hassan I saw alive for the last time, dragging his belongings behind Ali in a warm summer downpour, stuffing them in the trunk of Baba's car while I watched through the rain-soaked window of my room.

He gave a slow shake of his head. "Tired of everything," he repeated.

"What can I do, Sohrab? Please tell me."

"I want—" he began. He winced again and brought his hand to his throat as if to clear whatever was blocking his voice. My eyes were drawn again to his wrist wrapped tightly with white gauze bandages. "I want my old life back," he breathed.

"Oh, Sohrab."

"I want Father and Mother jan. I want Sasa. I want to play with Rahim Khan sahib in the garden. I want to live in our house again." He dragged his forearm across his eyes. "I want my old life back."

I didn't know what to say, where to look, so I gazed down at my hands. *Your old life,* I thought. *My old life too. I played in the same yard, Sohrab. I lived in the same house. But the grass is dead and a stranger's jeep is parked in the driveway of our house, pissing oil all over the asphalt. Our old life is gone, Sohrab, and*

*everyone in it is either dead or dying. It's just you and me now.
Just you and me.*

"I can't give you that," I said.

"I wish you hadn't—"

"Please don't say that."

"—wish you hadn't ... I wish you had left me in the water."

"Don't ever say that, Sohrab," I said, leaning forward. "I can't
bear to hear you talk like that." I touched his shoulder and he
flinched. Drew away. I dropped my hand, remembering ruefully
how in the last days before I'd broken my promise to him he had
finally become at ease with my touch. "Sohrab, I can't give you
your old life back, I wish to God I could. But I can take you with
me. That was what I was coming in the bathroom to tell you. You
have a visa to go to America, to live with me and my wife. It's true.
I promise."

He sighed through his nose and closed his eyes. I wished I
hadn't said those last two words. "You know, I've done a lot of
things I regret in my life," I said, "and maybe none more than
going back on the promise I made you. But that will never happen
again, and I am so very profoundly sorry. I ask for your *bakhshesh,*
your forgiveness. Can you do that? Can you forgive me? Can you
believe me?" I dropped my voice. "Will you come with me?"

As I waited for his reply, my mind flashed back to a winter day
from long ago, Hassan and I sitting on the snow beneath a leafless
sour cherry tree. I had played a cruel game with Hassan that day,
toyed with him, asked him if he would chew dirt to prove his loyalty to me. Now I was the one under the microscope, the one who
had to prove my worthiness. I deserved this.

Sohrab rolled to his side, his back to me. He didn't say anything
for a long time. And then, just as I thought he might have drifted to
sleep, he said with a croak, "I am so *khasta.*" So very tired.

I sat by his bed until he fell asleep. Something was lost between Sohrab and me. Until my meeting with the lawyer, Omar Faisal, a light of hope had begun to enter Sohrab's eyes like a timid guest. Now the light was gone, the guest had fled, and I wondered when it would dare return. I wondered how long before Sohrab smiled again. How long before he trusted me. If ever.

So I left the room and went looking for another hotel, unaware that almost a year would pass before I would hear Sohrab speak another word.

IN THE END, Sohrab never accepted my offer. Nor did he decline it. But he knew that when the bandages were removed and the hospital garments returned, he was just another homeless Hazara orphan. What choice did he have? Where could he go? So what I took as a yes from him was in actuality more of a quiet surrender, not so much an acceptance as an act of relinquishment by one too weary to decide, and far too tired to believe. What he yearned for was his old life. What he got was me and America. Not that it was such a bad fate, everything considered, but I couldn't tell him that. Perspective was a luxury when your head was constantly buzzing with a swarm of demons.

And so it was that, about a week later, we crossed a strip of warm, black tarmac and I brought Hassan's son from Afghanistan to America, lifting him from the certainty of turmoil and dropping him in a turmoil of uncertainty.

ONE DAY, maybe around 1983 or 1984, I was at a video store in Fremont. I was standing in the Westerns section when a guy next to me, sipping Coke from a 7-Eleven cup, pointed to *The Magnificent Seven* and asked me if I had seen it. "Yes, thirteen times," I said. "Charles Bronson dies in it, so do James Coburn and Robert

Vaughn." He gave me a pinch-faced look, as if I had just spat in his soda. "Thanks a lot, man," he said, shaking his head and muttering something as he walked away. That was when I learned that, in America, you don't reveal the ending of the movie, and if you do, you will be scorned and made to apologize profusely for having committed the sin of Spoiling the End.

In Afghanistan, the ending was all that mattered. When Hassan and I came home after watching a Hindi film at Cinema Zainab, what Ali, Rahim Khan, Baba, or the myriad of Baba's friends—second and third cousins milling in and out of the house—wanted to know was this: Did the Girl in the film find happiness? Did the *bacheh film*, the Guy in the film, become *kamyab* and fulfill his dreams, or was he *nah-kam*, doomed to wallow in failure?

Was there happiness at the end, they wanted to know.

If someone were to ask me today whether the story of Hassan, Sohrab, and me ends with happiness, I wouldn't know what to say.

Does anybody's?

After all, life is not a Hindi movie. *Zendagi migzara*, Afghans like to say: Life goes on, unmindful of beginning, end, *kamyab*, *nah-kam*, crisis or catharsis, moving forward like a slow, dusty caravan of *kochis*.

I wouldn't know how to answer that question. Despite the matter of last Sunday's tiny miracle.

WE ARRIVED HOME about seven months ago, on a warm day in August 2001. Soraya picked us up at the airport. I had never been away from Soraya for so long, and when she locked her arms around my neck, when I smelled apples in her hair, I realized how much I had missed her. "You're still the morning sun to my *yelda*," I whispered.

"What?"

"Never mind." I kissed her ear.

After, she knelt to eye level with Sohrab. She took his hand and smiled at him. "*Salaam*, Sohrab jan, I'm your Khala Soraya. We've all been waiting for you."

Looking at her smiling at Sohrab, her eyes tearing over a little, I had a glimpse of the mother she might have been, had her own womb not betrayed her.

Sohrab shifted on his feet and looked away.

SORAYA HAD TURNED THE STUDY upstairs into a bedroom for Sohrab. She led him in and he sat on the edge of the bed. The sheets showed brightly colored kites flying in indigo blue skies. She had made inscriptions on the wall by the closet, feet and inches to measure a child's growing height. At the foot of the bed, I saw a wicker basket stuffed with books, a locomotive, a water-color set.

Sohrab was wearing the plain white T-shirt and new denims I had bought him in Islamabad just before we'd left—the shirt hung loosely over his bony, slumping shoulders. The color still hadn't seeped back into his face, save for the halo of dark circles around his eyes. He was looking at us now in the impassive way he looked at the plates of boiled rice the hospital orderly placed before him.

Soraya asked if he liked his room and I noticed that she was trying to avoid looking at his wrists and that her eyes kept swaying back to those jagged pink lines. Sohrab lowered his head. Hid his hands under his thighs and said nothing. Then he simply lay his head on the pillow. Less than five minutes later, Soraya and I watching from the doorway, he was snoring.

We went to bed, and Soraya fell asleep with her head on my chest. In the darkness of our room, I lay awake, an insomniac once more. Awake. And alone with demons of my own.

Sometime in the middle of the night, I slid out of bed and went to Sohrab's room. I stood over him, looking down, and saw something protruding from under his pillow. I picked it up. Saw it was Rahim Khan's Polaroid, the one I had given to Sohrab the night we had sat by the Shah Faisal Mosque. The one of Hassan and Sohrab standing side by side, squinting in the light of the sun, and smiling like the world was a good and just place. I wondered how long Sohrab had lain in bed staring at the photo, turning it in his hands.

I looked at the photo. *Your father was a man torn between two halves,* Rahim Khan had said in his letter. I had been the entitled half, the society-approved, legitimate half, the unwitting embodiment of Baba's guilt. I looked at Hassan, showing those two missing front teeth, sunlight slanting on his face. Baba's other half. The unentitled, unprivileged half. The half who had inherited what had been pure and noble in Baba. The half that, maybe, in the most secret recesses of his heart, Baba had thought of as his true son.

I slipped the picture back where I had found it. Then I realized something: That last thought had brought no sting with it. Closing Sohrab's door, I wondered if that was how forgiveness budded, not with the fanfare of epiphany, but with pain gathering its things, packing up, and slipping away unannounced in the middle of the night.

THE GENERAL AND KHALA JAMILA came over for dinner the following night. Khala Jamila, her hair cut short and a darker shade of red than usual, handed Soraya the plate of almond-topped *maghout* she had brought for dessert. She saw Sohrab and beamed. "*Mashallah!* Soraya jan told us how *khoshteep* you were, but you are even more handsome in person, Sohrab jan." She handed him a blue turtleneck sweater. "I knitted this for you," she said. "For next winter. *Inshallah,* it will fit you."

Sohrab took the sweater from her.

"Hello, young man," was all the general said, leaning with both hands on his cane, looking at Sohrab the way one might study a bizarre decorative item at someone's house.

I answered, and answered again, Khala Jamila's questions about my injuries—I'd asked Soraya to tell them I had been mugged—reassuring her that I had no permanent damage, that the wires would come out in a few weeks so I'd be able to eat her cooking again, that, yes, I would try rubbing rhubarb juice and sugar on my scars to make them fade faster.

The general and I sat in the living room and sipped wine while Soraya and her mother set the table. I told him about Kabul and the Taliban. He listened and nodded, his cane on his lap, and *tsk*'ed when I told him of the man I had spotted selling his artificial leg. I made no mention of the executions at Ghazi Stadium and Assef. He asked about Rahim Khan, whom he said he had met in Kabul a few times, and shook his head solemnly when I told him of Rahim Khan's illness. But as we spoke, I caught his eyes drifting again and again to Sohrab sleeping on the couch. As if we were skirting around the edge of what he really wanted to know.

The skirting finally came to an end over dinner when the general put down his fork and said, "So, Amir jan, you're going to tell us why you have brought back this boy with you?"

"Iqbal jan! What sort of question is that?" Khala Jamila said.

"While you're busy knitting sweaters, my dear, I have to deal with the community's perception of our family. People will ask. They will want to know why there is a Hazara boy living with our daughter. What do I tell them?"

Soraya dropped her spoon. Turned on her father. "You can tell them—"

"It's okay, Soraya," I said, taking her hand. "It's okay. General Sahib is quite right. People *will* ask."

"Amir—" she began.

"It's all right." I turned to the general. "You see, General Sahib, my father slept with his servant's wife. She bore him a son named Hassan. Hassan is dead now. That boy sleeping on the couch is Hassan's son. He's my nephew. That's what you tell people when they ask."

They were all staring at me.

"And one more thing, General Sahib," I said. "You will never again refer to him as 'Hazara boy' in my presence. He has a name and it's Sohrab."

No one said anything for the remainder of the meal.

IT WOULD BE ERRONEOUS to say Sohrab was quiet. Quiet is peace. Tranquillity. Quiet is turning down the VOLUME knob on life.

Silence is pushing the OFF button. Shutting it down. All of it.

Sohrab's silence wasn't the self-imposed silence of those with convictions, of protesters who seek to speak their cause by not speaking at all. It was the silence of one who has taken cover in a dark place, curled up all the edges and tucked them under.

He didn't so much live with us as occupy space. And precious little of it. Sometimes, at the market, or in the park, I'd notice how other people hardly seemed to even see him, like he wasn't there at all. I'd look up from a book and realize Sohrab had entered the room, had sat across from me, and I hadn't noticed. He walked like he was afraid to leave behind footprints. He moved as if not to stir the air around him. Mostly, he slept.

Sohrab's silence was hard on Soraya too. Over that long-distance line to Pakistan, Soraya had told me about the things she was planning for Sohrab. Swimming classes. Soccer. Bowling league. Now she'd walk past Sohrab's room and catch a glimpse of books sitting unopened in the wicker basket, the growth chart unmarked, the jigsaw puzzle unassembled, each item a reminder of a life that could have been. A reminder of a dream that was wilting even as it was budding. But she hadn't been alone. I'd had my own dreams for Sohrab.

While Sohrab was silent, the world was not. One Tuesday morning last September, the Twin Towers came crumbling down and, overnight, the world changed. The American flag suddenly appeared everywhere, on the antennae of yellow cabs weaving around traffic, on the lapels of pedestrians walking the sidewalks in a steady stream, even on the grimy caps of San Francisco's panhandlers sitting beneath the awnings of small art galleries and open-fronted shops. One day I passed Edith, the homeless woman who plays the accordion every day on the corner of Sutter and Stockton, and spotted an American flag sticker on the accordion case at her feet.

Soon after the attacks, America bombed Afghanistan, the Northern Alliance moved in, and the Taliban scurried like rats into the caves. Suddenly, people were standing in grocery store lines and talking about the cities of my childhood, Kandahar, Herat, Mazar-i-Sharif. When I was very little, Baba took Hassan and me to Kunduz. I don't remember much about the trip, except sitting in the shade of an acacia tree with Baba and Hassan, taking turns sipping fresh watermelon juice from a clay pot and seeing who could spit the seeds farther. Now Dan Rather, Tom Brokaw, and people sipping lattes at Starbucks were talking about the battle for Kunduz, the Taliban's last stronghold in the north. That December, Pashtuns, Tajiks, Uzbeks, and Hazaras gathered in Bonn and, under the watchful eye of the UN, began the process that might someday end over twenty years of unhappiness in their *watan*. Hamid Karzai's caracul hat and green *chapan* became famous.

Sohrab sleepwalked through it all.

Soraya and I became involved in Afghan projects, as much out of a sense of civil duty as the need for something—anything—to fill the silence upstairs, the silence that sucked everything in like a black hole. I had never been the active type before, but when a man named Kabir, a former Afghan ambassador to Sofia, called and asked if I wanted to help him with a hospital project, I said yes. The small hospital had stood near the Afghan-Pakistani border and had a small surgical unit that treated Afghan refugees with land mine injuries. But it had closed down due to a lack of funds. I became the project manager, Soraya my comanager. I spent most of my days in the study, e-mailing people around the world, applying for grants, organizing fund-raising events. And telling myself that bringing Sohrab here had been the right thing to do.

The year ended with Soraya and me on the couch, blanket spread over our legs, watching Dick Clark on TV. People cheered and kissed when the silver ball dropped, and confetti whitened the screen. In our house, the new year began much the same way the last one had ended. In silence.

THEN, FOUR DAYS AGO, on a cool rainy day in March 2002, a small, wondrous thing happened.

I took Soraya, Khala Jamila, and Sohrab to a gathering of Afghans at Lake Elizabeth Park in Fremont. The general had finally been summoned to Afghanistan the month before for a ministry position, and had flown there two weeks earlier—he had left behind his gray suit and pocket watch. The plan was for Khala

Jamila to join him in a few months once he had settled. She missed him terribly—and worried about his health there—and we had insisted she stay with us for a while.

The previous Thursday, the first day of spring, had been the Afghan New Year's Day—the *Sawl-e-Nau*—and Afghans in the Bay Area had planned celebrations throughout the East Bay and the peninsula. Kabir, Soraya, and I had an additional reason to rejoice: Our little hospital in Rawalpindi had opened the week before, not the surgical unit, just the pediatric clinic. But it was a good start, we all agreed.

It had been sunny for days, but Sunday morning, as I swung my legs out of bed, I heard raindrops pelting the window. *Afghan luck,* I thought. Snickered. I prayed morning *namaz* while Soraya slept—I didn't have to consult the prayer pamphlet I had obtained from the mosque anymore; the verses came naturally now, effortlessly.

We arrived around noon and found a handful of people taking cover under a large rectangular plastic sheet mounted on six poles spiked to the ground. Someone was already frying *bolani*; steam rose from teacups and a pot of cauliflower *aush*. A scratchy old Ahmad Zahir song was blaring from a cassette player. I smiled a little as the four of us rushed across the soggy grass field, Soraya and I in the lead, Khala Jamila in the middle, Sohrab behind us, the hood of his yellow raincoat bouncing on his back.

"What's so funny?" Soraya said, holding a folded newspaper over her head.

"You can take Afghans out of Paghman, but you can't take Paghman out of Afghans," I said.

We stooped under the makeshift tent. Soraya and Khala Jamila drifted toward an overweight woman frying spinach *bolani*.

Sohrab stayed under the canopy for a moment, then stepped back out into the rain, hands stuffed in the pockets of his raincoat, his hair—now brown and straight like Hassan's—plastered against his scalp. He stopped near a coffee-colored puddle and stared at it. No one seemed to notice. No one called him back in. With time, the queries about our adopted—and decidedly eccentric—little boy had mercifully ceased, and, considering how tactless Afghan queries can be sometimes, that was a considerable relief. People stopped asking why he never spoke. Why he didn't play with the other kids. And best of all, they stopped suffocating us with their exaggerated empathy, their slow head shaking, their *tsk-tsk*s, their "*Oh gung bichara.*" Oh, poor little mute one. The novelty had worn off. Like dull wallpaper, Sohrab had blended into the background.

I shook hands with Kabir, a small, silver-haired man. He introduced me to a dozen men, one of them a retired teacher, another an engineer, a former architect, a surgeon who was now running a hot dog stand in Hayward. They all said they'd known Baba in Kabul, and they spoke about him respectfully. In one way or another, he had touched all their lives. The men said I was lucky to have had such a great man for a father.

We chatted about the difficult and maybe thankless job Karzai had in front of him, about the upcoming *Loya jirga*, and the king's imminent return to his homeland after twenty-eights years of exile. I remembered the night in 1973, the night Zahir Shah's cousin overthrew him; I remembered gunfire and the sky lighting up silver—Ali had taken me and Hassan in his arms, told us not to be afraid, that they were just shooting ducks.

Then someone told a Mullah Nasruddin joke and we were all laughing. "You know, your father was a funny man too," Kabir said.

"He was, wasn't he?" I said, smiling, remembering how, soon after we arrived in the U.S., Baba started grumbling about American flies. He'd sit at the kitchen table with his flyswatter, watch the flies darting from wall to wall, buzzing here, buzzing there, harried and rushed. "In this country, even flies are pressed for time," he'd groan. How I had laughed. I smiled at the memory now.

By three o'clock, the rain had stopped and the sky was a curdled gray burdened with lumps of clouds. A cool breeze blew through the park. More families turned up. Afghans greeted each other, hugged, kissed, exchanged food. Someone lighted coal in a barbecue and soon the smell of garlic and *morgh* kabob flooded my senses. There was music, some new singer I didn't know, and the giggling of children. I saw Sohrab, still in his yellow raincoat, leaning against a garbage pail, staring across the park at the empty batting cage.

A little while later, as I was chatting with the former surgeon, who told me he and Baba had been classmates in eighth grade, Soraya pulled on my sleeve. "Amir, look!"

She was pointing to the sky. A half-dozen kites were flying high, speckles of bright yellow, red, and green against the gray sky.

"Check it out," Soraya said, and this time she was pointing to a guy selling kites from a stand nearby.

"Hold this," I said. I gave my cup of tea to Soraya. I excused myself and walked over to the kite stand, my shoes squishing on the wet grass. I pointed to a yellow *seh-parcha*. "*Sawl-e-nau mubabrak*," the kite seller said, taking the twenty and handing me the kite and a wooden spool of glass *tar*. I thanked him and wished him a Happy New Year too. I tested the string the way Hassan and I used to, by holding it between my thumb and forefinger and pulling it. It reddened with blood and the kite seller smiled. I smiled back.

I took the kite to where Sohrab was standing, still leaning against the garbage pail, arms crossed on his chest. He was looking up at the sky.

"Do you like the *seh-parcha?*" I said, holding up the kite by the ends of the cross bars. His eyes shifted from the sky to me, to the kite, then back. A few rivulets of rain trickled from his hair, down his face.

"I read once that, in Malaysia, they use kites to catch fish," I said. "I'll bet you didn't know that. They tie a fishing line to it and fly it beyond the shallow waters, so it doesn't cast a shadow and scare the fish. And in ancient China, generals used to fly kites over battlefields to send messages to their men. It's true. I'm not slipping you a trick." I showed him my bloody thumb. "Nothing wrong with the *tar* either."

Out of the corner of my eye, I saw Soraya watching us from the tent. Hands tensely dug in her armpits. Unlike me, she'd gradually abandoned her attempts at engaging him. The unanswered questions, the blank stares, the silence, it was all too painful. She had shifted to "Holding Pattern," waiting for a green light from Sohrab. Waiting.

I wet my index finger and held it up. "I remember the way your father checked the wind was to kick up dust with his sandal, see which way the wind blew it. He knew a lot of little tricks like that," I said. Lowered my finger. "West, I think."

Sohrab wiped a raindrop from his earlobe and shifted on his feet. Said nothing. I thought of Soraya asking me a few months ago what his voice sounded like. I'd told her I didn't remember anymore.

"Did I ever tell you your father was the best kite runner in Wazir Akbar Khan? Maybe all of Kabul?" I said, knotting the loose end of the spool *tar* to the string loop tied to the center spar. "How jealous he made the neighborhood kids. He'd run kites and never look up at the sky, and people used to say he was chasing the kite's shadow. But they didn't know him like I did. Your father wasn't chasing any shadows. He just...knew."

Another half-dozen kites had taken flight. People had started to gather in clumps, teacups in hand, eyes glued to the sky.

"Do you want to help me fly this?" I said.

Sohrab's gaze bounced from the kite to me. Back to the sky.

"Okay." I shrugged. "Looks like I'll have to fly it *tanhaii*." Solo.

I balanced the spool in my left hand and fed about three feet of *tar*. The yellow kite dangled at the end of it, just above the wet grass. "Last chance," I said. But Sohrab was looking at a pair of kites tangling high above the trees.

"All right. Here I go." I took off running, my sneakers splashing rainwater from puddles, the hand clutching the kite end of the string held high above my head. It had been so long, so many years since I'd done this, and I wondered if I'd make a spectacle of myself. I let the spool roll in my left hand as I ran, felt the string cut my right hand again as it fed through. The kite was lifting behind my shoulder now, lifting, wheeling, and I ran harder. The spool spun faster and the glass string tore another gash in my right palm. I stopped and turned. Looked up. Smiled. High above, my kite was tilting side to side like a pendulum, making that old paper-bird-flapping-its-wings sound I always associated with winter mornings in Kabul. I hadn't flown a kite in a quarter of a century, but suddenly I was twelve again and all the old instincts came rushing back.

I felt a presence next to me and looked down. It was Sohrab. Hands dug deep in the pockets of his raincoat. He had followed me.

"Do you want to try?" I asked. He said nothing. But when I held the string out for him, his hand lifted from his pocket. Hesitated. Took the string. My heart quickened as I spun the spool to gather the loose string. We stood quietly side by side. Necks bent up.

Around us, kids chased each other, slid on the grass. Someone was playing an old Hindi movie soundtrack now. A line of elderly men were praying afternoon *namaz* on a plastic sheet spread on the ground. The air smelled of wet grass, smoke, and grilled meat. I wished time would stand still.

Then I saw we had company. A green kite was closing in. I traced the string to a kid standing about thirty yards from us. He had a crew cut and a T-shirt that read THE ROCK RULES in bold block letters. He saw me looking at him and smiled. Waved. I waved back.

Sohrab was handing the string back to me.

"Are you sure?" I said, taking it.

He took the spool from me.

"Okay," I said. "Let's give him a *sabagh*, teach him a lesson, nay?" I glanced over at him. The glassy, vacant look in his eyes was gone. His gaze flitted between our kite and the green one. His face was a little flushed, his eyes suddenly alert. Awake. Alive. I wondered when I had forgotten that, despite everything, he was still just a child.

The green kite was making its move. "Let's wait," I said. "We'll let him get a little closer." It dipped twice and crept toward us. "Come on. Come to me," I said.

The green kite drew closer yet, now rising a little above us, unaware of the trap I'd set for it. "Watch, Sohrab. I'm going to show you one of your father's favorite tricks, the old lift-and-dive."

Next to me, Sohrab was breathing rapidly through his nose. The spool rolled in his palms, the tendons in his scarred wrists like *rubab* strings. Then I blinked and, for just a moment, the hands holding the spool were the chipped-nailed, calloused hands of a harelipped boy. I heard a crow cawing somewhere and I looked up. The park shimmered with snow so fresh, so dazzling white, it burned my eyes. It sprinkled soundlessly from the branches of white-clad trees. I smelled turnip *qurma* now. Dried mulberries. Sour oranges. Sawdust and walnuts. The muffled quiet, snow-quiet, was deafening. Then far away, across the stillness, a voice calling us home, the voice of a man who dragged his right leg.

The green kite hovered directly above us now. "He's going for it. Anytime now," I said, my eyes flicking from Sohrab to our kite.

The green kite hesitated. Held position. Then shot down. "Here he comes!" I said.

I did it perfectly. After all these years. The old lift-and-dive trap. I loosened my grip and tugged on the string, dipping and dodging the green kite. A series of quick sidearm jerks and our kite shot up counterclockwise, in a half circle. Suddenly I was on top. The green kite was scrambling now, panic-stricken. But it was too late. I'd already slipped him Hassan's trick. I pulled hard and our kite plummeted. I could almost feel our string sawing his. Almost heard the snap.

Then, just like that, the green kite was spinning and wheeling out of control.

Behind us, people cheered. Whistles and applause broke out. I was panting. The last time I had felt a rush like this was that day in the winter of 1975, just after I had cut the last kite, when I spotted Baba on our rooftop, clapping, beaming.

I looked down at Sohrab. One corner of his mouth had curled up just so.

A smile.

Lopsided.

Hardly there.

But there.

Behind us, kids were scampering, and a melee of screaming kite runners was chasing the loose kite drifting high above the trees. I blinked and the smile was gone. But it had been there. I had seen it.

"Do you want me to run that kite for you?"

His Adam's apple rose and fell as he swallowed. The wind lifted his hair. I thought I saw him nod.

"For you, a thousand times over," I heard myself say.

Then I turned and ran.

It was only a smile, nothing more. It didn't make everything all right. It didn't make *anything* all right. Only a smile. A tiny thing. A leaf in the woods, shaking in the wake of a startled bird's flight.

But I'll take it. With open arms. Because when spring comes, it melts the snow one flake at a time, and maybe I just witnessed the first flake melting.

I ran. A grown man running with a swarm of screaming children. But I didn't care. I ran with the wind blowing in my face, and a smile as wide as the Valley of Panjsher on my lips.

I ran.

THE KITE RUNNER

READERS GUIDE

For more information on THE KITE RUNNER and
Khaled Hosseini, please visit www.riverheadbooks.com.

DISCUSSION QUESTIONS

1. The novel begins with Amir's memory of peering down an alley, looking for Hassan, who is kite running for him. As Amir peers into the alley, he witnesses a tragedy. The novel ends with Amir kite running for Hassan's son, Sohrab, as he begins a new life with Amir in America. Why do you think the author chooses to frame the novel with these scenes? Refer to the following passage: "Afghans like to say: Life goes on, unmindful of beginning, end . . . crisis or catharsis, moving forward like a slow, dusty caravan of kochis [nomads]." How is this significant to the framing of the novel?

2. The strong underlying force of this novel is the relationship between Amir and Hassan. Discuss their friendship. Why is Amir afraid to be Hassan's true friend? Why does Amir constantly test Hassan's loyalty? Why does he resent Hassan? After the kite running tournament, why does Amir no longer want to be Hassan's friend?

3. Early in Amir and Hassan's friendship, they often visit a pomegranate tree where they spend hours reading and playing. "One summer day, I used one of Ali's kitchen knives to carve our names on it: 'Amir and

Hassan, the sultans of Kabul.' Those words made it formal: the tree was ours." In a letter to Amir later in the story, Hassan mentions that "the tree hasn't borne fruit in years." Discuss the significance of this tree.

───────

4. We begin to understand early in the novel that Amir is constantly vying for Baba's attention and often feels like an outsider in his father's life, as seen in the following passage: "He'd close the door, leave me to wonder why it was always grown-ups time with him. I'd sit by the door, knees drawn to my chest. Sometimes I sat there for an hour, sometimes two, listening to their laughter, their chatter." Discuss Amir's relationship with Baba.

───────

5. After Amir wins the kite running tournament, his relationship with Baba undergoes significant change. However, while they form a bond of friendship, Amir is still unhappy. What causes this unhappiness and how has Baba contributed to Amir's state of mind? Eventually, the relationship between the two returns to the way it was before the tournament, and Amir laments, "We'd actually deceived ourselves into thinking that a toy made of tissue paper, glue, and bamboo could somehow close the chasm between us." Discuss the significance of this passage.

───────

6. As Amir remembers an Afghan celebration in which a sheep must be sacrificed, he talks about seeing the sheep's eyes moments before its death. "I don't know why I watch this yearly ritual in our backyard; my nightmares persist long after the bloodstains on the grass have faded. But I always watch. I watch because of that look of acceptance in the animal's eyes. Absurdly, I imagine the animal understands. I imagine the animal sees that its imminent demise is for a higher purpose." Why do you think Amir recalls this memory when he witnesses Hassan's tragedy in the alleyway? Amir recollects the memory again toward the end of the novel when he sees Sohrab in the home of the Taliban. Discuss the image in the context of the novel.

———

7. America acts as a place for Amir to bury his memories and a place for Baba to mourn his. In America, there were "Homes that made Baba's house in Wazir Akbar Khan look like a servant's hut." What is ironic about this statement? What is the function of irony in this novel?

———

8. What is the significance of the irony in the first story that Amir writes? After hearing Amir's story, Hassan asks, "Why did the man kill his wife? In fact, why did

he ever have to feel sad to shed tears? Couldn't he have just smelled an onion?" How is his reaction to the story a metaphor for Amir's life? How does this story epitomize the difference in character between Hassan and Amir?

———

9. Why is Baba disappointed by Amir's decision to become a writer? During their argument about his career path, Amir thinks to himself: "I would stand my ground, I decided. I didn't want to sacrifice for Baba anymore. The last time I had done that, I had damned myself." What has Amir sacrificed for Baba? How has Amir "damned himself"?

———

10. Compare and contrast the relationships of Soraya and Amir and their fathers. How have their upbringings contributed to these relationships?

———

11. Discuss how the ever-changing politics of Afghanistan affect each of the characters in the novel.

———

12. On Amir's trip back to Afghanistan, he stays at the home of his driver, Farid. Upon leaving he remarks:

"Earlier that morning, when I was certain no one was looking, I did something I had done twenty-six years earlier: I planted a fistful of crumpled money under a mattress." Why is this moment so important in Amir's journey?

––––––––

13. Throughout the story, Baba worries because Amir never stands up for himself. When does this change?

––––––––

14. Amir's confrontation with Assef in Wazir Akbar Khan marks an important turning point in the novel. Why does the author have Amir, Assef, and Sohrab all come together in this way? What is the significance of the scar that Amir develops as a result of the confrontation? Why is it important in Amir's journey toward forgiveness and acceptance?

––––––––

15. While in the hospital in Peshawar, Amir has a dream in which he sees his father wrestling a bear: "They roll over a patch of green grass, man and beast . . . They fall to the ground with a loud thud and Baba is sitting on the bear's chest, his fingers digging in its snout. He looks up at me and I see. He's me. I am wrestling the bear." Why is this dream so important

at this point in the story? What does this dream finally help Amir realize?

———

16. Amir and Hassan have a favorite story. Does the story have the same meaning for both men? Why does Hassan name his son after one of the characters in the story?

———

17. Baba and Amir know that they are very different people. Often it disappoints both of them that Amir is not the son that Baba has hoped for. When Amir finds out that Baba has lied to him about Hassan, he realizes that "as it turned out, Baba and I were more alike than I'd ever known." How does this make Amir feel about his father? How is this both a negative and positive realization?

———

18. When Amir and Baba move to the States their relationship changes, and Amir begins to view his father as a more complex man. Discuss the changes in their relationship. Do you see the changes in Baba as tragic or positive?

———

19. Discuss the difference between Baba and Ali and between Amir and Hassan. Are Baba's and Amir's betrayals and similarities in their relationships of their servants (if you consider Baba's act a betrayal) similar or different? Do you think that such betrayals are inevitable in the master/servant relationship, or do you feel that they are due to flaws in Baba's and Amir's characters, or are they the outcome of circumstances and characters?

Khaled Hosseini's next novel

about Afghanistan

will be published by

Riverhead Books

in the summer of 2006.